ALL THAT THIS ENTAILS

A Pride & Prejudice Variation

NOELL CHESNEY

Quills & Quartos
PUBLISHING

Edited by Debbie Styne and Gail Warner

Cover Design by London Montgomery Designs

ISBN 978-1-951033-59-0 (ebook) and 978-1-951033-60-6 (paperback)

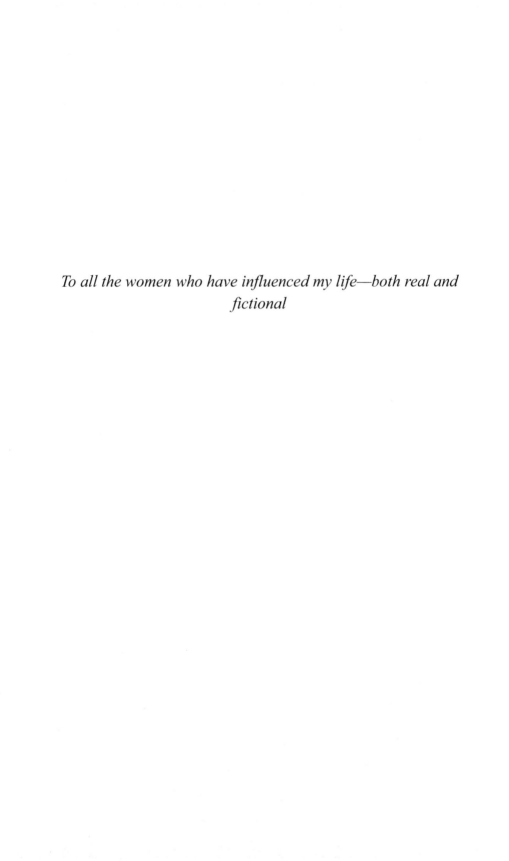

To all the women who have influenced my life—both real and fictional

TABLE OF CONTENTS

CHAPTER 1

Spring 1812, Longbourn

Elizabeth Bennet sat in a pretty wilderness in Longbourn's park contemplating the letter she had just received from her Aunt Gardiner. She was slightly disappointed her summer travel was to be delayed and more than a little concerned the new intended destination was to be Derbyshire.

Hearing a noise, she spied her father entering the area with a distracted look upon his countenance. He did not seem to notice her, so Elizabeth called out to him. He startled, then returned her smile, and walked over to her.

"Good day, my dear," he said as he sat down beside her on the bench. "Escaping the lamentations of your mother and Kitty, I see."

"I am enjoying the beautiful summer's day," she answered

with a laugh. "But you seem distracted. Shall I leave you to your solitude?"

Mr Bennet seemed discomfited at her mention of his distraction and looked at her as though he were determining something.

"Not at all. I believe I must discuss this with someone, as I shall have to tell the entire family about it very soon."

Elizabeth was somewhat surprised by the gravity of his answer.

"Do not be alarmed, Lizzy, it is only that I have received an interesting letter that will affect all our fortunes in a most astonishing way. But before I reveal the contents of this letter, let me tell you a little story.

"I have never told you a great deal about your Bennet relations, and that is where this story should begin. Your great-grandfather, John Bennet, was the Duke of Everard."

Mr Bennet stopped speaking when he heard Elizabeth gasp. He looked into her astonished face, but she quickly collected herself and nodded for him to continue.

"The Bennet family is an old and noble line. The original manor is in the north in Staffordshire, and by now the dukedom is quite large with many land holdings and a great deal of wealth—one of the largest in the empire, I believe.

"My grandfather had three sons. In fact, the Bennets had not produced any female offspring for many generations—a point that will be important later in this tale."

A small smile played at the corners of Mr Bennet's mouth, and Elizabeth found herself smiling in return. It was a rather ironic statement considering his current progeny, but her father was starting to speak again, so Elizabeth focused her attention back to his astounding revelations.

"Your grandfather James had a twin brother named

Alexander. There was also a younger son, Michael, who died as a child from illness. Though male children were a matter of course for the Bennets, this was the first set of twins to be born in the line. The duke was concerned for James, born only five minutes later than his twin brother but destined to inherit nothing, being in essence a younger son. So, the duke determined to provide a small estate for James and to instruct him alongside Alexander to ensure both young men knew all that being a landowner and peer would require. This small estate, as you have probably already guessed, is Longbourn.

"However, he wanted to ensure that the estate remain known as a Bennet holding and so entailed Longbourn only to male heirs, knowing the family's propensity for male children." Mr Bennet turned to look at his daughter and smiled. "Your grandmother was one of six girls, which is where I am sure the line was corrupted," he stated playfully, and Elizabeth laughed softly in response.

"But I am getting ahead of myself. Alexander and James were sent to the best schools and taught everything their father deemed necessary for their welfare. As a result, the boys were quite close during their childhood and early adulthood..." Mr Bennet's voice trailed off and a distant expression overcame his features as he looked out over the garden.

"You say they remained close only through their early adulthood?"

"Yes, my dear, for you see, on the eve of their twenty-fifth birthday, their father held a grand ball to celebrate. They had both just returned from a two-year tour of the Continent, and the duke desired to reintroduce them to the English aristocracy.

"The duke's health had been failing for nearly a year, and

he wanted to see Alexander married and hopefully with an heir before his death, so a ball was hosted in London, and every eligible female member of the *ton* was invited.

"The toast of the Season that year was a beautiful, charming, and of course, very wealthy young lady named Elizabeth Percy." Mr Bennet paused to mark his daughter's reaction. "Yes, it is your grandmother of whom I speak. She was introduced to the Bennet young men at the ball, and unfortunately, a destructive competition broke out between the brothers."

Elizabeth sighed. It was an age-old story but one that rarely had a happy conclusion.

"Both the brothers pursued her, but she loved your Grandfather James, and their married life was full of happiness. Alexander, unfortunately, was bitterly disappointed and broke all ties to his brother—a situation that saddened the duke and was never resolved before his death.

"Although your grandparents were happy, your grandmother's family was not. The Percys believed she should have married Alexander, who would inherit the title and a vast amount of property, whereas James was only the master of a small country estate and a younger son. As a result of her choice, they disinherited Elizabeth, and she retired to the country with her new husband."

The narrative momentarily brought to Elizabeth's mind the chance she had been offered with Mr Darcy's proposal in April, but she quickly pushed the thought away. Although she did think better of him, to have accepted his proposal at the time would have been purely mercenary because she did not love him then.

Then? Surely, I do not love him now? Elizabeth again pushed consideration of Mr Darcy from her mind to return her attention to her father. She knew he was far from finished with the conversation.

"So, what does all this have to do with your letter?" Elizabeth asked.

"The letter I received this morning, by express no less, is from an attorney in London whose client is none other than the present Duchess of Everard."

"Does she desire to heal the breach? Does she perhaps want to offer an olive branch?" she questioned impishly. Her father laughed softly at the allusion to Mr Collins.

"It is slightly along that vein, my dear."

"Surely, she cannot break the entail?"

"This involves an entail of a completely different nature— or more accurately, not an entail but an inheritance."

"What inheritance?"

"Well, to be precise, mine, and then in the future, yours and your sisters'."

Elizabeth was excessively diverted. "What exactly are you to inherit?"

"The dukedom, of course."

Mr Bennet kept a close eye on his daughter after this astonishing revelation. Elizabeth sat in shock, unable to fully comprehend her father's disclosure. As she reviewed his words, their meaning became clearer.

"Are you saying that you are to inherit a dukedom?"

"So it would seem, Lizzy, but again, I am getting ahead of myself. Let me finish my story.

"James and Elizabeth Bennet retired to Longbourn, and Alexander withdrew to Staffordshire to nurse his disappointment and help manage the family estates. I have already mentioned the duke was experiencing ill health at this time.

His desire to see his firstborn, his heir, married was still firmly fixed, as I understand.

"Alexander was persuaded to return to London for the remainder of the Season. There, he met Lady Anne Hutchinson. She was reported to be quite lovely, and of course, possessed wonderful connexions and a sizeable dowry. They married at the end of the Season, and the duke died within the next year before an heir was born or there was a reconciliation between his sons. Alexander, now the Duke of Everard, and his wife had two sons, Joshua and Nathaniel."

Elizabeth interrupted her father. "How is it that you know all the goings-on of these Bennets if your father never reconciled with his brother?"

"Your grandfather was always pained by the separation and endeavoured to keep abreast of his family's actions."

"And did he also keep you informed?"

"When I came of age, he related the story in its entirety. I confess I was as surprised as you are, my dear. I had no knowledge of the eminence of my father's heritage or the breach. However, after his initial disclosure, I decided not to pursue further information about my uncle and cousins. I did not believe I would ever meet them." He looked pensive after uttering this statement. "I may have been mistaken and would have been better served by maintaining my father's vigilance. Then I might not have been so shocked when I received this attorney's letter."

Elizabeth smiled. "Will I be privy to this communication?"

Mr Bennet nodded. "The attorney, a Mr Spencer, writes to tell me that the Duke of Everard has died in a shipwreck while escorting his brother and brother's family back from the Indies. This means there are no surviving descendants of Alexander Bennet.

"Joshua, the most recent Duke of Everard, and his wife,"—Mr Bennet paused to consult the letter in his hand for the necessary information—"Agatha, had no children. And the younger son Nathaniel, his wife, and children were all on the ship with the duke when it sank. My father would have been the next in line for the title had he lived, but it has passed to me. This is exactly what Mr Spencer has written to inform me. I shall be the Duke of Everard."

Elizabeth could hardly believe the disclosure her father had uttered with such little fanfare. Her head was full of numerous thoughts travelling in divergent directions, and she did not know which she should pursue first.

My father is a duke. I am the daughter of a duke! Elizabeth could hardly consider the statement. Her thoughts continued in this vein when she suddenly exclaimed, "Mama is a duchess!"

Mr Bennet laughed out loud at this declaration. "I believe that conclusion is correct! Mr Spencer states in his letter that the dowager duchess would like for my entire family to travel to Staffordshire to take up residence at Grancourt, the estate there. She believes, and here I quote from the letter, 'There is much that needs to be addressed as you assume the dukedom, and the duchess would like to acquaint herself with you and your family to help ease the ascendancy.' Lizzy, I believe we are summoned to Staffordshire!"

Having sufficiently calmed to heed the rest of her father's account, Elizabeth gave a soft laugh. "Of course we must answer this summons, but first let us return to the house and have some tea."

Elizabeth was by no means as completely recovered from the miraculous revelation as her statement implied, but she understood there was entirely too much to discuss and examine to continue to do so in Longbourn's garden. She stood, Mr Bennet followed suit, and they made their way back to the house.

The other Bennet ladies were sitting in the drawing room and were unaware of the drastic change in their circumstances. On the walk to the house, Mr Bennet suggested the disclosure not be made until he had an opportunity to respond to the missive from Mr Spencer and post it express, for he believed that it deserved an immediate reply. Elizabeth consented, and she and her father entered the drawing room as Hill entered with tea.

After the family finished, Mr Bennet immediately retired to his library. Elizabeth had resolved to tell Jane of her father's morning communication at the earliest possible moment. She needed Jane's consolation, as she was still feeling quite unsettled from the discussion with her father. Elizabeth suggested they attend to some tasks in the stillroom. She knew her mother would be busy settling the dinner menu, Lydia was in Brighton, and Mary and Kitty never entered that room.

As the two girls were sorting through drying herbs, Jane asked, "Is there something bothering you? You were unusually quiet earlier."

"I have been thinking about some things Papa and I discussed this morning."

Elizabeth paused. She had earlier received her father's permission to tell Jane, but she did not quite know how to do so without inflicting unnecessary shock. Upon reflection, she realised it was almost impossible to reveal such information without causing some distress, and she determined to be as straightforward as possible.

"Papa received a letter this morning that contained the most astonishing and wonderful news. It seems Papa is to be the Duke of Everard."

Jane looked up at her sister at this declaration and smiled. "Lizzy, do be serious. You are always teasing me."

However, as Elizabeth did not laugh or smile, Jane soon recognised her sister was in earnest. Jane abruptly stopped her work and sat down upon a stool. Elizabeth, seeing her sister's dismay, immediately began to relate the tale she had learned earlier that morning. The sisters spent above an hour in the stillroom discussing the revelations and comforting each other, for they were bewildered about how this would affect their future.

"I do not know what to think of this. What has Father determined to do?"

"He has written to the attorney to accept an invitation to Grancourt for our family. I believe he hopes to travel there within a fortnight." Elizabeth paused a moment upon realising how this development would affect her summer plans. "Oh, I must write to Aunt Gardiner, for I shall not be able to travel with them if we are to go to Staffordshire."

"That is a shame. I know you were looking forward to your trip to the Lakes."

"I received a letter from Aunt Gardiner this morning, informing me that our trip was to be delayed by a few weeks, and we would not travel as far as the Lakes but only to Derbyshire."

Elizabeth felt Jane's gaze upon her when she mentioned Derbyshire and knew Jane must be thinking of Mr Darcy's connexion to that region.

"I am sure that they will miss your company during their tour. Perhaps we should return and see whether Mama needs us?"

"I should like to talk to Papa and determine if he has made any other decisions. Will you come with me?"

"Of course, Lizzy."

The sisters tidied up the stillroom and made their way to Mr Bennet's library. They entered the room to find their father deep in thought as he sat at his desk. He looked up upon their entrance and smiled while inviting them to sit.

"I have told Jane the news, Papa. Have you written to Mr Spencer?"

Mr Bennet related all he had done for their journey to Staffordshire, including summoning Lydia home so they might depart quickly. "Shall we tell the others this news so they may also begin to realise their good fortune?"

"Of course we must tell them," Elizabeth said, "but certainly we can wait until after the first course. Knowing the raptures that will follow, we would not want to waste any of Cook's hard work."

Mr Bennet's eyes twinkled mischievously as he gestured his daughters out of the library. They made their way to the dining room where the rest of the family was already gathered for the evening meal. A few minutes into the soup course, Mr Bennet cleared his throat and addressed his wife.

"I received a letter today from an attorney in London. It contained some rather astounding information that will particularly affect the marriage prospects of our daughters."

This statement garnered Mrs Bennet's attention, and she looked up expectantly from her soup. Elizabeth warily eyed her father, knowing his inclination to vex his wife.

"In fact," he continued, "I believe we shall have no trouble marrying them off to wealthy men in the near future."

Mrs Bennet raised her spoon to her mouth and asked her husband how this feat was to be accomplished.

Timing his response perfectly, Mr Bennet pronounced, "I

have inherited the Dukedom of Everard, all the girls will be titled with large dowries, and you, my dear Mrs Bennet, will be the Duchess of Everard."

Mrs Bennet choked, spluttered, and then fainted.

CHAPTER 2

Mrs Bennet was revived and immediately escorted to her room by Jane and Mrs Hill. Elizabeth directed a disapproving stare towards her father that he ignored as he excused himself to his library and his port. This left Elizabeth the onerous task of explaining the situation to Mary and Kitty. She gave them a brief summary of their family history and answered their questions as well as she could. Luckily, both girls were shocked speechless by the disclosure, giving Elizabeth the chance to escape and retire early.

The following morning commenced with a rather late start to the Bennet family's routine. Mrs Bennet was indisposed and kept to her room but constantly called upon members of her family to attend her. Mr Bennet visited his wife in the early afternoon to explain more fully their new situation and to inform her of the invitation to Staffordshire. Although she did not entirely comprehend all the implications of the news, Mrs

Bennet understood well enough that she would need new clothes for herself and all the girls before they ventured north. To meet the Dowager Duchess of Everard would certainly require the finest lace!

Mr Bennet awaited only a reply from Mr Spencer, confirming the family's journey to fordshire, before he would undertake a trip to Brighton. His natural indolence was set aside in the face of such an immense undertaking, and he became rather impatient for a letter. However, just two days after his own express to town, Mr Spencer sent a return post. Two carriages from the Everard estate would arrive at Longbourn in a fortnight to convey the Bennets to Grancourt. After receiving this letter, Mr Bennet made immediate plans to travel to Brighton to fetch Lydia and left early the next morning.

In his note to the Forsters, he had given no reason for the curtailing of Lydia's visit other than a vague *family situation*. Lydia was understandably angered at her father's arrival and the end of her time with the officers, and for the first several hours of the return journey, she loudly lamented her father's unfairness. Mr Bennet finally succumbed to her expressions of grief and disclosed the true reason for her return. Her cries of woe instantly turned to shrieks of joy and raptures on the balls and parties she would attend in London.

With the return of the two to Longbourn, preparations for the journey north intensified. Elizabeth wrote a letter to her Aunt Gardiner, explaining the situation and apologising for her need to cancel her summer plans with them. Mr Bennet also wrote a note to Mr Gardiner in which he more fully explained the news as revealed in Mr Spencer's original communication.

After much fuss, visits to dressmakers, enthusiastic discussions, and occasional moments of amazement, the Bennets entered the large, fine carriages with the Everard coat of arms and began their journey north. Mr Bennet, Jane, and Elizabeth travelled in the first carriage, while Mrs Bennet and the remaining three daughters followed in the other. Their own small family carriage followed behind with servants and trunks. In this pleasant fashion, after two days on the road, they crossed into Staffordshire. Elizabeth became increasingly in awe of the beautiful countryside. It was so wild and untamed compared to the sedate woods and fields of Hertfordshire.

Towards the end of the third afternoon of travel, they arrived at Grancourt. The house was a large, rambling building set on a wide plain with hills and forests rising behind it. The sun turned the stone of the house a glowing gold, and towering, overarching trees flanked the avenue leading to the inner courtyard. It was an impressive sight, and they were all quite thunderstruck by its grandeur.

After alighting from the carriages, the Grancourt servants directed the Bennets to a spacious room, at the centre of which stood a handsome, finely dressed woman, whom all assumed to be the dowager duchess.

Duchess Agatha surveyed her guests with an intelligent eye and curtseyed to Mr Bennet. "Welcome to Grancourt, Your Grace."

"Duchess Agatha," he replied with a bow, "thank you for the invitation. May I introduce my family?"

The lady nodded and turned expectantly to the Bennet ladies. The duke continued with the introductions. "May I present my wife and my daughters." Motioning towards each of the girls, he stated, "Lady Jane, Lady Elizabeth, Lady Mary, Lady Catherine, and Lady Lydia."

At the pronouncement of her name, Lydia gave an unlady-like snort. The duke turned a gimlet eye towards his youngest daughter, the duchess blinked, and Jane blushed and looked down in mortification.

Elizabeth watched Duchess Agatha. For her part, she maintained an expressionless face except for a slight narrowing of her eyes. Elizabeth had for some time been contemplating exactly what type of woman the dowager would be. She dreaded another Lady Catherine de Bourgh and hoped for an intelligent yet forgiving and compassionate woman like her Aunt Gardiner.

Duchess Agatha's features softened slightly. "You are all very welcome." She gestured towards a set of couches and chairs in the centre of the room. "You must be tired from your journey and in want of rest and refreshment."

She rang for a servant, requested tea and refreshments be served immediately and then seated herself in a chair that commanded a view of the others as they sat down in the available places.

As the group was getting comfortable, Duchess Agatha's gaze wandered over her new relations. Watching her, Elizabeth understood she was inspecting them, and they were most likely falling short of expectations. She determined to make conversation.

"Your Grace, I am very sorry for your loss. To lose both your husband and his brother's family in such a tragic accident…"

"Thank you, Lady Elizabeth. It has been a most difficult time. The ship was due to land several months ago, and when it failed to arrive in London, enquiries were immediately sent out to determine its whereabouts. Unfortunately, the answer was a devastating one. Another vessel passed the wreckage and brought word of the ship's end. No one survived. My husband, his brother Nathaniel, my dear sister Margaret, along with their two children, all perished."

The dowager turned towards the window and a deep sadness seemed to descend upon her.

"You were a close family?" Elizabeth asked. "I am so sorry. I do not know what I would do if I were to lose loved ones."

Duchess Agatha returned her gaze to Elizabeth. "I met Joshua at the end of my first Season just after he returned from the West Indies, and we were married shortly thereafter. I loved him deeply. Meg was my twin, and we were inseparable until our marriages. Our husbands were brothers, and very close, so naturally our families remained on intimate terms. Nathaniel had remained behind in the Indies for several years, so he and Meg married later, which is also why their children were still quite young."

This statement startled Elizabeth, and her heart went out to Duchess Agatha. She considered what her own feelings would be were she to lose Jane or one of her other sisters, and in an attempt to comfort the lady, she offered a soft smile and placed her hand over hers.

"I know we cannot replace your family, but you now have five cousins, and we shall do our best to help alleviate your sorrow."

Duchess Agatha appeared touched by Elizabeth's genuine response. "You are very kind. Joshua and I always hoped for children but were never blessed, and I doted upon my sister's family. And though I will miss them all terribly, it will be wonderful to have young ladies in the house again. Having grown up with a twin sister, I have missed the companionship of women and know you will bring me comfort during this time of mourning."

Elizabeth felt an attachment beginning to form between them. "We will do our best, but you may find that six extra females in the house is more than you might wish."

Duchess Agatha smiled. "Time will tell, Lady Elizabeth."

The servants entered with the tea service and all conversation momentarily stopped while they were served. After all were settled with tea and cake, Duchess Agatha addressed the purpose of the Bennets' visit and turned to the duke.

"I suppose the letter from Mr Spencer quite astounded you when you received it?"

"Your supposition is correct, Duchess. I know we will have much to discuss in the upcoming days."

Conversation then turned to the journey from Hertford-shire and other mundane subjects. After a quarter of an hour, the duke yawned indiscreetly, and Duchess Agatha suggested they retire to their rooms for a rest and change before dinner.

"I have moved into another family apartment and have ordered the master's and mistress's chambers made ready for you. The ladies also each have a room in the family wing, and I have selected a maid for each of them." Turning to the duchess, she said, "I understand your own maid accompanied you."

"Yes, though I am sure I should require a French maid now. Sarah will hardly know how to do the latest coiffures, and without a proper one, I cannot show my face in London."

Duchess Agatha informed her that they could acquire new maids in London if so desired, but they would probably not travel to town for several months. The duchess was pleased with this explanation and allowed the housekeeper to show her to her rooms.

Duchess Agatha caught Elizabeth's eyes starting to roll and tried to hide the small smile forming on her lips, but Elizabeth comprehended it and smiled shyly in return.

Jane and Elizabeth were glad to be shown to adjacent rooms, and once they entered, discovered there was an adjoining door between their chambers. They thoroughly inspected both rooms and their vast dressing rooms. They teased each other about the number of gowns they would have to order to fill the racks and shelves.

Elizabeth was glad to note, although richly furnished, the entire house was neither gaudy nor uselessly fine, with less of splendour and more real elegance than the furniture of Rosings. A discreet knock announced the arrival of their maids, and after requesting they return in an hour to help them prepare for dinner, the maids were dismissed, and Jane and Elizabeth fell onto the bed in Elizabeth's chamber to rest before dinner.

THE FAMILY GATHERED TOGETHER AT THE ARRANGED TIME, and the footmen directed them to a small, informal dining room. The table was beautifully appointed, and the meal was cooked to perfection. Duchess Agatha was elegantly attired, far more fashionably than the rest of the party, though in mourning clothes.

As the dinner progressed, some comments by the duchess or Elizabeth's younger sisters caused Duchess Agatha's countenance to tighten with apparent disapproval. On the whole though, the dinner was a pleasant affair. During the last course, the dowager began to speak.

"It is delightful to have so many people at table. I am afraid it had become a rather dull affair with just Joshua and myself. Nathaniel and Margaret often stayed at Grancourt with their children, but they had been living at Bennet Hall, our estate on Jamaica, for the last three years. The holding was recently divested, and I was eagerly anticipating their return. We were a small family party, and it is pleasant to have more people with whom to converse. However, I know you must all be exhausted from your trip and the ensuing excitement, so I propose we retire directly after dinner."

Turning to the duke she said, "Could we perhaps meet tomorrow morning to discuss some of the particulars of the inheritance and estate affairs? I was informed before dinner that Mr Spencer has arrived. He should be prepared to review matters tomorrow."

"That will be agreeable, Your Grace."

"Good. If that is all settled, then I shall excuse myself. Goodnight."

"Excuse me, Duchess Agatha," the duke called and motioned her aside from the others as they exited the dining room. "I would like Jane and Elizabeth to be present during our discussions with Mr Spencer."

Duchess Agatha was clearly surprised by this request, and it showed plainly on her face.

The duke smiled and continued. "I value their sense and judgment. They are of an age and intelligence to understand the various nuances of this change."

"Would you also like the duchess to be present?"

"I do not think that will be necessary. My wife is overtired from the preparations and the journey and does not generally concern herself with financial and estate matters. I think she will be quite content to recuperate tomorrow. Perhaps a tour of the house could be arranged for my wife and younger daughters. Sometime in the afternoon perhaps?"

The duchess smiled and agreed to his requests.

THE NEXT DAY, ELIZABETH WOKE AT HER USUAL EARLY HOUR and summoned her maid. She was quickly dressed and left her chamber in search of the breakfast room. There, she found her father, Duchess Agatha, and surprisingly, Jane—who usually awoke later than Elizabeth—already seated and enjoying a companionable silence as they broke their fast.

"Good morning, Lady Elizabeth," said Duchess Agatha. "I hope you slept well."

"I did, thank you." Elizabeth served herself some tea and rolls and sat down next to Jane. "And thank you for assigning Carter as my maid. She is a treasure. She already had my trunks unpacked and all the clothes organised! And I am sure I have never been dressed as quickly and efficiently as I was this morning, though having a maid all to myself, rather than sharing one with five others, may account for a small part of this efficiency."

Duchess Agatha laughed softly. "There will be a great many things for which you will need to accustom yourself, my dear, and not sharing a maid will be but a minor one. In fact, once we are finished, we should adjourn to the master's study and meet with Mr Spencer."

Elizabeth turned a quizzical eye towards her father.

"I would like for you both to be present in the discussions with Mr Spencer," the duke explained.

Elizabeth was a bit surprised, but she was also thankful for this consideration. She did not want to miss any new revelations Mr Spencer might disclose. "Should we wait for Mama?"

"The duchess and I have arranged for your mother and

sisters to take a tour of the house this afternoon. The girls can surely find other amusements until then."

"I do not think Mary would enjoy the tour. Perhaps she could be directed towards a pianoforte or the library."

Duchess Agatha informed a servant to have Mary shown the music room after she had dressed and eaten. With the activities of the rest of the party determined, the four made their way to the study to meet with Mr Spencer.

THE ATTORNEY, AN ELDERLY GENTLEMAN, GREETED THEM formally. "It is an honour to meet you, Your Grace. Thank you for your prompt responses to my letters. I know Her Grace was anxious to meet you and proceed with the transition. There are some issues that need your attention—signing papers and such—and I am also at your service to answer any questions you may have regarding the inheritance and certain estate matters. There are, of course, stewards for each of the properties with whom you may wish to confer individually to gain better knowledge of each estate. I have been the family's attorney for many years, and my father served before me, so I am quite familiar with the terms of the title and its inheritance. Where would you like to begin?"

"First, I would like to dispense with the formalities of all these titles! If it is agreeable to you, Duchess Agatha, please call me Bennet, and pray call my wife Frances."

"And you must call me Agatha. We are family." She smiled at him. "Very good. That is settled."

The duke reflected for a moment and asked Mr Spencer the question foremost in his mind. "In your letter, you stated the original Patent of Nobility had some unique qualities. What exactly are they?"

"Ah, yes. As you know, this peerage title is an old one. As such, it does not follow the more modern rules of inheritance, meaning it can be inherited through the female line. The original patent charts a line of descent that follows one line only until all members are deceased. The males of each line have precedence, but then the females have precedence before the inheritance passes onto the next line or generation. So, if your cousin, Duchess Agatha's late husband, had any living children, whether male or female, the title would not have fallen to you. This would also have been the case had his brother or any of his children survived. It is only because all descendants of Alexander Bennet's line are deceased that the inheritance has moved onto the next family line, that of your father, James. He was never disinherited, so he is not exempt from the line of descent.

"Now, if you had a son, the title would naturally fall to him, but because you do not, your heir shall be the son of your firstborn daughter, both for the title and Everard estates. If no sons are born, then the oldest daughter of your firstborn child will inherit, followed by her firstborn son and so on. This prevents the title from dying out and becoming obsolete."

Elizabeth and Jane were speechless. Not being raised among nobility, they were never taught the minute details of peerage inheritance. They had only understood entails. This thought brought her cousin to Elizabeth's mind.

"So Mr Collins is not my father's heir?"

"He is the next in line after the duke's grandchildren," explained Mr Spencer. "He is still the heir to Longbourn. That entail was written recently and follows the more current practice of male-only descent. If you and all your sisters were to die before producing any children, then Mr Collins would inherit the Everard title and estates."

"Thank you for that thorough explanation," replied the duke. "What is the extent of the Everard estates?"

"There are eight country estates, of which Grancourt is the largest. Their total annual income is nearly seventy thousand pounds. There are also two London houses. Everard House is located on Brook Street in Grosvenor Square and has been the principal London house since it was built. The smaller house, Malvallet House, is currently leased to a distant cousin. There are various investments in companies and businesses that bring the total income to around one hundred-twenty-five thousand a year."

The sisters could not prevent a small gasp from escaping their lips. Elizabeth was thankful her mother was not present. If Mr Bingley's five thousand a year could produce raptures, Elizabeth did not want to contemplate the hysterics their father's income would generate.

But Mr Spencer was not finished with his explanation. "We have determined a fortune of forty thousand should be settled on each of your daughters upon their marriage with parental consent or when they reach the age of thirty."

"Do you not think the amount excessive?" the duke questioned.

"It is somewhat smaller than the common amount for ladies of their station, Your Grace, but there are five of them, and the estate would have a difficult time recovering from something larger."

Duchess Agatha, seeming to notice the duke's concern, interjected, "Let us return to that discussion later. We need to determine the time of your permanent removal to Grancourt."

Elizabeth startled at this statement. Of course they would move to Grancourt. Instinctively she knew it, but the thought of leaving Hertfordshire and Longbourn suddenly saddened her. Though she had thought she would be happy to live in Staffordshire, she would miss the woods and groves of her childhood home. But Elizabeth was not of a nature to brood over what could not be changed and soon found herself looking forward to the opportunities that living at Grancourt would provide. *My own maid for a start*, she thought impishly.

"Let us call for refreshments," Agatha said, "and then we can continue our discussion. We need to determine how to retrieve your belongings from Hertfordshire, when you want to go to London, presentations at court, announcements to newspapers, and numerous other details."

While they ate, Agatha questioned the girls about their accomplishments and education. She seemed pleased that Jane, Elizabeth, and to some degree Mary, were well read and that Elizabeth and Mary could play the pianoforte. Jane volunteered that Elizabeth also had a pleasing voice and way of performing. The statement caused Elizabeth to blush slightly and to tease her sister in response by reporting that Jane was a fairly accomplished horsewoman. All the girls had been taught needlepoint, cards, the serving of tea, and the other mundane actions gentlewomen would be called upon to perform.

Mr Spencer produced some papers for the duke to sign, and they drafted an announcement of the inheritance to be placed in some of London's prominent newspapers. The passing of Joshua Bennet and Nathaniel's family had already been reported several months earlier, and speculation was already rife among the upper echelons of society as to the identity of the next Duke of Everard. Agatha and Mr Spencer suggested a little forewarning of the imminent introduction of the new duke, duchess, and their family would somewhat alleviate the curiosity of the *ton*, at least until they came to London. Mr Spencer was dismissed with the newspaper announcement in hand. He would return to London in the early morning to see to legal matters.

The presentation at court of the duke and duchess could not take place until the following spring, at the beginning of the London Season. This would allow for ample time to move to Grancourt and even spend a little time in London to procure necessary items of clothing.

As the conversation turned to these matters, Agatha spoke. "I have been reflecting on your daughters' futures. May I be frank with you?" At the duke's nod, she continued. In this level of society, girls as young as Catherine and Lydia, and even Mary, would not be out in society when their older sisters are unmarried. I do not believe the younger girls are ready to be presented yet."

Elizabeth and Jane's eyes widened at this statement. They had often thought similarly, but their suggestions had never been heeded. They both turned to their father to judge his reaction.

The duke pondered a moment. "I believe you are right. What would you suggest we do?"

"The younger girls would all be served by attending school for a few years. Mary could attend a school I know of in the south that emphasises music. She could perfect her talent of the pianoforte and learn other instruments. I believe only a year or two would be necessary before you could bring her out into society again. Catherine and Lydia should probably attend for another three or four years. This would enable them to further their knowledge, and each might pursue another interest such as music or drawing."

Elizabeth interrupted. "I suggest Kitty and Lydia be sent to separate schools. This would allow them to make their own friends and develop independence from one another."

The duke nodded his agreement with this insight. "Well, ladies, I believe this course of action would be for the best." Turning to the dowager duchess, he said, "I shall need the names of some schools and will write to them directly to seek admission."

"Perhaps after the new year would be best. You can spend autumn in London, to shop for clothing and other necessities, and then spend the winter at Grancourt. Would you like to invite some relations or friends to spend Christmas here? I believe I shall visit my cousin's family if they can accommodate me."

"Surely, you would stay here. I am certain none of my family want to thrust you from the home you have known for so many years. And we enjoy your company so much." Elizabeth looked to her father and sister for support.

"Oh yes, Duchess Agatha," Jane responded. "Say that you will stay. You are our family now and should be here with us."

The duke added his entreaty. "You must always consider Grancourt your home. You are not a guest here. You are certainly welcome to visit your other relations if you desire, but it would be very agreeable if you would stay. Besides, I believe your advice will only become more invaluable as the Season approaches, for I surely cannot recommend which gowns to wear and which lace is most becoming!"

Agatha laughed delightedly, both at the duke's wit and the warm affection shown by Jane and Elizabeth.

"You entreat so sweetly that I must oblige and stay!" she said. Elizabeth clapped her hands in pleasure and Jane smiled. "So, shall we all travel to London in a few months? On the way back north, we can stop in Hertfordshire to ready the belongings you wish to bring to Grancourt." All agreed to this plan.

"I must admit," Elizabeth stated, "I shall be sad to leave Longbourn. We spent many happy years there. Although I shall have most of my loved ones with me, Aunt and Uncle Philips will remain in Meryton. Charlotte has already left, of course."

This statement again brought Mr Collins to mind, and she questioned her father. "Will Mr Collins and Charlotte be invited to live at Longbourn? It would not do to leave the house vacant."

"I shall write to him and make the offer, though Mr Collins may not desire to leave his esteemed patroness," the duke responded wryly.

The remainder of their sequestered time was spent discussing dates of travel and how they should spend their time at Grancourt. Elizabeth expressed a desire to become acquainted with the countryside. Agatha suggested she and Jane ride, as Grancourt had splendid stables, and it was the best way to view the estate. Elizabeth declared her preference for walking.

Agatha looked askance at her. "Is that so? I now recall you only declared Jane an accomplished horsewoman."

"I am not. I had a rather disagreeable argument with a horse when I was young, and it put me off them completely."

"I assume the horse won that argument?"

"Yes, he most emphatically did. I wanted to learn to ride, he did not want to teach me, which resulted in me laying on the ground with a broken arm."

"Oh Lizzy," Jane exclaimed, "that was years ago. You must have been seven years old. I have attempted time and time again to persuade you to try once more. It is so unlike you to fear something after so much time has passed."

"You really should try again, my dear," Agatha said.

"There are several very gentle mares in the stables that would suit you perfectly, and mounted is truly the best way to see the countryside around Grancourt. While walking is beneficial exercise, the northern landscape is less cultivated than Hertfordshire, and many trails and walks are too steep or rough to travel on foot. I would be happy to teach you. I have been riding since I was a young girl, and I assure you it would be quite safe and enjoyable." The duchess smiled, and Elizabeth found her apprehension weakening.

"Perhaps you are right. I shall think about it and let you know if I decide to accept your kind offer."

"Good. Now, I believe we have been locked up in this study long enough. The rest of your family must be wondering where we have gone. Shall we try to find them? Then perhaps later we could walk in the garden, and I could begin to acquaint you with Grancourt's splendid park."

"That sounds delightful," Elizabeth replied, and both she and Jane rose from their seats.

"Before we go," said the duke, "I have a request to make." He waited until the three had given their acknowledgement. "I would prefer not to inform the other girls about their upcoming attendance at school. Kitty and Lydia will both be bitterly disappointed not to participate in the Season next year. We shall have no peace over the ensuing months if they are informed early. I shall tell them after Christmas. Let us have a quiet autumn and winter, or at least as quiet as possible under the circumstances." The three accepted the duke's request, and they left to find the others.

Mary was in the music room, dutifully practising the pianoforte while valiantly trying to ignore the commotion produced by her mother and younger sisters. The duchess had thoroughly enjoyed her tour of Grancourt Manor. Upon seeing

Agatha, she immediately began singing the praises of the estate's material possessions. Elizabeth thought Agatha hid well her irritation at such vulgarity.

THE FAMILY SPENT THE REMAINDER OF THE SUMMER AT Grancourt. Elizabeth and Jane grew even fonder of Duchess Agatha and counted her only below their parents and the Gardiners in their affection. The three were most often found outside, exploring the countryside, for Elizabeth had relented to Duchess Agatha's gentle persuasion and was learning to ride.

Occasionally, the duke would accompany them, but he was happiest when firmly established in his large library with a glass of his favourite port. He would also seek sanctuary from his wife in the master's study, where the duchess did not attempt to interrupt him, being informed by her husband that essential estate business was conducted there, and any inter-ruption would be disastrous to the future of the dukedom.

The duchess spent the summer almost exclusively in Kitty and Lydia's company. They wasted entire days paging through fashion publications and planning their London shopping excursions.

Periodically, Agatha would devote a day to instructing the new duchess in the running of Grancourt and the expectations of the *ton*. She was still in sufficient awe of Agatha that when entirely alone with her, she displayed some modesty in an imitation of Agatha's demeanour.

In this way, the Duke of Everard and his family spent a pleasant summer. But sooner than they thought possible, the autumn was upon them. They ordered their trunks packed and made their way to London.

CHAPTER 3

Pemberley, Derbyshire

F itzwilliam Darcy stopped his horse on the rise overlooking his estate. He was relieved to be home again. The spring had been a difficult time—his mind in tumult and his spirit weighed down by introspection. Being on the grounds of Pemberley brought immediate solace to his wearied soul, and he looked forward to a day of solitude before the arrival of his guests on the morrow. After a few more moments of respite, he spurred his horse towards the stable.

He left his mount in the capable hands of a groomsman and began to make his way towards the manor house. Turning a corner in the path, Darcy stopped short at seeing strangers on his property. Being a private man, he had always dreaded the summer tradition of opening one's property to the inspection of visitors. However, over the prior months, he had spent a considerable amount of time examining his character.

After the disastrous proposal in April, he had carefully examined all of Elizabeth Bennet's accusations and had discovered she was correct in many of her assertions. Yes, some of her opinions had been based on misinformation and even lies, which he hoped had been corrected with his letter, but the other charges, *'your arrogance, your conceit, and your selfish disdain for the feelings of others,'* were too often correct. Darcy had only to recall the words of his marriage proposal. He had not at all considered Elizabeth's feelings. He had belittled and humbled her with his words about her family and connexions. He was condescending and patronising, and in some respects, no better than Lady Catherine!

The result of such introspection was the formation of many resolutions. He would become a better man. Gratitude filled his heart for Elizabeth and the opportunity she had inadvertently offered him. Although he could not have her love, he would live his life so that, if they were ever to meet again, she would approve of him.

Before him was a perfect chance to show his resolve. Elizabeth had declared that he did not converse easily with strangers because he would not practise. *Well, I will practise now!*

He approached the couple and bowed. "Welcome to Pemberley. I am Mr Darcy." He finished this short speech with a small smile and held his breath. The lady returned his smile.

"Good day, sir. I am Mr Gardiner and this is my wife. We thank you for your kind hospitality in allowing us to tour your estate. Your home and lands are beautiful, but no doubt you know that already."

"The finest we have seen," Mrs Gardiner added. "But pray

forgive us if we intrude upon your privacy. Your housekeeper assured us that the family was away from home."

Darcy was relieved this man and his wife appeared to be friendly and polite people. It made his attempt to practise much easier.

Waving away Mrs Gardiner's apology, Darcy said, "I was not expected until tomorrow but rode on ahead of my party to discuss some business with my steward. Have you just begun a tour of the park?"

"Yes, we were on our way to the stream. Your gardener assured us there are some lovely views along that walk. We shall go there now. Pray, do not let us disrupt your business."

Darcy surprised himself with the discovery that he desired to remain in their company and asked Mr Gardiner, "Would you like me to accompany you? I could point out some areas of interest."

His surprise apparent, Mr Gardiner readily assented after seeking his wife's approval. As the threesome made their way along the stream, they fell into a natural discussion of travel and the beauties of Derbyshire and Pemberley. Darcy found a like mind in Mrs Gardiner, who believed as he did in the superior merits of Derbyshire to any other county. The conversation flowed easily, and Darcy's gratitude for Elizabeth swelled anew. *To think of all the opportunities I may have missed due to my excessive reserve!*

They stopped at a particularly lovely spot upon a simple bridge. The area was unadorned, and the valley contracted into a small glen, bordered by coppice-woods. It was a charming place.

"Elizabeth would love this spot," Mrs Gardiner mused aloud.

Darcy visibly startled at this pronouncement. He had been

thinking the same thought, though undoubtedly of a different Elizabeth.

"My niece Elizabeth is a great lover of nature and would have adored this view. She was to have accompanied us on this trip but is instead traveling to attend to some family business." Mrs Gardiner paused and then said, "I believe you may be acquainted with her."

Darcy could not contain his surprise. He started to speak, swallowed, and tentatively asked, "What is the lady's name?"

"Miss Elizabeth Bennet of Longbourn in Hertfordshire," said Mrs Gardiner. "I understand she met you last autumn when you stayed with Mr Bingley."

"Yes, of course, and I saw her again in Kent when she visited her friend Mrs Collins." Darcy could hardly believe his misfortune. *Elizabeth could have been here at Pemberley! We might have been talking at this very moment!*

It had been too long since he had last seen or talked with her—too long since he had heard her delightful laughter or crossed verbal swords with her wit. He realised it would have been an awkward meeting, but he believed he could endure anything if only he could look into her enchanting eyes and show her that he had addressed her reproofs.

"I am sorry not to be able to see Miss Bennet again. I have witnessed first-hand her love of walking and exploring. I often came across her during her rambles. I hope she will visit Derbyshire another time, for someone with such a passion for nature would almost certainly gain much enjoyment from this county."

Mr Gardiner laughed. "Do not worry about Lizzy, Mr Darcy. I am sure that she is enjoying the wondrous countryside of Staffordshire just as much. After all, it is almost as far north as Derbyshire."

Only one county away! Cursed luck! What is she doing in Staffordshire? Mrs Gardiner said something about attending to family business. Is her family well? Is she well? He could tolerate the uncertainty no longer and unflinchingly enquired about the Bennets and their welfare.

To his surprise, the Gardiners seemed somewhat discomfited. "They are visiting relations for the summer, which prevented our niece from travelling with us. We were sad to lose her company, but she was needed, and we hope to meet together in the autumn or winter."

Although Darcy was disappointed and extremely frustrated at missing Elizabeth, he resolved to show the Gardiners every civility with the hope it would reach her ears, and she would think better of him. He would also not waste an opportunity to learn more of her.

Unfortunately, Mrs Gardiner chose that moment to announce it was time for them to return to Lambton, as they had a dinner engagement. Darcy escorted them back to their carriage and expressed his desire to meet again before they left the area.

"Perhaps I may be allowed to introduce my sister during your stay?"

"That is a lovely idea," agreed Mrs Gardiner. "We shall look forward to your call. We are staying at the Crown Inn and should be there for the week."

Darcy nodded and signalled to the driver. He watched the carriage disappear over the hill, his heart lighter than it had been in many months.

DURING THE FIRST MONTH OF INTROSPECTION FOLLOWING HIS proposal to Elizabeth, Darcy often found himself in the midst of an almost insurmountable despair and loneliness. Although he did not realise it until some weeks later, Georgiana had become extremely worried about his dark and sombre mood and thought he was perhaps still angry about her near elopement the prior summer. Unable to discover the reason for her brother's bad temper, she had solicited the advice of their cousin Colonel Fitzwilliam.

He answered Georgiana's letter by appearing at the Darcy's London townhouse. When the colonel was shown in, Darcy was slumped in a chair, staring vacantly out the library window. Colonel Fitzwilliam greeted his cousin, who barely deigned to respond, and took a seat. He then proceeded to ply Darcy with liberal amounts of brandy, and over the course of the evening, persuaded him to reveal the source of his melancholy. The entire history of Darcy's relationship with Elizabeth Bennet unfolded.

Fitzwilliam seemed sympathetic to Darcy's predicament but did not attempt to give him advice concerning his actions towards Miss Elizabeth. However, he did not hesitate to counsel him regarding his treatment of Georgiana. "You have completely neglected your sister, and she is worried about you," the colonel informed him.

Darcy flushed with shame at this pronouncement. He had not regarded Georgiana's feelings. Elizabeth's accusations that he had been selfish and unfeeling were sound. This was the beginning of his resolve to change his character. He would begin as soon as he was sober.

"You are correct, Fitz. I have been an appalling brother to Georgiana. I shall talk with her tomorrow."

"She is growing up. I believe you can share some of your problems with her. You do not need to shoulder them alone."

The cousins shook hands and Darcy followed the colonel's

advice, sharing his story with his sister the next morning. The resulting shift in their relationship had delighted both siblings over the last several months.

Darcy contemplated all this while standing on the front steps of Pemberley, awaiting the arrival of his sister and the Bingley party. He was excited to acquaint Georgiana with his unexpected good fortune the previous day. He knew she would understand his eagerness to spend time with the Gardiners and hoped to gain her approval of an introduction and possible invitation to a dinner at Pemberley.

The sound of a carriage alerted Darcy of his sister's approach. Bingley rode next to the carriage and nodded a greeting as he dismounted. Darcy approached the carriage, waving away the footman to open the door and assist his sister himself in exiting the carriage. Georgiana gave him a tired but grateful smile. The footman then approached, handing out Mrs Hurst first, then Miss Bingley, followed by Mr Hurst stumbling from the vehicle.

Darcy embraced his sister and, leaning down, whispered, "Welcome home, dearest. We must see to our guests first, but I would like to talk to you as soon as may be."

Looking up at her brother and noticing his smile, Georgiana seemed intrigued. Darcy turned to his other guests, welcomed them to Pemberley, and gestured them into the house. The party entered a large drawing room where the servants had laid out refreshments.

Miss Bingley immediately accosted him. "Oh Mr Darcy, what a terrible journey we have had! If only you had not left us yesterday. The trip would have been much more pleasant with your company."

"I regret the carriage was not to your liking, Miss Bingley. I had business with my steward that could not be delayed, and as I would have ridden alongside you, we would not have had much occasion to talk during the journey."

"Certainly, sir, we would not want to interrupt your business. Such a fine, grand estate as Pemberley must require an extraordinary amount of your time. And you are always so diligent in attending to everything."

She flashed a simpering smile, and Darcy controlled the urge to roll his eyes or retreat to the window. He offered his guests tea and food, and the group conversed for a quarter of an hour before Darcy suggested they retire to their rooms to refresh themselves from their *terrible journey*.

As Georgiana left the room, she caught her brother's eye, and after a quick wash and change of clothes, she joined him in his study. He directed her to a chair near him, which she took and turned to him expectantly.

"I have a surprise to share with you. When I first arrived home and was walking from the stable, I came across a couple touring the house and grounds."

"Oh? Did you know them?"

"I introduced myself to them," Darcy admitted somewhat sheepishly, "and we began a conversation. I was relieved to discover they were an agreeable and friendly couple, and I offered to show them some good views along the stream."

"Brother, I am astonished!"

"There is more. In the course of our conversation, I discovered that the couple, Mr and Mrs Gardiner, are Miss Elizabeth Bennet's aunt and uncle. She was to have travelled with them this summer but was called away to visit other family members. She is in Staffordshire for the entire summer, I believe."

Darcy paused to gauge his sister's reaction. Georgiana was speechless. Darcy did not leave her in suspense long.

"I would like to spend some time with them while they are in the neighbourhood. Mrs Gardiner spent some of her youth in Lambton and they are planning to stay at an inn there for a week before returning to London. I would like to introduce you, and I hope to invite them to dinner at Pemberley."

"Oh! But I do not know if I can!"

"I promise they are very pleasant and kind people."

Georgiana gave him a tremulous smile. "I would be happy to make their acquaintance."

Darcy smiled brilliantly. "Thank you, Ana." The use of her childhood name brought a sincere smile to Georgiana's face. "I would like to call on them tomorrow, if that is agreeable?" Georgiana nodded her acceptance, and she and her brother parted to dress for dinner.

THE DARCYS WERE BOTH EARLY RISERS COMPARED TO THEIR guests. They were able to break their fast alone the following morning. Darcy gave Georgiana a more detailed description of his first encounter with the Gardiners. He had also questioned Mrs Reynolds regarding the couple and received a favourable account, which he shared with his sister.

After they had eaten, they retired to the music room. Darcy presented a new pianoforte to Georgiana in honour of her birthday and requested she play for him. He was anxious to be in Lambton, but knew it was entirely too early for a polite call. He hoped his sister's music would calm him and help the time pass more quickly. They spent a pleasant hour in this manner until Bingley joined them.

Darcy informed him about their intent to visit some acquaintances in Lambton but did not name the Gardiners specifically. Darcy still harboured some guilt concerning his deception of his dear friend. He knew at some point he would have to confess his knowledge of Jane Bennet's presence in town last winter to Bingley, but he did not want anything to impede his visit. The time for disclosure would have to wait. He recognised the innate selfishness in this action but promised himself he would not delay too long and pushed the thought from his mind.

Not surprisingly, Bingley chose to remain at Pemberley and promised to make the Darcys' excuses to his relations once they awoke. Darcy and Georgiana left shortly thereafter and rode the five miles to Lambton to call upon the Gardiners.

They found them in their rooms at the inn. Mrs Gardiner had been in the midst of writing a letter, and Darcy wondered whether it was meant for Elizabeth, or even better, whether it contained information about Pemberley and Derbyshire.

He immediately moved to introduce his sister. Darcy was pleased that Mrs Gardiner, being a well-mannered woman, instantly drew Georgiana into conversation, leaving the men to talk. As he spoke with Mr Gardiner, Darcy looked towards his sister frequently and was relieved to see her begin to relax. Mrs Gardiner was a truly gracious woman, and Darcy was pleased he had sought an introduction for his sister.

Georgiana had little opportunity to make friends, and she was uneasy among most women of the *ton*. Women like Miss Bingley particularly discomfited her, with their strident voices and snide comments. Georgiana would benefit from an association with a woman such as Mrs Gardiner.

Darcy remembered Jane and Elizabeth had spent quite a bit of time with these relations and better understood the differences between them and their younger sisters. The influence of their aunt must have been great, and he was thankful Elizabeth had been so privileged.

Darcy also enjoyed himself. Mr Gardiner was sociable and open but was also well-informed and intelligent. Darcy was again ashamed that, only a few months ago, he would have refused an acquaintance with Mr Gardiner purely based on his residing in Cheapside and being in trade.

His conversation with Elizabeth's uncle ranged over many subjects, and Darcy relished the opportunity to converse with a man he could respect and admire. People so often deferred to his opinion that he rarely found someone who could meet him in intellectual discourse.

Elizabeth could as well and I often found myself at a disadvantage! She is my match in every way. How am I to live without her?

Pushing such thoughts aside, he focused again on the man before him. He recognised Mr Gardiner would also meet this standard. In fact, the man reminded Darcy of his father, though he was more loquacious.

The subject had turned to fishing, and Darcy invited Mr Gardiner to Pemberley to pursue that gentlemanly recreation. Mr Gardiner applied to his wife, and when she allowed they had no set engagements, the men agreed to meet in the morning to fish. Mrs Gardiner would join them later at Pemberley for dinner.

Mrs Gardiner asked Miss Darcy whether she would like to shop with her and an acquaintance and then join them for tea while the men were busy. Georgiana's companion, Mrs Annesley, had been granted some time to visit her sister before joining the Darcys at Pemberley. Therefore, Georgiana had no studies to attend to besides her music and was desirous to accompany Mrs Gardiner. Her brother agreed, and a time was determined for Georgiana to meet the ladies at the inn the following morning.

With plans firmly settled, the Darcys bid farewell and returned to Pemberley. Brother and sister were quiet on the return journey. Georgiana seemed pleased with her new acquaintances, and Darcy was also satisfied with the visit. He wished he could have mentioned Elizabeth in the conversation, but he was content that he would see the Gardiners for the better part of the next day. He hoped to question them about their niece and learn more about how she had fared over the past few months.

THE DARCYS RETURNED TO PEMBERLEY TO FIND A DISPLEASED Caroline Bingley.

"We have been quite desolate without you this morning, Mr Darcy. Where could you have gone so early?"

"I had some acquaintances in the village I wished to introduce to Georgiana, so we paid a call on them. I have invited them to dinner tomorrow. Mr Gardiner is going to come fish in the morning. Would you care to join us, Bingley?"

"That would be a pleasure."

"Oh yes," said Miss Bingley, "we would love to welcome any guests you invite to Pemberley."

He could not believe the presumption of the woman. Did she think she would serve as his hostess? "I am sure all my guests will be kind to the Gardiners. Now if you will excuse me, I must speak to Mrs Reynolds." He bowed and left the room to make arrangements for the next day.

CHAPTER 4

The next morning, a Pemberley coach drove Georgiana into Lambton. It brought her to the Crown Inn, where Mr Gardiner was waiting. He returned to the estate in the carriage to meet the gentlemen and left Miss Darcy in the care of his wife. The carriage would return again in the late afternoon to take Georgiana and Mrs Gardiner to Pemberley for dinner.

After greeting her hostess, a little of Georgiana's shyness returned, and Mrs Gardiner immediately sought to ease it.

"I am so pleased you could join us this morning. My friend Mrs Sullivan should be here shortly, and then we can venture into the village. Would you care for some tea before we leave?" Georgiana nodded, and Mrs Gardiner fixed a cup for her.

"Do you often come into Lambton when you are at Pemberley, Miss Darcy?"

"Not very often. I am afraid I am not familiar with the village."

"It has not changed much since I lived here, and Mrs Sullivan has promised to show us all the best shops. We shall be in good hands. It is wonderful to visit here. I enjoyed my childhood years spent in Derbyshire. As we discussed yesterday, no county can compare in beauty. I only wish my niece could have accompanied us as planned."

Georgiana could not believe her luck. She had resolved to question Mrs Gardiner about Elizabeth Bennet, and the good lady had just given her the perfect opportunity. However, she was not well versed in subtlety and pursued the subject frankly.

"I have heard much about your niece. My brother often wrote about the Bennets while he was staying with Mr Bingley and again when he met with Miss Elizabeth in Kent. I understand they spent quite a bit of time together while she visited her friend." This was the most Georgiana had spoken since meeting Mrs Gardiner.

The lady smiled at the young girl. "I too have heard about your brother from my niece. Perhaps we can all meet sometime when you are in London."

"I am sure my brother and I would be honoured to do so when we are next in town. May I send a note to you on our return to London in the autumn?"

"I would be delighted, and I will be sure to leave the direction before we depart for home."

A noise was heard in the corridor, and a servant knocked and entered the room to announce the arrival of Mrs Sullivan. Mrs Gardiner and Georgiana joined her and had a pleasant morning exploring the village. After several hours, the group returned to the inn to partake of a light meal and more conversation.

Georgiana rarely had such a satisfying excursion. After Mrs Sullivan left to attend to her children, Mrs Gardiner quickly changed for dinner, and they took the carriage back to Pemberley.

Upon arrival, Mr Darcy and Mr Gardiner were on the front steps to greet them.

"Good evening. We are so pleased you could join us for dinner," Darcy said, and taking Mrs Gardiner's and his sister's arms, he escorted the ladies into the house.

Mrs Gardiner looked to her husband, who appeared cheerful and smiled merrily. "Well, my dear, are we to partake of the gentlemen's plunder tonight?"

"That we shall, Madeline. Mr Darcy and I were quite successful today, though poor Mr Bingley could not catch a thing." Mr Gardiner looked significantly at his wife, her eyes wide at the mention of Mr Darcy's friend.

"I was unaware Mr Bingley was currently at Pemberley."

Darcy stiffened at Mrs Gardiner's reference to his friend. He forgot that Miss Bingley had met Mrs Gardiner. He now wished he had made his admission to Bingley before the dinner, as any mention of Jane Bennet's visit to London could be quite awkward.

Well, there is nothing for it now. I shall have to make a full confession tonight and can only hope Bingley will forgive me for my interference, Darcy resolved.

Miss Darcy departed upstairs to change for dinner, and the remainder of the group entered the drawing room. The gentlemen rose as Darcy made the introductions.

"It is a pleasure to see you again, Miss Bingley," Mrs Gardiner politely said.

"I knew the name Gardiner sounded familiar. You reside in Cheapside, do you not?" Miss Bingley asked.

Mr Bingley ignored his sister's question. "*Again,* Mrs Gardiner? Have you and my sister met before?"

"I met Miss Bingley when she called upon my niece Jane Bennet this last winter," Mrs Gardiner replied. Judging from his shocked expression, it was clear his sister had not mentioned the visit. "I understood you knew of Jane's being in town but were rather busy with Mr and Miss Darcy, so you could not accompany your sister when she came to call. I was sorry not to make your acquaintance."

Mr Bingley turned an icy glare towards Caroline. "I apologise, madam, but I was never informed of Miss Bennet's presence in London. If I had known, I would not have been too busy to call." He never once removed his eyes from his sister, who began to cower slightly under his dark glare.

"No apology is necessary. It appears there was a misunderstanding."

Mr Darcy felt the tension in the room mount and sought a way to dispel it. He had been angered that Miss Bingley had used both his sister and himself as an excuse and recognised her attempt to suggest a relationship between Bingley and Georgiana. He would never have condoned such manipulation. He was ashamed enough that he had deceived his friend and realised the hurt that Miss Bennet must have felt when she was made to believe Bingley was courting another. Miss Bingley's machinations were deplorable.

His resolve to make a clean breast of everything to Bingley strengthened, and he would do so tonight after the Gardiners left.

At the moment when Darcy feared the tension would overwhelm them and ruin the evening, Georgiana entered, followed by a servant to announce dinner. All felt a general relief as they moved to the dining room.

CHAPTER 5

Darcy was thankful for his foresight in arranging the seating for dinner. He sat at the head of the table with Georgiana on his right, followed by Bingley, Mrs Hurst, and Miss Bingley. On his left sat Mrs Gardiner, Mr Gardiner, and Mr Hurst. Caroline would be separated from her brother for the meal and would be too far down the table to converse easily with him, his sister, or Mrs Gardiner. Miss Bingley seemed incensed at her placement.

Bingley was silent at the beginning of the meal but soon composed himself and began to converse with the Gardiners. He asked numerous questions about their relations, which the Gardiners responded to politely but ambiguously. Darcy sensed their evasion at times and wondered at the nature of the *family business* that had called Elizabeth and the others to Staffordshire. He was too well-bred to enquire more directly, but he filed away every bit of information they revealed to examine at a later time.

The gentlemen reviewed their exploits of the day when the fish was served, and Mrs Gardiner and Georgiana recounted details of their shopping excursion. Miss Darcy expressed her enjoyment of the outing and told her brother she hoped to meet the Gardiners again upon their return to London. She also revealed Mrs Gardiner's promise to introduce her to the Miss Bennets when they were next in town.

Darcy was pleased with this development. "We would be honoured to visit you when we return. Georgiana is not yet out, but I had planned to take her to some of the amusements London offers. Perhaps we could all attend the theatre one night with supper at Darcy House afterwards?"

"That is a wonderful suggestion, Darcy!" Bingley enthusiastically exclaimed.

"A lovely idea," replied Mrs Gardiner. "I have given Miss Darcy the direction to our house in London, and when you arrive, she can send us a note. We can finalise plans then."

"And perhaps your nieces will be in town," said Georgiana, "that I might finally meet them."

"It is possible, my dear, but I do not know their plans following their summer trip."

"Are the Bennets travelling for the summer?" Mr Bingley interrupted.

"Yes, they are in Staffordshire for the summer, visiting relations."

"I hope everyone is well," Mr Bingley mused.

"I believe everyone is in excellent health," Mr Gardiner answered. He stole a sidelong look at his wife as he said it.

When the meal ended, the party moved to the music room. Earlier that day, Mrs Gardiner had suggested they perform some duets, with Georgiana on the harp while she accompanied her on the pianoforte. The duo moved towards the instruments to select some music. Darcy chose a seat with a clear view of the performers, and Miss Bingley seated herself in the chair next to him.

Once the ladies began to play, Mr Darcy was engrossed in watching his sister. She truly was proficient, but she also played with emotion few performers possessed. In fact, Mr Darcy could think of only one other who could command his attention so thoroughly during a performance.

If only Elizabeth were here… I have imagined evenings such as this so often. She would play to please me. She and Georgiana would be as close as sisters. The halls of Pemberley would again ring with the sound of laughter and music. She would bring happiness to my home. His reverie was interrupted by applause as the two performers finished.

Miss Bingley leaned towards him. "Your sister is better at her instruments each time I hear her," she whispered, attempting intimacy. "I am sure no other young lady can compare with her accomplishments. Luckily, Mrs Gardiner is sufficiently proficient to accompany her. Do you remember the poor talents of Miss Mary Bennet and her sister Miss Eliza? It is certain neither lady had the benefit of London masters as did dear Georgiana."

Darcy fumed at Miss Bingley's criticisms of Elizabeth but replied with composure. "True, they did not have the benefit of masters, but I do not believe I have ever had more pleasure than listening to a performance from Miss Elizabeth. And Miss Mary, I understand, is very diligent in her practise. Many young women would benefit from her example of conscientiousness. Too many are left alone to fritter away their time and develop bad habits, such as gossiping."

Darcy rose from his chair to move towards the pianoforte. "That was splendid, ladies."

"Thank you, Mr Darcy. This is a beautiful instrument. I understand you just purchased it."

"Yes," replied Georgiana, "for my birthday. Is he not a wonderful brother?"

"Yes, he is. You are very fortunate."

"I would have liked to have had a sister," Georgiana answered and turned to look significantly at Darcy. He could hardly believe her impertinence. It reminded him of Elizabeth. He was even more convinced they would like one another and his sister would benefit from knowing her.

Smiling, he raised one eyebrow. "That is hardly my fault, Georgiana, and the situation cannot be rectified now. You will just have to be patient."

Georgiana giggled, and Mrs Gardiner looked fondly at the siblings. "Perhaps, Miss Darcy, I could suggest a substitute until such time as your brother sees fit to find a wife."

"And just what did you have in mind?" Darcy asked warily.

"Actually, sir, it fits perfectly into our current plans. I have promised to introduce Miss Darcy to my nieces, and they will surely adopt her as an additional sister. What is one more girl in a family of five?"

Darcy could sense the mischief in this statement. He began to suspect Mrs Gardiner understood his feelings for Elizabeth. He turned a piercing gaze towards the lady, who returned his look with a half-smile.

Yes, she knows. And I may be able to use that to my advantage. She seems to support my suit. Perhaps I have found an ally.

He returned Mrs Gardiner's smile. "I would be happy to

accept your suggestion, ma'am. I am sure Georgiana will be pleased to make their acquaintance as soon as may be."

"Of course, and we shall look forward to your call."

With that, a silent bargain was sealed. The party ended soon afterwards, and the Darcys, along with Mr Bingley, escorted the Gardiners outside. They said their farewells, and all parted with feelings of goodwill and happy expectations for the future.

Bingley and Georgiana turned to enter the house, but Darcy stopped them. "Georgiana, I have a matter to discuss with Bingley. Will you make my excuses to the rest of our guests? Hopefully, we shall not be long."

"Yes, Brother."

Darcy nodded his thanks and led Bingley to the library. The time of his confession had come.

He gestured for his friend to seat himself and poured them both a generous brandy. The men had not separated from the ladies earlier that evening, and Darcy felt he would need a little liquid encouragement before his disclosure.

Bingley smiled vacantly, lost in thought. Darcy was not the type of man to delay once he had formed a resolution, so he straightened his shoulders and addressed his friend. *Hopefully, we shall still be friends after this night*, thought Darcy grimly.

"I have a confession to make to you."

Bingley looked at his friend and recognised the serious-ness of his countenance. He gathered his thoughts and motioned for Darcy to continue.

"I knew of Jane Bennet's time in London last winter." Bingley's smile disappeared. "Your sister told me Miss Bennet had called and the visit had been returned. I did not think you should see her. You did not appear to be over your regard for her. At the time, I believed Miss Bennet did not care for you, and I did not want you to be trapped in a loveless marriage. However, I have received some information that has changed my opinion regarding Miss Bennet's feelings." Darcy paused to judge the reaction to his revelation.

"What information did you receive that would alter your opinion?"

"I understand she cared for you and was disappointed when you left Netherfield."

"And where exactly did you receive such information?"

Darcy shifted his gaze towards the window. He feared Bingley would ask him this and knew that only complete disclosure would satisfy his friend.

"Miss Elizabeth Bennet told me when I was at Rosings this spring."

Bingley could not contain his shock at this statement. "Miss Elizabeth? I did not know that you had seen her again. Why did you not tell me sooner? I could have gone to Hertfordshire! I could have apologised to Jane months ago, begged her forgiveness for abandoning her, and continued courting her!" Bingley's voice rose with each successive thought. "How could you do that?"

"It was a misjudgment. I failed to realise the depth of Miss Bennet's feelings. Her manners were open and engaging, but I never noticed any sign of particular regard. I did not believe her heart would be easily touched, and her mother would have convinced her to accept your suit, no matter Miss Bennet's sentiments."

"How could you presume so much? Jane is a modest and genteel woman. What would you have had her do to demonstrate her affection? Would you have preferred if she had fawned over me and behaved the coquette, such as ladies do in your presence?" Darcy winced at these words, but Bingley continued. "I should have trusted my own judgment. I knew Jane's smiles were for me, and she felt a warm affection. Why did I not listen to my own heart? What must she think of me now? I left her without a word and then Caroline snubbed her! How can I overcome such obstacles?"

"I should never have presumed to counsel you—or more truthfully—to make decisions for you. It was arrogant of me. I did not take into account anyone's feelings. Miss Elizabeth severely chastised me for this behaviour, and I have been attempting to correct it. I am sorry for the pain I have caused. But there is hope. The Gardiners are aware of some of these events and are still willing to welcome you to their house."

Bingley seemed pensive. "That is true. And Jane is such an angel that surely I can gain her forgiveness." He paused as a sudden thought overcame him and he sat up in alarm. "What if she has met someone else? What if I am too late?"

"The Gardiners did not indicate Miss Bennet was attached to anyone. I am sure they would have imparted such knowledge. Mrs Gardiner seems a clever woman. I believe she understands our feelings for her nieces."

Bingley looked up sharply at his friend. "*Our* feelings for her nieces? Why exactly did Miss Elizabeth reveal her sister's feelings to you?"

Darcy felt himself blush deeply. He had not realised he had been so indiscreet. The emotions of the last few days and the brandy had made him forget himself.

"Come, Darcy, out with it. I can see you have more to confess."

Darcy sighed deeply and told Bingley the entire sad tale, including Wickham's treachery towards Georgiana. At the conclusion of the narrative, Bingley gazed sympathetically at his friend as though his anger and resentment had abated.

"Well, Darcy, it appears you and I are in a similar situation. What are we to do about it? I, for one, believe we should try again. And this time, I am sure we shall succeed."

Darcy softly smiled at his friend's optimism. "You still love Miss Bennet." It was a statement, not a question.

"Yes, and you still love Miss Elizabeth."

"I do."

"Then let us make our plans for September." He held out his hand, and Darcy shook it, their friendship assured.

"We shall, but first we must return to the music room. We have been away too long. Poor Georgiana will be beside herself. She is not accustomed to being a hostess."

"Yes, we must relieve Miss Darcy of that arduous task. I know my family is not easy to entertain."

The two men chuckled as they left the library and returned to the music room. They had been gone for almost an hour, and Bingley was feeling much happier after his conversation with Darcy.

He sat down on a sofa, a large grin on his face. "What a delightful evening!"

"Oh, Charles, please. It was so tedious," Caroline complained.

Bingley's countenance darkened. All of the anger for his sister returned. He directed an irate gaze towards her, and she shrank back in her seat in response.

"I cannot begin to describe how angry I am with you, Caroline. How could you keep Miss Bennet's visit from me?"

"Her visit to London does not change anything. Jane Bennet is not a worthy match for you. Think of the behaviour of her mother and sisters. And the Gardiners are not at all fashionable, and I might remind you, they are in trade."

"Do you forget our fortune comes from trade? Father was

a shipbuilder, a successful one, but a tradesman, nevertheless. You would not be accepted into half as many houses as you are were it not for your fortune and my association with Darcy. Mr Bennet is a gentleman."

"You exaggerate. The Bennets have nothing to recommend them. Their estate is hardly significant and is entailed away, and their connexions are appalling. The father is nearly absent, the mother is vulgar, and the sisters…"

"I have heard only good things about Miss Bennet and Miss Elizabeth," Georgiana bravely interrupted, though she was trembling slightly. Her brother looked at her proudly, and her spine straightened with his support.

Bingley continued. "I shall have no more criticism of the Bennets in my presence. Listen carefully, Caroline. I intend to court Miss Jane Bennet, if she will allow me. I have much to atone for, not excluding your rudeness. Now, if you do not mind, Darcy, I believe I shall retire."

Darcy nodded. Bingley bowed to Miss Darcy, turned on his heel, and strode from the room.

Miss Bingley sat crumpled in her seat, looking dejected, but she soon composed herself and retired to her room to write a letter. Mr and Mrs Hurst followed, leaving the Darcys alone.

Darcy chuckled softly, and Georgiana joined him with giggles of her own.

"I have never seen Bingley so fierce," he stated, "I did not know he was capable of such emotion."

"Nor I. Did you see Miss Bingley?" Georgiana dissolved into more giggles. "I noticed you did not declare your intent to pursue and court Miss Elizabeth, as Mr Bingley did in regard to Miss Bennet."

"I do not want to bring Miss Bingley's attention to that particular desire. I made the grievous mistake of telling her I admired Miss Elizabeth's eyes, and she relentlessly teased me afterwards. She was also rude to Miss Elizabeth. I shall not make the same mistake again."

"But you do intend to court her?"

"Yes, I do. But my task will not be as simple as Bingley's. My mistakes are more serious, and Miss Elizabeth is not as meek as her sister. The reunion of Bingley and Miss Bennet will hopefully ease the way, and I shall show Miss Elizabeth, by every civility in my power, that I have amended my character and taken her reproofs to heart."

"I have every faith in you. Miss Elizabeth will not be able to deny you when faced with your true and charming nature."

Darcy smiled at her sisterly bias. He was certain Elizabeth was capable of resisting him, but he would not quit until she was married to someone, preferably to him! He took his sister's arm and escorted her to her room.

MRS GARDINER HAD BEEN DISAPPOINTED NOT TO FIND A LETTER from either Jane or Elizabeth on their arrival in Lambton. This frustration subsided on the morning before their departure upon the receipt of a letter from Jane that had initially been misdirected. Mrs Gardiner was not surprised, for Jane had written the direction remarkably ill. Her pleasure increased upon opening the letter to find one from Elizabeth enclosed within. There was also a brief note for Mr Gardiner from his brother Bennet.

These letters were not in response to the ones she had sent from Derbyshire. She had written and posted one that morning recounting their dinner at Pemberley, and also some troubling information a friend from Lambton had revealed regarding the questionable behaviour of Mr Wickham.

She expected the girls' letters would contain accounts of their summer travels thus far and began reading. Jane's letter spoke cheerfully of Grancourt and the welfare of her parents and younger sisters.

Elizabeth's letter was perused more eagerly. She also described Grancourt, particularly admiring the countryside, and included her study of horsemanship. Mrs Gardiner was surprised that Elizabeth had endeavoured to learn to ride and wondered how this marvel had occurred. Her curiosity was soon answered when the letter described Agatha in great detail. Mrs Gardiner understood that Elizabeth had grown to respect and value the dowager duchess, and she was keen to make the good lady's acquaintance.

Elizabeth also included an account of the meeting with Mr Spencer, the details of the inheritance, and the plans to send the younger girls to school after the Christmas holidays. Mrs Gardiner was amused that Elizabeth's father intended to inform the girls of their upcoming schooling only at the last possible moment.

Elizabeth informed her aunt that the entire family would travel to London in the autumn. They planned to be there no later than the fifteenth of September. They would shop and see to some legal matters, spending about six to eight weeks in town. Her father desired to consult Mr Gardiner, and the family hoped to spend many hours in their company. They would not open the house to other visitors, hoping to conceal their presence in London and therefore not have to introduce the younger girls to any society.

Agatha would still be in mourning, though she intended to sponsor Jane and Elizabeth during their presentation the following Season. By spring, more than a year would have passed since her husband's death, and she would chaperone the girls during her second mourning.

Elizabeth also explained that the family would take up permanent residence at Grancourt. They would travel to Longbourn on their return to Staffordshire to supervise the packing and shipping of their belongings to their new home. Elizabeth concluded the letter with an invitation for the Gardiners to spend the entire month of December at Grancourt.

Mrs Gardiner was just reading her niece's adieu when the party from Pemberley was announced.

"We have come to call and say farewell until we meet again in September," Mr Bingley said.

"Thank you all for coming," Mrs Gardiner responded, "and thank you again for the lovely dinner we enjoyed the other night, Mr Darcy. I have written to my nieces describing your thoughtfulness and the delight we have found in your acquaintance. I am sure they will be grateful you were all so kind to us during our stay in Lambton."

"It was our pleasure," Darcy replied. "I hope your letter finds the Bennets well."

"I have just received and read letters from both Jane and Elizabeth. They are enjoying their stay in Staffordshire and are looking forward to a trip to London by mid-September." Mrs Gardiner looked pointedly at Mr Darcy.

"Perhaps we may meet with them as well then."

"Elizabeth informs me they have a great deal of business to attend to but hope to call upon us, and I am sure we shall host them for several dinners. When you get back to London, we can plan an evening together, if that is agreeable to you, Miss Darcy?"

"Oh yes, please," Georgiana responded. "May I write to you, ma'am?"

"Of course, my dear. You have the direction."

As the Gardiners had some calls to make in the village before they left the county, farewells and fond wishes for their next meeting were exchanged, and the threesome returned to Pemberley.

CHAPTER 6

The party at Pemberley became somewhat subdued after the departure of the Gardiners from Lambton. During the following fortnight, Miss Bingley was uncharacteristically restrained, though she still fawned over both Darcys. Mrs Annesley had returned to Pemberley, and with her, Georgiana's studies recommenced. She avoided Miss Bingley for a large part of the day, but evenings were always a trying time.

Miss Bingley did not insult the Bennets or Gardiners in her brother's presence, but she frequently expressed her frustration and resentment to her sister, who was always a willing listener.

Bingley was generally found riding around the park, in Darcy's study playing chess, or in conversation with his friend. Now that he was privy to Darcy's dealings with Miss Elizabeth, the friends found ample sources of conversation.

Sometimes they shared their memories, other times their hopeful plans.

Darcy spent many hours attending to estate matters and his other numerous obligations. His leisure was spent with Bingley or in the company of his sister. He saw his other guests only at mealtimes and in the evening.

THE MORNING MEAL WAS GENERALLY A QUIET AFFAIR FOR THE residents of Pemberley. Darcy read the London newspapers as he did every morning. Miss Bingley also read these publications, though most suspected she did so only because Darcy did, and she only read the society pages.

The calm of the morning was broken when Miss Bingley loudly shrieked, "It cannot be true!"

All movement abruptly ceased, and the others stared at her in alarm. She looked at the newspaper in panic.

"What on earth is the matter?" Bingley asked, a look of concern evident in his features.

"Forgive me. It is nothing, Charles."

"Surely, something prompted that outburst." Bingley snatched the paper from her hands and scanned the page. Clearing his throat, he read the article aloud.

Many months ago, we informed our readers of the tragic death of Lord Joshua Bennet, the Duke of Everard. His Grace was lost in a shipwreck, along with his brother, and heir apparent Lord Nathaniel Bennet. Lord Nathaniel's wife, Lady Margaret, and their two children also perished. Her Grace, the Duchess of Everard was in Staffordshire at the time of the tragedy. The duke had no children, and for some months the question of the legitimate heir has been unanswered. At last we are able to inform the public that he has been identified.

Mr Thomas Bennet, of Longbourn, Hertfordshire, cousin to the late Duke of Everard, will succeed to the title. The duke brings with him his wife, Frances Bennet, the Duchess of Everard, and five daughters, Ladies Jane, Elizabeth, Mary, Catherine and Lydia Bennet.

We convey our condolences to the family on their loss and anticipate their arrival in society.

The subsequent silence was palpable.

"Are not two of those the chits who stayed at Netherfield last year?" Mr Hurst enquired, breaking the strain. "That pretty, sickly one and the impertinent girl who did not play cards?"

Bingley directed a reproving stare at his brother. Mr Hurst failed to notice because he had already resumed eating.

Mrs Hurst seemed baffled. "But Jane never mentioned anything about the Everard Bennets when we questioned her about her connexions. Would she not have told us they were relations?"

"Someone must be in error," Miss Bingley answered.

Thankful for the years of practice hiding his emotions, Darcy calmly took up the other newspapers and scanned the society pages.

"There are identical articles in the other papers," he explained, keeping his face expressionless. "It must be an official announcement." Despite his calm demeanour, his thoughts and heart were racing.

No wonder the Gardiners were so evasive when answering questions about their relations. They must have been awaiting permission to make the knowledge public. How did I not make the connexion with Staffordshire and the Everard Bennets sooner? And how will this alter my suit with Elizabeth? He brushed these thoughts aside. He would need to carefully examine everything before he decided on a plan of action.

Georgiana looked at him anxiously. He smiled slightly and excused himself to meet with his steward.

The rest of the party remained in the breakfast room. Georgiana was worried about her brother. She knew the information was significant but could not fully comprehend the consequences it would have.

"What astounding news," stated Bingley, "and what good fortune for the Bennets."

"Everard is one of the richest titles in the land, and Agatha is one of the most influential women of the *ton*! This means Jane Bennet is now in her inner circle. Perhaps I should write to her. Surely, dear Jane will want the support of her friends at such a time," Miss Bingley remarked.

"But Caroline, why did Jane not tell us about her connexion when we asked her at Netherfield?" questioned Mrs Hurst. "Surely, she would want everyone to know!"

Georgiana noted Miss Bingley looked rather distracted. She was more diverted when Mr Hurst simply finished his breakfast and excused himself to take a nap. Obviously, such astonishing news did nothing to affect him at all.

Georgiana looked again towards Mr Bingley and became slightly worried by his pensive expression. She suddenly realised this announcement could affect his courtship of Jane Bennet, since she was now a member of the peerage. She would mention her concern when next she saw her brother.

DARCY SECLUDED HIMSELF IN HIS STUDY. AFTER ATTEMPTING to concentrate on business for an hour, he dismissed his steward. His mind would not focus. Too much had occurred over the last two weeks, and he needed to organise his thoughts.

He knew this morning's surprising information would influence his ability to court Elizabeth Bennet but not to what degree. The Bennet sisters would be avidly pursued when they were presented to the *ton*. Darcy was privy to some facts that would give him an advantage over the competition, but he wondered whether it would be enough to win Elizabeth.

Can I make amends for the horrendous way I have treated her since our first meeting? Does she think better of me after reading my letter? Can she forgive me?

He had given his word to the Gardiners that he would meet them in town, and he would honour that promise. *It would at least be a beginning. Hopefully, I can meet with Elizabeth before she is introduced to society.*

His meditations were rudely disrupted by a loud knock on the study door followed immediately by the entrance of a most unwelcome visitor—Lady Catherine de Bourgh.

"Aunt? What brings you to Pemberley? I was not informed."

"You can be at no loss to understand the reason for my journey hither."

"You are mistaken. I am not able to account for the honour of seeing you at Pemberley."

"I am not accustomed to being trifled with," her ladyship angrily replied. "I have travelled immediately from Kent to respond to a report of a most alarming nature. I understand that you have been associating with tradespeople and allowing your sister to as well. You allowed Georgiana to spend a day in the company of a Mrs Gardiner, a merchant's wife, and then invited the couple to dine. Are the shades of Pemberley to be thus polluted? Have you lost all sense of decency? Heaven and earth! How could you forget your station and the duty you owe to uphold the honour of the Darcy name? When Anne is your wife, she will prohibit such unacceptable behaviour."

Darcy listened to this tirade in silence, but could restrain himself no longer. "That is enough, madam. I am the master here and will choose to invite whomever I will to my home. I do not have to answer to anyone, least of all you. And once and for all, I am not going to marry Anne. My parents never spoke of this supposed betrothal, and I have no feelings for your daughter beyond cousinly concern for her welfare. That is my final word on the matter."

"You refuse to obey the claims of duty, honour, and gratitude? Obstinate, headstrong man!" Lady Catherine paused in her diatribe and narrowed her eyes at her nephew. "It is because of Elizabeth Bennet! That conniving hoyden has drawn you in. Her arts and allurements have seduced you and made you forget what you owe to yourself and all your family!"

Darcy's patience had reached its limit. He turned a dark glower towards his irate aunt. "Enough!"

Lady Catherine was not easily intimidated. "Is she what prevents you from marrying Anne? The upstart pretensions of a young woman without family, connexions, or fortune? Is this to be endured! But it must not, shall not be. Your alliance would be a disgrace. Her name would never be mentioned by any of us. You will be censured, slighted and despised by everyone!"

"You would do well, madam, to be in possession of all the facts before asserting such accusations. I am not engaged to Miss Elizabeth Bennet, or as I should more properly call her, Lady Elizabeth."

This statement finally halted Lady Catherine's diatribe.

She frowned at her nephew, but before she could continue, he addressed her.

"I assume your travels have prevented you from reading the London papers, so I will gladly inform you of a most extraordinary announcement. Mr Bennet, the father of the young woman you have been insulting, is the heir of the Duke of Everard, who passed away some months ago."

Lady Catherine sputtered, and her face grew alarmingly red. Darcy was afraid she would suffer from apoplexy. He took her by the arm and led her to a chair, forcing her to sit.

"It cannot be true!" exclaimed Lady Catherine, eerily echoing Miss Bingley's outburst.

"It was confirmed in all the London newspapers."

Lady Catherine gathered her resentment again and stood. "I do not believe it. You are saying this merely to justify your appalling behaviour. You are determined to have Miss Bennet. Her influence is pernicious and has affected your judgment."

"Believe what you will, but I assure you it is quite true," he answered with a forced calm. "Now, I insist that you leave Pemberley immediately. You have insulted me, and I will not allow Georgiana to be subjected to your abuse. I will have a servant escort you to your carriage." He strode to the door, summoned a servant, and turned to his aunt, gesturing to the open door.

Her ladyship lifted her chin in the air and regally left the room, yelling over her shoulder as she walked. "I am for Matlock immediately, and I shall inform the earl of your insolence. I take no leave of you, Nephew. I am most seriously displeased!"

He made no answer and without attempting to placate his aunt, watched her exit. Darcy remained in the doorway, his posture rigid, fists clenched tightly against his sides. He was furious, and he needed a moment to calm himself.

The weak assertions and imperious commands of his aunt were pitiful, and he did not seriously regard them. However, the insults hurled at Elizabeth were unforgivable. He vowed to cease all intercourse with Lady Catherine until she apologised.

But even more important at the moment was the source of her ladyship's information. There could be only one person who would enlighten his aunt about his association with the Gardiners, only one person who would imply he was attracted to Elizabeth. He marched down the hall in search of his guests.

After several minutes of fruitless searching, a passing footman directed him outside. He found the Bingleys and Hursts under a tent on the lawn enjoying the fine summer weather. Georgiana was with Mrs Annesley, studying French. She would mercifully not be a witness to the scene he was certain would unfold.

Miss Bingley looked up, appearing startled from her thoughts. Seeing his thunderous countenance, she immediately blanched.

"Miss Bingley, you have stepped outside all bounds of propriety and decency. I demand that you leave Pemberley. You are no longer welcome at any Darcy residence, and you would be wise never to speak to any of my relations again."

He turned to his dear friend and addressed him in a slightly softer tone. "You and the Hursts are welcome to stay at Pemberley for the remainder of the summer as planned, but I must insist that your sister leave as soon as may be. I can no longer abide her presence."

Bingley turned a horrified gaze to his younger sister. "What have you done?" When she did not immediately reply, he asked again. "What have you done to anger Darcy?"

"Tell him. Explain why my aunt has travelled for days to berate me."

She was trembling. Turning to her brother, Caroline said, "I-I am afraid I have...I have done something."

"Obviously. But what?"

"I wrote a letter to Lady Catherine de Bourgh."

"What possessed you to write to a woman to whom you are not acquainted?" Bingley asked. "And what did you write in that letter?"

"I-I wrote about the Gardiners' visit. I explained that the Gardiners are in trade, and that they are below her nephew in station. I informed her ladyship that Mr Darcy was allowing his sister to associate with them." Seeing Darcy's scowl upon her, she faltered again.

"What *else* did you put in that letter?" Bingley enquired.

"I may have implied Mr Darcy was infatuated with Eliza Bennet, and that she was attempting to trap him in marriage."

Though he had assumed as much, her statement made Darcy's fury burn still hotter.

Bingley shared his anger. "You have gone too far this time, Caroline," Bingley said through tightly clenched teeth. "Have your things packed immediately." He held up a hand when she attempted to interrupt him. "No, do not say anything. Louisa, perhaps you should escort Caroline to London. I will see that her belongings in my townhouse are packed and sent to your home." He turned his attention back to Miss Bingley. "I will call on our attorney when I return to town in September to see to your inheritance. You may have possession of it now. I will no longer supplement your income. You will have to live on your inheritance alone unless Louisa chooses to help you. I will remain in Derbyshire."

Mrs Hurst spoke in low tones to her husband, urging him

to quickly gather his things and call for their carriage. She ushered her sister to their rooms and instructed the maids to pack their belongings without delay. They would travel to London as soon as possible. The harried servants obeyed, and, later that day, the Hursts, along with a crushed Miss Bingley, entered the coach that would take them away from Pemberley for the final time.

CHAPTER 7

Georgiana finished her morning lessons and went in search of her brother and his guests. She unsuccessfully explored several rooms before finally coming upon Mrs Reynolds in the dining room, supervising the cleaning of the chandelier.

"Do you know where I can find my brother—or anyone for that matter? They all seem to have disappeared."

"Mr Darcy is walking in the park. I do not know the current whereabouts of Mr Bingley, but Mr and Mrs Hurst and Miss Bingley left for London about a quarter of an hour ago."

"But why?"

Receiving an inadequate answer from Mrs Reynolds, Georgiana considered the matter. It was highly out of character for their guests to leave without a farewell, especially considering Miss Bingley's usually excessive solicitude towards herself and her brother. She went in search of him.

She hastened to a pretty footbridge over the stream. It was a lovely spot, but not one that she or her brother frequented. However, since the Gardiners' visit, her brother was often found there. A small stone bench had been placed under a willow tree in compliance with his wishes. As Georgiana suspected, he was sitting on the bench, looking intently into the stream. He was lost in thought, and she had to call his name several times before he discerned her presence. He smiled at her, but it did not reach his eyes.

"Are you well, Brother?"

"Yes." His succinct answer was obviously untrue.

"Mrs Reynolds told me that it has been an extraordinary morning. What has happened while I have been conjugating French verbs?"

A pensive look overcame his features. "I hardly know where to start. So much has happened today. I have not had enough time to sift through it all."

Georgiana sighed. "You seemed so despondent when I came upon you earlier."

"I was not despondent. I was merely lost in thought. And I was still overcoming some of my fury from my interviews with Lady Catherine and Miss Bingley."

"What made you angry with them? Why was Lady Catherine here? Why have the Hursts and Miss Bingley left for London?"

"Enough!" He laughed softly. "One question at a time!"

Darcy gave a brief but altogether amazing account of the events of the morning. Shocked by all of it, Georgiana asked the first of many questions that came to mind.

"Why would Miss Bingley write such a letter to our aunt?"

"You know the reason. I told you I had once commented about my admiration of Miss Elizabeth's eyes, and I believe

71

Miss Bingley understood from the beginning what the outcome of that admiration would be. Consequently, she sought a way to discredit Miss Elizabeth, whom she considered a rival.

"She wrote to Lady Catherine with the hope that her ladyship would condemn such a connexion, and she certainly did. But Miss Bingley does not know my character. I have never listened to Lady Catherine or heeded her advice. And Miss Elizabeth has taught me that there is more to life than one's position in society.

"Our parents taught me good principles, but I was allowed to follow them in pride and conceit. I was allowed—encouraged, almost taught—to be selfish and overbearing, to care for none beyond my own family circle, to think meanly of all the rest of the world. But no more. I know what is of value now, and I will not succumb to any person's whims, demands, or manipulations. Caroline Bingley greatly misjudged me. I cannot tolerate such interference, so I ordered her to leave. I was sorry to inflict pain on Bingley, but I could no longer allow his sister to live under my roof. I have banished her from all the Darcy residences and warned her not to speak to any of my relations. You will be free from Miss Bingley's fawning."

Georgiana was speechless. She wanted to contradict her brother's assertions that he had been selfish and prideful—for he had always been generous with her—but she recollected his actions in Hertfordshire, specifically towards the Bennets, and even his presumptuous interference in Mr Bingley's affairs, and she knew that his assessment was partially correct. He was changing though. In essentials, he remained as good and steadfast as ever, but he was exerting himself more in company, and he was more considerate of others' feelings.

Georgiana was surprised at the severe penalty he had given to Miss Bingley. His remonstrance must have been merciless indeed, and she wished she could have been present before she swept the uncharitable thought from her mind.

"Poor Mr Bingley," she mused aloud, "to have such a sister. Sometimes I do not understand how they can possibly be siblings. We must find Mr Bingley. He must feel dreadful about what has happened, and you know he will blame himself for his sister's behaviour."

"Of course. Let us return."

Darcy stood, helped Georgiana up, and the pair walked to the house. As they approached the door, Georgiana stopped their progress.

"Did you really banish Lady Catherine from Pemberley?"

"Indeed. She deserved nothing less. She insulted both Lady Elizabeth and myself."

Georgiana looked to her brother, hoping for more details, but he did not comply.

"I will only add that you will also be free from our aunt's demands for the foreseeable future."

Georgiana smiled, linked her arm with her brother's, and they entered the house.

Darcy found Bingley slouched in a chair, deep in thought. He rose immediately when he heard Darcy enter.

"I must apologise for the pain my sister's actions have caused. I have never been able to control her. My failures have caused you extreme distress, and if you would rather I leave, I will do so without argument."

"I do not want you to go. You could not have stopped your sister because she acted without your knowledge. It is her fault alone. I do not hold you responsible in any way, so think no more on it. I am sorry if I caused you pain when I dealt with your sister so harshly, but I was too overcome by anger to do otherwise. I could have her here no longer."

"She is to live with Louisa from now on. She will have to change and offer a sincere apology before I accept her back in my house."

"Perhaps it was for the best." Darcy placed his hand on Bingley's shoulder. "Let us go to the dining room. There are some things I must tell you about our time in London come September."

"Of course. I can hardly wait to return to town. How fortunate the Bennets are to be reunited with their relations, for I have concluded they knew nothing of the connexion prior to this inheritance. We would have known about it otherwise."

"I am acquainted with the late duke and his wife, Duchess Agatha, and I never heard them speak of any family in Hertfordshire. The connexion must have come to light while searching for the heir. It does create some interesting ramifications."

"As well I know. It means that I have little chance of securing Lady Jane's hand. How am I to compete with society's elite, especially since I have already injured my suit by abandoning her last year?"

"Do not despair, my friend. Remember that we are on good terms with the Gardiners—an aunt and uncle that both Lady Jane and Lady Elizabeth highly regard. I sense Mrs Gardiner particularly supports us, even though she must surely have understood the change in the ladies' circumstances. We must cultivate this relationship prior to the Bennets' arrival in town."

He patted Bingley's back in encouragement. "We do not

know what the autumn will bring. You do not plan on giving up, do you?"

Bingley looked thoughtful for a moment before his features and his resolve firmed. "I do not. This morning's revelation certainly changed some things, but it does not make the situation hopeless. I will just have to work harder to win Lady Jane's affection."

"If you ever truly lost it."

Bingley looked surprised at this statement but finally nodded in agreement.

THE REMAINDER OF THE SUMMER PASSED PLEASANTLY. THE three friends enjoyed the northern countryside and each other's company, but all were eager to leave for town when the time of their departure arrived.

Darcy was unsurprised by Lord and Lady Matlock's response to Lady Catherine's interference. They both wrote amusing letters regarding the lady's visit to them at their Matlock estate to condemn the union and Darcy's supposed insolence. Lady Catherine had always been a source of entertainment for the couple.

They were most interested to discover that Darcy was familiar with the new Duke of Everard's family. Their letters pressed him for details, hoping to gain some prior knowledge before they were introduced to the *ton*. Darcy was vague in his replies, but promised to be more forthcoming when they met in London.

The members of the *ton* were either vexed or excited at the prospect of five extremely wealthy, elite, and single ladies entering London society. The reaction generally was determined by one's gender or the gender of a child one had the duty of marrying off. Young ladies of marriageable age and their matchmaking mothers were incensed. Single men, whether old or young, were delighted by such prospects.

Speculation was rampant. Some claimed the Bennet ladies were sure to be accomplished, charming, and beautiful. Others maintained they were known to be rather spoiled, insipid, and plain. But whatever the conjecture, the Bennets were the chief object of conversation among society.

The surprise was greatest among the small populace of Meryton and the environs surrounding Longbourn. That the Bennets, who all had known for so many years, could suddenly rise to such prestige was almost more than their country society could grasp. There were some natural feelings of envy, but they were short-lived, and most of the neighbourhood wished the Bennets happiness. Many of the mothers with single daughters rejoiced that the Bennet girls would no longer compete with their daughters for the available gentlemen.

Lady Catherine persisted in her indignation. When she could no longer deny the truth, she cursed the Bennets. She could not believe their audacity to rise to such precedence. That she, Lady Catherine de Bourgh, must make way for Elizabeth Bennet—she refused to call her Lady Elizabeth—enraged her! She vowed to use her influence to snub the upstarts.

She wrote letters to all her acquaintances, pointing out the impudence and impropriety of the Bennets as a whole and Miss Elizabeth in particular. She would have been infuriated to know the response her letters received, for the recipients were extremely grateful to her for gratifying their curiosity and giving them exclusive knowledge to share with their friends. Since Lady Catherine was unaware of the excited speculation her letters produced, she continued to supply the ladies of the *ton* with gossip.

Unfortunately for the Collinses, the anger of Lady Catherine necessitated their removal from Kent. Mr Collins had received a letter from Mr Bennet, informing him of his family's upcoming move to Staffordshire and inviting the Collinses to move to Longbourn in November. Mr Bennet had not mentioned the reason for such a move, and Mr Collins had been undecided. However, when the inheritance became known and Lady Catherine's spleen was vented upon her poor rector, his wife persuaded him to accept his cousin's offer of Longbourn.

They could not reside there immediately, but Mrs Collins proposed a stay with the Lucases prior to their inhabiting the estate, which her husband accepted with alacrity. The condescension of Lady Catherine was a privilege, but her fury was a burden. The Lucases graciously extended an invitation at their daughter's insistence, and the Collinses packed their belongings and travelled to Hertfordshire.

After the newspaper announcement was published, Charlotte received a letter from Elizabeth, giving a brief summary of events and an explanation. Charlotte was satisfied and was able to express the best of wishes to her dear friend.

Those who knew the Gardiners and their relationship with the new duke tirelessly questioned the poor couple. They looked forward to being reunited with their relations. The upcoming autumn would be entertaining indeed.

CHAPTER 8

On the first day of September, the Darcy carriage left Pemberley in the early morning to travel to London. Three of the carriage's occupants were restless and impatient to reach their destination.

After three days on the road, they arrived at Darcy House. They alighted from the coach, entered the mansion, and were divested of their traveling coats and garments.

"Welcome home, sir," the butler said. "I hope your journey was uneventful."

"Thank you, Haskins, it was. Is tea laid out?"

"In the blue parlour, sir."

"Excellent. Shall we?"

Mrs Annesley excused herself for the evening, and Bingley and Georgiana followed Darcy to a cosy parlour. The late afternoon sun was shining through the windows, giving an air of comfort and cheer to the room.

"It is good to be in London," Bingley stated.

Darcy glanced at him and smiled. He generally preferred the country to town, but he was exceedingly glad to be in London now. He prepared himself some tea and sank into a comfortable chair.

"It is. I believe I will have a quick cup and then dash off a note to the Gardiners."

"Not wasting any time, are you?" Bingley teased.

"Do not pretend you are not as eager to see them again. The Gardiners told us to contact them when we arrived, and I see no value in waiting."

"I am excited to see Mrs Gardiner again. I have enjoyed her letters for the past few months," said Georgiana.

In truth, they had *all* enjoyed Mrs Gardiner's correspondence. She would slyly include references to her nieces, which Georgiana had no hesitation sharing with her brother and his friend. The gentlemen had been more impatient for the arrival of the good lady's letters even than Georgiana. Mr Gardiner had written to Darcy, but he was much more circumspect, limiting his discussions to business. Darcy appreciated the man's shrewd mind, but he enjoyed reading his wife's letters much more.

"Will you include a note with mine?" Darcy asked.

"Yes, please. I will retire to my room to change and will ring for a servant when I have finished the letter. Perhaps I can include an invitation to dine."

"That is an excellent suggestion. Invite them for a night this week at their convenience."

"I shall. It should not take me but a few moments."

"Mrs Haskins will retrieve it from you."

Georgiana raised her eyebrow when informed he would summon the housekeeper to retrieve a simple note but said nothing, understanding that Darcy obviously did not want the note to go astray. She agreed and left for her chambers. Darcy moved to a writing desk and penned a quick letter to Mr Gardiner.

He then turned towards Bingley. "Will you stay at Darcy House? There is no reason for you to be alone when there is plenty of room for you here."

"Thank you, I believe I shall, though I do have some things to do to settle matters for Caroline."

They had avoided the subject of Miss Bingley, and Darcy sensed his friend's unease. "Do not fear mentioning her to me when you must. It is unavoidable, and I want you to feel you can confide in me. I fear there is a steep road ahead of us, and we must be able to discuss anything if we are to encourage one another."

"Of course. Thank you again, Darcy, and if you will excuse me, I will rest before dinner."

THE GARDINERS WERE PROMPT IN THEIR REPLY, ACCEPTING AN invitation to dine at Darcy House that Friday, on the condition that they be allowed to return the favour the following evening. Darcy agreed to the stipulation with pleasure. The note also invited Darcy to meet with Mr Gardiner at his place of work and for Georgiana to come for the day to spend time with Mrs Gardiner and be introduced to her children.

At dinner, when Darcy informed his sister of this invitation, she clapped her hands in enthusiasm. Mrs Gardiner's letters were full of her children's antics, and Georgiana was eager to meet them.

"Will you accompany me to the Gardiners' home before going to the warehouse?"

"I will take you there in the carriage and stay briefly. When I meet with him, I believe I will ask Mr Gardiner to dine with me at my club. Will you join us, Bingley?"

"That is a fine idea. It will give me something to look forward to tomorrow."

The Darcys and Bingley spent the remainder of the evening in the blue parlour involved in earnest conversation about their plans for the next eight weeks. They retired early, for the day had been full of activity. All three entered their chambers with smiling faces.

DARCY AROSE WELL BEFORE SUNRISE THE NEXT MORNING AND left the house to walk in nearby Hyde Park. It was a short distance from Darcy House on Grosvenor Square, and Darcy felt the need for fresh air. His mind was filled with conflicting thoughts. He was excited and anxious, energetic and apprehensive. At one moment he was sure that his desired outcomes would be achieved, then he found himself despairing at the long road ahead. He needed the peace and quiet of the park in the early morning to soothe his tension and shore up his resolve. He ambled in the park for an hour before returning to the house, his determination bolstered.

Upon his arrival, the inhabitants of Darcy House gathered together to break their fast. Georgiana chattered animatedly about her hopes for the day. Her brother and companion smiled indulgently, happy to see her in such good spirits.

Prior to leaving Derbyshire, Darcy had spoken with Mrs Annesley regarding his thoughts for their schedule while in London. He hoped to spend a large amount of time with Georgiana, which would preclude her studies. He offered Mrs Annesley the opportunity to suspend her charge's lessons during their sojourn in town, allowing her to visit with friends and family. She gladly acquiesced. Her time would be her own, leaving Georgiana in her brother's care. The group finished their meal and left for their destinations—the Darcys to the Gardiners and Bingley to his solicitor.

The Gardiners lived in a modest house on Gracechurch Street, close enough to Mr Gardiner's warehouses on the Thames to make the daily travel convenient. The Darcys were greeted graciously and introduced to the Gardiner's four young children. Mr Gardiner had awaited the arrival of Mr Darcy before heading to work, and after a few moments spent in conversation, the gentlemen left, promising to return in the late afternoon.

Georgiana was instantly delighted by the young Gardiner children. The girls were both sweet-tempered and gentle and appeared somewhat awestruck by the genteel young lady being introduced to them. The boys were well-mannered when they gave their bows. Mrs Gardiner quickly proposed an outing to a local park, and Georgiana eagerly consented. They spent a few hours playing games with the children, then returned to the house to eat. After the meal, the children were escorted to the nursery for afternoon lessons.

Georgiana and Mrs Gardiner spent the remainder of the day in pleasant conversation. A few of Mrs Gardiner's acquaintances called in the early afternoon and were introduced to Miss Darcy. Georgiana was initially shy with each introduction, but all of Mrs Gardiner's friends were so kind and amiable, she was soon at ease and contributed to the discussions. It was a delightful day, and spending time together would become a habit for the ladies over the next fortnight.

WHEN MR GARDINER took DARCY ON A TOUR OF HIS warehouses, his guest was impressed with the size and prosperity of the enterprise. Mr Gardiner was a successful man of business. His import company had become more lucrative each year. His income was already close to three thousand pounds annually and showed signs of increase. He had learned from his brother-in-law's indolence and endeavoured to provide well for his family. He was frugal in his savings and wise in his investments, while still enjoying the comforts of life. The family lived contentedly, not ostentatiously. Darcy's respect for the Gardiners grew.

Bingley joined them for luncheon at Brooks's. Darcy was pleasantly surprised when several acquaintances from his club greeted Mr Gardiner. He was well-known for his business acumen, and men often sought his counsel. He had been asked to join the club but preferred to spend his leisure with his family and had politely declined all offers of sponsorship. Darcy wondered that he had never made Mr Gardiner's acquaintance before, but he was thankful for the association now and for more than the reason of his being Elizabeth's uncle.

The gentlemen enjoyed a pleasant meal and a few games of chess before returning to Gracechurch Street to retrieve Georgiana. The bright smile on her face answered all her brother's questions regarding her thoughts on the day. The dinner invitation for Friday was happily anticipated by all.

Georgiana spent several days each week in company with Mrs Gardiner and her children, occasionally joined by Darcy and Bingley. Darcy became a great favourite with the boys, especially the youngest, Ethan, who declared, "Mr Darcy is almost as good at telling stories as Cousin Lizzy." Darcy smiled at such praise but professed he would never dare to compete with 'Cousin Lizzy' in anything.

Thus, the first two weeks of September passed pleasantly with affection growing between the families.

CHAPTER 9

The journey to London in September passed in a similar fashion as the trip to Staffordshire in June, with only the addition of Agatha to the first carriage and a few extra servants following behind.

The duke and his family started later than planned on the final day of the journey as a result of Lydia entirely unpacking her trunk the previous night and misplacing several items that had to be found. Consequently, they arrived at Everard House in the early evening, rather than the afternoon. The family ate an informal meal, and the duchess and her three youngest daughters retired to bed early. The duke decamped to the library to enjoy a glass of port and a good book. Agatha, Jane, and Elizabeth moved to a small room at the back of the house called the striped parlour.

"This is my favourite room," Agatha sighed as she sat

upon a comfortable sofa. "Joshua and I spent many happy hours here."

"It is a beautiful room," Jane remarked.

The walls were plastered in stripes of soft gold and cream, and the furniture was covered elegantly with silks and velvets of light greens, accented with blues. The colours had been muted by habitual use. The feeling was warm and inviting. Elizabeth walked to the terrace doors that overlooked a beautiful courtyard and garden.

"I believe this will become my favourite room as well, especially with the enticing prospect from these windows."

"You should open them, Lizzy," Agatha recommended. An affection had quickly grown, which had long ago secured the necessity for her to address Elizabeth informally.

"Hodges, the gardener, plants many aromatic flowers, and on a summer's night, you can often catch a scent of jasmine or nicotiana."

Elizabeth opened the terrace doors and let in the night's breeze. She inhaled deeply and did discern the aroma of a blooming jasmine vine.

"Well, the matter is settled. This is my favourite room."

"You have only seen two rooms and the foyer!" Jane observed. "Wait until our tour tomorrow and then decide. The house is large and has many rooms to explore. What of the library? Or the music room?"

"Oh, I am sure those will be fine rooms, but I would prefer to steal a book and curl up on this chaise by the doors and enjoy the summer evening. Is that not a splendid idea?"

Agatha replied in the same happy tone. "No need to steal anything, my dear. You are welcome to everything in Everard House, but please do remove your shoes before placing them on that chaise. I had a difficult time finding the perfect fabric and would not want it spoiled."

Elizabeth laughed gaily and proceeded to remove her slippers and reclined on the chaise in an affected pose. Duchess Agatha smiled indulgently, but this happy scene was interrupted by the arrival of the butler.

Along with his housekeeper wife, Mr Sheldon had enjoyed the running of Everard House for several decades. He entered the parlour clearly reluctant to interrupt but seeming to enjoy the levity within.

"Good evening, Duchess. Please pardon the interruption, but if you would be so kind as to inform me which visitors are welcome while you are in town, I will leave you to enjoy the rest of your evening."

"Of course, that does need to be determined. We are of a mind that our stay will be as unobtrusive as possible, but I am certain there will be many who will want to call and condole with me."

"Knowing your influence in society, there will be numerous members of the *ton* who will be grieved to hear of your husband's passing and will not give a thought to the five marriageable cousins you have inherited," Elizabeth said.

Duchess Agatha laughed softly. "Exactly, my dear, so we must be quite selective whose names appear on the list."

She turned to the butler. "Sheldon, we will need to discuss this. I shall ring for you when we have a complete list."

He bowed and left the room.

Duchess Agatha continued, "I believe we should limit the visitors allowed while we reside here the next several weeks. There will be many prying acquaintances who will call merely to gain a glimpse of you before anyone else. I think we can politely exclude all but family and the closest friends. We will of necessity have to venture into the city, for shopping particularly, and will certainly excite interest wherever we go. And I am sure you will want to visit with Mr and Mrs Gardiner frequently, as well as entertain them here."

She paused and both ladies agreed. "I thought so. Perhaps you can attend a concert or play, but we will have to discuss that with your father. So, let us decide who will have the honour to gain admittance into Everard House this autumn."

Elizabeth smiled and sat at the writing desk. "Mr and Mrs Gardiner and their children will be allowed." Elizabeth wrote down their names. "I was sorry not to travel with them to Derbyshire, and I will be glad to see them again." *And I have much to discuss with my aunt!*

"Is there anyone in addition to the Gardiners you want included? Perhaps some acquaintances of your father's?"

"We must consult Papa about that," Jane replied. "I shall go and ask him." She rose and made her way to the library, leaving Agatha and Elizabeth to finish the rest of the list.

"Are there any particular friends you wish to add, Lizzy?"

"I have not spent enough time in town to form any close friendships here, and my good friend Mrs Collins will hardly venture to London. No, I cannot think of anyone I need add. But what of you, Duchess, surely there are some friends you would include?"

"There are only a few. If you would please write down Lord and Lady Matlock and Mr Fitzwilliam and Miss Georgiana Darcy, that should suffice. Oh! And the Matlocks' sons, Lord Stephen Amherst and Colonel Richard Fitzwilliam."

Elizabeth stared at Duchess Agatha in astonishment, her pen suspended in the air.

"My dear, are you well?"

Duchess Agatha's voice brought Elizabeth back to her

senses. She had been unable to contain her surprise at the mention of Mr Darcy's name, but she quickly composed herself.

"You know the Darcys?"

"I do." Turning shrewd eyes to Elizabeth, she continued. "And it appears you do as well."

"I-I have a slight acquaintance with Mr Darcy," she responded and then turned a grateful look to Jane as she entered the room.

"Papa wants to remind us to be sure to include Mr Spencer," Jane said.

"Of course. I am sure Mr Spencer will be a regular visitor to discuss legal matters with the duke," Duchess Agatha began and then turned her attention to Jane. "My dear, Lizzy was just telling me that you know Mr Darcy. How did you meet him?"

Jane looked to her sister. "We met him last year when he stayed with a friend in Hertfordshire. Mr B-Bingley had leased Netherfield Park, three miles from Longbourn, and we were often in company with that party. Lizzy also saw Mr Darcy again in Kent at Easter while he visited with his aunt, Lady Catherine de Bourgh."

Elizabeth was impressed with Jane's calmness while discussing Mr Bingley, though she did notice the slight catch at his name.

"I have met Mr Bingley—a very amiable young man— though I cannot say I have heard much good of his sisters. The unmarried one has been in well-known pursuit of Darcy since she came out. I have told him he is too much the gentleman, and he should just have done with it and inform her she will never be mistress of Pemberley. But he does not want to hurt his friend, so he gallantly endures the sister."

Elizabeth had blushed at Duchess Agatha's words, especially when she described Mr Darcy as too much the gentleman. *How different were my own words only a few months ago!*

Elizabeth was in a state of agitation. She had already begun to think better of Mr Darcy. His letter had long ago acquitted him of Mr Wickham's false accusations. And though Elizabeth still harboured some resentment towards him due to his separation of Jane and Mr Bingley, she admitted that Jane's disappointment had been in part due to the work of her own nearest relations. Additionally, knowing of his attachment had excited gratitude in Elizabeth—and that feeling had recently been rekindled by a letter from her aunt.

She had received Mrs Gardiner's letters from Lambton with utter amazement and was exceedingly gratified by Mr Darcy's attentions to her dear relations. That he was unaware of the connexion but still introduced himself was a wonder and a divergence from his behaviour as known in Hertfordshire. His civilities to the Gardiners, his introduction of his sister, and the invitations to Pemberley were compliments of the highest kind.

Her aunt had slyly hinted he had asked after her specifically. *Why is he so altered? It cannot be for me. It cannot be for my sake that his manners are thus softened. It is impossible he should still love me.*

But such assertions had lost strength over the last several weeks as she had pondered the revelations. She had concluded that her reproofs at Hunsford had wrought a change in Mr Darcy, and she was anxious to meet him again. Whether her feelings were more of trepidation or anticipation, she was undecided, but Elizabeth knew she desired to meet him and judge for herself his altered manners.

And now Duchess Agatha acknowledged an acquaintance

with him, a rather close association if she meant to include him on their list of approved visitors. This thought allowed Elizabeth to collect herself.

"How do you know the Darcys, Duchess Agatha?"

"I have known the Darcy children since their births. Their mother, Lady Anne, was a friend of mine from school, and we remained close after our marriages. My sister and I were sent away to school at age fourteen. We were both worried about making new friends. There were not many young girls our age near our childhood home, so the opportunity of meeting so many new ones was both exciting and intimidating.

"Upon our arrival, we were introduced to numerous young ladies, all from the best families of society, but I was quickly drawn to two. Lady Anne Fitzwilliam reminded me of Meg— gentle but with a little more courage, and Susan Albright, a rear admiral's daughter, was exactly like myself. The four of us became inseparable from the very beginning. We spent our years at school mastering all the accomplishments virtuous young women should, as well as getting into as much mischief as Susan could concoct. I will not divulge any particulars of the tricks we played on our schoolmates, for I would not want to give Lizzy ideas." Jane and Duchess Agatha both laughed aloud at Elizabeth's indignant harrumph.

"We had our first Season together when we were eighteen. Susan was quickly snatched up by Anne's brother, Harold, the future Earl of Matlock. They had met several times during our school years, and I believe Harold only waited until her coming out to make official what they had decided between themselves years before.

"I met Joshua towards the end of the Season, after he had returned from the West Indies. Nathaniel returned to England several years later and met Meg while she stayed with us at

Grancourt. Her shyness had prohibited gentlemen from pursuing her, which is why she was still unmarried when she met Nathaniel."

"I wish we could have met your sister and her family."

Duchess Agatha smiled gratefully at Elizabeth. "I miss them. I was so excited they were finally coming home. At times it seems only yesterday that we were all together at Grancourt, and other times, I can hardly believe it has been eight months since I heard of the shipwreck—that I will never see any of them again in this life."

Elizabeth made her way to Duchess Agatha's chair and embraced her.

Jane said, "If you would like to finish your story another time, we understand."

"Not at all. Talking about them is a comfort to me, so let me continue." She wiped away a tear. "Now, where was I? Ah, yes! Anne was the third to marry. She did not meet George Darcy until the following Season. And I must take partial credit for the match. George was a good friend of Joshua's from his Cambridge days. He was a reserved but very kind man, and I introduced him to Anne at a dinner party. He was instantly smitten and courted her. Most of Anne's family was pleased with the connexion, particularly Harold and Susan. However, Anne's sister, Lady Catherine de Bourgh, considered the association beneath the daughter of an earl."

Duchess Agatha must have noticed Elizabeth's look of distaste when Lady Catherine was mentioned. "I see you are acquainted with Lady Catherine, Lizzy."

"As well acquainted as I ever wish to be."

"You need not be tactful with me, my dear. I know she is insufferable. Her domineering manners and pride are repulsive. I do not believe she ever liked me."

"Then we have that in common. She was extremely displeased by my impertinence."

"I can well believe it! Such a harridan!" Jane gasped at this epithet. "Do not be so shocked, Jane, you have not met her."

"True," Elizabeth replied, "but Jane never sees a fault in anybody. She is a true angel. Unlike you and I, for I have no scruples in agreeing with you about Lady Catherine."

"If only we could be as compassionate as Jane—but I digress. Lady Catherine had her eye on a marquess for her younger sister and was quite vocal in her vehemence against George Darcy. However, there was true affection between the couple, and Anne was her parents' favourite, so they were allowed to marry, to everyone's happiness except Catherine's.

"Joshua and I preferred the country, as did the Darcys, and we met together often, and our families remained close throughout the years. As Joshua and I had no children, we watched our friends' children grow and considered ourselves their aunt and uncle. Indeed, we were probably closer to them than many relations are to their nieces and nephews.

"We were all greatly saddened when Anne died after Georgiana's birth. George was lost without her, but he rallied himself for the children. Fitzwilliam was quite attached to his mother and suffered acutely. He was always a serious boy, a temperament that only intensified after his parents' deaths, particularly when he was left with the responsibility of Pemberley and Georgiana at the age of three and twenty."

Elizabeth coloured when reminded of the tribulations Mr Darcy had endured in his life. *I have treated him so unfairly and abused him so abominably! He must hate me now. I thought I was so clever in my dislike of him, when truly he was an honourable, generous man. What will I do when we meet again?* It was absolutely certain they would meet, for he was sure to call upon Duchess Agatha during their stay.

Duchess Agatha continued her story. "It was a sad time, but judging from the last letter I had from Georgiana a few months ago, I believe they are both in good spirits now. They made some new acquaintances this summer and were anticipating meeting them again during the fall. I am sure we will see the Darcys as well as Lord and Lady Matlock. Their older son, Stephen, is getting married in late December to Lady Frederica Sutton, daughter of the Earl of Falmouth. Susan's most recent letter informed me that the family would be in London for the entire autumn until the wedding—except perhaps their younger son, Richard. He is a colonel in the army and may not be granted leave until closer to the wedding."

"I am acquainted with the colonel," Elizabeth said. "He was visiting in Kent with Mr Darcy. I was introduced to him and spent some time with him while he stayed at Rosings."

"And how did you find Richard?" Duchess Agatha asked.

"I enjoyed his company. He is not a handsome man, but his manners are so pleasant and friendly. I believe my most entertaining evenings at Rosings were spent in his company."

Duchess Agatha frowned at these words. "Richard has always had charming manners. Poor Susan cannot understand how, with his ability to entertain young women, he has not yet found a wife."

"But I can answer that!" Elizabeth playfully responded. "In the course of a conversation we had, I came to understand, as a younger son, he cannot marry without some attention to money. I teased him that the price of the younger son of an earl could not be above fifty thousand pounds, but perhaps his habits require a much larger sum, and he will not submit to matrimony for anything less than double."

"I doubt his habits are so costly. Susan would hardly permit her son to become such a coxcomb."

"Then it must be attributed to his desire to find a woman who can give him as much happiness as his mother has his father."

"That is an admirable sentiment, my dear, but I am not certain that the colonel is such a romantic. Darcy would be more likely to ascribe that notion to his matrimonial prospects." Elizabeth coloured at this statement. "Now, it is getting very late, and I must attend your mother and younger sisters to the shops tomorrow, so I will need a long, restful sleep."

"I am not sure any amount of rest will prepare you for such exertions as you will meet tomorrow. You are truly courageous to have offered to escort them."

"Oh Lizzy," Jane admonished, "it will not be so horrible. And they will need Duchess Agatha's counsel."

"Not to mention her prudence, or Mama might spend our entire annual income on gowns and lace."

"Do not worry. I have developed a good excuse to forestall your mother's spending."

"And pray what have you devised?"

"The girls will only need morning gowns while they are at school, but they will become suspicious if they do not have ball gowns made, for they believe they will be attending the Season next year. I will simply persuade them that most young ladies of the *ton* will not have their clothes for the Season made until the newest edition of *La Belle Assemblée* is published. They will not want to be considered *outré*. We will have a few evening gowns made for the winter when the

Gardiners come to stay, but I believe I can prohibit other purchases."

"That is inspired!"

"At the risk of sounding immodest, I believe it is rather clever. However, when I go shopping with you and Jane, we should begin selecting some of your wardrobe for next year. I believe your tastes will not require the most modern Paris fashions, so we may purchase many of your gowns now, allowing next spring to be less hectic. Perhaps your Aunt Gardiner would like to join us."

"I believe she would greatly enjoy it. I am looking forward to introducing her to you. I believe you will like her."

"I have every confidence I will if she is all you have described. When will you visit her?"

"I would like to do so tomorrow while you are busy with my mother and sisters. Does that suit you, Jane?"

"That is a wonderful idea. It will be pleasant to talk with her when there are fewer distractions."

"I can only imagine the barrage of conversation our poor aunt will be subjected to when Mama and Lydia have her in their midst! So, to Gracechurch Street we will venture and assure ourselves of a few quiet hours spent in the company of our beloved aunt."

"Come, ladies," Duchess Agatha said, "and I will show you to your rooms. I hope you do not mind that you have been placed in adjoining chambers again."

"If my room adjoins Jane's, it is sure to become my *second* favourite in Everard House—after the striped parlour!"

The three ladies were laughing as they exited the room to retire to their chambers for the night.

CHAPTER 10

E lizabeth awoke early, and with the help of her maid, she was quickly dressed and readied for the day. She made her way to the breakfast room, hoping to enjoy a quiet hour of reflection before anyone else in the house stirred. She was a bit disappointed to find Duchess Agatha already seated at the table drinking a cup of tea. Elizabeth helped herself to some tea and a buttered muffin and took a seat across from the duchess.

"Good morning, Lizzy. Did you sleep well?"

"Yes, thank you. I am surprised to see you up so early. I thought you would want to be completely rested before your ordeal today," Elizabeth playfully responded, masking her frustration at not having time to herself.

"I assure you, I am not fearful of today's outing. You must remember that I have been in company with members of the *ton* for the last thirty years. I believe I can handle a few hours shopping with your mother."

Elizabeth could not help but smile at Duchess Agatha's sanguine attitude, but she was certain her thoughts would be less positive in the evening. "If you insist, but I *did* warn you."

"I will take your forewarning under advisement and promise not to be in a bad temper if I am proven wrong. But there is something I would like to discuss with you. May I speak frankly, my dear?"

Elizabeth was curious. "Of course. I hope we may always be honest with each other."

"As do I. So, let me come straight to the point. What is the nature of your acquaintance with Mr Darcy? I sensed you did not tell me everything last night."

Elizabeth's eyes widened. She had hoped the conversation last night would have satisfied Duchess Agatha, but as she pondered the situation, Elizabeth realised Duchess Agatha was too perceptive to let the matter rest and recognised that the duchess's prior association with Mr Darcy might be useful in better understanding his character. Elizabeth mustered her courage and took a deep breath.

"I would like to discuss this with you, but I am afraid of being interrupted. Could we perhaps take a walk where we will not be disturbed?"

"An excellent idea. Hyde Park is only a short distance from here. There are plenty of paths where we can find privacy for our talk."

Elizabeth smiled gratefully. "Let us gather our coats and gloves and be on our way."

The two ladies soon left Everard House, a footman accompanying them for safety. Elizabeth began her tale as they strolled.

"My acquaintance with Mr Darcy has been a thorny one. It did not start favourably. When Mr Darcy came to Hertfordshire, he was aloof and unsocial. He insulted me before we were even introduced, though it was a conversation I am sure he did not know was being overheard."

Duchess Agatha gasped in surprise. "How did he insult you? I consider him one of the most well-mannered men of my acquaintance."

Elizabeth smiled sheepishly. "The first night I met Mr Darcy was at a ball, where he refused to dance with anyone but members of his own party and refused introductions. His friend Mr Bingley approached him during the evening and offered to introduce him to me as a dancing partner, and I was close enough to overhear their conversation. Mr Darcy flatly refused, saying I was not handsome enough to tempt him, and he would not give consequence to young ladies who were slighted by other men. I laughed at the time, but as I have thought about that night, I realised his statements hurt my pride more than I was willing to confess.

"I quickly formed a dislike of him, and every time we met, his poor manners increased my prejudice. I allowed this aversion to mislead me when a young man, a lieutenant in the militia, came to Meryton and spread stories about Mr Darcy's supposed infamous conduct towards him."

"That cannot be! I know Fitzwilliam Darcy to be scrupulously honest and principled. I will concede he is oftentimes too serious, and he is uncomfortable in large groups, particularly if he does not know many people. I am ashamed that he was rude to you and offer no excuses, but he is truly a good and honourable man."

"I know all this now, but I was misled. At the time, one young man was making himself agreeable, and the other was taciturn and proud. Mr Darcy thought he was above his company, but I have reason to believe his manners have altered."

Elizabeth paused to gather her thoughts. She espied a stone bench off the path ahead and gestured to it. They left the trail to sit for a while.

"Mr Darcy and I were not the best of friends; however, Jane and Mr Bingley had grown quite fond of each other. From the first moment he met Jane, it was obvious Mr Bingley preferred her to anyone else in the neighbourhood, and we all thought he would propose before Christmas.

"He held a ball in late November and gave Jane every attention, but the next morning, he left for town, and his party followed almost immediately thereafter. Miss Bingley wrote a note to Jane, informing her that they would not return that winter. I never cared for Caroline Bingley—such a vain and haughty woman—but Jane, who never sees a fault in anyone, concluded Miss Bingley was trying to warn her of her brother's indifference.

"Mr Bingley did not return, and I convinced Jane to travel to London after the New Year and stay with the Gardiners. While there, she called upon Miss Bingley and Mrs Hurst. They were not happy to see her, and Miss Bingley did not return the visit until three weeks later."

"I told you I had not heard good things about Mr Bingley's sisters, and this only confirms it. Vain, selfish, conceited creatures."

"Yes, and even Jane could no longer be deceived by Miss Bingley's professed regard. She assured Jane that her brother knew of her being in town and insinuated an attachment between Mr Bingley and Miss Darcy that put an end to Jane's hopes."

"But that cannot be. Georgiana is but fifteen years old!"

"It was my conclusion then, and it still stands, that Miss Bingley hoped if her brother married Miss Darcy, Mr Darcy would be more likely to offer for her. It is a preposterous expectation, but I am convinced that is her belief."

"There is no limit to the woman's ambition. To imply such a thing to Jane! She had to have known Jane was attached to her brother. Such insolence! I will not forgive her for it. Poor Jane! Has she recovered from her heartache?"

"She still thinks of Mr Bingley as the most amiable man of her acquaintance and prefers him to anyone else, though she is exceptional at hiding her sorrow."

"Well, I am not sure I will be able to forgive Mr Bingley."

"Do not judge him too harshly, for I have things to relate that may acquit him. After Miss Bingley's visit, it seemed our association with the Bingleys and Mr Darcy was at an end. However, as Jane mentioned last night, I again met Mr Darcy in Kent. I was visiting my friend Charlotte, who had married our cousin Mr Collins, the current rector of Hunsford, the village close to Lady Catherine de Bourgh's estate, Rosings. I was only in Hunsford a fortnight when I learned Lady Catherine expected a visit from her nephews, Mr Darcy and Colonel Fitzwilliam. I was distressed by this knowledge, for I still harboured a poor, though misguided, estimation of Mr Darcy.

"The gentlemen called on us, and I entered easily into conversation with the colonel. Mr Darcy spoke hardly at all and only enquired after my family with the barest trace of civility. I teased him about Jane being in town, and he replied he had not been fortunate enough to see her. I had become certain he was involved in keeping Mr Bingley from my sister, not with any intention of forwarding a match with Miss Darcy, but because he disapproved of our family."

Elizabeth grimaced in remembrance, and Duchess Agatha patted her hand in sympathy.

"I knew Mr Darcy condemned my family's behaviour, and I believed he censured my impertinence. I constantly vexed and provoked him.

"I had walked out early one day and came across Colonel Fitzwilliam. We began a discussion about Mr Darcy that resulted in the colonel admitting that his cousin had recently congratulated himself on saving a friend from a most imprudent marriage—that there were some very strong objections to the lady. It could only have been Jane! I was incensed, and my agitation and tears soon brought on a headache, and I excused myself from the dinner invitation at Rosings. I was perusing Jane's letters when a visitor was announced. Imagine my surprise when Mr Darcy entered the room!"

Elizabeth, reliving the emotions of that fateful evening, could not immediately continue. It was a painful memory, but she had decided she would tell Duchess Agatha everything. She composed herself and took up the tale again.

"I was as polite as possible, though he was the last man I wanted to see at that moment, and I offered him a seat. He sat but was quickly up again and pacing the room."

Elizabeth remembered his speech that night had been full of passion, a passion she had never expected from the staid Mr Darcy. *You must allow me to tell you how ardently I admire and love you.*

"He proposed to me, but I was not of a mind to hear it, and he did not offer it in the most favourable way. He did admit he loved me and had for many months, but he also gave a recitation of the degradation he would feel from my inferiority in society and the family obstacles that would naturally result from our union."

"I cannot believe he would say such things in his proposal! How could he have strayed so far from propriety and decency? I am sorry you had to endure such rudeness. If I had heard it from anyone else, I would not believe it, but I am sure it occurred as you said. For shame, Fitzwilliam Darcy!"

"Yes, it was shockingly rude, but I confess I was not beyond reproach in my behaviour that evening. I confronted him with the stories I had heard about his conduct towards Mr Wickham, the militia lieutenant, and Jane and Mr Bingley. I accused him of behaving in an ungentlemanlike manner. I was callous and severe in my condemnation.

"He left the parsonage, and I dissolved into tears and retreated to my room to escape, for I did not feel equal to meeting anyone. The next morning, I arose after a fitful night and walked out to recover from the thoughts that had assaulted me. I hoped a long walk would clear my mind and conscience.

"I met Mr Darcy during my walk. He had ventured out solely to find me and put into my hands a letter, which he asked me to read, and then quickly left. I could not contain my curiosity, and so, ignoring the impropriety of his actions, I sat and eagerly read through the missive.

"It gave an account of his dealings with Mr Wickham, laying out their entire history. The two stories matched in many instances, but I was persuaded to believe Mr Darcy's account. A very frank confession, which I am not at liberty to divulge, forced me to acknowledge that Mr Darcy was entirely blameless throughout and Mr Wickham is not an honourable man. I received further proof of this when Aunt Gardiner wrote from Derbyshire. Mr Wickham had grown up at Pemberley, but upon quitting the neighbourhood, he left many debts, and there were rumours of his licentious behaviour with some of the tradesmen's daughters. Mr Darcy has been completely exonerated in regard to Mr Wickham, and I better understand his principled character now.

"Mr Darcy's letter also gave his justification for separating Jane and Mr Bingley. He had noticed Mr Bingley's preference for my sister, but as he observed Jane, he did not recognise any signs of particular regard. Upon reflection, I remembered Charlotte's comment suggesting that Jane was too reserved and that someone who did not know her character might be misled by her placidity. After acknowledging this possibility, and the lack of decorum exhibited by my family, I was forced to give some weight to Mr Darcy's observations.

"I have since become absolutely ashamed of my behaviour towards the gentleman. I abused him abominably, and although I do not regret my refusal of his offer, I wish that our acquaintance had progressed more amicably. I am afraid to meet him now."

"I can understand your apprehension, Lizzy, but you will certainly meet him. I know that he and his sister will call on us, but do not be fearful. Darcy is not resentful by nature."

"But that is exactly what I fear! Last year, he said he *was* of a resentful temper, and his good opinion once lost was lost forever. I have done nothing to gain his good opinion and everything to lose it!"

"You obviously did gain his good opinion or Darcy would not have proposed to you, though I am still astonished at his mode of declaration. But you need not be ashamed to meet him. Do you want his good opinion? Would you like him to renew his addresses to you?"

Elizabeth blushed. She felt a sincere interest in his welfare, but she did not know how far she wished that welfare to depend upon her.

"My Aunt and Uncle Gardiner met him while they were touring Pemberley," she shyly disclosed. "He was very kind and attentive to them. He did not know their connexion to me at first, but he introduced himself anyway. He also introduced his sister and invited them to dine at Pemberley. Miss Darcy spent a day shopping with my aunt, and my uncle fished with Mr Darcy and Mr Bingley, who was visiting for the summer.

"At dinner, my aunt revealed to Mr Bingley that Jane had visited London last winter and called upon his sisters. They had never informed him of it, and Aunt Gardiner reports that he was infuriated with them. I hope this acquits Mr Bingley somewhat, though perhaps he is a little too influenced by his friends and family."

"I suppose I can forgive him, though a young man of his age and independent fortune should not place such implicit confidence in others."

"His nature is obliging and modest."

"Very like Jane's. Do you suppose she would be happy to meet Mr Bingley again?"

Elizabeth hesitated. "I am not certain. I believe she would, but I do not know that it will happen. We are now as far above Mr Bingley as we were below him before."

"Yes, but he is Darcy's good friend, so it is likely you will meet him at some point."

"True, and he has become friends with the Gardiners as well."

"We shall just have to let things unfold. And we should probably return to the house. Your mother and your sisters will be anxious to begin their shopping."

Elizabeth smiled but then turned a serious glance to her

companion. "I have not shared this with anyone but Jane, and even then, I never told her about Mr Darcy's interference between her and Mr Bingley. I have related the contents of my Aunt Gardiner's correspondence with her, so she knows Mr Bingley was unaware of her presence in town and that he plans on pursuing a friendship with them, but Jane has not confided in me her expectations of meeting Mr Bingley again.

"I think it would be best if we kept this from the rest of my family, especially my mother. She was so eager to have Jane marry Mr Bingley last year, but I am not sure what her reaction will be were he to try courting Jane now that Papa has inherited the dukedom."

Duchess Agatha readily agreed to her suggestions. The conversation had been long, and both would be missed at Everard House, so they quickly proceeded home.

NEITHER LADY NOTICED THE TALL GENTLEMAN STEP OUT OF the nearby grove of trees. Darcy had made a habit of walking in Hyde Park each morning. He knew the Bennets had arrived the previous evening, for he had requested that his valet inform him of it immediately. Elizabeth was in town, and he had walked out that morning to review his plans for the upcoming months. His meditations had been interrupted by the sound of female voices, and he had looked up to behold a wondrous sight. *Elizabeth!*

He had watched the approach of Duchess Agatha and Elizabeth with excitement. He noticed they were in earnest conversation and would not interrupt them, but he could not forgo the opportunity to look upon the woman he loved.

She was more beautiful than he remembered. Her cheeks were flushed from the chill of the early morning, and her eyes were intense with the emotion of her discourse. He wondered what would give such animation to Elizabeth's countenance. He was delighted Elizabeth and Duchess Agatha had developed what appeared a close rapport, for Duchess Agatha was a woman he highly regarded.

He hid himself in a wooded area where he could command a full view of their faces without overhearing their conversation. Occasionally, small exclamations would reach his ears, and he thought he heard his name mentioned, though he could not be sure. Far too soon for his taste, they stood and returned home, but he was thankful for the short time he was able to see Elizabeth. He promised himself that it would not be long before he met her again, and this time he would leave a different impression.

CHAPTER 11

Duchess Agatha and Elizabeth returned to Everard House to find the rest of the family in the breakfast room. The duchess, Kitty, and Lydia were in high spirits. They eagerly anticipated their shopping expedition and were proposing outrageous ideas about the wardrobes they would purchase. Duchess Agatha attempted to rein in their exuberance. She smiled and informed the duchess of the need to delay such purchases.

The new duchess could not dispute Duchess Agatha's obvious knowledge of what was fashionable. "Of course! We were not even contemplating purchasing anything for next Season, were we, girls?"

Lydia replied to her mother with a derisive snort.

Duchess Agatha continued. "Today we should content ourselves with selecting simple and elegant fabrics for morning gowns. We should also have a few winter evening gowns made for when your family visits at Christmas. And of course, you should get new bonnets and coats. You will all need fur-lined pelisses and gloves, for the winters at Grancourt can be very cold. You are used to such mild weather in Hertfordshire compared to the northern climes."

The duchess could only nod in agreement, while Lydia and Kitty pouted that their purchases were to be curtailed. Mary stated she would rather stay at home.

"Lizzy and Jane, are you still planning to go to Gracechurch Street?"

"Yes," Jane responded, "we will visit there this morning, but we should be back later in the afternoon."

"Excellent. And perhaps in a day or two, I can accompany you both to the shops to begin your purchases as well."

"I do not see why Jane and Lizzy are not coming with us today," the duchess interjected.

"We would not want to overwhelm the modistes, Frances. Four women will be enough for them at one time. We have six weeks to see to everything. Jane and Lizzy can wait for another day."

Elizabeth smiled gratefully at Duchess Agatha, and her mother was placated for the moment, but she almost instantly admonished her younger daughters to hurry so they could set out. She bustled them out of the room to retrieve their outdoor clothing. Duchess Agatha turned to the duke.

"Bennet, you must see to some purchases yourself."

The duke looked at her quizzically. "I am sure it does not need to be attended to this moment. I will avail myself of the peace that will settle once you have all departed and spend the morning in the library. Joshua kept an excellent collection."

"I thought you might like to dispense with the task as quickly as possible."

The duke looked thoughtful for a moment. "Perhaps you are right. I think this afternoon might be a good time to visit my tailor, and I might also stop at my club, so please tell Frances not to expect me for dinner."

Elizabeth stifled a laugh at his avoidance of her mother. It appeared he would not be in company with his wife for more than the morning meal, which would be wise, considering her evening discourse would be full of lace! The duke left the breakfast room, and Duchess Agatha turned to her two remaining companions.

"Enjoy your visit with your Aunt Gardiner. I would like to meet her as soon as possible. Perhaps tomorrow?"

"I will ask," Elizabeth offered. "I am sure Mama will want to visit soon, and Jane and I will never refuse an opportunity to go there."

"Thank you, Lizzy. I should go now, but I will try to have us back in the late afternoon." She stood and left to find the duchess and the younger girls prepared for their outing. Jane and Elizabeth also rose, donned their coats, and took a carriage to Gracechurch Street.

When the ladies entered the Gardiners' parlour, they were immediately assailed by their young cousins. Ethan would not relinquish Elizabeth's leg until she had picked him up and showered his face with kisses. As she placed him on his feet, she noticed a young woman in a corner of the room, but her Aunt Gardiner soon commanded her attention as they embraced and exchanged greetings.

"My dears, it is wonderful to see you, but where are your mother and sisters?" Mrs Gardiner asked.

"They have gone shopping this morning," Jane replied.

"Mama was anxious to start that task as soon as possible. Duchess Agatha has accompanied them this morning, but she expressed a hope of meeting you soon and asked whether she could call with us tomorrow?"

Mrs Gardiner heard the young woman's intake of breath across the room and gestured for her to join them. "I would be delighted to meet her tomorrow." She turned to her guest. "May I present Miss Georgiana Darcy. Georgiana, my nieces Lady Jane and Lady Elizabeth."

Elizabeth was amused to hear her aunt introduce them so formally. Georgiana timidly curtseyed, but the smile on both Jane and Elizabeth's faces seemed to ease her shyness.

They were seated, and aunt and nieces began to converse. Mrs Gardiner answered questions about her trip to Derbyshire and the welfare of her children. Jane and Elizabeth recounted their impressions of Grancourt and Everard House, their growing relationship with Duchess Agatha, and their intended plans for the autumn. More than once, Elizabeth found Georgiana surreptitiously watching her.

"Miss Darcy, it is a pleasure to meet you. I have heard about you from many sources and must admit that I have been eager to make your acquaintance."

Georgiana smiled. "Thank you, Lady Elizabeth. I have heard much about you as well."

"I am not accustomed to being addressed with a title. To do so will surely give me airs that would be most unbecoming. If we are to be friends, you must call me Elizabeth. Besides, if we were to meet in public and you called out, 'Lady Elizabeth,' I am not sure I would remember to answer!" Mrs Gardiner and Jane laughed at Elizabeth's playful manner, encouraging Georgiana to join in.

"Of course, Lady—I mean, Elizabeth, if you will call me Georgiana?"

"It would be my pleasure."

Elizabeth's young cousin Beth, who at age six was showing signs of her namesake's nature, interrupted her. "Lizzy, may I not call you Lady Lizzy now that you are so rich?"

Elizabeth laughed delightedly. "Certainly not! When I must, I will endure the title, but only my most beloved family and friends can call me Lizzy. It is a mark of my fondness for you that you are allowed. Would you want to share that with everyone?"

Beth wrinkled her nose. "Oh no! I do not like sharing you with anyone! Even if Mr Bingley were to come today, I am sure we would send him away, though he is so very handsome."

"Though not as tall as Mr Darcy," interjected Diane, the Gardiners' seven-year-old daughter.

"And Mr Darcy is such a good storyteller—almost as good as you, Lizzy!" Ethan eagerly replied. "He told us the story of King Arthur and his knights, and he promised he would tell us about Robin Hood next. You still need to finish *Beauty and the Beast*," he pouted as he climbed up into Elizabeth's lap.

"I have not forgotten, dear Ethan, but not today," she responded as she cuddled the small boy. She turned to Georgiana again, desirous to learn more about her.

"I understand that you are fond of music and play exceptionally well."

"I do not play exceptionally well, but I am very fond of music. I understand you play the pianoforte and sing."

"True, but very ill indeed. Your aunt Lady Catherine told me I would not play at all ill if I took the trouble of practising, but I am afraid I am neglectful, and my talent suffers as a result. I would be delighted to hear you play." She looked at her aunt. "I understand you spent a day shopping in Lambton. Did my aunt tire you by insisting you visit every mantua-maker in the village?"

"Lizzy, for shame!" Mrs Gardiner replied with a laugh. "You will give Georgiana a poor opinion of me, since I have engaged her to spend a day with me in the shops here."

"I know your proclivity, Aunt, do not attempt to deny it. And why should you when Uncle has such vast resources at his disposal. Have you been to my uncle's shop, Georgiana?" The girl shook her head. "My uncle imports quite a bit from India, and there are so many beautiful things—silks, statues of ivory, spices, and tapestries. You will feel as though you have left England entirely! Perhaps you can take her, Aunt? I am sure she would enjoy it."

"That is a wonderful idea, but you and Jane should come with us. You are the best guide in the world, Lizzy. Everything is exciting to you, though you bother the poor clerks dread-fully with all your questions."

"I hope none of them have resigned on my account!" Elizabeth exclaimed. "Duchess Agatha is escorting us to the dress-maker's to purchase new gowns for the winter. Perhaps Georgiana can accompany us, and we can visit Uncle's shop during our excursion. Do you think your brother would approve of such a scheme?"

"I would love to come! And I am sure I can persuade him to allow it. I do not often get the chance to shop with friends."

"Did Miss Bingley never convince you to go with her?" Elizabeth asked, watching closely for a reaction. Georgiana wrinkled her nose, causing Elizabeth to laugh. "I can see the idea is not agreeable to you. Ask Mr Darcy and then write to my aunt with your answer."

"Thank you, Elizabeth, I shall do so directly when I see him today."

She smiled at the young girl's enthusiasm. They spent another hour in conversation, and Elizabeth quickly grew fond of Miss Darcy. She was obviously shy and only needed encouragement to be truly amiable.

The last of Mr Wickham's lies had proven false, for there was not a trace of pride in Georgiana Darcy. She often mentioned her brother and Mr Bingley and expressed a hope of them all meeting together. Jane and Elizabeth were both nervous at the proposal, but the introduction to Miss Darcy would help to ease any apprehension. Elizabeth was disappointed not to have any private discussion with her aunt, but she hoped they would have an opportunity soon.

Mrs Gardiner appeared delighted with the burgeoning friendship between Miss Darcy and her nieces. The group soon dispersed, for Jane and Elizabeth were expected back at Everard House.

CHAPTER 12

Duchess Agatha returned to Everard House after her shopping trip in a disturbed state. She had taken the duchess and the younger girls to dressmakers of good reputation, though not generally patronised by members of the *ton*, hoping to cause as little stir as possible. Duchess Agatha was sure to include some evening dresses in their purchases to assuage any suspicion, but she need not have planned such a contingency. The duchess, Kitty, and Lydia were so eager to be shopping in London, they soon forgot about ball gowns and lost themselves in dress patterns and fabrics.

The shops' proprietors were grateful for the enthusiasm and the access to wealth displayed by these new customers. Duchess Agatha was careful to avoid using titles, but the modistes were not ignorant that there were new heirs to the Everard dukedom. They were discreet, however, hoping to garner loyalty from these new members of the peerage.

The group spent several hours having measurements taken, choosing fabrics and trimmings, and enjoying the novelty of almost unlimited funds—or so it seemed to them. The duke had been generous with their allowance for this excursion, though he never intended to inform his wife and youngest two daughters of the exact extent of his wealth. Since the amount was so much more than usual, they were perfectly satisfied with the duke's current liberality. Duchess Agatha was able to leave the other ladies to themselves, for they had good taste, and only a few prohibitions were needed to confine the amount of dresses ordered and limit some of the more outrageous adornments. This allowed Duchess Agatha to spend some uninterrupted time with Mary.

As the middle daughter and not particularly close to any of her sisters or either parent, Mary was often neglected. She filled the void of companionship by turning to books and music. Duchess Agatha had become aware that Mary only needed a little guidance and attention, and she was most willing to supply it.

Duchess Agatha realised she would never be as close to Mary as she was to Jane and Elizabeth, but she hoped to nurture some sort of friendship with her. She took Mary in hand and questioned her about her tastes in fabrics and patterns. She made gentle suggestions of styles she believed would better suit Mary and flatter her colouring and figure. Mary began to blossom under such notice, confirming Duchess Agatha's expectations that a little interest would benefit the young woman.

Late in the morning, as the duchess was being fitted for a gown and Duchess Agatha and Mary were debating a choice of red muslins, Kitty and Lydia stepped outside the shop to get a breath of fresh air. A few minutes after their exit, Duchess Agatha noticed they were missing and went in pursuit of them. She found them just outside the shop's door, conversing with a handsome young man.

She approached the group with a look of disapproval on her face. It was dangerous for young ladies to walk about London and converse with strangers, and she was of a mind to reprove them for their thoughtlessness. The trio turned towards her at her approach, and Kitty introduced the young man as a Mr Wickham, whom they had known in Meryton, where he was a lieutenant in the militia.

This information immediately called to mind her morning conversation with Elizabeth. She had mentioned Mr Wickham was the young man who had spread lies about Darcy. Duchess Agatha kept her expression impassive as she accepted the introduction of the scoundrel, for he must be the worst sort of reprobate to fabricate malicious rumours about a man as honourable as Fitzwilliam Darcy.

She had to admit that Mr Wickham was charming, and she better understood Elizabeth's initial regard for him. If Darcy's manners had been as disagreeable as Elizabeth described, Mr Wickham's appeal would be a welcome contrast. However, Duchess Agatha was not deceived by his charm. She ended the conversation as quickly as she could and ushered the girls back into the shop.

WICKHAM WAS DISAPPOINTED TO SEE THEM LEAVE SO QUICKLY. He had planned their *surprise* meeting with the hope of renewing their acquaintance. When Lydia Bennet had left Brighton early, Wickham was hardly aware of her departure.

His finances had become dire, and he was wrapped up in his own concerns. He was forced to leave Brighton and the militia because of his mounting debts and had travelled to London, hoping to evade the various authorities that were certain to be tracking him. His associate, Mrs Younge, helped him to find accommodations in a very poor section of the city.

He had been in hiding for several weeks when he read an interesting notice in one of the newspapers—Mr Bennet was to inherit a dukedom. The Bennet girls were heiresses! He asked Mrs Younge to discreetly enquire about the Everard estate and learned it included a London townhouse on Grosvenor Square, a good indication the title was a wealthy one.

Wickham immediately began scheming. He was well-liked in Hertfordshire, and the Bennets had been some of his strongest advocates. His optimism was slightly dimmed when he recalled his last conversation with Miss Elizabeth. Her opinion of Darcy seemed to have improved, and although she did not specifically imply she discredited any of his professed history with him, he had not tried to distinguish her further, and they had parted civilly. Wickham wondered whether he could restore her previous regard. He was certain she had preferred him, and he would have pursued her if she had only ten or twenty thousand pounds. Now she most likely had a great deal more, and she was titled as well! And if he could not secure *Lady* Elizabeth, one of her sisters would do just as well.

Lydia always seemed partial to me and jealous of the attention I gave to Elizabeth. She is a silly chit, but a man could stomach a lot for a large dowry and access to the best of London society.

He had begun spying on Everard House and was one of the

first to know of the Bennets' arrival in town. He stationed himself outside the house early in the morning, hopeful of meeting one of the ladies, but he had withdrawn into the shadows when Elizabeth left the house in the company of a footman and a woman he assumed was Duchess Agatha. He had no desire to encounter Elizabeth in that situation.

He continued to wait after Elizabeth and her companion returned to the house, and his patience was soon rewarded. Mrs Bennet—or Her Grace—exited the house exclaiming loudly for her daughters to hurry and not waste any of their precious shopping time. Mary, Kitty, and Lydia soon followed and entered a stately carriage, followed by the woman he had seen earlier with Elizabeth. She told the driver the name of an establishment and was assisted into the carriage. Wickham had overheard the destination and immediately made his way there.

He waited outside a store opposite the one named as their destination. He was becoming impatient when he finally beheld Kitty and Lydia stepping out onto the pavement. When no others followed, Wickham made his way across the street and called their names. Lydia waved at him, and encouraged by her demeanour, he gallantly bowed and fell into conversation with the two girls.

Wickham had barely expressed his pleasure in meeting them so *unexpectedly*, when a regal woman in mourning clothes approached them. It was the same woman who had walked out with Elizabeth, and he was soon introduced to her. His assumption that she was Duchess Agatha had been correct, but she showed no signs of recognising him, and he grew confident that she was unaware of his falling out with Darcy. Unfortunately, her arrival abruptly ended their conversation, and she propelled Kitty and Lydia back into the shop.

He was frustrated at their early departure, but he was by no means discouraged. Wickham was convinced it was only a matter of time before he would be dining at Everard House and would win the hearts of one of the fair Bennet ladies. A few more *surprise* encounters would be needed, but he was resourceful and had high expectations of his success.

DUCHESS AGATHA WAS DISTURBED BY THE ENCOUNTER, though her concern was slightly lessened as she listened to the girls' chatter.

"Mr Wickham is such a handsome man," Lydia exclaimed, "though I do not know why he was not wearing his regimentals. He looks so much better in them."

"A man is nothing if he is not in regimentals."

"And he is only a lieutenant. Now that we are so rich, I do not think I can abide anything less than a general or a lord!"

"Oh! A lord would be ideal!"

"Next Season, we may even meet royalty. Princess Lydia! What a good joke that would be!"

Kitty nodded in eager agreement, and Duchess Agatha had to suppress a smile. The girls would be in for quite a shock when their father's plans for the following year were finally disclosed.

The group returned to the house shortly after this exchange. The duchess was fatigued from the excursion and in need of a rest. Mary withdrew to the music room, while Duchess Agatha, Kitty, and Lydia entered the main drawing room to partake of tea.

Duchess Agatha was glad to see that Jane and Elizabeth had already returned from their aunt's home. She could not relate her news immediately, however, because Kitty and

Lydia commandeered the conversation and regaled their older sisters with visions of the dresses ordered and bonnets purchased. Jane listened attentively, but Elizabeth quickly tired of the discussion and made her way to a seat near Duchess Agatha in a corner of the room.

"Lizzy, I would like to discuss something with you that occurred during shopping. It has put my mind into some agitation."

Elizabeth smiled knowingly. "I gave you fair warning."

Duchess Agatha laughed softly. "No, it was not that. It was not terribly distressing to take your mother and sisters shopping. They have good taste, and I was able to spend some time with Mary."

"Pray do not leave me in suspense. My alarm grows by the minute."

"At one point during the day, Kitty and Lydia stepped outside the shop. I followed them as soon as I realised they had disappeared and found them in conversation with a handsome young man. They introduced him to me."

"I am not surprised that Kitty and Lydia, particularly Lydia, made the acquaintance of a handsome young man. They are terribly forward. Hopefully, their upcoming years at school will teach them more decorum and caution."

"Oh, no, you mistake me. They were not talking with a stranger. It was Mr Wickham, whom you all met in Hertfordshire."

Elizabeth's eyes widened and then her brows knitted together in a frown.

Duchess Agatha perceived her reaction, and her concern grew. "I remembered his name from our discussion earlier."

"What is he doing in London? I thought his regiment was stationed in Brighton?"

"I cannot answer that, but you told me he is not an honourable man. I cannot think it wise for your sisters to be meeting him."

"What did they say? How did he act?" Elizabeth questioned, the disquiet evident in her voice.

"I did not hear much of their conversation, but it must have been brief, for I followed them almost immediately after they left and hurried them back into the shop directly after my introduction to Mr Wickham. Remembering your earlier warning, I was concerned for the girls. I believe they are unaware of his true character."

"Jane knows of it, and you and I, of course, and that is all. We did not see the need to inform the rest of the neighbourhood. The prejudice against Mr Darcy was so violent, and since Mr Wickham was to leave soon, we did not think it would signify. Mr Darcy had not authorised me to make his communication public. We chose to remain silent. Looking back, that may have been the wrong decision."

"I think you made the right one at the time, but things are different now. Your fortunes have risen significantly. Every person imaginable will seek out you girls, many of them unsavoury and avaricious. Mr Wickham struck me as such a man, and Kitty and Lydia do find him handsome, though they believe his rank of lieutenant is not high enough for them now."

Elizabeth smiled wanly at this statement. Duchess Agatha was glad to faintly lift the sombre mood but continued in a serious tone.

"If a person of your acquaintance is known to have a licentious character, then it must be disclosed to every member of your family. It is the only way to prevent calamity. Let us make your father aware, and he can decide how to best disseminate the information. But I do not believe the girls should be allowed to go anywhere without proper supervision. Your mother is an inadequate chaperone, for she is not vigilant enough. It will fall to Jane, you, myself, and hopefully your father, to provide suitable protection."

"I think it is the best course for now. Hopefully, Papa will be willing to listen this time. He did not listen when I urged him not to send Lydia to Brighton. She was invited to travel with the wife of the regiment's colonel, a silly and frivolous young woman, not at all adequate to chaperone Lydia around a town where hundreds of soldiers were encamped. Papa thought she would learn her own insignificance when in the presence of so many other young women competing for the soldiers' attention.

"I heartily disagreed with him. Lydia is an incorrigible flirt, and our parents have never checked her behaviour. I feared her conduct would increase the censure of our family. Luckily, we were all called to Grancourt, and my father fetched her before she got into any mischief."

"Let us hope she will learn better manners. I believe your father is more conscious of his duty to his daughters now. Agreeing to send the girls to school, knowing the tantrums that will result, shows his resolve, do you not agree?"

This comment finally provoked a sincere smile from Elizabeth. "Yes, and we must help him, for the tantrums you prophesy will thoroughly test it. We must not allow him to relent in order to restore peace."

Duchess Agatha chuckled softly. "Have no fear, Lizzy, for sending them to school will ensure a longer-lasting peace, of which the duke is probably very aware." Elizabeth smiled wryly in acknowledgment. "But, before we part, I would like to discuss Mary with you, and I would like for Jane to hear as well."

Kitty and Lydia had finally relinquished Jane's attention in order to withdraw to their rooms and sift through their closets of existing clothing. Duchess Agatha called Jane over and related her day's experience with Mary. She encouraged the girls to bestow a little more consideration on their middle sister. Expressing dismay at their lack of sisterly concern, they promised to spend more time with Mary.

Elizabeth immediately repaired to the music room and spent the afternoon in gentle direction of Mary's choices of music and attempted to instil some insights of artistic expression. She chose pieces that would show Mary's skill at the pianoforte without the need for singing, for no matter how much Mary practised, she would never have a tolerable singing voice. Mary welcomed the attention, and both sisters felt the afternoon was pleasantly spent. They agreed to repeat it regularly.

Elizabeth was delighted with her successful efforts and the positive change it produced in Mary and was grateful to Duchess Agatha for the suggestion.

THE DUKE SPENT THE MORNING IN HIS LIBRARY BUT VACATED the house before the return of his wife and youngest daughters. He decided to heed Duchess Agatha's advice, and he visited his tailor. Luckily, he had retained the services of the late duke's trusted valet, Dawson.

As Mr Bennet, he had not had his own manservant and was still becoming accustomed to the idea, but he was thankful for the man now. After initial measurements were taken, the duke left the choice of waistcoat colours and fabrics to the very capable Dawson.

He entered his London club, hoping to spend a quiet afternoon reading the book he had brought along. However, he soon found himself the centre of attention. He had not spent much time in London since his marriage and only occasionally visited Brooks's, so he was amused at the interest he garnered.

As he was playing chess and renewing the acquaintance of old friends, many gentlemen approached him and introduced themselves. He invited them to sit and converse with him. Initially, the duke was entertained and diverted, but as the afternoon lengthened, his dismay heightened. He discovered he and his family were one of the main topics of conversation among the *ton*. There were even several ongoing bets in the gentlemens' clubs of London regarding his family. He was interrogated about everything but most especially about his five daughters.

The duke hid his growing consternation with his cynical wit, evading all specifics, and causing extensive frustration among the gentlemen. The situation reinforced his duty to guard his daughters, and he returned home, his mind full of the rules he would put into effect to protect the girls and keep them safe from society's rakes.

On his return, the duke found Duchess Agatha, Jane, and Elizabeth in the striped parlour. After greetings were exchanged, Elizabeth addressed her father.

"Duchess Agatha brought something to our attention that must be discussed. While shopping, Kitty and Lydia ventured outside unaccompanied and fell into conversation with a male acquaintance. Fortunately, Duchess Agatha almost immediately returned them inside, but it raises the issue of ensuring a proper chaperone while we are in London."

"Who was this male acquaintance?" queried the duke.

"It was Mr Wickham, whom I have come to know is not a reputable man."

The duke turned shrewd eyes upon Elizabeth. "I see. I had already determined that I will accompany your mother and sisters whenever they leave the house, and this only strengthens my decision. While dining at my club today, I was made acutely aware of the danger my wife and daughters are in due to this inheritance. I feel an obligation to personally attend you on all subsequent outings."

"Surely, Papa, you do not mean to go with us everywhere?" Elizabeth asked

The duke vehemently shook his head. He understood her confusion. In the past, he had always chosen to escape them when possible.

"No, I have shirked my responsibility long enough. From this point onward, I will fulfil my obligation to your mother and sisters. No one else has the authority to check their behaviour, and I have been remiss in that duty. If you could have seen the bets being placed at Brooks's—how quickly my daughters would marry, in which scandals they would be caught! I could hardly restrain my anger, knowing how easily Kitty and Lydia could fall into a trap.

"I remember your advice to me this spring, Lizzy, and have finally acceded to your wisdom. I trust you and Jane, for you have sense and intelligence, but you must promise me to take all precautions. I could not bear it if any of you came to harm."

He looked earnestly at his eldest children, both of whom were fighting tears. Jane rose to embrace and comfort her father. He held her close for a moment and then releasing her said, "Let us find your mother and sisters. I have some directives for them. They will not be happy, but it is necessary."

He straightened his shoulders, and the ladies followed him out of the parlour and to the main drawing room.

THE DUCHESS HAD COMMANDEERED THE ROOM FOR HER personal use. It was the stateliest of the main rooms, fitting her idea of what was appropriate for her rank. When the duke entered, his wife and younger daughters were involved in their usual pursuits. Mary was reading, while the duchess, Kitty, and Lydia discussed their morning shopping excursion. The duchess was surprised by her husband's entrance, not knowing he had returned. She immediately launched into a recitation of the day's activities, outlining their many purchases. The duke raised his hand to halt her torrent and adopted a commanding tone.

"My dear, I am glad you had a pleasant day; however, there are a few things I need to discuss with you and our daughters. This will be a serious conversation, and I need undivided attention from all of you." He looked directly at each person in the room, keeping his gaze on Lydia until she abandoned her task of trimming her bonnet and rose to sit on a sofa near the others. When he was certain they were all listening, he began.

"I heard some rather distressing gossip today at my club. Apparently, there is much speculation about my family, particularly my daughters and how soon they will be advantageously married."

Lydia seemed giddy at this information and could not restrain her glee. "I am sure I will be the first! Kitty and I have already talked about the beaux we will have. All the handsome and rich young lords will want to court us. It will not take long for any of us to be married, even Mary."

The duchess nodded her head in enthusiastic agreement. "Oh, my dear Lydia, of course none of you will have trouble finding rich and handsome husbands. I knew from the moment your father announced the inheritance that all my lovely daughters would be advantageously matched within months."

The duke looked daggers at his wife and youngest daughter and icily voiced his displeasure with their outbursts. "You will not be getting married in the next few *years*, let alone in months, for you will not be meeting any gentlemen. I absolutely forbid Mary, Kitty, and Lydia to leave the house without being accompanied by either myself or Mr Gardiner. No introductions to strangers will take place, and you will not be attending any events besides family dinners or evenings with the Gardiners."

Lydia's shock and indignation were instant, and she immediately began bewailing the unfairness of her father's commands, Kitty burst into tears, and Mary looked on indifferently.

"You cannot do this! I want to go to balls and parties," Lydia cried. "We have already purchased gowns for them. Mama, you must stop this. It is not fair that we should be so restricted when Jane and Lizzy are free to do whatever they please!"

The duke interrupted her tirade. "It will do no good to beg your mother, Lydia, for she will also be kept under vigilant watch. Our newfound status in society and our wealth will make you all targets for the worst sort of rogues and scoundrels. I will not allow you to gallivant about town and be at the mercy of kidnappers who would hold you for ransom."

"Kidnapped! Oh my dear, I had not thought of that possibility. I could not survive such an ordeal. My nerves would be the death of me! Of course we will want your constant presence to prevent such a thing."

Lydia's shrieks increased with her mother's desertion to her cause. "It is not fair! Jane and Lizzy are just as likely to be kidnapped!"

"That is true," the duke sardonically replied, "but they have more sense than you and Kitty and have earned my trust. You girls will have to do the same before I lift these restrictions. But, until such a time, my edicts stand. I will brook no argument. If you are disobedient, you will not be allowed to leave the house at all, and we will depart immediately for Hertfordshire. Have I made myself understood?"

Lydia glared at her father, which he returned, until she was forced to nod her head in reluctant agreement. Kitty followed Lydia's lead as did Mary.

Elizabeth was proud of her father, but also desired to relieve the oppressive tension in the room. "I think Papa is wise to be so mindful of our safety. I will set a good example by requesting permission to walk in Hyde Park each morning the weather allows. I promise never to go unaccompanied and will keep to the main paths."

The duke smiled fondly at his favourite child. "Be sure to take the most imposing footman possible. Do you have a recommendation, Agatha?"

"I believe Thomas will do very well. He is by far the largest and most fierce looking of all the male servants. The gentlemen of the *ton* will be too afraid to approach Lizzy in his forbidding presence."

"Excellent, have Sheldon send Thomas to my study, and I will instruct him in his new duty to safeguard Elizabeth during her morning walks." Turning to his wife, he asked, "What are your plans for the morrow, my dear?"

"We were to call at the Gardiners to introduce Duchess Agatha."

"Ah, good. I will be happy to accompany you on that errand, for I need to discuss some issues with my brother. Shall we leave for Gracechurch Street at ten?"

The duchess accepted and the duke left the room for his study to meet with Thomas.

CHAPTER 13

U pon entering the breakfast room early the next morning, Elizabeth was pleased to find it empty except for a young maid delivering some freshly baked scones. Elizabeth served herself some tea, hastily ate, and left the room to don her outdoor clothing. She rang for Thomas, who appeared quickly, and the two left Everard House for Elizabeth's walk in Hyde Park. Thomas, undertaking his new commission zealously, kept several paces behind Elizabeth, but his eyes constantly scanned the surroundings. They entered the park, Elizabeth following the main thoroughfare, lost in thought.

She relished the opportunity for quiet reflection. Her days had been busy for the past two months, and she had been in almost constant motion or conversation since the family's arrival in London. Her current meditation involved the evening's final discussion. She was extremely proud of her father's action and resolve.

Elizabeth was not blind to her father's faults. He was not unloving, but he was too often indifferent. However, since the inheritance was revealed, he had begun to take a keener interest in his family, particularly his wife and youngest daughters, whom he had frequently neglected.

Elizabeth welcomed the changes and hoped the girls, especially Lydia, would benefit in time. Her rumination was halted by the sound of someone calling her name. She turned to the source and valiantly repressed a frown to greet Mr Wickham civilly.

"My dear Miss Bennet, what an unexpected pleasure to meet you!"

"It is *unexpected* indeed. What a coincidence for you to meet both my sisters yesterday and myself this morning in such unforeseen circumstances! It must be Providence."

Wickham momentarily faltered. She watched as he affected ignorance and smiled his most charming smile.

"Then I must thank Providence for such a splendid occurrence. I hope you have fared well since the last time we met?"

Thomas moved closer. "Pardon me, madam, do you know this man?"

She smiled in reassurance. "He is a passing acquaintance."

She returned to her conversation with Wickham. "I am in perfectly good health, thank you."

"And how long will you be in town?"

"Some weeks."

"Is there anything in particular that has brought you here at this time of year?"

"Shopping."

"Ah yes. I met your sisters while they were on that errand. I was also introduced to a relative of yours, Duchess Agatha. I did not realise she was your relation. I do not remember her being mentioned in Hertfordshire."

"Our acquaintance was so trifling, it would be unreasonable for you to know everything about my family."

Wickham frowned at this response.

Elizabeth grew weary of Mr Wickham's presence and conversation. She could hardly believe he had the audacity to approach her and attempt to renew their association. Their parting in the spring had been civil, but Elizabeth believed he understood her changing opinion and had no desire to meet him again. That Mr Wickham was aware of her family's elevation in fortune she did not doubt, and as a result, all his intentions and actions were suspect. She had just resolved to unceremoniously dismiss him and leave him in no uncertainty of her present attitude when a deep voice stopped her.

DARCY HAD LEFT HIS HOUSE TO TAKE HIS EXERCISE IN HYDE Park, secretly hoping to see Elizabeth. After walking the main path for several minutes, he recognised her form up ahead. She was talking with a gentleman, and a large man, who appeared to be a servant, was standing close by. As Darcy neared, he realised Elizabeth's companion was none other than Wickham! He was about to retreat when he noticed that Elizabeth was not smiling, and her countenance seemed irritated. She had often turned such an expression on him, so he could now correctly identify its meaning. He decided to interrupt the discussion and hoped Elizabeth would not be angry at his interference.

He approached them and called her name. She turned, and recognising him, bestowed such a brilliant smile upon him that he stopped short, his heart skipping a beat. *How often has she looked at me in such a way in my dreams?* He blinked away his surprise and tentatively returned her smile.

Elizabeth greeted Darcy with a warm salutation. Wickham instantly paled and took several steps backwards. Darcy noticed his retreat and inwardly smiled at the reaction, but he could only spare a moment's thought for Wickham when Elizabeth was before him and smiling so beguilingly.

"Lady Elizabeth, good morning."

Elizabeth looked discomfited, likely still unused to the change in her address. "Good morning, Mr Darcy." They bowed and curtseyed and then Darcy turned to his old childhood companion.

"Wickham," he said tersely.

Ignoring Darcy, Wickham turned back to Elizabeth. "*Lady Elizabeth?*"

"Mr Wickham," Elizabeth intervened, "should you not be on your way? We would not want to keep you from any business you might have. After all, something very *particular* must have brought you to town, else you would be with your regiment."

She smiled innocently, but Wickham smirked, obviously not fooled. He hastily bid them both goodbye, hurrying away to re-evaluate his next strategy.

With feeling, Elizabeth declared, "I am glad he is finally gone! One second more and I would have had Thomas remove him from the park. He is completely insufferable!"

Darcy startled at this outburst and looked at her in bewilderment. Elizabeth flushed when she realised her mistake, and Darcy sought to ease her embarrassment.

"I would have gladly helped Thomas in such an endeavour."

Elizabeth started to smile but was almost immediately self-conscious again.

Darcy realised that this was their first meeting since Hunsford. He had slighted the woman he loved and her family, and she had properly rebuked him for his callousness and self-ishness. He had given her his letter with the hope that the truth would amend her opinion of him.

Has she forgiven me? Has her estimation of me improved? How can I show her that I have attended to her reproofs? How can I show her that I still love her?

These deliberations kept them both silent until roused by a cough from Thomas.

"I should return home. My family will be gathering to eat, and I would not want to worry anyone needlessly. Thomas has been charged with accompanying me but has other duties."

"Will you allow me to escort you?"

She hesitated for a moment and then nodded. He offered her his arm, and they headed towards Grosvenor Square.

Darcy was elated to be in her company, close to her as they walked side by side, but he was careful to be as decorous as propriety dictated. Inwardly, he was euphoric. He could sense Elizabeth was still somewhat embarrassed. She was quieter than usual and looked straight ahead. He recognised this was an opportunity to demonstrate his improved manners, to show her that he was practising as she had admonished him to that spring evening in Kent.

"I made the acquaintance of the Gardiners while they were touring Derbyshire. They said you travelled to Staffordshire this summer. Did you like the countryside?"

"It is a beautiful county. I had never travelled so far north and was delighted with the rugged terrain and the wildness of the landscape."

"It is certainly not as tame as Hertfordshire, but that county has many charming views and prospects as well. I have grown rather fond of it."

"I have a great affection for Hertfordshire, but I am certain you know I will be moving north."

"You refer to the inheritance. I read the announcement in the papers. Will you be permanently removing to Staffordshire then?"

"Yes, we will make a short stop at Longbourn to oversee the packing of our belongings, then the family will settle at Grancourt."

"I have fond memories of visiting Everard and Duchess Agatha there. The park is vast. Everard helped teach me to ride, and we roamed all over the estate."

"Duchess Agatha has been teaching me to ride. She has been extremely patient, for I was a reluctant student. As a child, I took a bad fall from atop a horse. I still prefer to walk, but I am grateful for her urging, or I might have missed many beautiful aspects of the manor."

Darcy was pleased. "I had always wondered why you did not ride. I assumed your indomitable spirit would not allow you to fear horses, but your childhood experience is a reasonable explanation. I know of several gentlemen who refuse to ride for the same reason, but they have not overcome their fear as you are attempting to do. It is very commendable."

"You are too good, for you, of all people, know the faults of my character. I am a selfish creature, and for the sake of giving relief to my own feelings, care not how much I may be wounding yours." She lowered her eyes. "I can no longer delay the apology I owe you. I abused you abominably the last time we met and allowed the flattery of a scoundrel to hinder my reason. Please forgive my lack of discernment and the cruel words I hurled at you."

Darcy was astounded that Elizabeth believed she owed him an apology. His conduct was inexpressibly painful to him, and he could not let her linger under such a misapprehension.

He stopped their progress. "What did you say of me that I did not deserve? Although your accusations were formed on mistaken premises, my behaviour to you at the time had merited the severest reproof. It was unpardonable. I cannot think of it without abhorrence."

"We will not quarrel for the greater share of blame annexed to the evening. The conduct of neither of us, if strictly examined, would be irreproachable. Let us begin anew, for we have both, I hope, improved in civility. You must learn some of my philosophy. Think only of the past as its remembrance gives you pleasure."

Elizabeth smiled and held out her hand. For a moment, Darcy looked deeply into her eyes, and seeing absolution and a hint of something he could not quite identify, raised her hand to his lips and bestowed a gentle kiss on the back of her glove.

Elizabeth blushed deeply, and sensing her reaction, Darcy could not help but hold her hand longer than proper. Seeing the footman step closer, he reluctantly released Elizabeth's hand and tucked it into the crook of his arm while resuming their previous pace.

They ambled the remainder of the way to Grosvenor Square in companionable silence. At the steps of Everard House, Darcy bowed and again kissed Elizabeth's hand, and she smiled shyly at him before ascending the stairs and entering the house.

Darcy could not prevent a sigh from escaping his lips. The encounter had been more poignant than he had envisaged. Her sweet apology, her indignation with Wickham, her permission to escort her home—all bespoke her exoneration of his past conduct. Elizabeth did not resent the past. She believed the words of his letter.

His hope strengthened, and he returned to Darcy House.

CHAPTER 14

Elizabeth remained distracted, and her cheeks were still warm when she entered the breakfast room. She had been contemplating her meeting with Mr Darcy and was relieved that the first one was over and appeared to have been successful. They had forgiven each other of past mistakes, but she was still undecided about his current opinion of her. However, she could not help but be optimistic in the face of his gallantry in both accepting her apology and rendering his own. *And he looked very handsome this morning.*

Other gentlemen had kissed her hand, but it had never produced a shiver throughout her entire body as Mr Darcy's had done. Elizabeth was roused from her contemplations by her father's morning greeting.

The duke and Duchess Agatha were seated and had been enjoying breakfast when Elizabeth entered the room. Both appeared amused by her lack of awareness of their presence.

"Did you enjoy your walk this morning, Lizzy?"

Elizabeth felt her face redden even more. "It is a very beautiful morning."

"Have you been running? You look flushed."

"Papa, the daughter of a duke does not run."

"At least not in a public park, but I know well that you have run all over the paths surrounding Longbourn. Do not attempt to deny it."

Elizabeth smiled sweetly at him and served herself some tea before taking a seat across from Duchess Agatha.

"I met some acquaintances during my walk this morning."

The duke looked pointedly at Elizabeth. "Is that so? Where was Thomas? Did I not explicitly state my daughters were to be protected? I trusted you to have better sense, Lizzy. Who were you so *lucky* to stumble upon?"

"I met Mr Wickham. I told him how astonished I was by the coincidence of him meeting my sisters yesterday and myself this morning when we all thought him to be in Brighton with the regiment."

The duke looked thoughtful at this statement. "Wickham, you say? I had not paid particular attention to the name of the man you mentioned yesterday. That is a twist of fate. It must have been Providence."

"Those were my exact words, Papa!" Elizabeth said with a laugh.

"And who else did you meet on your walk?"

Elizabeth hoped her father would forget her mention of another acquaintance. She was still a little discomposed by her conversation with Mr Darcy and wished she had some time for quiet reflection.

Her father cleared his throat in obvious expectation of her answer.

She smiled apologetically. "Mr Wickham and I had only been conversing for a few minutes when we were pleasantly interrupted by Mr Darcy."

"Pleasantly interrupted? One walk in Hyde Park and my daughter is accosted by two men and nothing is done to prevent it? I should speak to Thomas immediately. He obviously is derelict in his duties."

"Do not blame Thomas. He did intervene, but I assured him the men were known to me. I was not in any danger."

"Not in danger? This is London, Elizabeth!"

"I was about to dismiss Mr Wickham when Mr Darcy approached. Mr Darcy is a gentleman well-known to us, and Duchess Agatha can speak to his character."

The duke turned to Duchess Agatha. "I did not know you were acquainted with the gentleman."

"Fitzwilliam Darcy is a fine young man, though a little too serious."

"If I recall correctly, our Lizzy was not good enough for that gentleman in Meryton, but as the daughter of a duke, she is now handsome enough to tempt him?"

Elizabeth frowned at this allusion to Darcy's previous disdain. She did not like being reminded of the insult to her vanity that had produced such a rash judgment of him.

Duchess Agatha did not let the comment go unanswered. "Bennet, that is somewhat unfair. I do not condone Darcy's behaviour towards Lizzy that night, for it was exceptionally rude, but it is not his typical conduct. I am sure if he were aware she had heard him, he would be deeply mortified and would have apologised profusely."

Elizabeth recalled her previous conversation with Duchess Agatha regarding this subject and was again ashamed of her lack of discernment. She understood Mr Darcy's poor reputation was partly due to her. She had openly expressed her bad opinion and had forwarded the bad opinion that others, including her father, still held of him. She had to correct her mistake if she were to be allowed to meet Mr Darcy again. *And I must meet him! I do not understand why I suddenly feel this urgency, but I know that we must meet and come to know each other better.*

She hesitated, aware of the awkwardness of her position, but she put her pride behind her. "I believe that we all, and myself particularly, have misunderstood Mr Darcy's character. I admit my vanity was wounded by his slight, but I reacted badly. I met with Mr Darcy again in Kent when I was staying with Charlotte. He was visiting his aunt Lady Catherine de Bourgh, and he was more agreeable in company there. I have come to understand that he was not in the best humour last autumn when visiting with Mr Bingley, and I have begun to change my opinion of him. He was very amiable in the park this morning, and I was grateful for his interruption, for Mr Wickham was trying my patience."

The duke raised his eyebrows at this pronouncement. Elizabeth noted his reaction and realised she had only vaguely alluded to Mr Wickham's dishonourable character. She would have to reveal her knowledge.

"During our discussion last night, I forgot to inform you of something important that regards Mr Wickham. I have heard from several reliable sources, including Aunt Gardiner, that he is known for dissipated and licentious behaviour and should not be trusted around young ladies. I know he attempted to elope with a young girl of a good family, and I fear Mr Wickham may attempt the same with one of us now that our circumstances have so advantageously altered. He obviously arranged a meeting with both my sisters yesterday and myself today. I was relieved you had already reached a similar conclusion and so forgot to inform you of Mr Wickham's actions specifically, but I do not trust him to have relinquished his goals. I fear he will try again in the future."

"Thank goodness Darcy was there to extricate you, Lizzy," Duchess Agatha said, appearing mollified, though the duke seemed somewhat pensive.

Jane and Mary soon joined them, so their discussion ceased. The rest of the family arrived shortly, and within the hour, they were preparing to visit the Gardiners.

THEY DESCENDED ON THE GARDINERS JUST AS THE CHILDREN were settling into morning lessons. The ruckus caused by the duchess's and Lydia's entrance allowed the duke to steer Mr Gardiner towards the study after he hastily greeted his sister and the children.

Elizabeth waited for a lull in her mother and youngest sister's exuberance in order to introduce her aunt to Duchess Agatha. The women easily fell into conversation, and a rapport was soon established.

Unfortunately, the duchess almost completely monopolised the conversation. She spoke long about the grandeurs of Grancourt, the opulence of Everard House, their shopping the previous day, her joy of the inheritance, and her designs for her daughters' marriage prospects. Her expectations of the upcoming Season were splendid.

Elizabeth, Duchess Agatha, and Mrs Gardiner admirably restrained their mirth. An invitation for the Gardiners to dine at Everard House in a few days was given and accepted.

The morning passed quickly. The ladies were joined for luncheon by the duke and Mr Gardiner who had closeted themselves away for several hours. The duke was uncharacteristically grave during that time, arousing Elizabeth's curiosity about their discussion.

A light rain began to fall that afternoon, preventing anyone else from calling on Mrs Gardiner. After their tea, the duke and Mr Gardiner again retreated to the study as the ladies moved to the parlour to continue their conversation. Elizabeth renewed the shopping scheme they had discussed and volunteered to write a note inviting Miss Darcy to accompany them in two days.

Duchess Agatha raised an eyebrow and Elizabeth blushed. "Miss Darcy was visiting here yesterday when Jane and I called. We were introduced, and I invited her to accompany us on our shopping expedition. We promised to take her to my uncle's shop as well. I hope you do not mind?"

"Of course not. I am sure she would be delighted to accompany us, and I have not seen dear Georgiana for more than a year."

"So you know the Darcys?" Mrs Gardiner asked.

"Yes, very well. My husband and I were close friends of their parents as well as their aunt and uncle, the Earl and Countess of Matlock."

"They both speak very fondly of Lord and Lady Matlock."

"They have been like another mother and father to them. I believe you would like them as well, Mrs Gardiner, and I would be glad to introduce you to them during my stay in town."

"That is very kind. Mr Darcy has promised me the same."

"I understand you met Darcy and Georgiana while you were touring Derbyshire this summer and visited Pemberley?"

"That is correct. We were sorry to intrude on Mr Darcy's privacy at first, but he was very understanding and attentive."

She looked at Elizabeth. "We had the honour to dine at Pemberley one night, and it was a very enjoyable affair."

Elizabeth coloured at her aunt's reference, and Duchess Agatha exchanged a significant look with Mrs Gardiner.

It was late afternoon when the Everard party left. Promises to see each other soon were exchanged, and the families and friends parted in happy anticipation of meeting each other often over the coming months.

CHAPTER 15

Following his meeting with Lady Elizabeth, Darcy returned to his home but did not enter. He looked up at the imposing edifice but could not make his feet climb the stairs. He felt as though the walls would be too confining for the strength of his present emotions. He abruptly turned on his heel and strode again in the direction of Hyde Park.

Though his thoughts were racing and jumbled, he was aware of a pervasive feeling. He was absolutely elated! He shook his head to order his thoughts.

At first he had been excited just to recognise Elizabeth and was hopeful of an opportunity to talk with her. But noting she was in conversation with that rogue Wickham forced him to question whether her initial warm greeting was likely caused by her displeasure with Wickham's presence, or that she might have been thankful for anyone who would interrupt her discourse with the blackguard. This thought caused his elation to diminish slightly, but he was again encouraged as he remembered the rest of their conversation. She had only hesitated slightly when he offered to escort her home, and she had been welcoming while they discussed Staffordshire.

And then had come her amazingly unexpected apology! To think she believed she owed him one after the awful way he had treated her since the beginning of their acquaintance caused a painful twinge in his heart. He hoped his own apology was sufficient for Elizabeth to understand the deep remorse he felt.

He recalled her hand held out in absolution and the tingling of his lips as he placed a small kiss on the back of her hand.

Elizabeth blushed, I am certain of it. Did she feel the same shiver I did? he wondered. He remembered her words that he should think on the past only as its remembrance would bring him pleasure. *I am sure this memory will bring pleasure for days to come, until I am able to see her again.*

After a thorough review of their encounter, he allowed the feeling of elation to again sweep over him. He found the bench that Elizabeth and Duchess Agatha had sat upon the previous day and allowed himself the unusual opportunity of feeling nothing but excited anticipation. However, there was one thing Elizabeth had said that brought a feeling of unease.

When she had so clearly but civilly dismissed Wickham, she had stated that something *particular* must have brought him to London, and he had a sudden suspicion that the particular business that brought Wickham was mercenary. He must have read about the duke's rise in fortune and come to London specifically to pursue the ladies.

A distressing thought crossed Darcy's mind. Had he been lying in wait to encounter Elizabeth during her walk? It was not beyond the scoundrel's capacity to create an opportunity to meet her. Darcy resolved to investigate his suspicions, and he immediately rose from the bench and made his way home.

After securing himself in his study with a cup of strong coffee, he wrote several letters. His solicitor, his cousin Colonel Fitzwilliam, and a man named Danvers would each receive one, requesting information on Wickham's current activities and circumstances.

Darcy had used Danvers' services before when looking into possible business interests. He was discreet, thorough, and slightly unsettling in his ability to find secret but highly important information. He rang for a servant to immediately post the letters and then made his way to the breakfast room where he found Georgiana and Bingley.

"I wondered what had happened to you," Georgiana said, looking up. "You are usually the first to rise."

Darcy smiled fondly at his sister. "I went for a walk in Hyde Park and had some business letters to write. Are you well this morning, Ana?"

"I am, thank you. Are we still to call on Lord and Lady Matlock today?"

"Certainly, my dear. We have not seen them since our return to town. Had the countess not been so busy preparing for Amherst's wedding, I am sure we would have received an admonishment for our neglect. I am surprised Lord Matlock has not called on us yet, just to escape talk of weddings. He must be spending an inordinate amount of time at his club."

Georgiana giggled softly at this observation.

His aunt's letters had been full of wedding details.

Amherst's intended, Lady Frederica Sutton, was a beauty and the only child of the wealthy widower, the Earl of Falmouth. The wedding was to be held in December and would be the highlight of the winter season. Hundreds of prominent guests were invited to the ball that same evening, and Lady Matlock, a talented hostess, was helping her soon-to-be-daughter plan the formidable event, in lieu of Lady Frederica's late mother.

"Bingley, would you like to join us this morning?"

"Thank you, but not today. I promised Mr Gardiner I would procure a book that belonged to my father. I will have to go to my townhouse and search for it in the library. It is likely to take me hours to find the blasted thing. You know how little I frequent that room."

Darcy raised his eyebrows in amusement. "We may call at Everard House afterwards. Lady Matlock and Duchess Agatha are old friends, and I suspect my aunt will want to visit her. Georgiana informed me that the Everard ladies and Duchess Agatha are to call at Gracechurch Street this morning to intro-duce the Gardiners to Duchess Agatha. So, if you would like to join us, meet us here at one o'clock."

Bingley's face lit up at this information. "I would not miss that visit for the world! Pray that I meet with quick success in my mission!"

Bingley immediately rose from his chair and exited the room, failing to close the door. The Darcys could hear him excitedly call for his coat and hat and the front door slam as he hurried out. They exchanged an amused look, finished their meal, and prepared to call upon their Matlock relations.

KENTON HOUSE, THE LONDON HOME OF THE EARL AND Countess of Matlock, was situated in Berkeley Square, so the

Darcys took their carriage. Upon arrival, they were shown into a large parlour, where they found Lady Matlock seated at an enormous table covered in fabric swatches, sheaths of paper, and other bits and pieces required for planning the social event of the year. The butler announced their presence, and Lady Matlock stood to greet her niece and nephew with hugs and kisses upon the cheek.

"What a pleasant surprise! Pray say you have come for a lengthy visit, so I may escape these dreadful plans for a while!" She linked her arms through theirs and led them to a settee. "I have planned any number of events and soirées over the years, but this endeavour is overwhelming. Your uncle abandoned me months ago. He says I have taken to reciting menus in my sleep. How long have you been in town?"

"About a fortnight, Aunt."

"A fortnight! And you are only now calling upon me? For shame, young man!"

"I did send my card upon our arrival. The letters from the earl told of your hectic schedule, and I did not wish to distract you. I know this is a very important event."

"Distract me? But that is precisely what I need! Lady Frederica is engaged the entire day with some old school friends, and you must spend the day with me. I will send for your uncle and cousin. They are at Brooks's. That is where they can be found these days."

Darcy and Georgiana exchanged smiles at this statement as their aunt wrote a brief note and summoned a footman to deliver it.

"I am surprised I have not met his lordship at his club, for I have been there a few times since I arrived."

"He and Amherst have also been spending quite a bit of time at Angelo's and Jackson's, though I have told Amherst that a month before the wedding he will not be allowed to participate in any pugilism. It would not do to have the groom standing at the altar with a bruised eye."

Georgiana looked shocked at this pronouncement.

"Do not worry, my dear, your cousin rarely participates at Gentleman Jackson's, though he is becoming quite proficient at fencing, so I am told. I am sure he will challenge you, Darcy, so I hope that you have been practising as diligently as you usually do."

"I have fenced a few times since our arrival, but Georgiana and I have been kept rather busy with some new acquaintances, the Gardiners. I am certain Georgiana has written to you about them."

"Of course. It is the family related to Agatha's newfound relations, correct?"

Darcy searched his aunt's face, knowing her curiosity about the duke and his family. He had promised to give more explicit information regarding his connexion to them and wondered what he would be persuaded to divulge.

"The Gardiners are charming people!" Georgiana exclaimed. "They have the most adorable children. Ethan, their youngest, is the sweetest little boy. And Beth asks the most amusing questions. I met Lady Jane and Lady Elizabeth yesterday, and they have invited me to go shopping with them and Duchess Agatha. They are both very beautiful, and Lady Elizabeth is so kind and lively. We are all going to the theatre soon, and I am so looking forward to it."

Georgiana blushed when she realised the exuberance of her chatter, but her aunt patted her hand fondly. "I am glad that you have made some new friends, my dear. I would like to meet the Gardiners. If they have acquired your approbation, I am certain I will be delighted with them."

"Would you and Uncle like to join us for our evening at the theatre?" Darcy asked. "As you know, my box is large enough to accommodate us all, and we will be returning to Darcy House afterwards for a light supper. You did say you would welcome a distraction."

"That sounds delightful. Have you settled on a date?"

"We are to go a week Friday, to see the production of *Much Ado About Nothing*."

"I will confer with your uncle, and if we have no fixed plans, we will be happy to join your party. Now," she continued, fixing Darcy with a pointed stare, "tell me everything about the new duke and his family. I must admit, Agatha has been secretive in her letters and only mentioned the amazing circumstances after they had been revealed in the newspapers. To think that I, her oldest friend, found out such news the same time as everyone else! Unthinkable! I wrote to her immediately, chastising her, but she is still withholding information. I am certain of it! You must divulge all you know.

"There is enormous speculation about the new Everards, and I will need the ability to correct any gossip that could be harmful to their entrance into society. I will not have Agatha and her new relations embarrassed or anxious. Nobody has seen them or knows anything about them besides Lady Catherine, and I cannot trust her word. In fact, she is the cause of much of the negative speculation. You cannot allow her to prejudice London society against the duke and his family."

Darcy observed his aunt. Her face bore an innocent expression and her arguments were logical, but he was wary he would be manipulated into revealing more than he desired.

His absolute honesty with Colonel Fitzwilliam, Georgiana, and Bingley about his history with, and present feelings for, Elizabeth already made him feel more vulnerable than he ever had before. He would have to make his intentions known eventually, but he would guard his words carefully in the meantime.

"I promised I would tell you more about them, but perhaps we should wait until Uncle and Amherst are here. I would prefer to tell it only once."

Lady Matlock narrowed her eyes. "Then you and Georgiana must stay for dinner. I am certain my curiosity will not be satisfied quickly." When Darcy hesitated, Lady Matlock asked, "Do you have other plans for the day?"

"We thought we would call on Duchess Agatha this afternoon."

"Agatha? Is she in town? Why has she not written and advised me of her arrival? I do not know what is happening to her. We have never kept secrets from each other."

Lady Matlock appeared quite incensed with her friend, and Darcy sought a way to prevent her displeasure. "Perhaps the duke has asked for her silence. The Gardiners were evasive about the Everards when we met them this summer. They did not mention anything until after the official announcement in the newspapers. I believe everyone was sworn to secrecy."

"That has never mattered in the past, but I see what you are trying to do, and I will hold my temper until I can speak with Agatha. Could you postpone your visit to Everard House until tomorrow? Richard arrives this evening, and if he is free, I am sure he would like to call with us, as Agatha is his godmother."

Darcy again hesitated. He wanted to see Elizabeth as soon as possible, but he knew one day would not make a material difference.

He grudgingly acceded. "Certainly, we will stay. I must

write a note to my friend Bingley, though. He was to meet us later and call with us at Everard House."

"He is welcome to join us if he would like."

"Thank you. Now, if you do not mind, I will go to the library and await Uncle's return. I dare say you and Georgiana would like a little time alone."

"That is a splendid idea. I will have Martin inform you when they have arrived and will tell Cook to set an extra place for dinner, should your friend decide to join us."

Darcy left his aunt and sister to write his note to Bingley, thankful for the time to settle his thoughts and determine exactly what he would tell his Fitzwilliam relations.

"Now, Georgiana, tell me more about your new friends."

"Oh, I have had such a wonderful two weeks. Fitzwilliam met the Gardiners while they were touring Derbyshire this summer. Mrs Gardiner spent some of her childhood in Lambton, and they were taking in the local sights, including Pemberley. My brother came upon them while they were touring the park and spoke to them."

Lady Matlock's eyebrows rose with this information about her generally shy nephew, but Georgiana did not notice and continued telling her aunt the details of their visit, including the reaction of Miss Bingley to it all.

"How did your brother meet Lady Jane and Lady Elizabeth?"

"Their estate is located just three miles from the one Mr Bingley leased in Hertfordshire. They all met last autumn when my brother accompanied Mr Bingley to Netherfield. They were often in each other's company at assemblies and evenings with other neighbours. Lady Jane and Lady Elizabeth even spent a few days at Netherfield when Lady Jane fell ill, and her sister attended to her. Fitzwilliam met Lady Elizabeth again in Kent. She was visiting a friend at Hunsford. Has Richard told you anything about their Easter visit? He met Lady Elizabeth there as well."

"No, my darling son has not mentioned a thing about it." Lady Matlock had quite forgotten that he had accompanied Darcy to Rosings that spring. She had had access to a direct source of information on the Everards all along!

Amherst's wedding preparations have softened my mind! She shook her head. *I will be sure to rectify this mistake as soon as Richard arrives, though the rascal should have divulged what he knew when I mentioned the duke and his family in my letters!*

"They were introduced in April. I was finally able to meet Lady Elizabeth yesterday. I had heard many wonderful things about her. My brother described her in his letters last fall, and she is very dear to the Gardiners. She was so kind to me yesterday, and I look forward to our shopping trip. I hope we will go in a day or two."

Lady Matlock looked fondly at her niece. She had not seen Georgiana this excited for several years. "I hope to meet this paragon of a young lady. Agatha has not been forthcoming, and your brother has been worse, and now I find my own son has withheld information from me." She laughed. "I shall have to determine just punishment for this conspiracy."

A knock sounded on the door and Lord Matlock entered the room, followed by Lord Amherst and Darcy.

"Susan, my dearest," Lord Matlock's voice boomed as he approached his wife, "and Georgiana! How lovely to see you!"

"Georgiana has just given me a brief history of your introduction and subsequent meeting in Kent with Lady Elizabeth, but I wish to hear your account of it, young man."

Darcy sighed in mock vexation. "Very well, but make yourself comfortable, for it is a long and convoluted history."

"I am sure we will all be vastly entertained."

DARCY PROCEEDED TO RELATE HIS DEALINGS WITH ELIZABETH. He did not divulge his innermost feelings or his disastrous proposal, only confessing to admiration and esteem for her beauty, wit, generosity, and intelligence. He divulged enough for his aunt to surmise the regard he held for the young lady but no more.

Lord and Lady Matlock both reproached him for his interference in Bingley's affairs, but noting his repentant attitude and confession to his friend, they quickly moved on to evaluate Miss Bingley's behaviour. The Matlocks could not suppress amusement at that woman's antics.

Bingley joined the family just as a light rain began to fall. He was a wonderful source of information on the lovely Everard sisters, and Lady Matlock questioned him unceasingly about their accomplishments and appearance. He gave his own impressions of the Gardiners, and Lord Matlock and Lord Amherst recognised the name and disclosed their own knowledge of Mr Gardiner, who was held in high esteem among wealthy gentlemen and the aristocracy for his success in business and gentlemanly manners.

The party was joined by Colonel Fitzwilliam at dinner. His mother gently scolded him for withholding information from her, which he deflected by suggesting that his army duties had pushed the news from his mind.

The evening was comfortably spent with cards and music,

as the rain grew more persistent against the windows. The group determined to meet the next morning to pay a call on the Everards, if the weather permitted. The Darcys and Bingley then returned home in anticipation of the call to Everard House on the morrow.

CHAPTER 16

Unfortunately for the residents of London, a hard, driving rain continued unceasingly for four days. Those foolish enough to venture into it were instantly and completely drenched.

The inhabitants of Darcy House became increasingly restive. Darcy attempted to read or attend to business matters, but the others often found him pacing the hallways or staring out windows and cursing the rain. Bingley amused himself at billiards or in pleasant recollections of the previous autumn. Georgiana busied herself with her pianoforte, practising several new pieces she had purchased. Lady Elizabeth had written to her, promising a note outlining their shopping excursion would be dispatched immediately once the rain ceased. Every knock on the door and every letter in the salver addressed to Georgiana was anticipated with bated breath, only to bring a gust of cold rain and disappointment.

At last the interminable rain ceased, and the day dawned bright and sunny. A mist rose from the evaporating rain on the streets and walks. Miss Darcy and Mrs Annesley were in the breakfast room when a footman entered with a note for Georgiana. The hand was instantly recognisable, even though Georgiana had only received one other missive from the writer.

Dear Georgiana,
At last the sun shines, and ladies may venture forth from their houses to rob the shops of their treasures! Would you care to join our party at ten o'clock to plunder the wares of Bond and Oxford Streets?

Please send your reply with the servant who awaits you. If you can persuade your brother to relinquish your company for a few hours, we shall arrive at your home to escort you. Please say you will join us, and invite Mr Darcy and Mr Bingley to come for refreshments at half past four at Everard House afterwards. I eagerly await your response.

Yours &c.
Lady Elizabeth

P.S. I have not forgotten my promise to give you a thorough tour of my uncle's shop.

GEORGIANA GAVE A SMALL SQUEAL OF DELIGHT AND QUICKLY rose, making her way to her brother's study. Upon being admitted, she found him staring out the window at the sunshine. He turned to greet her with a smile, and his eyebrows rose at seeing her obvious excitement. She wordlessly handed him the note from Lady Elizabeth and watched the emotions flit across his face.

DARCY HAD HOPED THAT THE CHANGE IN WEATHER WOULD produce the long-awaited missive from Elizabeth. He had been staring out the window towards Everard House, willing Elizabeth to write. When Georgiana entered with a blinding smile on her face, he knew his wish had been granted. He was thankful when she handed him the note, allowing him to enjoy Elizabeth's missive, even though it was addressed to his sister. He admired the elegance of her hand and smiled in happiness at the display of her wit. He was wistful that his sister would spend the entirety of the day with Elizabeth while he would be forced to find something to occupy his time and thoughts. Delighted surprised filled him when he read the line inviting Bingley and himself to Everard House.

"Elizabeth," he whispered, the sound barely audible and the word indistinguishable to his sister, but she could not mistake his happiness.

"May I go? I must write immediately, for it is already almost nine. Please, Fitzilliam?"

"Of course you may," he replied distractedly, re-reading Elizabeth's note. "There is paper and ink on my desk."

Georgiana sat down eagerly to write her acceptance. "What shall I answer for you and Mr Bingley?"

"Yes, we shall come."

"Should you not ask Mr Bingley?"

This question shook Darcy from his thoughts, and he smiled sheepishly. "I hardly need ask him, but I probably should."

He rang for a footman to find Bingley then sank into a chair to read Elizabeth's note for a third time. He lingered over her mention of him in the short missive. *Is she as eager as I to meet again, to finish our conversation started in the park?*

Darcy realised he would be meeting her among members of her family and also in the presence of Duchess Agatha. He debated over the amount of attentiveness he should show. He would have to reveal his preference for Elizabeth soon, but he was unsure of his reception among the Everards. The impression he had made almost a year ago in Hertfordshire had not been favourable.

He knew Mrs Gardiner would be welcoming and had attempted to correct the family's opinion of him, but he had no idea whether she had met with success. Darcy had not seen Duchess Agatha since before her husband left for Jamaica, and although he had sent a letter of condolence when informed of the duke's death, he had not written to her since the knowledge of the duke's heir had been disclosed. She was a perceptive woman and would be alert to any particular attention he gave Elizabeth. He wondered whether Duchess Agatha would look with favour upon his desire to court and marry Elizabeth. He believed she would at least be an ally but could not be certain.

A thought as clear as crystal entered his mind. *Elizabeth is all that matters. She must never be made to doubt my preference for her. She must be aware of my intention this time. I shall just have to win everyone's approval, including hers. No one must mistake my intent, so I shall pay her every attention she deserves. I am done with hiding.* That resolution made, he returned to reading Elizabeth's note.

He was grateful for her attention to Georgiana. That Elizabeth expressly remembered the promise to view Mr Gardiner's shop proved her thoughtfulness. He welcomed their growing friendship, knowing the benefits Elizabeth's influence would bring to his dear sister.

These pleasant reflections were interrupted by the arrival of Bingley. He was informed of the invitation and readily accepted. Georgiana completed her note and dispatched it with the waiting Everard footman. The next hour would be a long one.

Just after ten o'clock, a commotion was heard in the front hall. Darcy opened his study door to observe his sister donning her bonnet and coat. He shut the door and strode quickly to the window facing the street, hoping to catch a glimpse of Elizabeth. A moment later, Georgiana was helped into the Everard carriage by a liveried footman. The door was shut, and the horses put into motion. Darcy would have to wait until the afternoon to see her, but his thoughts the entire day would not stray far from where Elizabeth and his sister were in London. He invited Bingley to join him at Brooks's, hoping to keep them both distracted until the afternoon.

THE EVERARD COACH MADE ITS WAY INTO CHEAPSIDE. THE morning would start at Mr Gardiner's shop. The party arrived at Gracechurch Street, and Duchess Agatha and Mrs Gardiner elected to remain at the Gardiner house to further their acquaintance. Jane, Elizabeth, and Georgiana, followed by two footmen, walked the few streets to Mr Gardiner's place of business. To call it a shop was an understatement. Gardiner Emporium was a large, handsome building of several stories filled to the brim with delights from around the world. Georgiana was enchanted.

The shop was organised according to the country of origin.

The ground floor was occupied with the native products of England, and the first-floor displayed goods from the Continent—France, Germany and Italy. The girls browsed through the items quickly and made their way to the top floor.

Georgiana could not repress a gasp of delight. The atmosphere was positively exotic. Elizabeth had not overstated the magnificence of Mr Gardiner's wares. Georgiana felt she was in the wilds of some foreign land. In every corner and with every glance, there were beautiful treasures to behold. The air was scented with ginger, cardamom, and cinnamon. Vibrant-coloured silks were draped over tables and chairs. Striking statues and pottery decorated with delicately painted scenes stood on pedestals.

Elizabeth directed the group through items from India, Africa, China, and some rare artefacts from the West Indies' ancient civilisations. The shop was quite busy, but the staff was attentive to the three girls. The clerks were well acquainted with Jane and Elizabeth and were always delighted to show them newly arrived goods.

Georgiana found an exquisitely carved wooden inlaid box, which Elizabeth persuaded her to buy. The young girl also secretly bought two soft Kashmir shawls. The sisters rarely purchased items from their uncle's shop, for things were rather expensive, but their expanded allowances granted them the capability of indulging their fancies. Jane bought a jade-handled brush set, and Elizabeth discovered a jewelled hair comb in the shape of a dragonfly with a matching brooch. Georgiana bought the matching cravat pin to give to her brother, causing Elizabeth to blush prettily. As they were completing their purchases, a clerk notified the ladies that Duchess Agatha and Mrs Gardiner were awaiting them in their carriage in front of the store. They quickly made their way out of the building and, after securing their bundles, headed towards the modiste shops.

Unlike the shopping trip with the duchess and the younger Everard ladies, Duchess Agatha directed the driver to the fashionable shops of the London *ton*. She and Mrs Gardiner had discussed the idea of gently introducing the girls to society before their official presentation in the spring. Duchess Agatha was well-known to the owners and patrons and would be able to guide the ladies in their purchases and introductions.

For the next several hours, they selected patterns, fabrics, bonnets, gloves, and all the other accoutrements of a lady's wardrobe. Jane and Elizabeth's tastes were elegant and refined, and although decisive, they were also amenable to suggestions from the two older ladies, particularly in regard to spending more lavishly than they previously would have done.

Georgiana was also fitted for several new gowns, particularly for a lovely dress to be worn to the theatre. At the mention of this event, she hinted to Elizabeth that she would be pleased to see her in attendance. Elizabeth smiled but did not respond further.

During their outing, numerous women of Duchess Agatha's acquaintance approached the party. All expressed condolences on the tragic loss of her family but quickly displayed their curiosity to be introduced to her companions. The introduction of Mrs Gardiner would typically have garnered no particular attention, but as the friend of Duchess Agatha and the aunt of the Everard ladies, she was accorded unusual civility. No one wanted to offend Duchess Agatha and her illustrious cousins.

Jane and Elizabeth acknowledged each new acquaintance with an ease and friendliness that surprised the ladies of the *ton*. Elegant, poised, and agreeable, they would be significant competition for the bachelors of London society. A few women raised their eyebrows to see Miss Darcy in company with the Everard relations. Mr Darcy was considered one of the prime catches among the presently available young men, and the fact that there was already an intimacy between the Darcys and the Everards was somewhat vexing.

Elizabeth was amused to see the reactions she and Jane caused among Duchess Agatha's acquaintances. Most were impertinently curious, unashamed to ask questions that were easily evaded. A few were welcomed warmly by Duchess Agatha and introduced readily, showing they were intimate friends.

One introduction was especially interesting. While at a milliner, Duchess Agatha approached an elegant woman. The two embraced and talked briefly, brushing away a few tears that had escaped down their cheeks. They turned and made their way to Elizabeth's party.

The lady took Georgiana's hand and addressed her. "You did not tell me that you would be in the shops today. How are you faring, my dear?"

"I am well, Aunt. And you?"

"I am quite busy these days, but I am well. Lady Frederica and I are out purchasing some things for her trousseau. Would you do me the honour of introducing me to your friends?"

"Certainly. May I present the daughters of the Duke of Everard, Ladies Jane and Elizabeth, and their aunt, Mrs Gardiner. Ladies, my aunt, the Countess of Matlock." The women performed their curtseys.

"I am delighted to meet you both. I have heard about you particularly, Lady Elizabeth, from my numerous relations. In fact, almost my entire family has made your acquaintance.

Even my sister-in-law, Lady Catherine de Bourgh, has had the pleasure."

Elizabeth sensed a test in this conversation, but she would not be intimidated and chose to answer in her usual manner.

"They have been negligent towards myself as well, for they have told me little of you. I owe all my knowledge of your ladyship to Duchess Agatha. I have promised her not to divulge too many of your school day antics, but her stories have made me eager to meet you. We should remedy your relative's disregard and further our acquaintance. Would you care to come for a visit tomorrow at Everard House?"

Lady Matlock smiled. "That would be lovely, but I am afraid I must decline. I am hosting a small party for my future daughter-in-law tomorrow afternoon. Would you and Lady Jane care to come to us tomorrow? Georgiana will be there, as will her brother and my son Richard, whom I understand you met in Kent. Agatha, you must come as well. I know that you are still in mourning, but it is for Amherst's wedding and will be quite a small gathering."

"Oh Susan, your definition of *small* is generally very different from mine!" Duchess Agatha exclaimed. "How many are invited? Fifty? Sixty?"

Lady Matlock laughed. "You always did exaggerate. There will only be twenty or so. I am sure Lady Frederica would be pleased to have some young women there her own age, for the majority of the party are ancient Fitzwilliam relations." A pale blonde beauty about Elizabeth's age approached the group. "Ah, here she is now."

Lady Matlock performed the introductions. Lady Frederica's expression did not change from the rather bland smile on her lovely face, and during the short time the group conversed, she did not contribute a single word. She left them when another acquaintance greeted her.

Duchess Agatha accepted the invitation for the morrow after some hesitation, prompting Jane and Elizabeth to also acquiesce. Lady Matlock turned to Mrs Gardiner and promised to invite her to visit another day so they could become better acquainted, and the ladies parted to travel to their destinations.

As they neared Everard House, Elizabeth's excitement and trepidation grew. She had thoroughly enjoyed her day. She was thankful to be away from her mother and younger sisters and in the company of the women she loved most in the world. Miss Darcy had become increasingly more open as the day progressed, and their friendship was developing well. But now Elizabeth and Jane would meet again with the gentlemen who had caused so much heartache and distress the previous year. The ladies made their way into the striped parlour to await the gentlemen's arrival.

Elizabeth knew she and Mr Darcy had made their peace and were on the path of friendship, but she wondered whether she should move beyond that with him. The possibility that he desired more had been sparked by the kiss on her hand following their walk in Hyde Park.

I must let his actions be my guide, but I must also be cautious. If Mr Darcy shows a desire to renew his addresses, I must be certain of my own heart, for I would not want to raise hopes that would cause him any pain, should I decide against his suit. I shall be friendly, but not overly attentive. There is the whole of next Season to become reacquainted with him. I shall not repeat my hasty judgments of last year. With this resolution, her thoughts turned to her dear sister.

Jane and Mr Bingley had not met since the night of the Netherfield Ball. Elizabeth, prompted by comments by

Duchess Agatha, had finally informed Jane of all the events of the winter and spring. That Mr Bingley had been ignorant of her presence in town last winter, through the manipulations of his sisters and Mr Darcy, had been a blow. She could no longer believe in the innate goodness of people. When she learned Mr Bingley had broken from his sisters due to their interference, her heart ached for the pain she had caused his family, no matter how inadvertently. She shared only a few of these feelings with Elizabeth, and although Jane's countenance was tranquil, Elizabeth sensed her cheerfulness had been lessened by the situation with the Bingleys.

Jane had avoided the topic since, and Elizabeth had not forced her confidence, even when Duchess Agatha had suggested the gentlemen join them for the afternoon. Elizabeth was anxious for Jane and gave her hand a small squeeze as they sat on a settee. A knock on the door sounded, and Jane stiffened slightly.

A footman entered the room. "Mr Darcy and Mr Bingley," he announced.

CHAPTER 17

Darcy's eyes instantly sought Elizabeth. She was seated next to her sister and looked as beautiful as ever. His smile rose reflexively, eliciting an upward tilt of her lips in a welcoming response. He bowed, prompting Bingley to do likewise.

Duchess Agatha stood and approached the young men. "Darcy, you are looking well."

Darcy bowed over her hand. "Thank you, Duchess Agatha, you do as well."

Turning to Bingley, she said, "It is a pleasure to see you again, sir."

"Please accept my sincere sympathy for your loss. Darcy always spoke so fondly of you and the duke and of the time he spent at your estate. I am glad to be in your company again."

He then turned his smile to Jane, who startled and blushed

to have his attention so fixed on her. "Lady Jane, Lady Elizabeth, how wonderful to see you again. I hope you are well."

"Thank you, Mr Bingley, we are quite well." Lady Jane smiled tentatively, and Bingley was decided. He sat opposite her, not relinquishing her company for the remainder of the afternoon.

Elizabeth and Darcy exchanged amused glances and then he turned towards his sister, who was seated next to Mrs Gardiner. "Georgiana, did you have a pleasant time?"

"It was splendid. Have you been to the Emporium? It is absolutely magnificent. Elizabeth showed me all the treasures from India and Africa. The entire top floor is an exotic wonderland."

Darcy turned towards Mrs Gardiner. "Did you finally persuade my sister to buy something for herself?"

"I was not there to persuade her, sir." Darcy's eyebrows rose, but Elizabeth interrupted.

"My aunt and Duchess Agatha did not accompany us to my uncle's store. Some footmen from Everard House escorted us, and my aunt met us there afterwards to attend the other shops. Jane and I convinced your sister to purchase a lovely wooden box from Shanghai. I believe she will keep her secret letters and trinkets in it, so you must have her show it to you before you will no longer be welcome to view its contents. We women must have some secrets."

Darcy smiled at Elizabeth's teasing and unconsciously touched his waistcoat pocket where he had secreted Elizabeth's note to Georgiana. He had not returned it to his sister, hoping she would not remember its existence. He could not surrender it to anyone else's keeping, for it was the only thing he had of Elizabeth's.

Darcy took a seat next to his sister, and once the tea was

poured and the food served, the group settled down to chat. Georgiana was as animated as any had ever seen her. She dominated the discussion, detailing the items in Mr Gardiner's shop that had caught her fancy. The unexpected introduction to Lady Matlock was also shared, and Darcy smiled broadly when informed that he would be seeing Elizabeth the next day at his aunt's gathering.

"Lady Matlock has been extremely curious to meet you all. Georgiana has been filling her ear with stories."

"As I understand it, the countess has felt rather neglected to wait so long for an introduction. You and Colonel Fitzwilliam should be heartily ashamed of yourselves for such disregard, for as Lady Matlock said, even Lady Catherine has had the pleasure of my company."

Darcy's laugh was immediate and warm. "I shall be happy to rectify the situation, Lady Elizabeth. I promise I shall do everything in my power to bring you and my aunt in company together as often as possible so you may become better acquainted. We are all to go to the theatre on Friday to see the new production of *Much Ado About Nothing*. I know you are fond of Shakespeare, for I remember you eagerly perusing a copy of *A Midsummer Night's Dream* while you attended your sister at Netherfield."

"I do not recollect."

"It was on Saturday, the day before your departure. We sat in the library for about half an hour, and after you left, I glanced at the title of your book and no longer wondered about your absorption in your reading. Shakespeare is a favourite of mine, particularly his comedies. Would you and Lady Jane care to join us in my box to see the play? The Gardiners are coming as well as Lord and Lady Matlock. We shall dine at my home afterwards. It should be an enjoyable evening, and it would add to my pleasure to have you attend." His gaze never wavered from her face.

Elizabeth was slightly breathless. He had astonished her by remembering such details. At last she smiled. "I would be happy to attend, but I must first ask my father."

"Ask me what, Lizzy?"

Everyone turned in surprise to see the duke standing in the doorway of the parlour. No one had noticed his entrance, though it seemed he had been silently watching for some time.

"Mr Darcy has invited Jane and me to attend the theatre on Friday. Aunt and Uncle Gardiner are also invited."

"You and the duchess are welcome to join us as well, Your Grace," Darcy added. "It is a new production of *Much Ado About Nothing*."

"Ah, one of your favourites, is it not, Lizzy? Well, my dear, if you and Jane would like to go, shall we accept Mr Darcy's kind offer?" He looked towards his favourite daughter shrewdly, but she masked her feelings well.

"I would like to go. Jane, what is your opinion?"

"Though I am not as avid a reader of Shakespeare as you, Lizzy, it does sound like an enjoyable evening."

The duke turned to address Duchess Agatha. "My wife does not enjoy Shakespeare. Would you mind entertaining her and the younger girls for an evening, Agatha?"

"Being that I cannot attend while in mourning, it would be my pleasure. Darcy's box is in a wonderful location with an excellent view of the entire stage. As I recall, Darcy, your mother loved the theatre and insisted your father take her to almost every production when they were in town."

He smiled at this recollection. "Mother encouraged me to read all the great plays so I would more thoroughly enjoy them when I saw them performed. I was only able to attend with her once before her death. We saw Mozart's opera *The Magic Flute*, and at twelve years old, I fell instantly in love with Pamina and begged my parents to let me learn to play the flute."

"And did they agree?" Elizabeth questioned, her eyebrow raised in that endearing way that made Darcy's heart race. "Did you learn to play the flute to tame wild beasts?"

"Unfortunately, they refused, and I was heartbroken, but the next week my father gave me a new gun, and I shot three birds, which cured my love for the beautiful Pamina."

"Ah, the fickleness of youth."

"Yes, but my affections are no longer so easily changed." He looked pointedly at her.

The duke narrowed his eyes. "I accept your kind invitation on behalf of my daughters and myself. We shall be happy to join your party on Friday." There was a distinct edge to the duke's voice.

"I am honoured, Your Grace." He turned towards his friend. "Thank you for a very pleasant afternoon and for your kind attentions to Georgiana. Bingley, we should leave now."

"It was our pleasure, Mr Darcy," Elizabeth warmly acknowledged. "Georgiana, do not forget we must return for the final fitting of your new gown on Thursday. Shall we call for you at ten o'clock?"

Georgiana looked to her brother for confirmation then gave her agreement. She impulsively embraced her friend. "Thank you so very much, Elizabeth."

"You are most welcome. We shall see you tomorrow."

"Of course! I had almost forgotten my aunt's invitation. I shall see you almost every day this week!"

"Yes, you poor dear! I am sure you will soon grow tired of my company."

"That is not possible," Darcy interrupted, "for no one could tire of your delightful company. We shall see you tomorrow then." He raised her hand and lightly kissed it, making sure not to linger in the presence of the duke.

"Yes, tomorrow," Elizabeth whispered.

Darcy smiled, bowed to the other occupants of the parlour, and escorted his sister from the room.

"Good afternoon, Your Grace, ladies," Bingley said as he bowed and took his leave.

THE DUKE TURNED TO THE LADIES REMAINING IN THE ROOM. "It appears you had a pleasant visit."

Mrs Gardiner replied, "The Darcys and Mr Bingley are very agreeable company."

"It was good to see Darcy and Georgiana again," Duchess Agatha responded. "Georgiana has grown so. She reminds me very much of her mother at that age."

"Miss Darcy is a very sweet girl," Jane replied, "and it was good to meet with some old acquaintances."

"Mr Bingley appeared in good health," Elizabeth teased Jane.

"As did Mr Darcy," Mrs Gardiner replied, "would you not agree, Lizzy?"

The duke coughed and changed the subject. "Agatha, does the Everard estate have a box at the theatre?"

"It is currently being leased until the spring. Joshua and I had planned to remain the entire summer, autumn, and winter in Staffordshire, so we leased the box to friends visiting from France, Comte and Comtesse de Vymont. Hélène is a distant cousin of mine. She and her husband had grown weary of Bonaparte's regime and sought refuge in England. I am not sure when they will return to Saint-Clouz, their estate near Angers."

"That is the same cousin who is currently leasing Malvallet House, correct?"

"Yes, of course."

"I am to meet with Comte de Vymont tomorrow."

"Ah, you and François should get along splendidly. The turn of your minds is very similar."

"Then I shall look forward to the introduction. Perhaps his wife should accompany him so that you may visit with her as well?"

"When is Comte de Vymont expected?"

"Not until the afternoon."

"I am engaged to attend Lady Matlock's afternoon party with Jane and Lizzy, so I shall have to meet with Hélène another time."

"Ah, the afternoon party with Lord and Lady Matlock. I had almost forgotten. It appears you three will be spending an inordinate amount of time among the Darcy relations this week."

Elizabeth and Duchess Agatha eyed him with suspicion

"Do not worry, ladies. Let me form my own opinion. I have not spent enough time in company with Mr Darcy. Perhaps an invitation to join me for a nuncheon at Brooks's would be wise."

"An excellent notion, Bennet. I am certain once you have spent some time with Fitzwilliam Darcy, you will not prevent him from forming a friendship with your daughters."

"A friendship, you say? As Shakespeare declares, 'Friendship is constant in all things save in the office and affairs of love.' Friday shall be an interesting evening." He stood. "I shall see you ladies at dinner."

. . .

Elizabeth and Jane had spent half the night in conversation. Jane's attempts to discount her delight in seeing Mr Bingley again were summarily dismissed by her sister.

"Now that this first meeting is over, I feel perfectly easy. I shall never be embarrassed again by Mr Bingley's presence. I am glad we shall see him at the theatre on Friday. It will then be publicly seen that, on both sides, we meet only as common and indifferent acquaintances."

"Yes, very *indifferent* indeed," said Elizabeth. "Oh Jane, take care. I think you are in very great danger of making him more in love with you than ever. Mr Bingley never left your side the entire afternoon, he was attentive to your every word, and his face positively lit up when you agreed to attend the theatre."

"His attention to me was not nearly as particular as Mr Darcy's was to you," Jane responded slyly. Elizabeth startled at her sister's observation and at her actually declaring it.

"He *was* very particular. I must admit I am grateful for his continued preference."

"Grateful? Is that all?"

"I do not know yet. I have never enjoyed his company more than I did this afternoon. And I found myself desiring to please him, to keep him smiling and laughing. I cannot be certain though, so I have resolved to be cautious in my dealings with him."

"You must take care as well. I fear you are in danger of smiling too brightly and making Mr Darcy swoon."

Elizabeth laughed loudly at the image of the formidable Fitzwilliam Darcy fainting. "That is rather unlikely, but I shall give your warning due consideration. Unfortunately, I do not have your serenity. I am afraid my emotions are easily discerned."

"Particularly when you give them voice, dear Lizzy."

"My impertinence is well-known, and I must check it or I shall set the tongues of the matrons of the *ton* waggling at my impudence." She smiled and quirked her eyebrow. "Though, as a duke's daughter, there will surely be a certain leniency shown me. In consequence, there appears to be no true incentive to guard my words, and I shall just have to fare as I have in the past."

"You are incorrigible."

The girls bid each other goodnight and slept soundly until late morning. So it was that Elizabeth found herself in Hyde Park at ten o'clock, rambling the main drive, closely followed by Thomas.

She realised she was searching for a certain gentleman. This action surprised her, and she reflected again on the previous afternoon. Jane was correct that Mr Darcy's attentions towards her were quite pointed. She was glad his intentions were marked so as to leave no doubt in her mind. She would have to give him some encouragement, but exactly how much she had not yet determined.

I cannot be other than myself. I shall let my heart guide my actions. And even though my instincts are not entirely unassailable, they have rarely steered me wrong. Now that I am more aware of Mr Darcy's true character, let our interactions be genuine, and events will unfold as they may. With this resolution firmly in place, she returned to Everard House to wait until the afternoon gathering at the home of Lord and Lady Matlock.

CHAPTER 18

Duchess Agatha escorted Jane and Elizabeth to Kenton House. When they were announced, Elizabeth noticed all in the room were unknown to her, except her slight acquaintance with Lady Matlock and Lady Frederica. The countess approached them immediately and warmly embraced her friend.

"Thank you for coming, Agatha. Perhaps you can salvage this gathering from becoming a frightful bore."

"Is Richard not here to perform that task? It usually falls to him."

"He is coming with Darcy and Georgiana." Lady Matlock then turned to the Everard sisters, and with voice slightly raised, welcomed them. "I am delighted you could come. Let me introduce you." She directed them towards Lady Frederica and two men in the centre of the room.

"You remember Lady Frederica?" The young ladies

performed their curtseys and exchanged civilities. Then her ladyship turned towards the older of the two men, a distinguished man of about sixty years with the hint of a smile. "May I present my husband, Lord Matlock? My dear, Lady Jane and Lady Elizabeth, the Duke of Everard's eldest daughters."

"Delighted to meet you both," he jovially responded, bowing over each of their hands. "I have heard much about you from my nephew and niece, the Darcys. May I present my son Viscount Amherst?" Jane and Elizabeth turned to the younger man, and Elizabeth instantly recognised the resemblance between the viscount and his brother.

"Ladies," Amherst replied with a bow, "I appear to be the last of my family to make your acquaintance. A pleasure."

"But Lady Matlock assured us there would be many Fitzwilliam relations to meet today," Elizabeth responded, "so I'm certain there will be other introductions."

"Indeed. I suppose I am still smarting from the knowledge that Richard has had the pleasure of your acquaintance long before I have."

"Did he lord his superior knowledge over you? He was most eloquent on the subject of his plight as a younger son, so he was most likely extremely arrogant. But do not be distressed, my lord, for you have met Lady Jane before your brother. You may consider the scales even."

Lord Amherst laughed in delight. Those few in the room who had not been paying attention to their group turned their glances towards the merry cluster. Most had been casting surreptitious glances at the ladies since their arrival.

"I now have the advantage, but I shall not for long, for it appears my brother has arrived with my cousins." He motioned towards the drawing room door, through which Colonel Fitzwilliam, Darcy, and Georgiana had just entered.

Darcy's eyes locked with Elizabeth's and his smile blossomed. Elizabeth, though becoming slightly more inured to his heated stares, still found her breath hitch and her heartbeat quicken. Her smile rose instinctively. The moment was broken as Colonel Fitzwilliam made his way to their group.

"Miss Bennet!" he called but quickly corrected himself, "*Lady Elizabeth*, it is wonderful to see you again."

"Do not distress yourself. I am still more familiar with my former appellation."

"Indeed, but it behoves a gentleman never to do anything that may offend a lady."

Elizabeth watched as Darcy narrowed his eyes at his cousin, but the colonel kept an innocent expression on his face.

"I must accede to you then, Colonel," Elizabeth continued, "for Duchess Agatha has assured me that you are quite the expert at courting young ladies."

"Quite," Lady Matlock interjected, "though he is not quite an expert at following through with his attentions."

"Mother, dear," Colonel Fitzwilliam responded, "you know my plight as a younger son. I cannot marry just anyone."

"Now you see, Lord Amherst," Elizabeth said, "I am well aware of your younger brother's difficulties, and now it is time for you to even the scales."

"As you wish." Turning to his brother, he indicated Jane, who had been quietly talking with Lady Frederica. "Richard, allow me to present Lady Jane."

Jane turned towards Fitzwilliam and gave a small smile while performing her curtsey. Fitzwilliam stood transfixed for a moment before remembering to bow in return and give a civil reply.

"And are the rest of your sisters here?" Fitzwilliam abruptly asked, his eyes quickly scanning the room's occupants. "Or the duke and duchess?"

"No," Elizabeth replied, "only Jane, Duchess Agatha, and I have come today. You will meet my parents another time, I am sure. Are you to attend the theatre on Friday?"

"Yes, Darcy has invited me."

"Then I shall introduce you to the duke that evening, for we are engaged to go as well."

"As part of our party?"

Elizabeth nodded.

"Excellent! Now we shall have a merry time indeed."

"Your parents and cousins' presence would have prohibited your enjoyment, Richard?" Lord Matlock teased.

"But of course! You and my mother would be absorbed in the play, and Darcy would be brooding over something. Georgiana's delight in the performance would help, but nothing could compare to the company of two lovely young ladies."

Elizabeth laughed, causing more furtive glances from Lady Matlock's other guests.

"Your assumption is incorrect, Fitzwilliam," Darcy interrupted, then looking pointedly at Elizabeth continued, "for I know that *Much Ado About Nothing* is a favourite of Lady Elizabeth. It will be likely she will also be absorbed in the performance."

"Your memory is excellent."

"It is a favourite of mine as well. I have always enjoyed the banter between Beatrice and Benedick."

"'I wonder that you will still be talking, Signior Benedick. Nobody marks you'."

Darcy smiled at Elizabeth's quickness and immediately responded,"'What, my dear Lady Disdain! Are you yet living'?"

"'Is it possible disdain should die while she hath such meet food to feed it as Signior Benedick? Courtesy itself must convert to disdain, if you come in her presence'."

"'Then is courtesy a turncoat. But it is certain I am loved of all ladies, only you excepted'." Elizabeth blushed as Darcy paused, but soon he resumed quoting. "'Thou and I are too wise to woo peaceably'."

Darcy looked at Elizabeth. She visibly started at the abrupt change in dialogue, but quickly regaining her senses and feigning innocence replied,"'I would not deny you; but, by this good day, I yield upon great persuasion; and partly to save your life, for I was told you were in a consumption'."

Darcy's posture stiffened, knowing well the line that followed this and shoring up his courage, he leaned slightly towards Elizabeth and quietly stated,"'Peace! I will stop your mouth'." His eyes moved to her lips.

Elizabeth had not expected him to respond. She assumed he would know the line that should follow her own quote, but such an open avowal in front of his family was a revelation. She dared to raise her eyes to meet his, and her stomach fluttered at the emotions his gaze held.

No, Mr Darcy, there is not a doubt left as to your intentions. But I shall not be so easily wooed, peaceably or not.

She turned her head to survey the group's reactions to their exchange. Knowing how Duchess Agatha and Jane would react, she looked to her new acquaintances. Lord and Lady Matlock appeared curious while Lord Amherst and Colonel Fitzwilliam bore amused expressions. It was the narrowed eyes and pursed lips of Lady Frederica that puzzled Elizabeth.

Catching Elizabeth's gaze, Lady Frederica gained her intended's attention. "Amherst, my father has arrived. Shall we go and greet him?"

"Of course, my dear, at once," he replied and, taking her arm, guided her over to a portly older man who had just entered the room. Lady Frederica cast an icy glance at Elizabeth before departing, leaving her more confused than before.

"I must thank you again for letting Georgiana accompany you yesterday, Lady Elizabeth."

Turning her attention away from Lady Frederica, Elizabeth smiled in encouragement for Darcy to continue.

"She would not be satisfied until she had shown Colonel Fitzwilliam and me everything of interest at Mr Gardiner's shop."

"You have been to Gardiner Emporium?"

"We went this morning, and it is as impressive as everyone has claimed."

"I have many happy childhood memories exploring the nooks and corners in search of hidden treasure. Everything was fascinating to my young eyes. Did you find something, Mr Darcy? A box of your own?"

Darcy looked surprised. "Yes, a lovely chinoiserie piece."

"And will it serve the same function as Georgiana's—to hide all your keepsakes?"

"We men must have some secrets."

She smiled as she recognised her earlier statement, but Lord Matlock calling for Darcy's attention disrupted their conversation. Lady Matlock took the opportunity to introduce Jane and Elizabeth to the rest of the guests.

The Everards remained only a short time longer, with no further conversation between Elizabeth and Darcy, but later that night, she looked back on their exchanges that afternoon with satisfaction and eagerly anticipated the Friday night excursion to the theatre.

THE DARCYS REMAINED AT KENTON HOUSE FOR DINNER THAT evening. After the men had enjoyed their port and politics, they joined the ladies in the drawing room.

Lady Frederica finally found her opportunity to speak and turned to her hostess. "Thank you for such a delightful afternoon. It was a splendid gathering, and Father said he was very glad to see I would be among such noble company."

"The pleasure was mine, Frederica, and I hope your father knows he is always welcome at Kenton House."

"Thank you. And what a delight to meet some of your intimate friends. You have often mentioned Duchess Agatha, but to meet Lady Jane and Lady Elizabeth! My friends will be envious of me. I had not realised you had invited them to our little *family* gathering."

Lady Matlock ignored both the insincerity and the haughtiness in Lady Frederica's statement and simply nodded her head, but Lady Frederica was not deterred.

She turned to her future brother-in-law. "Lady Elizabeth would do very well for you, Colonel. You seem to have similar natures."

"Not at all," he replied indifferently, not even turning his attention from his card game. "She is too quick for me. Her wit would have me eviscerated within five minutes of an engagement, let alone a lifetime of marriage."

"Come now, she is tolerably pretty and will have an exceptional dowry. Surely, you would not consider courting her to be casting your pearls before swine."

"She is quite a beautiful creature as is her sister. I am sure they will have the gentlemen of the *ton* at their feet next Season. No young woman's introduction into society in the last decade will compare. I would bet a guinea on it."

"First you would have to borrow that guinea from me, Richard," Amherst replied, seeking to divert Frederica's ire before Lady Matlock was insulted by her rudeness.

"Actually, I am quite in the flush at the moment. Perhaps a game of billiards is in order? What say you, Darcy?"

He agreed and the three cousins rose to leave, but Lady Frederica was not finished.

"And what is your opinion, Mr Darcy? Will Lady Jane and Lady Elizabeth become quite the sensation your cousin predicts? The elder sister is quite lovely, but Lady Elizabeth is rather plain in comparison. And quoting Shakespeare? Everyone will think she is a bluestocking!" Lady Frederica laughed softly in derision, which she quickly stifled as Darcy turned towards her with a black look on his face.

"The ability to quote Shakespeare hardly qualifies a woman as a bluestocking, madam. It is rather refreshing to have intelligent conversation rather than discussing the latest style of evening dress. And having known the ladies for many months now, I consider them some of the finest women of my acquaintance. Lady Elizabeth is a particular friend of my sister, and I could not wish for a better influence on Georgiana. Now, if you would excuse me."

Darcy bowed stiffly and turned on his heel to leave the room. Amherst and Fitzwilliam followed in his wake, the elder brother rather embarrassed and the younger suppressing a grin.

Lady Frederica sat perfectly upright in her chair, left to all the satisfaction of having forced Darcy to say what gave no one any pain but herself. Lord and Lady Matlock were extremely displeased with the entire proceeding—not that they faulted Darcy for defending the young lady against Lady Frederica's abuse. In fact, Darcy's immediate desire to shield Lady Elizabeth from Lady Frederica's criticism deeply underscored their belief that their nephew was in love with the young heiress. He had openly flirted with her in a way neither of them had ever witnessed from their usually taciturn nephew. They could not fault his taste. There was vivaciousness in Lady Elizabeth's attributes and a spark in her rather fine eyes. Both looked forward to a deeper acquaintance with her.

Lady Matlock was particularly incensed with Lady Frederica's audacity to censure her choice of guests and with the young woman's rudeness towards her son and nephew. She was a formidable and influential woman of London society and had been for several decades, and she was not about to allow such insolence in her future daughter.

She turned to Lady Frederica and with a false smile, addressed the young woman in a soft but commanding voice. "My dear, I am pleased you enjoyed my gathering this afternoon. You are always a welcome guest, though soon you will be a member of the household—something we all anticipate.

"It was a shame you could not spend more time in Lady Jane and Lady Elizabeth's company. My dear friend Duchess Agatha is confident they will create quite a stir when they are introduced next Season, and you know the influence she has on the *ton*. Any young woman who is their friend will enjoy privileges and opportunities not permitted others. I do hope you make an effort to know them, for I am certain you will be in their company often. Georgiana, perhaps you could tell us about the day you spent with them?"

Georgiana was happy to comply, and Lady Matlock deftly steered the conversation away from controversial topics.

Lady Frederica was forced to relent for the moment, but

she was not placated and silently vowed to rebuff all advancements of friendship with Lady Elizabeth.

WHEN THE TRIO ARRIVED AT EVERARD HOUSE, THE LADIES repaired to the striped parlour as was their custom. Duchess Agatha asked Elizabeth for her impression of the afternoon.

"I liked Lord and Lady Matlock very well indeed. Lord Amherst and Colonel Fitzwilliam share very similar natures."

"Yes, Amherst and Richard are like their parents, particularly their father. They are both quite jovial and entertaining. What did you think of Lady Frederica, Amherst's intended?"

"I do not know what to think of her. I only exchanged the briefest of civilities with her, yet I do not believe that Lady Frederica approves of me."

"Why would you think that? I found her very amiable," Jane replied.

"I believe Lady Frederica is rather jealous of you, Lizzy," said Duchess Agatha.

"Jealous of me? Whatever for?"

"She is envious that she is engaged to Amherst when she would rather be engaged to the man who is currently paying you court."

"I am not being courted by anyone."

Duchess Agatha smiled at Elizabeth's embarrassment. "Indeed? Quoting Shakespeare to tempt a man to kiss you at his aunt's house?"

"I did no such thing!" Elizabeth exclaimed, blushing a deep red.

"It was a well-known fact among the *ton* that Lady Frederica attempted to catch Darcy's attention during her debut Season. She had likely assumed her beauty, wealth, and good connexions would cause him to succumb. She pursued him relentlessly, and although he was always unfailingly polite, he had not once shown a preference for her.

"At the end of the Season, she reluctantly discontinued her pursuit, and the following year, she consented to be courted by Lord Amherst. I suspect she attempted to persuade herself that Amherst was the better choice, for he was titled, but her pride had been badly wounded, and Lady Frederica has never fully forgiven Darcy for his indifference."

Duchess Agatha told Elizabeth and Jane what was known to only a few—that the Matlocks had endeavoured to dissuade their eldest son from his choice of bride. They sensed her hard-heartedness and worried that their warm and gregarious son would be unhappy with her. The young viscount would not be persuaded, however. He proposed, she accepted, and the wedding was to take place in December.

"And poor Darcy! He finally shows a preference for a lady, and she torments him mercilessly. His control is exemplary. I am certain if you two had been alone in that room, he would have followed that quote to its logical conclusion. You must not tease him so, Lizzy. You must decide your own mind soon and not raise his expectations. I do not believe you could find a better man for a husband and father, but you must decide whether you will allow him to court you properly. He is too in love with you to have you break his heart, should you refuse his affection a second time. And do not deny it," Duchess Agatha continued when Elizabeth appeared on the point of interrupting her. "He loves you ardently, and he is not attempting to hide it from anyone—your father yesterday, his own relations today ."

"I know you are only concerned for my happiness. I promise to be kind and consider Mr Darcy's feelings. After all,

I once accused him of wilful disdain for the feelings of others, and I do not want to be cut by my own words. I do not know whether a man once rejected would ask a second time."

"Given proper encouragement, I am certain he will."

"Shall we wager a new pair of gloves on it?"

"Two pairs, one silk, one leather, and you have a wager, Lizzy," Duchess Agatha responded. Jane shook her head in rebuke while Elizabeth and Duchess Agatha shook hands to seal their bargain.

"There is still one thing you mentioned that has me puzzled. You have told us of Lady Frederica's designs on Mr Darcy—yet she is engaged to his cousin. Surely she does not still harbour any inclination towards him?"

Duchess Agatha smiled at Elizabeth's naiveté. "Frederica is rather upset that you appear to have succeeded where she has failed. You possess the attention of a certain gentleman from Derbyshire who has been one of the most widely pursued bachelors of the *ton* for the last five years. Darcy has not shown the slightest interest in *any* young lady except you. And his interest is quite blatant. Lady Frederica will certainly not be the only one to be jealous of you."

"Do not worry. My courage always rises with every attempt to intimidate me."

"I would expect nothing less." She took Elizabeth's hand. "You and Jane will be placed in a very influential position, and men and women, young and old, married and single, will vie for your attention, and not always for altruistic purposes. I trust your judgment, but it may be lonely or frustrating at times. You will have to rely on one another for affection and comfort. I promise to help you navigate through the difficulties. You will be able to make some true friends, but most of your associations will be with shallow people, hoping to gain your approbation to advance their own positions."

Jane frowned at the prospect, for she was still disposed to think well of people, despite her interactions with the Bingley sisters. "Thank you, Duchess Agatha. We appreciate your guidance and encouragement."

"Of course, my dear. But it is time to change for dinner now."

They rose and retired to their rooms.

CHAPTER 19

Darcy was disappointed to miss Elizabeth's company on Thursday when the ladies went to the modiste with his sister, but his appointment for the day was not one he could ignore. He had been surprised on Wednesday morning to receive a request to meet with the duke the following day at Brooks's. He realised Elizabeth's father had easily discerned his attentions towards her, and a reckoning was imminent.

Darcy was not prone to nervousness, for he had been his own master for many years; however, this upcoming interview induced a feeling of anxiety not experienced since his schooldays.

Elizabeth was the obvious favourite of her father, and Darcy had not made the best impression the prior autumn. Without knowledge of his former regard, his marked attentions now could seem mercenary, and Darcy was uncertain what Elizabeth had shared with her father and his current estimation of him. This insecurity assaulted Darcy as he climbed the steps of his club and was led to a private chamber where His Grace was seated at a table studying a chessboard. The footman announced his presence, and Darcy bowed respectfully and awaited the duke's response.

He scrutinised Darcy slowly and carefully. His perusal was surprising, for they had been acquainted for over a year, though Darcy believed the duke had not paid particular attention to him. He motioned for Darcy to seat himself across from him.

"Thank you for the honour of your invitation, Your Grace."

The duke raised an eyebrow in perfect similitude of his second daughter. "Perhaps we could be a little less formal. *Your Grace* is rather stiff, would you not agree?"

Darcy smiled almost imperceptibly. "Duchess Agatha's husband used to say that."

"Did he? I am not surprised from what Agatha has told me. What did you call him?"

"I called him Everard as my father did."

"I am afraid I am no more familiar with that appellation, though I should most likely accustom myself to it. Will Bennet suffice? "

"Certainly, sir."

"Can I interest you in a game of chess? You play, I presume. And something to eat or drink?"

"Thank you. Yes, sir."

The duke and Darcy ordered their meals and began a chess game while they waited. Both were masters and enjoyed the competition in companionable silence. After an hour of play, with the duke the victor, Darcy realised his reprieve had ended.

"You play very well. Where did you learn?"

"My father taught me from a young age. The winters in the north are quite cold, trapping everyone inside, and chess is a common pursuit. My father was a member of a club here in town and would play matches through correspondence."

"I have not played such a challenging game for some time. As you know, I had no sons to teach. Elizabeth learned, but she generally preferred to read, and I am not a sufficiently diligent correspondent to play games through the post, though my brother Gardiner has suggested it. I understand that you met the Gardiners this summer while they toured Derbyshire."

Darcy sensed the direction the conversation was headed. "I had the honour of making their acquaintance while they toured Pemberley. I was pleasantly surprised to discover they were related to some of my Hertfordshire friends."

"I understand that you were also pleasantly surprised to meet with some of your *Hertfordshire friends* while you visited your aunt in Kent."

Darcy's posture stiffened at this reference, not certain what the duke was implying. "Yes, I met with the Collinses and Lady Elizabeth. They dined at Rosings, and we spent several evenings in their company."

"Ah, no assemblies then. Did you find the company more *tolerable* than last autumn?"

Darcy looked momentarily bewildered, but as realisation dawned, a feeling of utter mortification caused his face to redden.

She heard me! What cruel twist of fate persuaded me to attend that blasted assembly? It is no wonder she despised me so completely if that was the first impression I left with her. Arrogant, disdainful, ungentlemanlike! That short exchange with Bingley was the start of Elizabeth's disapprobation.

"Your Grace," he began, "I did not realise, that is—I did not intend for that remark to be overheard. I had not the slightest idea your daughter was so close. I cannot begin to excuse such behaviour. I was in a foul mood, but that is no reason to have behaved so rudely. I am truly—"

Darcy's expression of regret was halted by a wave of the duke's hand. "Do not apologise to *me*, young man. That is for another's ears. However, it was well-known last autumn that you did not look favourably upon my daughter. Things have obviously changed."

The duke looked hard at Darcy, and he understood that only the complete truth would be tolerated.

"Your Grace, I beg your indulgence, for I do have an explanation, but it is rather lengthy."

"I have no pressing engagements this afternoon. I am quite at leisure."

Darcy gathered his courage, turned to the father of the woman he loved, and began to reveal the most protected secrets and hopes of his heart.

Half an hour later, both men slumped in their leather chairs. The duke again perused the young man seated across from him, but Darcy perceived an improved esteem and respect now. There were some of Darcy's actions the duke had naturally censured, but he had also acknowledged that Darcy was young and in the midst of a passionate admiration for a very spirited woman for which his life experience had ill prepared him.

"That is quite a story, young man. You do realise I must ask you what your intentions are regarding Elizabeth."

Darcy's mien was serious. "My intentions are the most honourable. I love Lady Elizabeth, and I intend to win her hand. If she consents, I would like to marry her, with your permission, of course."

"Thank you for your candour, Mr Darcy. I shall not say anything to Elizabeth on this subject for now. Allow me to enjoy her company for the next several months. Goodness knows that come spring, I shall hardly see Elizabeth or Jane for all the parties they will attend with Agatha." He rose from his chair. "And now I should return to them."

Darcy stood and followed him, "I regret if anything I said today offended you or caused you any pain."

"I am not offended. I admit I am embarrassed to realise all I failed to observe this past year. Elizabeth is not the only one to question her discernment where you are concerned, and first impressions do not always stand when tempered with new knowledge. Agatha has been singing your praises, you know."

"She is very kind, but she is somewhat prejudiced."

"Indeed, but she is also very perceptive, would you not agree?"

Darcy could not find a response to this question that would not sound boastful, so he merely nodded once in acknowledgement.

The duke laughed softly. "Modesty may make a fool seem a man of sense, Mr Darcy."

"*Adolescentem verecundum esse decet*—modesty becomes a young man, sir."

The duke laughed aloud at this rejoinder. "I shall have to remember how well-read you are, Darcy. Until tomorrow evening."

The duke offered his hand, which Darcy shook, and the two men took their leave of each other with a new understanding.

CHAPTER 20

The next evening, the Everard coach made its way quickly through the London streets and was one of the first to arrive at Covent Garden. The trio alighted and entered the theatre. Elizabeth wore a new gown of deep violet silk. Her chestnut curls were piled on top of her head with a jewelled hair comb, leaving several ringlets to drape along her face and neck. Her eyes were immediately drawn to the tall figure of a gentleman in immaculate evening dress standing at the centre of the spacious foyer. Elizabeth smiled at Darcy, not bothering to disguise her happiness.

He performed a perfect bow. "Good evening." His words seemed to constrict his throat.

The group made their way to the Darcy box and greeted the occupants already assembled. Elizabeth introduced her father to Colonel Fitzwilliam, and the duke launched into a discussion of the Napoleonic situation with the colonel.

Bingley immediately garnered Jane's exclusive attention. Elizabeth seated herself next to Georgiana and began to discuss a piece of music she was attempting to learn.

"Lady Elizabeth, allow me to say how beautiful you look tonight," Darcy said. "I am pleased you could join us this evening." Elizabeth smiled and thanked him. "I must say that your selection of jewellery is quite fascinating. What exquisite pieces you are wearing!"

Darcy adjusted his cravat, drawing attention to the pin his sister had insisted he wear. Elizabeth easily recognised the matching adornment that Georgiana had purchased for her brother.

"Your sister has superb taste, does she not?" Elizabeth arched her eyebrow at her young friend.

Georgiana bit her lip and smiled shyly.

"Indeed. Perhaps she can find me a wife to match as perfectly as our dragonflies."

Elizabeth was spared having to respond by the entrance of Lord and Lady Matlock. Introductions were made, and Lord Matlock joined the discussion with the duke and colonel, while Lady Matlock sat beside Elizabeth to enquire about Duchess Agatha. Darcy returned to the foyer to greet the Gardiners upon their arrival.

THE THEATRE WAS FILLING WITH PEOPLE, AND DARCY WAS surprised by the high attendance. Most of the *ton* would still be at their summer homes, but many of their town acquaintances had informed them of the duke's arrival, and they had returned to London early in hopes of meeting the new Everards. A few lucky gentlemen had espied the duke at Brooks's, and the Fitzwilliam relations had shared their accounts of meeting Jane and Elizabeth.

As Darcy crossed towards the entrance doors, he caught several fragments of conversation regarding the Everards, and he silently blessed the duke for his foresight in suggesting the party arrive early. Darcy hoped to keep the presence of the duke's family secret, allowing them to enjoy the play without unwanted solicitations and interruptions.

He observed the Gardiners' arrival and quickly escorted them to his box. Most of the occupants were already seated in preparation for the beginning of the performance, and the necessary introductions were quickly accomplished.

Darcy was disappointed not to find an open seat anywhere near Elizabeth. She was surrounded by his sister, aunt, Mrs Gardiner, and the duke. He was forced to seat himself almost as far away from her as the box permitted, and he resigned himself to gaze upon her lovely face unimpeded. The orchestra soon announced the start of the play, and all, except Darcy, turned expectant faces towards the stage.

His eyes refused to focus on anything other than Elizabeth. He followed the play through her reactions. He could discern that it was well performed, for a smile of delight lingered on Elizabeth's lips. When the dialogue of the first act reached the quotes he and Elizabeth had exchanged, her eyes shifted in his direction. He held her gaze for several moments until her attention was drawn away by a comment from his sister.

At the first interval, the gentlemen of the party left the box in search of refreshments. Lord Matlock and Colonel Fitzwilliam greeted some friends, while His Grace steered Bingley to a table on the far side of the room. Darcy watched his friend's countenance turn ashen while talking with the duke, and he could guess the topic under discussion, since only yesterday he had received a similar interrogation. A voice interrupted his thoughts.

"I say, Darcy, is that you?" Turning around, he watched the advance of a tall, well-built gentleman. A small smile played on Darcy's lips, and he extended his hand in welcome as the newcomer approached.

"Newbury, it is good to see you!"

Lord Christopher Thurston, Earl of Newbury, was a friend of Darcy's from their days at Eton and Cambridge. After Colonel Fitzwilliam, Lord Newbury was Darcy's closest friend. The young earl had been living abroad the last several years due to the ill health of his mother. Her passing the previous year had allowed Newbury to return to his concerns in England and he had arrived in London only two days prior.

He was a handsome man, almost as tall as Darcy but with lighter colouring. His skin was quite tan from the time spent along Mediterranean coasts, but his most striking aspects were green eyes the colour of spring grass and a blinding smile. In temperament he was similar to Colonel Fitzwilliam, amiable and charming, but edged with a decided cynicism. He had inherited a rather wealthy earldom when he was only fourteen and was therefore subject to the machinations of the *ton* matrons from an early age. He and Darcy had often provided each other respite during the London Season. The two friends had corresponded regularly over the years and were pleased to be in each other's company again.

"I must say I am surprised to see you in town, Darcy. You usually hide away in the country until Advent."

"I have accompanied my sister to town for some diversion."

"Is your sister out already?"

"Georgiana is sixteen, and although not officially out, I

decided to bring her to London to enjoy some of the delights of town."

"When did you ever find anything about London society delightful?"

"I did not say London society. I merely referred to the concerts and exhibits found here."

"Such as this evening, I presume? Which of the lovely ladies in your box is little Miss Darcy?" Darcy's eyes narrowed slightly, which Newbury ignored. "I know Lady Matlock, and one of the women is obviously of middle age, so I can narrow my guess to the remaining three. Considering the ages of the younger ladies, which is difficult to determine from across the hall even with the aid of my opera glass, I would venture Miss Darcy is the blonde in the white gown sitting next to the exquisite creature in violet. Am I right?"

"That is correct," he warily replied.

"And just who is the exquisite creature in violet? Or the lovely blonde in pale blue?"

"They are the nieces of Mr Gardiner, a business associate of mine, as well as Georgiana's friends."

"Gardiner?"

"He owns a large import business as well as several shops. The largest is Gardiner Emporium."

"No, that is not it," Newbury murmured, then hearing the bell sound to announce the play's continuance, he turned towards Darcy. "I shall remember why that name sounds familiar eventually. Enjoy the rest of your evening. We should meet for a fencing match."

"I shall be here through Christmas. Amherst is marrying in December. There should be ample opportunity for me to soundly thrash you."

"Touché, Darcy, but beware. I have been studying in Italy and have a few new tricks up my sleeve."

"I look forward to the challenge."

The men shook hands and returned to their seats for the second act. On his return, Darcy found the seating slightly rearranged, with the only open seat on the end of the front row next to Elizabeth. She graced him with a small smile on his entrance and returned to her conversation with Mrs Gardiner. Darcy gingerly sat down. His arm gently brushed against Elizabeth's, and his skin under his lawn shirt warmed in response. He had desired her closeness earlier that evening, not accounting for the terrible distraction her nearness would prove. *Be careful what you wish for, Darcy.*

As the curtain was raised, he realised that if he had had difficulty focusing on the play during the first act, his situation was much more dire now. He could smell her perfume, a heady gardenia fragrance, and he turned and leaned towards her slightly to better imprint the scent in his memory. He released an audible sigh, causing Elizabeth to turn in his direction.

"Are you well, Mr Darcy?"

Their faces were quite close in the dark box, and Darcy had to restrain a strong urge to lower his lips to hers. "Never better, Lady Elizabeth."

"Are you enjoying the performance?"

"I am enjoying the evening."

He could sense her raised eyebrow at his reply, but she shifted her attention back to the stage without responding. The remainder of the second act was a pleasant torture for Darcy, and he exited the box reluctantly during the next interval.

He spoke with several acquaintances, and as he ascended the stairs for the third act, he noticed Amherst conversing with

Newbury. His friend raised his eyes, and when they alighted on Darcy, he first glared then winked before returning to his seat. Darcy was puzzled by the odd exchange, though it was clear the members of the Darcy party had piqued Newbury's curiosity.

Darcy returned to his box, disappointed to find the seating arrangements of the first act restored. At the conclusion, the group gathered their belongings and made their way to the carriages to take them to Darcy House for a late supper. He had no further opportunity to question his friend about his odd behaviour and resolved to meet with Newbury as soon as possible to discuss it.

Thoughts of his friend were soon pushed aside as the coach pulled up to Darcy House. The servants had outdone themselves in preparation for the evening, and Darcy was anxious to make the best impression possible and leave Elizabeth with a pleasant memory that would dispose her more favourably towards him.

He handed Georgiana out of the carriage and ascended the stairs. As the Everards made their way up the steps, Darcy caught Elizabeth's eye and bowed over her hand.

"Lady Elizabeth, welcome to my home."

He tucked her hand in the crook of his arm and escorted her into the house. Darcy led Elizabeth into the drawing room to a chair beside Georgiana. The remainder of the party entered the room and took up seats, chatting amiably about the performance until supper was announced.

Darcy again offered his arm to Elizabeth to escort her to the dining room. He had placed the duke on his right as was proper, followed by Jane, Lord Matlock, and Lady Matlock. Elizabeth was on his left, then Bingley, Colonel Fitzwilliam, and Mr and Mrs Gardiner. Georgiana took her place opposite her brother as hostess. Her smile was hesitant as she asked her guests to sit and signalled the footmen to begin serving.

The atmosphere was relaxed, the food excellent, and conversation flowed freely and amiably with all the guests predisposed to enjoy each other's company.

"I hope that everything is to your liking, Lady Elizabeth."

"Exceedingly so. I could almost imagine that someone had been spying on me, for your staff has prepared many of my favourites."

"My own tastes are similar to yours, which is why I have always employed an English cook, though I admit that we have a French bakery deliver some delicacies on occasion."

"Do you have a sweet tooth, sir?"

"I admit to a preference for *mille-feuille*. Mrs McGregor has staunchly refused to prepare something she cannot pronounce, forcing me to find other means of securing a morsel from time to time."

"Do not let him fool you, Elizabeth," Georgiana interrupted. "He would eat sweets for every meal were he allowed. If my brother did not ride and fence, he would certainly burst a button on his breeches."

Georgiana immediately blanched when she realised the impropriety of her statement. Her brother looked at her in astonishment, but Elizabeth began to laugh softly, dispelling the awkward moment.

"Let us be thankful then that Mr Darcy is so diligent in his exercise. I do not believe I have ever tasted *mille-feuille*. What is it?"

"Layers of puff pastry and pastry cream. I generally order it flavoured with orange." He turned to a footman. "James, would you please inform Mrs McGregor that we shall require the *mille-feuille* now?" The servant nodded and began to leave, but Elizabeth interrupted him.

"I can be patient and wait until after the meal is over. All good things come in their proper time, Mr Darcy," Elizabeth admonished with a smile. "The anticipation will make the reward of our patience that much sweeter."

"And what will be the reward for my patience, Lady Elizabeth?" He looked at her pointedly.

"You will receive your just desserts."

"I can tolerate just desserts this evening, Lady Elizabeth, if you will promise to sing for us tonight."

Elizabeth arched her eyebrow in thought. "One song for a taste of *mille-feuille*? Is this a fair exchange, Georgiana?"

"It is delicious."

"I shall acquiesce if you will promise to play a duet with me." Georgiana hesitated for a moment, then straightening her shoulders, she agreed. "Excellent. Very well, Mr Darcy, I shall sing."

"A song of my choosing."

"Perhaps, though that was not part of our bargain."

"Lizzy," the duke interposed, "I would be pleased to hear you sing that Scottish air you were practising yesterday."

"Your Grace," Darcy began, well aware the duke was gently reminding him of his promise, "a Scottish air would be delightful."

"I do not have the sheet music, Papa."

"My sister may have it," Darcy replied. "You and she can look through the music when we return to the drawing room."

Soon after their exchange, Darcy rose from his seat to signal the end of the meal, and due to the lateness of the hour, the gentlemen disposed of the customary time spent away from the ladies. The party made their way to the drawing room where Elizabeth and Georgiana immediately repaired to the pianoforte to make their selections.

Georgiana's collection of music was quite extensive due to Darcy's constant purchases for his sister, and she quickly found the Scottish folk song, *The Rising of the Lark*, and placed the sheets on the instrument for Elizabeth's performance. The others took their places and prepared for the entertainment.

Darcy's seat gave him an unobstructed view of the performers. He could not take his eyes from Elizabeth as she sat at the instrument and arranged her skirts about her. She softly touched the keys, then with a small smile towards Georgiana, she began.

Darcy was enraptured to hear her again. The chosen song was sweet and the melody simple, but it was over too quickly. Elizabeth stood to curtsey, and Darcy interrupted the applause.

"Lady Elizabeth, that was lovely. May I induce you to sing another?"

"Was the agreement not for *one* song, Mr Darcy?" Her eyebrow rose in that endearing way, causing Darcy's dimples to appear in a wide smile.

"This song would be entirely owing to your benevolence, milady."

"A clever trick. Do you have a particular request, sir?"

"I know just the one, Elizabeth!" Georgiana responded before her brother could. She quickly searched through the music, and finding her choice, sat at the instrument herself. "Do you know it?" she asked. Elizabeth examined the selection and a blush rose in her cheeks.

"Yes, I do, but..."

"Perfect! This is one of my brother's favourites, and my

voice is too weak to sing it, so I generally only perform the accompaniment. Shall I play for you?"

Elizabeth hesitated, then said she was willing. The opening bars of *Voi Che Sapete* filled the room.

Darcy was transfixed by Elizabeth's song. He had been surprised by his sister's choice as the lyrics were quite ardent in their description of the young Cherubino's love for the countess. He was not surprised by Elizabeth's obvious reluctance; however, her compliance caused his breath to catch in his throat. He could not prevent the yearning that entered his heart and was expressed through his gaze as she lifted her eyes to meet his. *If only she were singing of her true feelings.*

He could not prevent the wild imaginings her song produced—escorting her to the opera as his wife, evenings spent at Pemberley with her singing for him, nights spent showing her his love.

Her gaze remained fixed on him for the entirety of the song, and a hope he had not allowed himself to contemplate was kindled. He knew he still had much for which to atone, but he truly, unfailingly believed for the first time that Elizabeth's heart was within his grasp. It was softening towards him, and he would do all in his power to turn that partiality into a deep and abiding love, the kind of adoration he felt for her.

Her song concluded, and the applause woke Darcy from his reverie. Elizabeth reluctantly broke their exchange to acknowledge the others' praise, after which she fixed a sharp gaze on him.

He was troubled by the displeasure he saw, inasmuch as he could not understand it. Unfortunately, he had no opportunity to question her, for Lady Matlock was pressing Elizabeth and Georgiana to perform a duet.

Darcy did not understand what had caused her sudden ire. The prior moment had seemed perfect, only to be quickly replaced by uncertainty again. He could not allow another misunderstanding to mar their encouraging progress and devised a plan to have some private discourse with Elizabeth. At the conclusion of the duet, he boldly approached her with a plate of *mille-feuille.*

"Your reward, my lady." She rose from the bench and accepted the plate graciously. Her indignation seemed to have faded as quickly as it had arisen. "Lady Elizabeth, allow me to tell you how much I enjoyed your performance. My mother sang that song quite often for my father. It holds a tender place in my heart."

She was forestalled from replying when Darcy continued. "I feel you were not entirely happy after you concluded your song. If there is anything I have done to offend you, I wish to apologise. In truth, I have a great many things for which to apologise, one of which your father brought to my attention the other day."

Elizabeth appeared curious and somewhat confused.

"I did not know you had overheard me the night of the Meryton Assembly. It was a rude and thoughtless remark. I was in a foul mood, and Bingley was prodding me relentlessly to dance. I know that is not a valid excuse for such abominable behaviour. I mistakenly appraised you that evening, to my detriment, as we both know. I am exceedingly sorry for my comments. Can you ever forgive me?"

Elizabeth looked down at her hands before replying. "I must admit I was reflecting on that very night myself. However, I am trying to adhere to my own philosophy of only remembering the past as it gives me pleasure, and that particular occasion does not, so I suggest we remember it no more."

"I shall gladly follow your advice once I secure your forgiveness."

"Then you are forgiven."

"Thank you. May I also request the honour of dancing with you at every ball or assembly where we might both be in attendance, to make amends for my prior behaviour?"

Elizabeth's musical laughter rang out at this outlandish request coming from the usually staid Mr Darcy. "That is a rather difficult promise to keep. How will you accomplish it? How will you anticipate our mutual presence at such events?"

"We gentlemen must have some secrets, Lady Elizabeth."

Elizabeth laughed again at his reference to their prior conversation. "Touché!" Elizabeth took a bite of the pastry she had been holding. "This *is* delicious, sir. May I enquire which bakery you frequent?"

"You are avoiding the question, madam."

Elizabeth only smiled and took another bite of her dessert. Darcy sat back in his seat and folded his arms across his chest, patiently awaiting her answer. She was saved from responding by the interruption of Lord Matlock.

"I saw Newbury this evening, Darcy. Apparently, he is newly returned from Italy. I understand his mother finally succumbed to her illness."

Darcy cast a look at Elizabeth which informed her he would not forget their conversation before turning to address his uncle. "Yes, sir. She died a year ago, but Newbury stayed on the Continent to observe his mourning."

"Newbury, you say?" enquired Mr Gardiner. "Christopher Thurston, Earl of Newbury?"

Darcy turned towards Mr Gardiner. "Yes. Do you know him?"

Mr Gardiner hesitated, looking to his wife before answering. "I am his godfather."

Darcy was astonished. "How is it that he never mentioned you? I have known Newbury since Eton, and he has never talked about you, though he thought your name sounded familiar tonight when I mentioned you and your nieces were my guests."

"Thank you for your discretion, Darcy," the duke sardonically replied.

"I knew you wished to avoid any unsolicited introductions, Your Grace, but had I known Newbury was associated with Mr Gardiner, I would have invited him to the box to renew his acquaintance."

"Do not worry," Mr Gardiner replied. "I have not seen Newbury since his christening." The gentleman said no more, further rousing the group's curiosity.

"Edward," Mrs Gardiner prodded, "they are Christopher's friends. They cannot be unaware of his family's unhappiness."

"You are wise as always, my dear. Mr Darcy, did you ever meet Lord Newbury's parents?"

"I met his father a few times, but he died when Newbury was quite young. His mother was always rather sickly. She never came to London, and the few times I visited Mendon Manor, she appeared only briefly for meals."

Mr Gardiner nodded in agreement with Darcy's statements. "Walter, Lord Newbury's father, was a friend of mine from Cambridge. I was several years younger, and we were from different social circles, but we forged a strong bond. After Walter graduated, we kept a correspondence, and once I ventured into business, we would meet in London whenever he visited. He married quite young in an arrangement with his cousin, Beatrice Ravensdale." Mr Gardiner paused, seeming to consider his choice of words. "It was not a happy marriage.

Lady Newbury, as you noted, was always sickly, and after the birth of Christopher, ceased all contact with her husband.

"Walter spent a great deal of time in London, and we saw each other often. He was exceedingly proud when his son and heir was born and asked me to be his godfather. At the christening, when Lady Newbury was made aware of my identity, she was appalled by Walter's choice. I was not titled and did not have an estate, but it was too late to change anything. She demanded Walter relinquish our friendship in exchange for her...*company*, and I understood his desire to have more children, so I encouraged him to agree.

"It was a difficult choice for Walter, I know, and I missed his friendship. He made arrangements with his butler and steward to write to me and keep me apprised of his son's progress, but I have never met him. I suppose I should call upon him now."

After Mr Gardiner's explanation, the silence of the room felt oppressive. Darcy attempted to evaluate this new information regarding his friend. Newbury only hinted about his parents' sad marriage, but these details explained more fully his friend's cynicism regarding matrimony.

"Mr Gardiner, would you like me to accompany you when you call on Newbury?"

"That would be most welcome."

"My pleasure. I believe Newbury will be glad to make your acquaintance. He has always lamented the early loss of his father, and your friendship and close association with him would be a blessing, I am certain."

"Thank you. I wish things had been different, but the choices seemed so limited at the time. I understand he is a fine young man, and I only hope I can add some benefit to his life."

"Of course you will, Edward, as you do to all who know you," the duke responded, "but I believe it is rather late, and we should be going."

The ladies rose from their seats and extended their farewells. Georgiana and Darcy escorted the Everards to the door.

"Oh Elizabeth," Georgiana exclaimed, "I had such a marvellous time! When shall I see you again?"

"Do you ever go for walks, Georgiana?"

"Fitzwilliam and I walk constantly when at Pemberley."

"Would you like to join me for a walk tomorrow if the weather is fair? I try to go out early each morning, but after such a late night, perhaps sometime tomorrow afternoon would be better?"

"I have a music lesson in the afternoon, but we could go in the morning, if that is your preference. Fitzwilliam generally walks in Hyde Park most mornings. Should we meet there?"

Elizabeth looked at Darcy. "Would eleven o'clock be convenient for you?"

"I would not miss it for the world, Lady Elizabeth."

"That is an excellent idea, Lizzy," the duke intervened. "We shall look forward to seeing you tomorrow. Thank you for a delightful evening."

"It was my pleasure, Your Grace. Until tomorrow." He bowed to the duke and Lady Jane, then looking intently at Elizabeth he said, "I shall count the hours until the morning." He raised her hand to his lips.

Elizabeth softly responded, "Mr Darcy," in barely more than a whisper. She turned and took her father's arm and walked across the square to Everard House. Darcy watched until the party was enveloped in the darkness of Grosvenor Square before returning to his remaining guests

CHAPTER 21

The next morning, the Darcys and Bingley arrived at
Everard House as the chimes were ringing the eleven
o'clock hour. They entered the foyer and were greeted by the
duke, who teased them about their punctuality.

Lady Jane and Lady Elizabeth soon joined the group, and
after donning their coats and gloves, they all set forth into the
beautiful morning. During the walk to Hyde Park, they were
separated by gender, the men following the ladies, followed by
Thomas. As they gained the wider main path of the park,
Bingley strode forward and ensconced himself among the
females. The ladies had been discussing the merits of the
previous night's performance, and Bingley began regaling
them with stories of plays put on at Cambridge by his
schoolfellows. The duke and Darcy were content to listen to
their chatter.

The park was not busy in the morning hours, but Darcy

was a well-known figure, and several acquaintances stopped him. He was loathe to introduce the ladies to any of the gentlemen who detained their group, especially considering their openly admiring stares and obvious interest. Most were friends, and Darcy knew he would be severely interrogated the next time he ventured into his club. He was certainly aware of the speculation revolving around town concerning the Everards, and now he would be considered a primary source of information.

Darcy sensed the duke's growing discomfort with the attention their party was garnering, and at the next turn, he called out to the forward group. "Lady Elizabeth, are you not partial to wooded country lanes?"

Elizabeth stopped and turned in his direction, her eyebrow raised in amusement. "I am, sir."

"I believe the turn ahead will take us on a lovely path very reminiscent of the Hertfordshire landscape. Would you like to lead us?"

"I am not familiar with the paths of London. I would not want to get us all lost. I am sure you would be a much better guide. Perhaps you should lead."

"Certainly." He stepped forward and offered her his arm, his heart swelling when she took it without hesitation.

Then turning to the duke, he continued. "This path is not frequented by as many people. It is generally considered too sheltered and not at all conducive to being seen by acquaintances."

"That sounds perfect, Darcy. Lead on," the duke replied, clapping him on the shoulder and propelling him forward, forcing Darcy to relinquish Elizabeth's arm. The two men led the party forward, veering off onto the suggested path.

They ambled along companionably for several moments

when a feminine giggle drew the group's attention to the side of the path. A gentleman was very improperly inclined towards a young woman as she leaned against a tree and giggled indecorously. He drew his finger along the side of her neck, and Elizabeth and Jane both gasped just moments before their father's voice rang out forcefully.

"Unhand my daughter immediately!"

The man drew back sharply at this command and turned to face the approaching party. He blanched and took several retreating steps, but Darcy moved forward quickly and secured his arm in a crushing grip. He signalled Thomas to grab the man's other arm.

"Do not move, Wickham," Darcy said menacingly.

Lady Lydia staggered backwards and gasped in astonishment to see her father and eldest sisters advance towards her. Although she initially seemed tempted to laugh at the situation, her father's glowering visage instantly forestalled her mirth.

The duke looked positively livid. His lips were pressed into a thin, almost imperceptible line, and his hands were clenched by his sides. He took several moments to compose himself and then addressed his wayward daughter in a quiet, commanding tone.

"Lydia, return directly to the house with your sisters. Jane, have your mother order the servants to begin packing. We shall be leaving London immediately. I shall return shortly, once I have dealt with Mr Wickham."

His eyes never strayed from the rogue's face, and Elizabeth watched her father anxiously. She attempted to address him, but he forestalled her.

"Not now, Lizzy, please. Mr Bingley, would you kindly escort the ladies back to Everard House?"

Bingley nodded and motioned for the ladies to precede him. Lady Jane turned to Georgiana, who appeared quite pale, and gently directed her away. Lady Lydia only hesitated briefly before skirting around her father uneasily and following behind Jane.

Elizabeth did not immediately obey, and she turned pleading eyes towards Darcy. He nodded slightly, and she smiled wanly before rushing to join the group returning to Grosvenor Square. She cast one more glance at the remaining men before she disappeared around a bend and was lost to Darcy's gaze.

DARCY NEVER HAD ANY INTENTION OF LEAVING THE DUKE alone with a scoundrel like Wickham, but he was extremely gratified by the trust Elizabeth placed in him as she silently beseeched him to stay with her father. Her trust in his ability to protect one of her most cherished relations sparked warmth in his heart, and a glimmer of a smile played on his lips before his attention was called back to the present by the squirming of the man he held in a vicelike grip. Thomas was roughly searching through Wickham's clothes, looking for weapons, but he did not find any. Darcy's hold tightened, causing Wickham to grimace in pain.

The duke stared sternly at the villain, and Darcy recognised both the duke's anger and his indecision. As a father, he would be tempted to call Wickham out, but Darcy knew such a course could prove disastrous to both the duke's life and his family's reputation.

Prudent, rational decisions were needed, and Darcy had some knowledge at his disposal he hoped would help persuade the duke towards a right course.

He gathered his thoughts and addressed the older gentleman. "Your Grace, this man is absent from his regiment without authorisation."

"I know. He approached my daughters shortly after our arrival in London, and Lizzy warned me about him. My brother Gardiner and I had him put under surveillance, and Danvers informed us of his desertion from his regiment."

"Mr Danvers has informed me of the same, as well as the many debts he owes."

"You know Danvers?"

"I do."

The duke chuckled slightly, confusing Darcy. "Danvers could have mentioned you were also having Wickham investigated. It would have saved me money. He was paid twice for the same undertaking, that rascal."

His merriment soon subsided, as Wickham struggled to break free of his captors, and Thomas wrenched his arm behind his back, causing Wickham to yelp in pain.

The duke continued. "I shall tell you about Danvers another time, Darcy. First, I must deal with this... *person*," he stated while turning his attention back towards Wickham.

"Might I suggest we hand him over to the military authorities? My cousin is a colonel and would know the proper punishments that should be imposed."

The duke turned away and began walking towards the main path of the park. Darcy turned to follow when his prisoner attempted to address him.

"Darcy, how dare you—"

Darcy squeezed harder, causing Wickham to cry out again. "How dare *you*, Wickham," Darcy hissed, leading Wickham to follow the duke, Thomas following suit. "Do not tempt me, for I have every reason to throttle you right now as you well know. And do not think for a minute I shall only deliver you to the militia. There is also the little problem of your owing well over a thousand pounds to various merchants, not to mention your debts of honour left unpaid. The debt collectors will be grateful to see you as well. I wonder if it will be Newgate or the noose for you."

Wickham paled visibly and his steps faltered, but Darcy was not inclined to be compassionate. "You will finally receive the proper retribution for all the harm you have caused. God willing, you will not be able to injure anyone else, and my family and those I care for will be shielded from you."

Some of Wickham's bravado returned. "Ah yes. How is little Georgiana? Has she recovered from her folly and heartache? She was desperately in love with me, you know."

Darcy suppressed the rage he felt and stoically pressed forward along the path, but Wickham continued to taunt his boyhood friend.

"And the lovely Bennet ladies! How fortunate for them that their precedence and wealth has raised them to the level where you will finally condescend to know them. How is the lovely Elizabeth? I could have—"

Wickham was unable to finish his invective as Darcy punched him squarely in the jaw. A second punch to the gut dropped the rogue to the ground, writhing in pain.

"Never mention my sister or Lady Elizabeth's name again or you will have far more to fear than debtor's prison! Have I made myself understood?" Darcy towered over Wickham, and when the blackguard nodded meekly, he signalled to Thomas. The footman roughly hauled an unsteady Wickham to his feet.

The duke stood facing them at the intersection to the main path, having witnessed the violent exchange. Darcy and

Thomas dragged Wickham towards the duke, and when they reached him, the older man patted Darcy on the shoulder.

"Let us get him to the authorities. The quicker, the better."

Thomas took sole possession of the now subdued prisoner as the group left.

WICKHAM PUT UP NO FURTHER RESISTANCE AND WAS HANDED over to the military authorities. Danvers was summoned to give witness to Wickham's other crimes, and it was decided that desertion would take priority over Wickham's various debts.

Later, the three men were released to return to their homes. Before boarding their carriages, the duke jovially chastised Danvers for charging twice for investigating the same individual. He explained to Darcy that Danvers was an old school fellow of Mr Gardiner's and was a small investor in that man's business. Danvers was unashamed of his decision to charge both men for investigating Wickham, claiming the discretion and confidentiality he assured his clients would have been broken by refusing the other's request. His Grace chuckled good-naturedly at this reasoning, and the men parted amicably.

The duke and Darcy returned to Everard House late in the afternoon. Darcy was told his sister and Bingley had returned to his home hours previously. All the Everard ladies were busy supervising the packing and arranging for their departure early the next day, and Darcy determined it would be rude to interrupt them.

Finding no reason to linger, he shook hands with the duke and returned to his home, exceedingly disappointed not to have seen Elizabeth one last time. He would not see her again until the Season next spring and was crestfallen not to have had a chance for a private farewell. He had hoped their last leave-taking would have been heartrending but full of promise, not a sad and angry affair due to her sister's recklessness.

Fortunately, he had a stock of memories to buoy him up through the long winter without her, and that thought pervaded his mind as he entered the foyer of his home. Immediately upon entrance, he heard the strains of the pianoforte and turned his steps towards the music room.

Georgiana was seated at the instrument playing a melancholy tune. He waited until the piece concluded before addressing her. Despite his focused attention in the park earlier that day, he had noticed Georgiana's strained visage upon seeing Wickham and Lady Lydia. He motioned to a settee and the siblings sat together, Darcy explaining the potential consequences of Wickham's actions. Georgiana was understandably distraught, both by seeing Wickham again and by the possibility of his death or imprisonment. Darcy took his sister in his arms and calmed her. When told of the Everards' planned departure from London, he consoled Georgiana by reminding her they would meet again in the spring.

TWO DAYS LATER, DARCY ENTERED HIS CLUB. BEFORE SETTING off to conduct some business, he had seen his sister to the Gardiner's where he would join her later for dinner. Knowing he would be relentlessly questioned about the Everards and his encounters in Hyde Park earlier in the week by the unceasingly curious among his acquaintances, he had contemplated avoiding his club. He determined to get the worst of it over, accepted an invitation to play billiards with a friend, and shored up his forbearance as he entered the foyer of Brooks's.

He had not taken more than two steps into the main room when he was accosted by one of the gentlemen he had met in Hyde Park, who was quickly joined by others. Darcy dodged their questions expertly, though many of them were quite impertinent and a few so crude Darcy had difficulty restraining himself. He kept his answers as brief as possible and was quite glad to impart the knowledge that the entire party had left London and would not return until the spring. When his patience had reached its limits, he excused himself from billiards, and left to keep his dinner engagement with the Gardiners.

Darcy entered the house on Gracechurch Street and took a deep, relaxing breath. He always felt a sense of calm descend upon him when he was there and was thankful for the friendship he had developed with the family. He heard laughter coming from the sitting room and waved his hand to dismiss the servant, knowing the way quite well. There appeared to be a merry party gathered, larger than he had expected, but remembering the resolutions formed after Hunsford, he squared his shoulders and entered through the open door, only to be arrested completely by the sight before him.

Elizabeth sat on a sofa, Ethan cradled in her lap, and the rest of the room's occupants gathered around her as she told a story. She was even lovelier than he remembered, for her face was flushed with enthusiasm for her tale. He was enthralled by the picture she portrayed, but his reverie was soon disrupted as Ethan discovered his arrival.

"Mr Darcy!" the young boy exclaimed as he scrambled down from his cousin's lap to run to the newcomer and wrap his chubby arms around Darcy's calves. Darcy crouched down to the boy's level to give him a handshake in welcome.

"Cousin Lizzy is telling us the story of Hansel and Gretel," he explained as he tugged Darcy's hand to lead him to the sofa where Elizabeth was seated. "You have come for the best part. They just reached the gingerbread house!" Ethan reclaimed his seat on Elizabeth's lap, leaving Darcy the only option left in the room—on the sofa directly beside her.

"Mr Darcy, it is delightful to see you again."

"I did not expect to see you here this evening. I was under the impression you had left London." He raised his eyebrows in curiosity, but before she could reply, Ethan begged for the continuation of the story.

Elizabeth picked up the tale, and Darcy's eyes scanned the room to take in the other occupants. His sister and the other Gardiner children were eagerly listening to the story. Lady Jane, with Bingley close beside her, sat slightly separated from the group, talking in hushed tones so as not to interrupt. Duchess Agatha was seated beside Mrs Gardiner, and both ladies acknowledged him with a smile.

As his eyes rested upon the last person present, he recognised him with a small start of surprise. Newbury was seated in an armchair by the fire. He gazed at Darcy for a moment with an unreadable expression, then winked and turned his full attention to Elizabeth. It was the second time Newbury had winked at him, and Darcy could not decipher its meaning. Darcy's eyes narrowed slightly, but his good humour was restored as he listened to Elizabeth.

She was a splendid storyteller, changing her voice to suit the different characters and focusing her attention on her young audience. Darcy relaxed, shifting in his seat, which caused his thigh to brush Elizabeth's gently. She faltered slightly in her words, so Darcy repeated the action discreetly, and although the colour rose in her face and neck, she did not lose her place again. He relished in her maidenly blush but refrained from pushing her further and moved his leg back to its original position. She pursed her lips slightly in chastisement, but her reprimand was belied by the twinkle of amusement in her eyes. The story was soon over, and the children and Georgiana enthusiastically applauded their approval.

"Little Ethan did not exaggerate when he praised your storytelling abilities, Elizabeth. Was that not wonderful, Brother?" Georgiana exclaimed.

"I thought it a thrilling rendition of the story. I was glad such a surprise awaited me this evening."

"Yes, Darcy," Newbury said, "I am sure you were quite surprised by my presence here. I had recognised the name Gardiner at the play the other night, do you recall? I searched through my father's papers and discovered Mr Gardiner is my godfather and so paid a call on him this morning. We had quite a lengthy chat, and he offered to introduce me to his *nieces* who are staying with the family for a se'nnight."

Darcy could not fail to notice the emphasis in his last statement, but before he could answer, Mr Gardiner entered the room along with the servant to announce dinner. Duchess Agatha claimed Newbury's attention, so Darcy had the pleasure of escorting both Elizabeth and his sister into the dining room. He had no hesitation in placing himself between the two ladies for the duration of the meal.

Darcy's curiosity was finally gratified when he garnered Elizabeth's attention between courses.

"I was pleasantly surprised to find you still in London. I understood the entire family to have left two days ago."

"That was my father's initial plan, but Duchess Agatha reminded him that Jane and I had made some purchases that required our continued presence for fittings, so he allowed us to stay for a week. We shall travel to Hertfordshire then."

"And then on to Staffordshire?"

"Not immediately. We shall stay at Longbourn for a fortnight to organise the packing of our belongings that will be shipped to our new home. It will also allow us to visit and take our leave of the neighbours."

"That will be a bittersweet task, will it not?"

Elizabeth smiled warmly. "I confess, it will be. Longbourn has always been my home. Grancourt is very beautiful and I understand the necessity of our removal there; nevertheless, I shall miss my friends."

"And all your favourite paths."

Elizabeth's smile grew wider. "Of course, for I am an excellent walker, though I do say it myself."

Elizabeth's attention was drawn away by a question from Duchess Agatha, and Darcy sat back in contentment and sipped his wine as he surveyed the scene. His gaze finally fell upon Newbury, whose intense expression was fixed on his face. Darcy recognised that he owed him an explanation regarding his evasiveness at the theatre and was afforded an opportunity when the ladies adjourned to the parlour, and Mr Gardiner was called away by his butler, leaving the friends alone to enjoy their brandies and cigars.

Darcy stood and walked around the table, holding out his hand in greeting. "I am grateful for the chance to apologise for my behaviour at the play. The duke was concerned about garnering unwanted attention, for he does not plan on introducing his daughters to society until the spring. At the time, I was unaware that you were Mr Gardiner's godson. If I had known, I would have introduced you, but Mr Gardiner did not inform me of the relationship until later at supper. Please forgive me if it appears I deceived you."

"Mr Gardiner's *nieces*, Darcy?"

"Well, it was entirely true," Darcy answered, bringing forth a reluctant laugh from Newbury.

"Entirely true and entirely misleading. But you are forgiven, though I thought that every deception was an abhorrence to you."

"Ah, but I only asked to be forgiven if it *appeared* I deceived, for I did not actually deceive you as you have already concurred."

Newbury laughed more genuinely at this twist of words. "It is good to see you again, Darcy."

"You as well, my friend. I am glad you have made Mr Gardiner's acquaintance. Once I knew of your connexion, I offered Mr Gardiner my company when he called upon you, but it seems my help is unnecessary."

"You can imagine my shock when I learned my godfather's identity. I had never heard his name spoken by either of my parents. To satisfy my curiosity, I turned to my father's journals and correspondence and became aware of the entire sad business. You know I have never been close to my mother or held her in any special regard. I have always granted her the respect due her, but I now understand what a truly cold and unfeeling woman she was.

"I immediately resolved to introduce myself to Mr Gardiner and called upon his place of business—the one you had so thoughtfully supplied. We had a long chat about his friendship with my father, and I shall be glad to further the acquaintance. But now you must inform me of your own association with him and his lovely *nieces*."

"I met the family last autumn while I stayed in Hertfordshire with Bingley. He had leased an estate not three miles from theirs, and we were often in company. This was all before the inheritance of the dukedom, of course."

"And you had no inkling that they were related to the Everards?"

"No one had any suspicion. Even as close as my parents were to the late duke and his wife, I had never heard of the connexion until I read the announcement in the newspapers."

"I have heard of almost nothing else since my return. I shall be quite popular now that I have met them myself."

"I was serious when I mentioned the duke's preference to keep his family—"

"I know, I know. I have already been warned by Mr Gardiner. Besides, I do not believe I want to have Lady Elizabeth's interest drawn away by a competition. She is a beautiful woman."

"Indeed."

"And extremely wealthy and connected."

"Yes."

"And of course witty and charming."

"Without question."

"And you are completely besotted with her."

Darcy's eyes widened, and he hesitated only a moment before replying, "I am. I have been for almost a year now."

"Then why are you not married to her?"

"Our acquaintance did not get off to the best start."

"Meaning you were your usual taciturn, disagreeable self when you met and probably offended her."

Darcy's colour rose, confirming Newbury's assumption. "Something of that sort."

"She seems to have forgiven you."

Darcy released a pent-up sigh. "Yes, but only just, and I am still a far way off from gaining her affections."

"Is that your goal?"

"It is my hope."

"Hope alone will not be enough, you know. You will have fierce competition." Darcy's gaze narrowed to slits, causing Newbury to laugh. "Not from me, Darcy!"

His shoulders relaxed, and Darcy smiled somewhat sheepishly at his friend. "Forgive me, but I saw your interest in Lady Elizabeth earlier, and that blasted wink you gave me was very disconcerting for I could not comprehend its meaning. I know there will be unrelenting interest in her next spring, and the thought of it makes me incredibly jealous."

"The wink was just to tease you." Newbury slapped his friend on the back. "Your Lady Elizabeth is quite safe, but will one of the other sisters do for me?"

Darcy turned a sceptical eye towards his companion. "Lady Jane is quite spoken for, as I am sure you have witnessed throughout the evening."

"One could hardly miss it."

"And the three younger girls are full young. Sorry to disappoint you."

"I may have to start a wager of my own about you and…"

"Do not finish that sentence."

The young earl laughed heartily at this threat and rose from his seat. Mr Gardiner had returned and suggested they should all join the ladies. Darcy stayed behind for a moment, but eager to be in Elizabeth's company again, soon followed the two men to the sitting room where Elizabeth and Georgiana were entertaining the group with duets on the pianoforte. He chose a chair close to the performers and relaxed into his seat to enjoy the music.

After a few songs, Elizabeth stood and left Georgiana in sole possession of the instrument. She glanced around the room, and when her eyes lit upon Darcy's wide smile, she took the seat next to him and turned her attention back to the pianoforte.

"You and my sister play very well together."

"Your sister plays very well. I fudge my way through the difficult passages."

"It was beautiful, Lady Elizabeth."

She smiled. "Thank you."

The two sat in silence through several more pieces before Georgiana relinquished her position and joined them.

"You play exquisitely, Georgiana," Elizabeth began. "You have quite shamed me, for I have never taken the time to practise as you have and will therefore never become a true proficient."

"You have a wonderful sense of expression. You only need work on your fingering. And your voice is beautiful. I wish I could sing half as well as you."

"Duets seem to suit us both."

Georgiana changed the subject. "When shall you call for me tomorrow, Elizabeth?"

"I thought that since our first walk was so abruptly ended," Elizabeth explained to Darcy, "that we might renew the scheme before I left town."

Darcy's confusion turned to instant delight. "Are all the original participants included in this invitation?"

"Well, as my father is most decidedly not in London, we shall have to find a suitable substitute. Perhaps Duchess Agatha would like to join us?"

Hearing her name mentioned, the lady rose and made her way over to the threesome. "Perhaps I would like to join you in what?"

"I have invited Mr Darcy and Georgiana to accompany me

on another walk tomorrow, but Papa is not here to escort us, and Uncle Gardiner will be at work. Will you come?"

Duchess Agatha shook her head. "I promised Jane I would help her tomorrow at the milliner's. She is having bonnets adjusted."

"Of course, I had forgotten." Elizabeth pursed her lips.

"I am sure that with Mr Darcy escorting you both, it would be perfectly safe."

"You do not think Papa would mind after what happened the other day?"

"Your father would not mind if you were to walk with your friends in a small, little-known park. Will that be acceptable to you, Darcy?"

"Quite acceptable. Ten o'clock?"

"I look forward to it."

The party soon dispersed for the evening, two members hoping fervently the weather would be fine and clear the next day.

CHAPTER 22

The inhabitants of London were blessed with a brightly shining sun the next morning, and the Darcys were prompt in their arrival to escort Elizabeth on a walk. When she greeted them, Elizabeth asked whether they would mind the company of the four Gardiner children and their nurse. Assured they would be welcome, the group set off. Upon arrival at the park, the children, their nurse, and Georgiana scampered off towards the pond to feed the ducks, leaving Elizabeth alone with Mr Darcy. He brought her close to his side.

Elizabeth could not deny she was affected by being so near. Her mind was distracted by the scent of his cologne, and her heart began racing slightly. She knew she would have to engage him in conversation or else become entirely insensible. She gathered her courage and began.

"You must allow me to thank you for your help the other

day. I know it was an unpleasant encounter, and I regret it was my sister who forced you to undergo such mortification as to have to interact with Mr Wickham, but I appreciate the assistance you lent to my father. I was very concerned about his reaction, and I believe you helped him to remain sufficiently calm to seek out a reasonable resolution."

Darcy gave her fingers a gentle squeeze. "You have no need to thank me. Knowing Wickham as I do, I had no intention of leaving your father in his presence unprotected. As to my mortification, there was none. If I had done as I should have years ago and exposed his true nature to the world, Wickham would not have been free to impose on your sister."

"I understand your reason for not expounding on your past dealings with him. You would not want to hurt Georgiana."

"I concede that was my main purpose, but I also confess I am a very private man, and I was embarrassed to expose my affairs to strangers. However, it was abominably prideful of me not to consider the danger he would pose to others and not do what I could to help prevent it. I could have mentioned his dissolute tendencies without specific reference to Georgiana."

"I can understand the concern of saying too much, but you acted as you saw fit at the time in order to protect a beloved sister, and no one can fault you for that."

"You are most generous, but I fear I do not warrant such praise."

Elizabeth turned to look at him with a small smile playing at the corners of her lips. "You must learn to accept a compliment more graciously, sir."

He grinned in response. "Your wish is my command, madam."

"That is much better," she commended, but her voice became more serious as she continued. "You have every reason to be proud of Georgiana. I understand you have been primarily responsible for raising her for the last five years."

"I share that responsibility with Colonel Fitzwilliam and have also been aided by his parents."

"True, but she has spent the majority of her time in your company, and as she is a gentle, kind, and well-behaved young lady, you can take credit for much of her upbringing."

"I believe she has inherited her sweet disposition from my mother."

"What did we just discuss about accepting compliments?"

He chuckled at this rebuke. "My sincere apologies, Lady Elizabeth. I shall try harder to adhere to your wise counsel."

"You had better practise then, for we both know you will not become a true proficient otherwise. Now, shall we try again?" She cleared her throat. "Thank you for the assistance you lent my father and for accompanying him to the proper authorities."

"You are most welcome."

"There, was that difficult?"

"Completely painless, madam, especially as I have come to highly regard the duke."

Elizabeth looked askance at her companion. "Yes, it appears you and my father have developed a friendship. I am curious as to when this came about, for I thought you had not spent much time in each other's company."

Darcy looked distinctly uncomfortable with the conversation.

"Come now, sir, you had best confess."

He led Elizabeth to a bench along the path, and they sat down. "Your father invited me to meet him at his club last Wednesday."

"Such a short answer is insufficient to diminish my curiosity."

"He noticed my attentions to you the afternoon at Everard House and wished to enquire about my intentions regarding you. I told him about Hunsford."

Elizabeth's breath caught at this statement.

"Forgive me if I spoke out of turn."

"No, do not apologise. I should have confided in my father. He would certainly have been less surprised," she wryly commented.

They were silent for a time before Darcy had the courage to continue. "You did not ask about my answer to your father's question."

Elizabeth was quiet for several more moments. She then boldly turned to face him. "What was your answer, Mr Darcy?"

He gazed at her unwaveringly and in a firm voice replied, "I told him I intended to win your hand in the spring."

She blinked once in response. "The spring?"

"Yes, your father asked that I wait, for he desires to enjoy your company this winter without thought for the upcoming Season when you and your sister will be presented."

"Yet, you have not waited."

"I will not lie to you."

Elizabeth's smile returned. "You did not have to lie, and if I remember correctly, you quite obviously challenged me to enquire further so you would be forced to reveal your intentions."

"True, but you did not have to rise to the challenge."

"You know my courage always rises with every attempt to intimidate me."

"I confess I was hoping you had not changed in that particular."

Elizabeth could not repress a laugh. Darcy's grin widened. He gently took her hands in his own.

"I have wronged you in the past, and you have graciously forgiven me. I know I do not deserve a second chance, but I shall plead for one, nevertheless. Will you tolerate my attentions when you return to London in the spring? Will you allow me to show you all that is in my heart and to try to please a woman who is worthy of being pleased?"

Elizabeth could not look away from the intense gaze of the gentleman seated next to her, holding her hands so tenderly within his own. She had never felt as overwhelmed by her feelings as she did at that moment and felt she would not refuse him anything if he were to ask.

"Yes, Mr Darcy," she responded breathlessly, "you have my permission."

He raised her hands to his lips and placed a soft kiss on the gloved palm of each before releasing them. "Thank you. And may I also take this opportunity to solicit your hand for every supper dance at every ball during the upcoming Season?"

"I believe we have discussed this. How are you to ever know which balls we shall be attending?"

"Quite easily. I intend to have my sister beg you to correspond with her, and she will keep me privy to all the balls."

"You know I shall not refuse such a request, but I may not divulge my schedule to Georgiana as readily as you assume."

"I have other sources of information."

"Duchess Agatha? Well, as it seems I am outwitted for the time being, I shall accept and will leave my supper dances open, but only until after the first set. If you have not confirmed your attendance once the last note of the first set fades, be warned that I shall accept another offer. I cannot be left without a partner. It would appear as though I were being slighted by other men."

Darcy rolled his eyes at her as he stood and offered his arm, and they gaily chatted of inconsequential things as they ambled towards the pond. The remainder of their time in the park was spent amusing the children. Darcy helped the Gardiner boys in their attempts to catch frogs, and Elizabeth joined the girls in making chains from the last wildflowers of the summer.

The group returned to Gracechurch Street, and the Darcys were invited to stay for the evening, which they immediately accepted. Bingley and Newbury joined them at dinner as well, and a pleasant evening was had by all.

As Elizabeth, Jane, and Duchess Agatha would be required at the modistes for most of the remainder of their time in London, it would be the last gathering of the friends for the immediate future. However, the day before their departure, the trio called at Darcy House to take their leave.

Georgiana was disappointed to lose the ladies' company so quickly and shed a few tears. Elizabeth embraced her gently and comforted her with the knowledge that they would meet again in March and reminded her that her cousin's wedding was fast approaching, as well as the Christmas season with all its attendant festivities.

Georgiana pleaded with Elizabeth for a promise to correspond, causing Elizabeth to look pointedly at Mr Darcy. His smile was knowing, and Elizabeth felt the blush rise in her cheeks. She gave her promise to Georgiana, and Darcy and Bingley attended the ladies to the door.

The Everards returned to Gracechurch Street to spend a final night before venturing to Hertfordshire the following morning. Darcy watched the carriage drive away with a lingering warmth in his heart. He had Elizabeth's acceptance of his suit, and that would be enough—for now—to face the long winter in Derbyshire.

Next year, I shall have you beside me, Elizabeth! he silently promised himself as he turned and entered his home.

CHAPTER 23

The family spent a fortnight at Longbourn after the arrival of Jane, Elizabeth, and Duchess Agatha. The majority of their time was spent gathering and packing those belongings that would travel with them to Staffordshire.

However, the Duchess of Everard could not neglect the opportunity to flaunt her new status in front of her old neighbours. She visited and bragged to all her old friends who received her calls with generally well-disguised jealousy. No one in Meryton desired to offend such an illustrious person, for even though she was rather ungracious, she was a peer of the realm.

Her eldest daughters were greeted with more heartfelt welcomes, and there were many who would truly miss Jane and Elizabeth with their permanent removal to Grancourt. Elizabeth attempted to walk as often as she was allowed. Mr Darcy had been quite correct that she would miss all her favourite paths, and Elizabeth spent many hours traversing the familiar landscape of her childhood.

After arriving at Grancourt, the family settled into their new home rather easily. The house was large and well-staffed, and little was required of the ladies to keep it running efficiently.

Duchess Agatha immediately began instructing the duchess in the roles she would be expected to assume and the manners she would be required to display. The former Mrs Bennet surprised her entire family with her ability to imitate Duchess Agatha in almost every particular. True, she was still sometimes affected by nerves and would never be the most informed woman, but her sensibility became less, especially when not in the company of her youngest daughter.

Lydia was in disgrace with her family—her parents in particular. Her father's reasons for disapprobation were quite sound, considering the warnings he had given and her wilful disobedience of them. The duchess was quite vexed to have her stay in town curtailed by Lydia's actions, causing her to rant whenever the girl was in her presence. Lydia, unaccustomed as she was to being the source of her mother's displeasure, found herself avoiding her company. She was most often found alone in her rooms, sullenly reading a gothic novel or leafing through fashion publications. She joined the family at mealtimes, and although Jane and Elizabeth attempted to include her in conversation, she generally pouted and tried to avoid her mother's notice and retired to her rooms almost immediately after the end of the meal.

Jane and Elizabeth continued their attentions towards Mary. Having so little to do with household matters, they devoted their time to improving their accomplishments. Elizabeth and Mary practised their music, each becoming more proficient, and Mary was rapidly improving her sense of expression. They read books of various subjects—except Fordyce's sermons—and discussed them at length, finding joy in the opinions of the others and in the sisterly camaraderie that strengthened with each interaction.

Kitty, being somewhat abandoned by her usual companion, found herself more in company with her older sisters. She was initially hesitant to include herself, for she did not often understand their conversations and felt inadequate by comparison, but their gentle encouragement, especially Jane's, eventually persuaded her to join in. Elizabeth was quite surprised to discover Kitty had a wry sense of humour, and with more frequent exposure to literature and intelligent conversation, Kitty's sense and disposition began to slowly improve.

The duke was often immersed in the business affairs of his estates, finding them much more extensive and complicated than those of Longbourn. Of necessity, his habitual indolence diminished, and he began to spend more time in his family's company. He was pleasantly surprised and gratified with the changes that were taking place among the Everard ladies, and the evenings, which he had so often dreaded in Hertfordshire, were now anticipated with something akin to enjoyment and delight.

Thus passed the time before the Gardiners joined their relations for Christmas. They were welcomed effusively and were to stay some weeks in Staffordshire. The late duke and his lady had often entertained, and since Joshua Bennet's death and Duchess Agatha's mourning, the house had been sombre. The servants of Grancourt seemed pleased to have so many people present for the holidays. The addition of four young children was especially delightful. The servants outdid themselves in decorating the entire estate with all the trappings of the festive season.

Skating and sledding parties were planned, nights were filled with charades and impromptu pantomimes, and Duchess Agatha revealed the presence of an elaborate puppet theatre that entranced the young Gardiner children. Elizabeth, with the help of Kitty, composed several plays for them to perform, and on Christmas Eve, the entire party held a spontaneous dance in the grand ballroom. Little Andrew and Lydia, who had recovered some of her high spirits, filled in as gentlemen, while Mary and Duchess Agatha took turns playing reels on the pianoforte.

Later, as Mr Gardiner read the account of the Saviour's birth from the Gospel of Luke, a peace and contentment settled on the family. All understood the blessings they had been given, and they retired that night in the knowledge that those they cherished most were happy and safe.

ONLY A WEEK REMAINED IN THE GARDINER'S VISIT WHEN IT became necessary for the duke to discuss his plans for his youngest daughters' immediate future. The family had gathered in the music room following dinner and were about to take up their evening pursuits when the duke loudly cleared his throat, gaining the attention of all in the room.

"We have had such a joyous Christmas, and I am indeed grateful for all of my dear family. I am glad we were able to gather together, for soon many of us will be parting."

"Oh, my dear," the duchess interrupted, "we shall certainly miss the Gardiners once they have returned to London."

"Yes, that is true, but they are not the only ones who will be departing."

"Are we also returning to town?" asked his wife, turning an icy glare towards her youngest daughter. "Our last visit was shortened so abruptly that I did not complete everything I had hoped to do."

"No, my dear, we shall not be returning to town. I speak of our daughters leaving us."

A thoroughly confused expression appeared on the duchess's countenance. "Why are our daughters leaving us?"

"Not all of them will be. Jane and Elizabeth will stay here until their presentation."

"But what of Mary, Kitty, and Lydia?"

"I have decided that they will attend school to finish their education."

Silence ensued—stunned silence on behalf of those without prior knowledge of this information. For all of the duchess's newfound decorum, this revelation could not be responded to with anything approaching civility.

"Finish their education? There is no cause for that. I have taught them everything they need to know. They have all been in society and know everything they need to in order to capture a wealthy husband. What can a school teach them their mother cannot?"

"My dear Frances," soothed Duchess Agatha, "I know all the girls have been out in Meryton society, but that cannot be the case in London. It is just not done to have the younger sisters out before the older ones are married. Besides, we shall have enough to do presenting both Jane and Elizabeth to the *ton*. We cannot possibly hope to do everything adequately and give each girl her due if we have to make plans for five at once."

The duchess listened to this advice with her newly gained sense and at once saw the wisdom of it. She also realised the plan would give her the opportunity of presenting the other girls over the next several years, which would keep the focus on her daughters for a prolonged period of time.

"It will be as you say, Agatha," the duchess replied. A silent sigh of relief was released by several in the room at the duchess's quick acquiescence. "What school will the girls be attending?"

"Mary will spend a year at a school near London known for its musical education," the duke explained. "The Gardiners have graciously agreed to take her when they return to town. Kitty and Lydia will attend schools here in the north. Kitty will go to Mrs Pixton's Finishing Academy, and Lydia has been accepted into The Middleton School for Girls here in Staffordshire. They are all expected by mid-January. I shall escort Kitty and Lydia and see them settled in, and then I shall return here until we go to London for the Season."

"So we shall be going to London as well?" Lydia excitedly queried. Her father directed a stern look in her direction before addressing her question.

"Until you have proven you can spend your time productively and learn some propriety, you will not step a foot within ten miles of London. Middleton School is well-known for its strictness, and until I have excellent reports of your improved behaviour, you will remain there. You will be allowed to visit the family here during the summer and at the holidays, but I expect you to apply yourself diligently."

Lydia huffed and stomped out of the room. The duke sighed resignedly and turned to his other younger daughters.

"Well, girls, what have you to say?"

"I shall be grateful for the opportunity to improve myself, Father," Mary replied with proper solemnity, for she had not shed all of her seriousness, despite the increased time she spent with her older sisters.

"And you, Kitty?"

Kitty looked almost as confused as her mother had initially, but she happened to glance towards Jane and Elizabeth, both with encouraging smiles lighting their faces.

"I shall miss you all, but I shall also be grateful to learn more and see if I can make you proud, Papa," she shyly replied.

The duke could not help but smile at this response, and in an unusual show of affection, he approached Kitty, leaned towards her, and placed a soft kiss on her forehead.

"You are a good girl. Take this time to expand your mind and increase your accomplishments, and I am certain you will make me proud."

Kitty blushed at this show of fatherly esteem, unaccustomed as she was to being the centre of anyone's attention, particularly her father's.

"I believe you ladies have much preparing to do, for we shall leave at the end of the week."

Turning to his wife, he continued. "My dear, I believe you and Agatha purchased several gowns for the girls that they will need to take, but they are only allowed two trunks each, so be sure to have them packed wisely. I have some business to attend to, and I would like your opinion, Edward, if you would?"

His brother assented, and the men retreated to the duke's study. The duchess stood immediately and called for Mary and Kitty to accompany her so they could begin planning for their departure.

Duchess Agatha turned towards the remaining women and smiled indulgently. "That was far easier than I expected."

Elizabeth laughed merrily. "Indeed. Mama was quite easily persuaded that their schooling is for the best. You have produced such a change in her. You have spent so many hours with her, and she has adopted your good behaviour."

"Yes, Duchess Agatha," Mrs Gardiner responded, "you have truly helped Fanny, and we are all extremely grateful. Now, if only you could work some of your magic on Lydia."

"It will take much more than magic, I am afraid. I believe it will take a miracle!"

"Now, Lizzy, that is not kind," Jane gently admonished.

"You are right, as always, but I do worry about Lydia. I know she is still young, and I hope her schooling will help her overcome her more pernicious weaknesses, but I am afraid her character is so decidedly fixed through the indulgence and indolence under which she has been raised that we shall not see a marked improvement, and she will continue to make unwise decisions."

"Then let us hope she will apply herself over the next several years and surprise us all."

Elizabeth smiled at Jane fondly. "I shall apply myself just as diligently and promise not to make a prejudiced judgment until Lydia has been given a chance to redeem her character."

"That is sound, Lizzy," Duchess Agatha said, "for we all know what can happen when one is prejudiced and does not see a person's true character." She looked pointedly at Elizabeth at the conclusion of this statement.

"I have already apologised to Mr Darcy, as you well know."

"And you appeared to have developed a friendship," she hinted, causing Elizabeth to blush profusely.

"Yes, we have become friends."

"Your reaction appears to be a little severe, considering he is only a friend. Can your face turn any redder, do you think? Shall I continue to tease you?"

Elizabeth laughed. "I know what you are doing and will keep you in suspense no longer. I have agreed to let Mr Darcy call on me when we return to London."

"Call on you? For what purpose?"

"I am certain I do not need to elaborate."

"But I would have you do so anyway, for I cannot help but tease you, and as I am certain you have put Darcy through much worse torment, it is only fitting I should help to even the scale somewhat."

Elizabeth smiled widely. "Very well. You will hear it all."

Elizabeth proceeded to tell them of all her recent dealings with Mr Darcy, including their conversation the night of the theatre outing when he apologised for his initial slight as well as their walk in the park when he reserved all her supper dances for any ball they both attend.

"Well done, Darcy!" Duchess Agatha exclaimed. "What a clever young man! And how is he to be certain he attends all the same balls?"

"He is using dear Georgiana."

"Brilliant! You, of course, would not deny informing Georgiana of your plans, and she will report to him."

"I agree it is clever, but I have warned Mr Darcy that I shall only reserve the dances if he is present before the first set ends. You know how much he enjoys a ball, so now he will have to attend from the beginning through supper at least in order to achieve his scheme."

The ladies all laughed at Elizabeth's gentle torture of Mr Darcy.

"Well, I believe you quoted Shakespeare perfectly,"

Duchess Agatha said. "You are both 'too wise to woo peaceably.' I believe it will be a very entertaining Season!"

"And you owe Duchess Agatha two pairs of gloves, Lizzy," Jane reminded her. The ladies laughed, and after another hour in genial conversation, they retired to their rooms for the night.

THE LAST WEEK OF THE GARDINERS' VISIT PASSED pleasantly. Only Lydia, who returned to sulking in her rooms, did not share in the happy family atmosphere. At the end of the week, two carriages departed Grancourt. The first headed south towards London, carrying the Gardiners and Mary, who would be deposited at her school before the family continued to Gracechurch Street. The second carriage was occupied by the duke and his two youngest daughters. The duke was surprised by the moistness in his eyes as he watched his daughters depart for their schools, but he quickly collected himself, returned to his coach and to Grancourt.

CHAPTER 24

The Darcys and Bingley had remained in London and were saddened to see the Everard party depart for the north. They had become happily accustomed to seeing the ladies frequently, and to know they would be separated until the spring brought gloom. However, the continued presence of the Gardiners until their own journey to Grancourt helped to lift their despondency. The intimacy between Darcy House and the home on Gracechurch Street continued to strengthen.

Lord and Lady Matlock also dined several more times with the Gardiners, and their admiration for the fashionable and friendly couple increased with each interaction. Lady Matlock had invited Mrs Gardiner to several gatherings, and the matrons and hostesses of the *ton* also grudgingly approved of her, especially when they discovered she was aunt to the Everard ladies. Mrs Gardiner survived their cordial interrogations graciously without revealing much concerning her esteemed nieces.

When the Gardiners departed for Staffordshire, there was not much time for the Darcys and Mr Bingley to become downcast. The Advent season was fast approaching, and Bingley would travel with the Hursts and Miss Bingley to visit relations in Lincolnshire. He would be gone for six weeks, and then he was to visit a school friend until the start of the Season. The Darcys' time would be filled with family events, particularly the upcoming marriage of their cousin.

The wedding of Lord Amherst and Lady Frederica Sutton was to be an elaborate society affair. In addition to the ceremony itself, several engagement balls and soirées had also been planned in honour of the couple, hosted by both Lady Matlock and Lady Frederica's friends.

As close relations, the Darcys were required to attend, and although they generally preferred to avoid such grand social galas, their recent time spent with the Gardiners and Elizabeth had softened their reserve.

The members of the *ton* were amazed and thrilled with the change in the young, handsome Darcy heir. The matrons of society believed the marriage of his older cousin would induce him to choose a wife as well. While he remained polite, Darcy never singled out any young woman.

There were whispers about his intimacy with the Everard family, as witnessed by their attendance at the theatre with him, and there were circulating reports that Lord and Lady Matlock had met them and approved. The knowledge that the eldest daughters of the duke were beautiful and charming irritated these esteemed ladies tremendously, and they redoubled their efforts to win the heart of the dashing and rich Mr Fitzwilliam Darcy for their daughters.

Darcy was as embarrassed and frustrated with these machinations as ever, but he had learned how to better disguise his aggravation. Elizabeth had corrected him, and he had taken the lesson to heart. He was less taciturn in company, and when among his family and close friends, he smiled and laughed often.

The change was remarkable, and no one was more intrigued—and angered—by it than Lady Frederica. Her desire to win Darcy had never completely abated, and to see him now improved in manners only incited further ire, for she correctly surmised the change was due to Lady Elizabeth.

There was little she could do but bide her time until a proper revenge against her rival could be accomplished. For the time being, she smiled at her intended husband and prepared for her nuptials.

THE WEDDING OF LORD AMHERST AND LADY FREDERICA WAS scheduled for the Saturday before Christmas. Lady Catherine de Bourgh and her daughter, Anne, had arrived in London the Saturday before the wedding, but she had refused to speak to Darcy beyond the slightest required civilities. She had not forgiven him for his behaviour towards her in the summer when he had her removed from Pemberley. A summons to Lord Matlock's study upon her arrival in town had extracted a promise that she would not cause a scene during his son's nuptial celebrations.

Lady Frederica was a beautiful bride. She shimmered in a pale blue satin dress and was resplendent in pearl and diamond jewels. Colonel Fitzwilliam stood up with his brother, and Lord and Lady Matlock were seated next to Lady Catherine and Anne. The ceremony proceeded without incident, and numerous guests arrived at the Matlock's London house to partake of a wedding breakfast.

Darcy had promised Lady Matlock he would not remain in the shadows during the ball that was to be held in celebration of the wedding that evening. Since he resolved not to single out any lady, he asked his sister for the first dance of the evening. Georgiana was nervous to dance in front of such a large gathering, but she allowed her brother to lead her to the dance floor. She danced the next sets with her cousins and uncle and then sat down for the remainder of the ball.

Darcy did not fare as well. He danced the second set with Lady Matlock but knew after that he would be forced to ask women not of his family party. But first, he was required to dance with the bride.

He was not unaware of Lady Frederica's hope of becoming the next mistress of Pemberley. He had done nothing to encourage her but understood she had been severely disappointed, nevertheless. He had been surprised when Amherst had begun paying court to her and even more astonished when she had accepted his cousin's proposal. He was concerned for his cousin's future happiness. Darcy was afraid Lady Frederica would bring misery to Amherst, for although she was beautiful, wealthy, and well-connected, she was cold and calculating.

As his new cousin finished dancing with Colonel Fitzwilliam, Darcy approached her and asked for the next dance. She smiled at him and accepted. He led her to the set and braced himself for half an hour in her company.

They had been dancing for several minutes when she addressed him. "Well, Darcy, of what shall we speak?"

Her words were so reminiscent of Elizabeth's pert conversation at the ball at Netherfield that Darcy could not suppress a smile. Lady Frederica clearly misjudged that his smile was meant for her and returned it.

"It was a beautiful ceremony, madam. You must be very happy to have married my cousin."

Lady Frederica's smile slipped at this reply. "Amherst is everything a woman could hope for in a husband."

"I hope you will be happy together."

Darcy continued to lead the conversation through innocuous and inane topics until the dance was over, when he returned Lady Amherst to her new husband.

"Thank you for taking such excellent care of my wife," Amherst said.

Darcy turned to walk away, leaving a clearly vexed bride. He danced the remaining sets during the evening with the married ladies of his friends and acquaintances to preclude raising any hopes among the unmarried young women. He and his sister were among the last to leave, and Lady Matlock embraced them both as they departed for their carriage.

THE NEWLY MARRIED COUPLE HAD DEFERRED THEIR WEDDING trip until the summer and were to remain in London. The members of the *ton* soon began paying calls, and it quickly became apparent that the affection in the marriage was solely on the viscount's side. Lady Amherst was never improper, for she had been taught well, but she ignored her husband when in company, while he continuously courted her attention.

It was not unusual in their circle of society, but there were still whispers. Many speculated when Amherst would take a mistress to provide the affection that was obviously lacking in his marriage. Lord and Lady Matlock watched these developments with increasing concern.

Darcy and Georgiana spent most evenings with their Matlock relations to celebrate the Christmas holiday. They usually enjoyed such times, but there was an underlying tension among the family ever since Lady Amherst joined them. The Darcys could not but see the imbalance of affection between their cousin and his new wife, and there were several extremely uncomfortable instances when Lady Amherst flirted openly with Darcy. She would sit too close to him, speak too intimately, and laugh too loudly at his occasional jests. All this Darcy bore with extraordinary equanimity until Christmas Day.

The family had attended church and enjoyed a pleasant afternoon trading gifts and laughter. A delicious meal had been consumed, and Georgiana had consented to play carols on the pianoforte. Darcy sat on the sofa nearest the instrument to better view his sister as she performed and was pleasantly reflecting on the happiness he had experienced for the last several months, when Lady Amherst sat down next to him, too closely to be considered proper. Darcy attempted to move away but was prevented by the arm of the sofa. He silently cursed his lack of foresight in choosing it instead of a chair. Lady Amherst placed her hand on his forearm and leaned into him to whisper, ostensibly to avoid disturbing Georgiana as she performed.

"Your sister plays beautifully. It is obvious you have provided the best masters to teach her."

"She practises most diligently. She has a natural talent that I could not but help encourage."

"I am certain you are a very generous brother."

Darcy merely nodded his head and fixed his attention on

his sister, hoping to avoid further conversation, but Lady Amherst would not be thwarted.

"It is a shame other young ladies do not pursue their education as diligently as Georgiana. I understand the Everard ladies neither play nor draw. That shows a shocking lack of attention to what accomplished ladies should be taught. It comes as no surprise, considering they were raised in the country and with no expectations of being introduced to superior society."

Darcy would have preferred to ignore her, but he could never let an insult to Elizabeth remain unchallenged.

"I had thought you better informed, madam."

Lady Amherst looked momentarily confused, but her eyes narrowed as she replied, "I attended one of the best finishing schools. My father was very attentive. He knew what would be required of a lady in my position."

"I am certain your father was as attentive as you say. I was merely surprised you were not more aware of the Everard ladies' accomplishments. Two of the sisters play the pianoforte, and Lady Elizabeth is an especially gifted singer as well. I am sure I have not heard anything that brings me more pleasure than to hear her sing while my sister plays.

"The two youngest sisters draw. I have seen several of their sketches while visiting their relations. I suppose I should not be surprised by your lack of knowledge," Darcy paused and looked directly at Lady Amherst before continuing in a soft but stern tone, "for since you are a happily married woman, you have no need to keep informed about the young ladies of society who are no longer your rivals. It will not affect you at all that the Everard ladies will be the talk of the upcoming Season, for you will be focused on your own home and husband and will have no time to gossip about them."

Lady Amherst blinked at the veiled threat in Darcy's words and could only nod silently in response.

His eyes held hers for a moment longer, ensuring his warning was clear, then he rose and joined his sister at the instrument. The Darcys departed soon after the exchange, leaving behind a fuming but wary Lady Amherst.

CHAPTER 25

Georgiana and Darcy departed for Pemberley a few days after the contentious exchange between Darcy and Lady Amherst. They welcomed the change in scenery and the return to their ancestral home. Each felt their most comfortable at Pemberley. It was there, at their beloved estate, they were at their least reserved, and the autumn spent in London among their new friends had brought even more tranquillity to their lives. Darcy was especially pleased to know that even though he would not see Elizabeth for several months, she was only thirty miles away in the neighbouring county.

Elizabeth was an excellent correspondent, and Georgiana received weekly missives. The letters were full of the activities and antics of the Everards, written in such a sweet, witty style that the Darcys found hours of delight reading and rereading them during the evenings in Derbyshire. With the arrival of each new letter from Lady Elizabeth, a happy mood infused the household.

Darcy attempted to restrain his impatience and always allowed Georgiana to read her letter privately first to ensure that there were no confidences to be kept secret. Most times, after thoroughly enjoying Elizabeth's letter and somewhat purposefully prolonging her dear brother's suspense, Georgiana would simply hand the sheets of paper to him. Darcy would linger over Elizabeth's words and received a small jolt of pleasure any time she would mention him, whether specifically or indirectly.

They were highly entertained by Elizabeth's account of the duke's announcement informing his family of Mary, Kitty, and Lydia's upcoming schooling. He knew Ladies Jane and Elizabeth would be much better received by the *ton* without the unseemly behaviour of their younger sisters to distract from their own charms and accomplishments. London society loved nothing more than to see those above them brought low by scandal, and lack of decorum would be excellent fodder to ridicule what most society matrons would consider their daughters' fiercest rivals.

Darcy was worried about the upcoming competition as well. Although he had received Elizabeth's permission to call on her, Lord Newbury's initial interest in Elizabeth had manifested that she would be assiduously sought out by every male member of the *ton*. Darcy understood well that not all members of the aristocracy followed the moral dictates of society in order to achieve their schemes, and it was not unusual for a woman's reputation to be purposefully ruined in order to force a marriage. He knew he would have to keep a keen eye on everyone in Elizabeth and Jane's company. He promised Elizabeth he would attend every ball or soirée she did, not only to dance with and pay court to her, but also to dissuade other gentlemen. It was a fine line to walk. He wanted her to enjoy her debut Season, but he did not want her falling in love with any man but him.

Such thoughts occupied Darcy throughout the long, cold Derbyshire winter. He busied himself with estate matters, reading, billiards, and hours spent in his dear sister's company, but nothing had the power to distract him long from thoughts of Elizabeth. His mind would often drift to Grancourt, pondering what Elizabeth might be doing at that precise moment. Darcy gained new insights into Elizabeth's life and character with each missive Georgiana received. He had taken to hoarding her most recent letters in his waistcoat pocket to be removed often when he felt her absence most strongly.

THE REMAINING FEMALE INHABITANTS OF GRANCOURT WERE kept extremely busy with preparations for the upcoming Season. Duchess Agatha instructed the duchess, Jane, and Elizabeth in all that would be expected of them during the coming months, particularly their presentation to the queen. The ladies spent a memorable afternoon in the large attics of the estate searching through trunks of gowns.

The mode of dress for a court presentation was quite formal and required outdated but specific requirements. Dozens of gowns worn by the previous ladies of the house were carefully removed and regarded before being dismissed, and Elizabeth could not contain her laughter as some of the more outlandish fashions were presented.

At last, Duchess Agatha discovered a trunk tucked into the back corner of the attic. Her eyes slightly misted as she reverently opened the dusty chest, revealing two exquisite white gowns, one decorated with small seed pearls and the other embroidered with tiny silver flowers. Gasps of pleasure escaped Jane and Elizabeth as Duchess Agatha gently pulled the dresses from the chest.

"These were the gowns Meg and I wore to our court presentation." A tear traced down Duchess Agatha's cheek as she recalled that special day shared with her dear sister.

Elizabeth reached for Duchess Agatha's hand. "How you must miss her!"

"Every day, Lizzy, but I am grateful the Lord has seen fit to bless me with you and Jane in my life. I can see no better way to show my gratitude than to insist you two wear these dresses for your own presentation."

"I would be honoured," Jane demurely acquiesced.

Elizabeth was hesitant. "Are you certain? We would not want to make you uneasy."

"I remember that day with fondness. We were incredibly nervous, of course, but we were so thankful to have each other. You and Jane are as close as Meg and I ever were, and I trust you will gain the same comfort from each other that we did on such a momentous occasion. I believe it can only add to your confidence to wear these gowns that have already comforted two young and foolish girls. And the gowns could bring you luck, for at the risk of sounding immodest, I believe Meg and I were quite the sensation."

"Indeed, it had nothing at all to do with these stunning dresses." Elizabeth proffered a mischievous smile.

"Not a thing."

The two women suppressed their laughter for as long as possible before dissolving into a fit of rather unladylike giggles while Jane looked on in quiet amusement.

Hearing the noise, the duchess appeared at the attic door.

"What on earth has gotten into you, Lizzy? Have you not been listening to anything Duchess Agatha has taught you? Is this the proper conduct of a young lady about to be presented to society? My poor nerves cannot cope with all this racket, and I am certain you will not be able to attract a single gentleman if you persist in braying like a barnyard animal!"

Duchess Agatha and Elizabeth exchanged glances. Finally composing themselves, Duchess Agatha distracted the duchess by manoeuvring to show her an extremely elaborate gown.

"This would be absolutely perfect for your court presentation, my dear Frances."

Elizabeth and Jane exchanged smiles at the easy manner in which their friend handled the duchess. They called for a maid to collect the Beauchamp sisters' gowns to have them made ready for the spring.

FINDING THE APPROPRIATE GOWN WAS ONLY THE BEGINNING OF their training. Duchess Agatha required them all to endure hours of walking in the grand ballroom, dragging long sheets behind them in order to learn how to properly walk and curtsey. The duchess had a bit of difficulty with the full court curtsey, which required the lady to bend her knee almost to the ground, and she toppled over more than a dozen times.

There were also lessons in deportment and how one addressed their speech and correspondence to various levels of the aristocracy. Duchess Agatha even hired a dancing master from London to instruct the Everard ladies in the newest dances, particularly the waltz. The duchess was rather scandalised by this, and even Jane was slightly hesitant, but Duchess Agatha insisted it would soon be common at balls, and it would not do to have the Everards unprepared or out of fashion. Elizabeth found she loved the graceful dance once she had mastered the steps.

Duchess Agatha also deemed it wise to begin introducing the newest Everards to the more prominent members of the neighbourhood. Several intimate dinner parties were planned to make these introductions. Duchess Agatha was selective in her choices and invited only those who would favourably report on the meetings, hoping to ease the girls' upcoming introduction to London society. She was not ignorant of the rumours and speculation surrounding Jane and Elizabeth and hoped to gain many allies before thrusting them amongst the wolves of the *ton*.

Duchess Agatha suggested they host a larger party, requiring the guests to stay at Grancourt. The sisters were somewhat reluctant initially, but Duchess Agatha persuaded them that it would be an important part of their education. Jane and Elizabeth would be required to assist their mother to plan and host several such events each year, and this gathering would be relatively small in comparison. When the ladies finally agreed, plans were made to invite about twenty guests to Grancourt for a weekend in the middle of February.

The duke did not look forward to the upcoming frivolities with excitement. He had maintained an extremely busy schedule since the beginning of the new year and the removal of his youngest daughters. The ducal estates and business matters were vast and complicated, and he was only beginning to familiarise himself with them.

He was, however, quite enjoying the work. As a young man, he had derived great pleasure from his studies. It was only after a few years of marriage that indolence had over-taken him. His wife, though lively and beautiful as a young woman, did not have the intelligence or education to challenge his mind. He had, therefore, retreated to a world of books in order to keep his mind active. Looking back, the duke realised it had been within his power to broaden his wife's understanding, and it was negligence he would forever regret. He was extremely grateful to Duchess Agatha for the improvement she had made in his wife.

Having the responsibilities of the dukedom thrust upon him had reignited his energy. He would never be a man who anticipated socialising with excitement—similar to Mr Darcy —but he was more willing to interact with his family, and his conversation, particularly when addressing his wife, had begun to lose the biting cynicism to which his relations had become accustomed.

He was pleasantly surprised by his new neighbours once the introductions were made. They were generally people of sense and education, and he enjoyed the atmosphere of intelligence and accomplishment that infused the gatherings. However, he was always grateful when they returned to their estates, and his own home returned to a more tranquil state. The invitations had been sent, however, and in a fortnight, twenty guests would descend upon the steps of Grancourt.

The household was put into a flurry of preparations. Duchess Agatha guided the duchess, Jane, and Elizabeth as they discussed menus, directed the cleaning of guest rooms, and decided upon possible activities. Mrs Wallace, the housekeeper, and Prichard, the butler, were both extremely helpful and knowledgeable. The new Everards gained confidence in their ability to plan and organize such a large gathering, and an air of anticipation fell upon the entire estate. The designated weekend was finally upon them, and the Everards' invited guests began arriving.

The necessary introductions were made, and the guests

assembled in the grand drawing room to refresh themselves and converse before retiring to rest before dinner.

Elizabeth chatted with an elderly couple from the neighbouring county. The gentleman had been a great friend of her grandfather James while they were at Cambridge and told some rather amusing anecdotes. She did not notice the most recent and last expected arrivals as they entered the room until she heard her name called.

Elizabeth found herself in a vigorous hug from a young lady, while her brother looked on in amusement. She could not respond, the surprise of the pair's arrival having completely discomposed her.

"Lady Elizabeth, what a pleasure to see you again," the gentleman said.

Elizabeth finally regained her composure and elegantly curtseyed. "Welcome to Grancourt, Mr Darcy."

CHAPTER 26

Elizabeth's surprise was genuine. She glanced towards Duchess Agatha who unsuccessfully tried to restrain a satisfied smirk. Elizabeth narrowed her eyes at her mischievous relation and then returned her attention to the newly arrived guests.

She reached for Georgiana's hand. "How wonderful to see you! Did you have a pleasant journey?" She guided her young friend to a sofa where they sat and began a conversation.

Darcy looked on in contentment as the two women he loved best talked animatedly. He had not failed to notice the exchange between Elizabeth and Duchess Agatha and surmised the older woman had not informed her of their invitation. At that moment, Elizabeth graced him with a brilliant smile, and he knew his presence was welcome.

As he turned to survey the room, he caught the eye of the duke. *I am not so welcomed in that quarter, it appears.*

Darcy inclined his head a fraction in deference and was surprised when the duke beckoned him. He made his way to the older man, greeting a few acquaintances along the way. He made a quick but exact bow.

"Your Grace, thank you for inviting my sister and me to Grancourt."

The duke arched a brow. "You are most welcome, Mr Darcy, though I am certain you know that other than providing the funding, I had no part in it. It was entirely the ladies' doing, from menus to guest list."

Darcy detected the underlying warning in his statement. He had no desire to irritate the father of his beloved. He nodded his acknowledgement of the warning and began a discussion of the Grancourt estate and the upcoming spring plantings.

Darcy's attention was often drawn towards Elizabeth as she moved about the room, conversing with others, but he valiantly kept his place beside her father until the guests began to leave for their chambers.

Seeing an opportunity to speak to her, he excused himself, collected his sister, and made his way towards Elizabeth.

ELIZABETH HOVERED NEAR THE DOOR AS SHE SAW THE siblings advance. She had been extremely surprised to see them. She knew Duchess Agatha must have concocted a scheme, and she was at the centre of it. She would have to wait for the plan to unfold, but she had to admit she was pleased they had come.

Elizabeth studied Darcy as he approached her. Her eyes met his, and he quickened his pace in response, which inspired a heady feeling of power within her.

He once declared he ardently admired and loved me. Do those feelings remain and with the same fervour? To be loved by such a man would be exhilarating, but would it make me happy? His visit will provide an opportunity to know my own mind.

"Lady Elizabeth, Georgiana and I were very pleased to receive an invitation for this gathering."

"I am delighted you both could come," Elizabeth replied. "I hope the winter has been pleasant."

"Oh yes," Georgiana responded, "we had a lovely Christmas, and my cousin's wedding was beautiful."

"I wish Lord Amherst and Lady Amherst joy." A slight frown marred Mr Darcy's face that Elizabeth did not fail to notice but chose to ignore. "Has it been as cold in Derbyshire as it has been here?"

"It is not any colder than it usually is at this time of year," answered Mr Darcy.

"I suppose I am just used to the milder weather of Hertfordshire, for it has seemed quite chilly to me when I attempt rambles about Grancourt."

Darcy smiled at this statement. "That would certainly account for it. In time, your thin southern blood will adjust to the climate."

"I shall be forever grateful to Duchess Agatha for insisting that Jane and I purchase fur-lined coats and gloves. It seemed extravagant at the time, but now I cannot step out of doors without them. They will be most beneficial for some of the activities we have planned for your visit."

"What have you planned for us?" Georgiana enthusiastically queried.

Elizabeth smiled indulgently at the young woman's excitement. "Why, Georgiana, I cannot spoil the surprises that are in store!" She pouted at Elizabeth's refusal to elaborate, causing Elizabeth to laugh. "You will know soon enough, for the plan for the entire weekend will be presented at dinner tonight. In fact, you had better go to your rooms and refresh yourself. I am sure your journey was tiring, and dinner will be served in two hours."

"I confess I am a little weary. I hardly slept last night because of my excitement."

"Come, I shall show you to your rooms." The two young ladies linked arms and turned towards the door.

Elizabeth turned back towards Darcy and addressed him. "You may follow us, sir."

They exited the drawing room and began their ascent up the grand staircase. Elizabeth led the way to the main guest wing and suddenly stopped.

"I am afraid I do not know which rooms Duchess Agatha has assigned to you."

"Were you not instrumental in helping plan the festivities?"

"Naturally, but it appears Duchess Agatha made some amendments of her own and failed to acquaint the rest of us with them. I cannot show you to a room that has either not been prepared or prepared for someone else entirely!"

Darcy chuckled. "Perhaps there is room near the kitchens? Or in the stables?"

"Surely you do not mean for your sister to sleep in the stables! I am heartily ashamed of you. I had been led to believe that you are the best of brothers!" Georgiana giggled as Elizabeth led her down the corridor. "We need to speak with Mrs Wallace. She will surely know what arrangements have been made."

Turning towards the gentleman with a devilish glint in her

eye, Elizabeth continued. "We shall have a footman escort you to the stables, sir."

Elizabeth turned on her heel, and propelled Georgiana down the hallway, leaving an amused Darcy to follow them. They happened upon Mrs Wallace almost immediately who quickly steered the Darcys to their proper apartments, adjacent to one another and far away from Grancourt's illustrious stables.

ELIZABETH ATTEMPTED TO SPEAK TO DUCHESS AGATHA BUT could not find her wayward relation and eventually returned to her room to prepare for the evening. She took more care than usual in choosing her gown and allowed Carter to dress her hair elaborately. As the time for dinner approached, she dawdled at her dressing table and mused on the upcoming gathering.

The guests Duchess Agatha had suggested all appeared to be amiable. She had been nervous about the weekend but now looked forward to it with eager anticipation—more so now that the Darcys were present. Many of the guests were older, and while Elizabeth appreciated the opportunity to expand her acquaintances, the festivities would be more pleasant with other young people. There were two other young ladies in the party, daughters of one of Duchess Agatha's schoolmates, who were accompanied by their husbands. One other was the Honourable Timothy Dynham, grandson of Earl and Lady Bradshawe, with whom Elizabeth conversed prior to the Darcys' arrival. Mr Randolph Leventhorpe of Chetwin Hall, the estate nearest Grancourt, had accompanied his widowed mother. The Darcy siblings would add to the merriment the younger guests would enjoy.

Carter applied the final touches to her mistress's appearance and pronounced her ready. Elizabeth smiled at herself in the mirror, rose from her seat, and left her chambers, excited at the prospect of an enjoyable evening.

THE GUESTS ARRIVED IN A TIMELY FASHION AND WERE SHOWN into the dining room. Their number necessitated the use of a large table, and Darcy was slightly disappointed when he found both his and Georgiana's name cards at the end of it, almost as far from Elizabeth as possible. He was seated towards the duke's end with his sister on his left and Countess Bradshawe on his right. A young couple he was not acquainted with sat across from him. Elizabeth was seated near Duchess Agatha and her mother at the far end of the table. There was a young man, also unknown to Darcy, seated next to Elizabeth, and they were engaged in animated conversation. Darcy's lips pursed as he studied the pair. The young man was handsome and appeared of a lively disposition, and Elizabeth clearly enjoyed his company. As an acquaintance of Duchess Agatha, the man had to be a person of quality and wealth, and as the stirrings of jealousy began, Darcy wished he could be privy to their discussion.

He was soon engaged in conversation with those around him and found himself agreeably distracted. The food was sumptuous, and the discussions were intelligent. He recognised he had not been so entertained for many months. Although he was generally reserved, his natural reticence could not disavow such excellent company.

The couple across from him was soon introduced as Mr and Mrs Andrew Sinclair. Mrs Sinclair was the younger daughter of one of Duchess Agatha's schoolmates, and her husband had an estate in Staffordshire. Mrs Sinclair indicated a couple seated farther down the table as her sister, Lady Holcott, and her husband, Sir Walter. Darcy soon found himself forming new friendships, and even Georgiana was encouraged to cast off her shyness by the kindly Mrs Sinclair.

Darcy could not resist taking several glances towards Elizabeth throughout the meal and was discomfited each time he saw her laughing with her neighbour. His discomposure was eased somewhat when he found Elizabeth glancing in his direction, and they exchanged a few discreet smiles.

The dinner progressed happily in this manner until the duchess, after a prodding from Duchess Agatha, rose from her seat and asked the ladies to follow her to the music room. The gentlemen remained behind to enjoy cigars and brandy. Not inclined to smoke, Darcy procured a glass of liquor, and surveying the room, found the Earl of Bradshawe engaged in conversation with Elizabeth's dinner companion. Determined to be introduced, he walked resolutely in their direction.

The earl, an old acquaintance of his grandfather and father's, noticed his approach and smiled. "Darcy! It has been an age since we met."

Darcy shook the older man's hand affectionately. "It is a pleasure to see you again."

"That cannot be Georgiana with you, can it?"

"Georgiana has grown up right before my eyes. Your wife subjected her to a thorough questioning about her studies during dinner."

"Well, Lady Bradshawe must be kept well informed." The earl indicated the young man standing beside him. "Have you met my grandson? Timothy, this is Mr Fitzwilliam Darcy of Pemberley in Derbyshire. Darcy, my grandson, the Honourable Timothy Dynham."

The two gentlemen bowed respectfully to one another. Darcy could not help but take the measure of the man he now considered a rival for Elizabeth's attention. A quick assessment revealed that Mr Dynham was a few years younger and only slightly shorter than himself. He was fair in colouring with an athletic form and a ready smile. Darcy was put in mind of his good friend Bingley. He was also the grandson of the earl, so his connexions would be impeccable. He met the young man's gaze and was a little startled to realise he was also under scrutiny. He raised himself to his fullest height.

"Mr Dynham, I have known your grandfather for many years, and I am glad to have the opportunity to meet you."

"The pleasure is mine. I admit I know you by reputation."

Darcy raised an eyebrow, inviting an explanation, and Mr Dynham seemed happy to supply one. "I attended Cambridge only a few years after you, and my classmates and I tried valiantly to best some of the records you set. You left quite a mark by the time you graduated. I believe some of your achievements still stand to this day."

"I had some friends who spurred my competitive nature and was fortunate enough to sometimes come out the winner."

"Only *sometimes*, hmm? Your mastery of chess is legendary, as are some of your accomplishments in debate."

Darcy was beginning to become uncomfortable, but Dynham continued. "I was extremely gratified when I finally took your record in fencing."

"And which one is that?"

"The most recorded wins." Mr Dynham smiled, and Darcy finally understood his companion's motive for the conversation.

"Is that so, Dynham?" The young man nodded in triumph.

"And by how many matches did you beat the previous record?"

"Ten, sir."

"Do you still fence?"

"As often as I can."

"And did you happen to bring a foil with you?"

"Indeed I did."

"As did I. Perhaps you would care to try your luck against the previous record holder?"

Dynham's smile widened significantly. "I would be honoured. At dinner, Lady Elizabeth was so kind as to outline the plan for the weekend, so I know that there is some time set aside tomorrow afternoon for members of the party to pursue their own activities."

Darcy succeeded in controlling the surge of jealousy that began at Mr Dynham's reference to his time spent in Elizabeth's company. He would be happy to put this young pup in his place by beating him at fencing.

"Timothy, this is a splendid idea!" the earl interjected. "I have not seen you fence for several years. I am sure your grandmother would appreciate the opportunity to watch you, that is, if Darcy does not object?"

"Anything for the countess's entertainment."

"Perhaps we should join the ladies and procure my wife's approval."

"Excellent idea, Grandfather, for I would very much like to return to Lady Elizabeth's company. She is a rather fetching creature, would you not say, Mr Darcy?" The young man turned towards Darcy and almost took a step back at the dark glare he received.

"I have had the privilege of knowing Lady Elizabeth for well over a year. She and my sister are regular correspondents, and I spent quite a bit of time in her company this fall among her mother's relations. The duke is rather protective of her, as anyone who loves her would be." Darcy directed a pointed stare at Mr Dynham at this pronouncement.

Dynham seemed unwilling to be intimidated. With a smile, he said, "I understand that as something of an elder brother to Lady Elizabeth—considering her close friendship with your sister—you mean to warn me, but I promise I do not intend to trifle with the lady's affections. My intentions are strictly honourable."

The earl, sensing the increasing tension, chose to interrupt. "Come, Timothy, we must not keep your grandmother waiting," he loudly proclaimed, gaining the attention of the other gentlemen. Taking his grandson by the elbow, he steered him out of the room and in the direction of the ladies.

Darcy, struggling to overcome his pique, remained as the rest of the men began filing out. He could hardly believe the man's audacity! Had he not been sufficiently explicit in his warning?

I shall have to monitor him closely and not let him near Elizabeth alone!

Realising that Dynham was already making his way towards her while he was left stewing in the dining room, Darcy quickly collected himself, strode out of the room, and reached the doors of the music room before the earl and his grandson. Upon entering, his eyes instantly sought out Elizabeth, and he found her in conversation with Lady Bradshawe. Blessing his luck, Darcy made his way towards them, knowing that his contender would be second in at least this instance. The ladies looked up at his approach and smiled.

"Darcy," Lady Bradshawe began, "I was just telling Lady Elizabeth of the time you and your cousin fell into the lake at our estate. Imagine my surprise when she informed me she met Colonel Fitzwilliam this Easter at Rosings."

"That is true, and I found the colonel quite charming, though he failed to tell any stories of his youthful misadventures. Perhaps Mr Darcy would care to finish the tale, for you cannot quite remember the cause of their fall."

Darcy was reluctant, but seeing Mr Dynham approaching, he decided to keep Elizabeth's attention focused on him by relating the remainder of the story.

"We had been playing hide-and-seek with our other cousins. The colonel's elder brother had not yet been discovered, and we both set out to look for him. We were crossing the bridge over the lake and decided to use its height to survey the park and determine whether we could catch any glimpse of him or of a possible hiding spot we had overlooked. We were involved in an earnest discussion about the merits of a certain copse as a good area for concealment when Amherst snuck up behind us and gave us both a violent shove. We tumbled over the low wall of the bridge and toppled into the lake."

Elizabeth laughed gaily. "And what became of Lord Amherst? I am sure such an act could not pass without some form of retribution."

Darcy smiled at her intuition. "Let us just say Amherst did not find himself alone when he went to sleep that night, for there were several slimy frogs slipped into his bedclothes."

Elizabeth's musical laughter continued. "I shall have to ensure that any tricks I play on you will not be traceable to me."

Dynham interrupted. "Grandmother, Mr Darcy has agreed to a fencing match with me. Grandfather suggested you might like to be a spectator."

"I would be delighted to watch such a match. I have never

seen you fence, but I know you broke a record of some sort while at Cambridge, is that correct?"

Dynham smiled smugly. "Well, yes, madam. In fact, I bested Mr Darcy's record." He again looked exultantly at Darcy.

The countess turned to Elizabeth and asked, "My dear, would you like to accompany me?"

"I have never seen a fencing match, Lady Bradshawe."

"All the more reason for you to attend with me. They are quite exciting. I am certain you would enjoy it."

"When will it take place?"

"Tomorrow afternoon, Lady Elizabeth," Dynham answered. "I would be honoured if you would attend."

He looked beseechingly at her, but Elizabeth turned towards Darcy to gauge his opinion of the request.

He smiled softly at her. "Lady Elizabeth, please come." She gently nodded. "Lady Bradshawe, I am certain your grandson would like to honour you by winning, so I will take this opportunity to solicit the favour of Lady Elizabeth. Will you grant me a token to bring me luck in tomorrow's match?"

Dynham's eyes narrowed at this charming and effective ploy. Elizabeth pulled a white silk handkerchief edged in delicate lace from her sleeve.

"Gallant knight," she teased, "would you be so kind as to carry this token tomorrow so that you may overcome all foes?"

Darcy took possession of the handkerchief and Elizabeth's hand between both of his own. "It would be a pleasure, milady," he whispered as he placed a light kiss upon her fingers.

The air between the two immediately sobered with this declaration and show of attention, and a rosy blush spread across Elizabeth's face and neck. Darcy looked intently into her eyes, but the moment was broken as Dynham again interrupted.

He imitated Darcy by asking his grandmother to favour him with a token, and she obliged by offering a fan. A few of the other guests had joined the group throughout this conversation and were all interested in observing the fencing match, so it was agreed that the entire party would assemble tomorrow afternoon to witness it.

The men then began a discussion of fencing and the different schools and styles of the sport. The duchess asked several of the young ladies to entertain the group with some music, and Mrs Sinclair and Lady Holcott performed a lovely duet on the pianoforte and harp.

If Elizabeth's countenance remained rosy for the rest of the evening, it could be attributed to her frequent looks in Darcy's direction and the bit of lace peeking out of the breast pocket of his coat.

CHAPTER 27

The next morning, the repast was informal, allowing the guests to choose their seats. When the Darcys entered, Georgiana immediately sought a place next to Elizabeth. Darcy was increasingly grateful for their friendship, for it allowed him the ready excuse to place himself across from them and enter into conversation.

He filled a plate for his sister and himself and then thoroughly enjoyed his eggs and sausages as he watched with delight as Elizabeth coaxed giggles from Georgiana with tales of the Gardiner childrens' Christmas visit. His seat faced the door of the room, which allowed him the sight of Dynham entering. His initial look of frustration was quickly schooled into a smile when he noticed Darcy's position near Elizabeth and no vacant chairs left nearby.

Dynham filled his plate and chose a seat near the Sinclairs and Mr Leventhorpe. He cast surreptitious glances in Darcy's direction throughout the meal, but Darcy kept his satisfaction well-concealed. Jane and Duchess Agatha soon entered and seated themselves after relaying that Her Grace would be unable to join them until later in the morning. The party finished their meal, and the plans for the day were announced. Those brave enough to face the winter weather would enjoy a sleigh ride around the estate, while the others would entertain themselves playing cards.

The young guests applauded the idea of the sleigh ride, and the ladies departed to collect their warm clothing as the gentlemen retreated outside to see to the sleighs. Darcy followed leisurely, keeping to the back of the group, and then remained indoors. He was determined to be Elizabeth's escort for this activity and was soon rewarded as he saw her descend the stairs in a deep red velvet cloak lined with soft white fur, her dark curls tucked under a white bonnet. She looked like a winter sprite as she walked, pulling white gloves over her delicate hands. Once she reached the bottom of the staircase, Darcy stepped forward and offered her his arm. She smiled as she took it, and he led her outside.

The air was brisk, and Elizabeth turned her face upwards to catch the sun, closing her eyes and breathing in the invigorating crispness of the winter morning. Darcy was enchanted, and he quickly espied a smaller sleigh, large enough for a driver and only one other occupant, and steered her towards it. He assisted Elizabeth into the seat, adjusting the hot bricks around her feet, and then joined her, settling a warm blanket over them. Taking up the reins, Darcy nodded to the groom attending them to release the horse's head, and with a flick of his wrist, they were off before any of the others had even entered their sleighs.

He felt only slight guilt at leaving his sister to fend for

herself, but he knew that between Jane and Mrs Sinclair, Georgiana would be in good hands. Darcy stole a glance at Elizabeth and shifted in his seat to bring them closer. Elizabeth shivered in response.

"Are you cold?"

"Not at all, sir."

"You will be sure to tell me if you are."

"Of course." Elizabeth turned slightly in her seat to look behind them. "We seem to have outstripped the rest of the party, Mr Darcy. Perhaps we should wait for them."

"They will catch up," he replied.

Elizabeth then turned towards her companion and unconsciously shifted closer to him. The sky was a vibrant blue and the countryside glittered as the sun sparkled off the snow-covered ground. The horse pulled the sleigh effortlessly, and Darcy was the happiest he had been in years. He turned the horse towards the woods, slowing their pace as they entered a well-worn path that Darcy remembered led to a lake. The tree branches overhead were coated with ice, giving the appearance that they were made of glass. Darcy felt rather than heard Elizabeth's sigh of contentment, and before he even realised it, his hand had released the rein, and his arm slid around Elizabeth's shoulder, drawing her close. She lightly rested her head on his shoulder as she gazed up at the icy canopy. Darcy held his breath and could hardly believe his good fortune. He wished he could see her beautiful face, but it was hidden by the brim of her bonnet.

They travelled in companionable silence through the woods until the trees began to thin, and they crested a slight hill to see the lake spread before them. Elizabeth leaned forward in her seat, dislodging Darcy's arm, as she took in the lovely scene. The lake was covered in a thin layer of ice, and a pair of deer was poised at the far shore. Catching sight of the approaching conveyance, they gracefully darted off into the woods.

"Beautiful." Elizabeth whispered softly.

"Indeed," Darcy replied, his eyes never once wavering from the intoxicating sight of the woman at his side. Elizabeth appeared unaware of his meaning as she was entranced by the landscape.

The jingle of bells on a horse's harness broke through the tranquillity, interrupting their contemplation of the winter scene. The other sleighs had followed their tracks, and Dynham's sleigh pulled up alongside theirs. Jane, Georgiana, and Mr Leventhorpe also occupied his vehicle, and the Holcotts and Sinclairs brought up the rear.

All remarked on the beauty of the vista, and some bottles of warm cider and savoury pastries were produced.

Darcy climbed down from the sleigh to retrieve the drinks and refreshments. Elizabeth cupped the bottle in her hands, warming them, and turned to him, a soft smile lighting her features.

"Thank you for this," she said, lifting the bottle of hot cider to her lips. Her countenance was rosy and flushed from the wind and hot drink and, Darcy hoped, from their shared moment before the rest of the party arrived.

Dynham had also disembarked from his sleigh, dispersed some treats to its occupants, and made his way to the two of them.

"You departed so quickly I was afraid that something had frightened the horse."

"Not at all," Darcy returned.

"Are you certain? I would be more than happy to drive

Lady Elizabeth back to the house if you would feel more comfortable with a less spirited animal."

Darcy's hands clenched around his cider bottle. "That will not be necessary. I have been handling determined horses for more years than you, and I am quite capable of driving this sleigh."

"I believe the horse was just eager to be off, Mr Dynham," Elizabeth replied diplomatically. "It is a beautiful morning after all, and I admit I was just as impatient once I had stepped outside. Did you enjoy your ride, sir?" Elizabeth continued, effectively steering the conversation, and the group was soon discussing Grancourt's park and its more notable features.

The wind began to increase, and the gentlemen suggested a return to the house before the ladies caught a chill.

Darcy remounted the sleigh and drove around the lake to retrace their path through the woods, the other sleighs following close behind. He knew he should not try to outpace the others on the return ride, despite the great temptation to be alone with Elizabeth again, so he kept a moderate pace once they exited the woods onto the meadow leading up to the house.

Too soon for Darcy, they arrived at the entrance and disembarked their sleighs. They repaired to the drawing room where the other members of the party were involved in several games of whist. Georgiana persuaded Elizabeth, Mrs Sinclair, and Lady Holcott to retreat to the music room to plan some musical entertainment for the evening. Darcy entered into conversation with Sir Walter and Mr Sinclair. Mr Leventhorpe, a rather shy young man, joined their discussion once the topic of bird hunting was broached. Apparently, he was a rather fine shot. Dynham was kept in conversation with his grandmother, Duchess Agatha, and Jane.

The duchess joined the party at midday, and everyone entered the dining room to partake of a hearty meal. Hot soups, stews, and crusty breads with butter were the fare of the day, and everyone devoured their food with gusto, especially those who had spent the morning in the chilly winter air. The group had divided into male and female, and Darcy entered the fray of gentlemanly discourse, casting only a few glances towards the ladies' end of the table throughout the meal.

When all had eaten their fill, Dynham rose from his chair and addressed Darcy. "Are you ready to be beaten, sir?"

Darcy slowly folded his napkin, placed it on the table, and stood. "I am at your disposal whenever you are ready to lose."

Dynham smirked at this rejoinder and bowed to his opponent. Darcy bowed in return and then turned to Elizabeth. He pulled her handkerchief from his breast pocket and extended his hand to her.

"My lady, allow me to escort you to the field of battle."

She stood and placed her hand in his. He tucked it into the crook of his arm and led her upstairs to a wide hall that had been deemed the best location for the match. The servants had removed the carpet and lined chairs along the walls for the spectators to view the contest. Small tables with drinks and sweets had also been scattered between the seats. Darcy guided Elizabeth to a spot with a view of the centre of the hall, gallantly bowed, and then placed a lingering kiss on her hand. Her warm skin against his lips created a delicious sensation, and Darcy quickly withdrew to the place where his valet had appeared carrying his foil to collect himself. He would need to focus all his attention on his opponent to be victorious, and Elizabeth, though an exquisite distraction, was a distraction, nevertheless.

And I will be victorious! Dynham needs to learn his place, and I am more than willing to provide a lesson in humility.

Darcy had become more sanguine about his position in Elizabeth's affections after that morning's excursion, but he did not want to allow any room for doubt or significant competition. He would win, he was certain, but more importantly, he would win graciously, which he knew would hold more weight with Elizabeth.

Darcy removed his coat and rolled up his shirt sleeves to allow more fluid movement. He and Dynham had agreed to retain their waistcoats in deference to the presence of the ladies, knowing it would somewhat limit their abilities. They would also each wear a padded plastron, for though the tips of their foils were covered with a cork button, accidents were not completely preventable.

He turned to the assembled party and determined that Dynham was prepared. Meeting Elizabeth's eyes, he bowed and tucked her handkerchief into his waistcoat pocket. Dynham bowed to his grandmother and handed her fan to his valet to hold. The two men met in the centre of the hall, and Sir Walter, acting as referee for the match, outlined the rules the gentlemen had agreed upon the previous evening. Once Darcy and Dynham consented to the provisions, they took their positions, and Sir Walter pronounced, *"En garde!"*

Dynham attacked immediately, causing Darcy to retreat several steps. However, Darcy had learned from a renowned fencing instructor the need to learn one's opponent's style and strategy. He unwearyingly parried Dynham's advances, astutely observing and looking for signs of weakness. After several minutes of allowing Dynham the offensive, Darcy riposted and scored a point.

Dynham looked momentarily stunned before acknowledging the hit. The men retreated and each took a sip of water before returning. When play was resumed, Darcy again allowed his rival to take the offensive. Dynham was a capable fencer, but Darcy had almost immediately determined his technique. He attempted to use speed, intimidation, and aggressive thrusts in the hope of surprising his opponent. This left him open on his weak side, and a patient rival had but to wait for the opportunity when Dynham turned in order to score a hit. This Darcy did, and with a quick movement, he had scored another point.

Dynham was rapidly losing his composure and requested an immediate reengagement. Darcy acquiesced, recognising his opponent's agitation would soon result in his loss. Sir Walter called for the match to resume, and this time, Darcy attacked swiftly and decidedly. His attack was precise and extremely intricate. Dynham had difficulty parrying, and before long, Darcy had scored another hit and won the match.

Darcy stepped back, and Sir Walter declared him the winner. He bowed to his baffled challenger, who numbly bowed in return, still reeling from his unexpected defeat. Darcy then extended his hand towards Dynham who took it warily.

"Very well played, sir. I can see that you have studied Dardi extensively."

Dynham could not help but smile at this show of sportsmanship. "Thank you. I confess I was surprised by your initial passivity, but apparently, I was astoundingly wrong to interpret reserve as meekness."

Darcy merely smiled. The lesson had apparently been learned.

There was polite applause for both competitors. Elizabeth rose from her chair, and Darcy swiftly made his way to her side. He bowed and she curtseyed, still playing the role of medieval knight and maiden.

"Well done, sir. Congratulations on a commendable win."

"Thank you, madam."

"It was very exciting, but everything happened so quickly. I hardly knew you had begun before it was over." She smiled archly and dramatically fluttered her eyelashes, causing Darcy to chuckle. She was quite adept at acting a coquette.

Stepping a little closer, he whispered so that only she could hear. "It is customary in such cases for the knight to claim a reward from his lady."

Elizabeth instantly sobered. "Is that so?"

"Indeed. I shall have to determine an appropriate prize."

"Choose wisely." There was both a warning and a challenge in her statement, and Darcy knew it would not do to affront Elizabeth's sense of decorum. She was playful and unaffected, but she was still a lady.

"I shall," he responded seriously. "Did you enjoy the match? I know it was your first experience with fencing."

"That is not entirely true."

"But I heard you inform Lady Bradshawe that you had never witnessed a fencing match."

"Well, that is true, but I am a great reader, you know." At that statement, they both smiled in memory of Miss Bingley's outrageous declaration. "There are many novels and histories in my father's library that discuss fencing."

"Ah, but that is not the same as seeing it for oneself."

"True, but as you can see, I have had *some* experience. However, it was quite exciting. The movements are so swift, and it may seem incongruous, but for a sport that has the potential for causing tremendous injury, it is rather graceful."

Darcy smiled at this observation. "Not incongruous at all,

for I have always felt there was an almost dance-like quality to the sport, rather like watching a cruel ballet."

"That is a perfect description."

They were then joined by Georgiana who congratulated her brother. Darcy and Dynham both retired to their rooms to freshen themselves after their exertions, and the others dispersed throughout the house until it was time to dress for dinner.

ELIZABETH DRESSED EARLY, AND WANTING A MOMENT TO herself, made her way to the library. She was thankful to find the room deserted. Although usually a sociable person, she was somewhat overwhelmed by the number of houseguests currently at Grancourt. To have so many relatively unknown persons staying at one's home was a trifle tiring. She was genuinely impressed with the guests Duchess Agatha had selected and already determined that both Lady Holcott and Mrs Sinclair would make dear friends—and helpful allies during the upcoming Season—but she needed a slight reprieve from the responsibility of entertaining.

She selected a volume of poetry by Wordsworth and ensconced herself in a comfortable chair close to the fire. She was so intent on her reading that she failed to hear the door open or notice the entrance of the gentleman who currently observed her.

"You *are* a great reader, madam," said Darcy.

She laughed softly. "My father read to me from Wordsworth when I was very young. He has always remained a favourite for that reason."

Darcy nodded, and when she craned her neck to venture a

peek at *his* book, he turned it towards her so that she could read the title.

"*The Iliad*? Heavy reading before dinner."

"I did not know there were restrictions set forth for what one should read before certain meals."

"Of course there are. Such reading would make you entirely too sombre, and therefore, a poor companion at dinner, especially if you were seated next to a young lady."

"Ah, I see. I must have you write a list of appropriate selections."

"I would be happy to oblige you, sir." She rose from her seat, walked to a nearby shelf, and selected a book. When she returned, she held it out to him, and he chuckled when he recognised her choice.

"*Aesop's Fables*?"

"Certainly. It is entertaining but also highly instructional, for there is a moral within every tale."

"I remember you are also an expert on proper topics of conversation during a ball. Perhaps you should write a guide so that others could benefit from your counsel."

"I would never presume to be an expert on anything, and according to some ladies, I do not have the necessary skills even to be deemed accomplished." Her smile was impish at this further reference to Miss Bingley, and Darcy grinned in response.

"I consider you to be one of the most accomplished ladies of my acquaintance."

Elizabeth would have decried his statement, but he had not finished speaking.

"Lady Elizabeth, I have decided upon my reward."

She swallowed and then held her breath for a moment.

Darcy hesitated, then slowly reached out and gently

grasped her hand that was twisting a lock of hair. Her hand fell away, but he twirled his finger so the ringlet was wrapped tightly around it.

"A lock of this. That is all I ask."

His request was intimate but not entirely indecorous. His eyes were fixed on his finger entwined in her hair. Darcy met her gaze to confirm her agreement and then produced a small penknife from his pocket, pulled the curl taut, and smoothly cut off an inch.

When their eyes met again, there was a tenderness in his gaze that deeply touched Elizabeth's heart, and she knew that she was falling in love with him.

"Thank you," he whispered, and she could only smile warmly in return, for she was incapable of speech after such a moment. He excused himself to secure his treasure.

DARCY AND ELIZABETH WERE ONCE AGAIN SEATED AWAY FROM each other, but Darcy was glad to note that Mr Dynham was also partnered with others. Darcy spent the evening with some friends of Duchess Agatha's who were also well-known to his parents, while Elizabeth was seated with the Holcotts and Sinclairs. Darcy had escorted his sister into dinner and had left her in the company of Jane, Duchess Agatha, and the Leventhorpes. During a pause between courses, he was surprised to find Georgiana in earnest discussion with the shy Mr Leventhorpe, seated to her right.

Dinner proceeded in the same fashion as the prior evening with intelligent and lively discourse and delicious food. Later, the ladies performed several combined pieces they had practised earlier in the day.

After they had finished, the party was astonished when Mr

Leventhorpe approached the pianoforte, where Georgiana had remained, picked up the violin, and the two commenced to play a beautiful duet. Darcy, in a discussion with his sister later that evening in their shared sitting room, apologised to Georgiana for his abandonment of her during the sleigh rides, and she quickly granted her brother forgiveness. Darcy also discovered the duet had been the content of Georgiana and Leventhorpe's intense conversation at dinner. Apparently, not only was Mr Leventhorpe a fine shot, but a talented musician as well.

Darcy had had little interaction with Elizabeth throughout the remainder of the evening, but as he was preparing for sleep, he opened one of the drawers of his lacquered box and inhaled deeply of the gardenia scent emanating from Elizabeth's lock of hair. He climbed under the covers, fortified by many pleasant reminiscences of the day.

CHAPTER 28

E lizabeth awakened from a most pleasant dream. She could not remember the details, but she woke with a smile on her face and, hopping quickly out of bed, donned her dressing gown, and darted to the window seat overlooking the hibernating rose garden. She pulled a soft blanket over herself and gazed at the beauty of the winter scene outside her window. The sun was just rising amid clouds of glowing pink. *Like swirls of cake icing,* she thought and then giggled at the childish imagery her mind had produced.

She heard her maid bustling around in the dressing room and knew Carter would soon enter with a morning cup of hot chocolate—a rather decadent habit Elizabeth had adopted since coming to live at Grancourt. She snuggled into the blanket more securely, and her thoughts turned towards the previous day.

She had fallen in love with Fitzwilliam Darcy. She could

no longer deny it. How it had happened and when it had started she could not determine but, she knew it to be so. His attentions yesterday had been pronounced, but so tender, that any woman would be hard-pressed to resist him. He was intelligent and honourable, and above all, he respected her. He appreciated her wit and abilities, and he thought she was beautiful and accomplished. He had humbled himself and listened to her admonishments and had adjusted his behaviour accordingly.

He had not changed in essentials, for Mr Darcy was already the most excellent sort of man, but he had altered some of his habits in order to be more solicitous to those around him, and he continued to make an effort at conversing with strangers, although his shyness would tempt him to act otherwise. He had taken her words to heart and acted upon them which proved he was not a prideful man, but amenable to change, and it had been under her influence. Surely, this demonstrated the depth of his affection and reverence for her.

Elizabeth now comprehended he was exactly the man, who in disposition and talents, would most suit her. His understanding and temper, though unlike her own, answered all her wishes. Their union would be to the advantage of both. By her ease and liveliness, his mind had been softened and his manners improved. And she would benefit from his judgment, information, and knowledge of the world. They were both of consequence and wealth, although hers was rather greater than his now. It would be a splendid match, and moreover, she knew she would be exceedingly happy.

This final thought brought a radiant smile to Elizabeth's face, and when Carter entered bearing a tray of the expected drink, the maid was arrested by the happiness that suffused her mistress's countenance.

"Good morning, Carter. It is a splendid morning, is it not?"

"Yes, ma'am. Shall I place your chocolate on the table?"

"Oh, no, will you please bring it here?" Carter handed the steaming cup to her mistress and turned to depart. "Will you please prepare my warmest riding ensemble? I do not want to waste another minute of this beautiful day."

"Certainly, ma'am, everything will be ready for you." Carter then departed to perform her duties.

Elizabeth barely lingered over her drink before she entered her dressing room to be prepared for her ride. Soon, she was bundled up against the cold and heading towards the stables. She greeted several of Grancourt's servants as she merrily made her way down the path. Upon entering the building, she abruptly stopped. Before her stood the unmistakable form of Mr Darcy, leisurely feeding an apple to her horse. He had not yet noticed her, and she took the opportunity to study him.

Elizabeth was left somewhat breathless at his handsome face and tall figure. While she had always acknowledged his good looks her recent awareness of her affection for him, combined with his fine-looking features, created a more pronounced reaction than previously. She composed herself and stepped more fully into the building.

Her movement finally caught his eye, and he turned towards her. "Good morning, Lady Elizabeth."

"I had it on good authority that you had been given a room, but perhaps there has been a mistake, and you have been forced to sleep in the stables after all. I am certain a room in the house can be arranged for you. Perhaps near the servants' quarters, for you would be in no one's way in that part of the house."

"You are all graciousness."

"It is my duty as hostess to ensure the comfort of all the guests."

"We shall add it to the list of your many accomplishments, madam. May I enquire about your presence here?"

"Why would any person be in a stable on such a beautiful morning?"

"I myself have come for a ride, but I cannot account for your being here."

"To ride as well, sir."

Darcy appeared surprised by this response. Perhaps he had not realised she had become accomplished enough to venture out alone in the winter. "Would you mind if I joined you, or would you prefer solitude?"

"Your company would be much appreciated. I am still fairly new to riding, and your expertise might become indispensable."

"At your service. Which horse?"

"The one you were just spoiling, sir."

Darcy grinned sheepishly then turned to Elizabeth's horse to lead it from the stable. "This is a stunning animal."

"I shall take you at your word, for I am no judge of horse-flesh. Her name is Lily. Duchess Agatha selected her for me. She is quite gentle and was her sister Margaret's horse when she visited Grancourt."

A groom helped Elizabeth mount and then went to retrieve Darcy's stallion.

"I remember Lady Margaret," Darcy said, "a sweet-natured woman, rather the opposite of Duchess Agatha in many traits, but they were extremely close. In fact, the sisters remind me of you and Lady Jane."

"I would have liked to have met her. Duchess Agatha is still quite desolate over her loss."

"Yes, to lose one's family, especially all in one tragic occurrence, would be exceedingly difficult. I suspect your family's presence has helped to alleviate her sorrow."

Elizabeth detected the hint of sadness in Darcy's voice when he mentioned losing family and was reminded he had lost both his parents at a fairly young age. She still had so much to learn about this man and recognised that now would be the perfect moment to begin. As he finished mounting his horse, a large chestnut-coloured stallion, Elizabeth resolved to take advantage of the opportunity presented to her.

"I hope we have brought her some comfort. Did it help to have your family nearby when you lost your parents?"

"It was a great comfort to have my Matlock relations with me when my father died." He spurred his horse forward, and Elizabeth followed his lead.

"I knew my father had been sick, but I had been away at school, and once I returned home, I was surprised at the suddenness of his decline. He had delayed calling for me so I could finish my studies, but it left us very little time with each other before he died.

"My mother died when I was fourteen, and my father and I had grown close to each other during the intervening years. We would often ride together around Pemberley as he taught me about the management of the estate. My father was a great man, very generous, and he was my closest confidant. There are still moments when I doubt myself or my choices, and I wish for his guidance and counsel."

"I feel fortunate to have never lost anyone who was close to me. I love my parents for their own unique characteristics, though I confess that I am particularly close to my father."

"You and your father do seem to share some similarities."

"Do you comprehend me so well then, sir?"

"I would never claim that, though I can presume secure knowledge of some of your preferences."

"Is that so? And to which preferences do you allude?"

"You are a student of character and you love to read—both traits I believe your father possesses as well. You prefer hot chocolate in the morning and take your tea with honey and lemon and never with milk. You wear a gardenia scent, and during the day, you favour gowns of light spring colours, but you almost always wear darker shades, the colour of jewels, in the evening. When you perform, you select pieces of music that are simple in composition, not too technical, but full of feeling and expression. You finish your fish course but never take cooked carrots, and your sweet tooth is as pronounced as mine. You are well-read but gravitate towards poetry and Shakespeare. And...you bite your bottom lip when you are contemplating something, just as you are doing now."

It was a habit from Elizabeth's childhood that her mother had never successfully eradicated. She had not realised he had studied her *so* thoroughly. She was initially discomposed, but she quickly comprehended this was another demonstration of his affection. His love was not the work of the moment, an infatuation that would fade, but a deep, abiding feeling that had survived a refusal and many months of suspense and grown into steadfast devotion. He knew her likes and dislikes, he understood her flaws, and loved her in spite of them. He had suffered the mortification of renewing the addresses that had once been so cruelly rejected.

Darcy had halted his mount while reciting his list and was watching her.

With a smile, she said, "I see that I have much to learn about you in return, for I have absolutely no idea what colour waistcoat you prefer."

"I hope you will have a lifetime at your disposal to make your discovery."

"I am beginning to believe that I would enjoy just such an endeavour, Mr Darcy. I *can* say with certainty that your favourite dessert is *mille-feuille,* and you enjoy fencing and riding."

Darcy chuckled at this rejoinder. "Would you like to give our mounts some more vigorous exercise?"

The couple gently raced their horses for another half an hour before returning to the house. Elizabeth silently vowed to spend as much time in Mr Darcy's company as possible during the remainder of the visit.

DARCY AND ELIZABETH RETURNED TO THEIR ROOMS, AND after divesting themselves of their riding clothes, performing the proper ablutions, and donning garments more appropriate for the remainder of the day, they made their way to the breakfast room. They arrived at the same time, and Darcy held the door open for Elizabeth as she entered, complimenting her on her lovely sea-green muslin frock.

They were the last to arrive for the meal, and all eyes were upon them as they took their seats. Darcy offered to fill a plate for Elizabeth, and she acquiesced. He chose several of her favourite dishes and asked a servant to bring her a cup of hot chocolate.

When Elizabeth entered with Darcy, Mr Dynham looked exceedingly annoyed at first, but his scowl lasted only a moment before his features transformed into a more gentlemanly mien.

"You are getting a fairly late start to the morning, Lady Elizabeth," Dynham observed.

"Yes, where have you been, my dear?" her father asked. "You are usually one of the first ones up and about the house."

"I have not changed my habits in the slightest. I woke with the dawn, and the day looked so lovely, I decided to take a ride before breakfast. By a lucky coincidence, Mr Darcy was of the same mind, and we met quite fortuitously in the stables. He gallantly offered to help rescue me from any snowbanks should Lily become unruly."

The duke chuckled at his daughter's exaggeration.

"Now, Lizzy," Duchess Agatha drolly admonished, "you know if there were any trouble to be had, it would be by your instigation, and you should be ashamed of yourself for impugning poor Lily's behaviour. I am sure Meg never had the slightest problem from that horse."

"I am sure Lily was on her best behaviour with Lady Margaret, but certainly a horse can detect when it bears a rider that is not only inexperienced but too headstrong for her own good. I imagine Lily is only waiting for the perfect opportunity to prove her dominance."

Mr Dynham interrupted. "If you would like some advice to better help you control your horse, I would be more than happy to assist you."

Elizabeth raised her eyebrows at the suggestion. "I assure you such assistance will not be necessary. Duchess Agatha has been a most competent teacher. Lily and I shall have our battle of wills, and I am sure I shall emerge victorious—eventually. I only hope I do not sacrifice too many dresses to the mud in the process."

"Lizzy!" Duchess Agatha laughed. "We spent too many hours determining the proper cut and fabric, not to mention the lace!"

"It would be a shame," Darcy answered, "for you look particularly fetching in spring-coloured muslins."

Elizabeth would not yield under Darcy's teasing. "Why thank you, sir. Does that mean I do not look as well in jewel-coloured gowns?"

Darcy bit back a grin. "You continue to wilfully misunderstand me and express opinions that are not your own. Though you look fetching in spring-coloured muslins, you look absolutely ravishing in jewel tones." He gazed intently at her, and she leaned almost imperceptibly closer to him.

"Is your vanity sufficiently appeased now, Lizzy?" the duke queried as he rose from his chair. "Before your arrival, the gentlemen had been discussing a chess tournament to be held this morning. Would you care to join us, Darcy?"

The duke's expression brooked no opposition, so Darcy agreed and exited the room with the other gentlemen. They headed towards the library where the ever-efficient Grancourt servants had already arranged several chess boards throughout the room.

"I would like the chance to play you again, Darcy. I remember you are quite skilled."

"I am at your leisure, Your Grace."

The two settled into chairs around a board, and the other men dispersed throughout the room, some beginning their own games and others making selections from the extensive collection of books.

"I believe you agreed to call me Bennet."

"Indeed, sir, but it somehow feels improper to do so. These men were all friends of Duchess Agatha's husband, and it will serve you in the future to have them remember that you are now the Duke of Everard."

"Even so, please address me as such when the others are not present."

Conversation dwindled as the game progressed. The men were evenly matched, and the game required their undivided attention. When it became apparent the duke would win, and Darcy was merely manoeuvring pieces to delay the inevitable, the duke relaxed back into his chair and studiously scrutinised the young man before him.

Darcy moved a rook, which would postpone his loss for another turn, and when he glanced up, he noticed the duke's observation of him.

"You are not keeping your promise to me."

Darcy swallowed the lump that had formed in his throat and deliberated over his reply. He could not lie, but he did not want to further offend Elizabeth's father. Honesty had always served him well, and he resolved never to prevaricate with the duke.

"No, sir, I have not. But I have kept a promise I made to myself and your daughter."

"And what promise might that be?"

"I promised I would never leave Lady Elizabeth in doubt of my intentions. I made the mistake once of hiding my feelings from her, and the result was disastrous. I will not make the same mistake twice. I am sorry if that has compelled me to break my word to you. It is not something I have taken lightly, but with all due respect, Lady Elizabeth's feelings must come first, and I will not have her suffer if it is within my power to prevent it."

"Dynham has taken a keen interest in Elizabeth."

Darcy's jaw clenched. "I have noticed."

"That is why I am releasing you from your promise to me.

It would be unfair to allow that man to pay court to Lizzy and not grant you the same courtesy."

Darcy's tension eased immediately. "Thank you, Your Grace. It was becoming impossible to keep both my promises, and I am truly sorry that my pledge to you was the one that necessarily gave way."

"It would appear that you have made some progress with my daughter. What hope has Lizzy given you?"

Darcy toyed with the chess pieces in front of him, spinning a pawn with his finger. "She tolerates my company."

"So now you are tolerable enough to tempt *her*?"

When Darcy looked up, he recognised the same teasing glint often found in Elizabeth's fine eyes. Determined to treat the duke's taunting as he would his daughter's, Darcy tipped over his king.

"I hope so, sir."

"Well played, Darcy."

The men reset the board and played another game, and the duke was again the victor. They each played some of the other gentlemen as well before leaving to join the ladies.

CHAPTER 29

While the gentlemen were busy playing chess, the ladies amused themselves by painting. The estate's conservatory was an idyllic spot for such an activity, providing lush foliage carefully maintained throughout the winter as well as sweeping vistas of the snowy landscape through the windows. All the women tried their hand at the art, producing generally genteel results. However, towards the end of the morning, a challenge had been issued by Duchess Agatha to produce the best portrait—the prize to be a lovely ivory fan.

Two ladies accepted the challenge, and the men entered the room to find a charming scene—Jane posing with Lady Holcott and Mrs Sinclair as impromptu Grecian goddesses. Tablecloths draped around them and a pair of garden shears nearby attested to the plunder of the conservatory's plants to produce the vine headdresses. Both Georgiana and Elizabeth, backs to the door, were intently studying the easels before them as they attempted to capture the scene on canvas. The duchess, along with the older ladies of the group, were seated in chairs observing the proceedings. The gentlemen stopped near the doorway, loath to disturb the obvious amusement of the women.

"Georgiana, I cannot mix the proper colour of green!" Elizabeth exclaimed, still unaware of the men's entrance. "How am I ever to compete with your superior skills if I cannot finish a single leaf on Jane's headdress?"

Georgiana looked at Elizabeth's work and her nose wrinkled. "You are not even trying! You have painted the entire headdress blue! And Mrs Sinclair's hair is certainly not violet!"

"I told you I had no skill at painting, but you insisted I make an effort. And now you mock my endeavour? Shame on you!"

"You have not made a concerted effort at all. You have only spent fifteen minutes in the attempt."

Elizabeth adopted a supercilious tone and continued. "Your brother will be mightily disappointed that your education has been so lacking that you do not exhibit the proper manners towards your hostess. Do you not know that my father is the Duke of Everard? You should be flattering me and telling me my painting is by far the most accomplished you have ever seen. And then you should laugh at me behind your palette. Is that not how the ladies of the *ton* behave?"

The ladies all laughed at this bit of foolishness.

Darcy stepped forward. " Lady Elizabeth," he began, startling the ladies, "I would appreciate you not instilling such tendencies in my sweet, innocent sister." He looked at her canvas and stifled a laugh. It was a riot of clashing colours, and the scale of the figures was extremely exaggerated. "And my sister is quite correct, for that is one of the most horrid paintings I have ever laid eyes on."

Elizabeth laughed delightedly, not in the least offended. "It *is* rather ghastly. I would have assumed that the masters you hired for your sister would have been more talented, but I shall take her under my wing, and she will perfect her technique in no time, I assure you."

Darcy chuckled at her impertinence and complimented his sister's work, which was actually quite lovely. Mr Dynham approached the group to view the canvasses. He made a vague comment to Elizabeth on her use of colour.

Elizabeth smiled slightly in response. "Now that you gentlemen are here, perhaps you would be willing to judge our endeavours? You see, there is an exceptionally fine ivory fan at stake to the lady who can produce the best portrait."

The gentlemen stepped forward to examine the works of art. Many of the men tried to be diplomatic when commenting on Elizabeth's attempt, but her father had no such compunction.

"What a complete waste of canvas! Perhaps you should trade in your paintbrushes for some more sheet music, Lizzy. I believe your time would be much better spent practising your singing, for at least we are assured you have some talent in that area."

Elizabeth acknowledged her lack of artistic skills with amiable grace and announced Georgiana the unanimous winner of the contest. Duchess Agatha presented the fan, and Elizabeth's mother invited the guests to adjourn to the dining room to partake of a light meal. The models were helped out of their costumes and much laughter accompanied the group into the dining parlour.

The seating was again informal, and Dynham secured a chair next to Elizabeth, but he was visibly disappointed when the Darcys placed themselves opposite her. The conversation revolved around art and the different exhibits that had been seen by the members of the group. Darcy told of his experiences in Italy, viewing some spectacular frescoes, particularly Michelangelo's *The Creation* on the ceiling of the Sistine Chapel. Mr Dynham related his recent visit to the British Museum and the special lecture he had attended on the Rosetta Stone and the hope it would provide the key to translating ancient languages.

When the meal was finished, the guests parted to enjoy their own pursuits for the afternoon. Mr Dynham might have hoped to spend more time in Elizabeth's company, but he was thwarted by his grandparents' request that he discuss a letter recently received from his father.

Darcy, knowing he had somewhat neglected his sister, invited Georgiana to take a walk with him, as the day was proving to be rather fine for the season. She quickly agreed and left to retrieve her outdoor garments. Darcy overheard Elizabeth tell Jane she would meet her in the library in a few minutes and then followed her out of the room. He called out to stop her progress.

Elizabeth turned to acknowledge him, and he quickly caught up to her. Darcy held a napkin he had retained from the meal. She opened her mouth to question him, but he prevented her.

"Be still."

Her eyes widened, but Elizabeth complied. He slowly

brought the cloth to her cheek and tenderly wiped it. She was made speechless by his action.

"Violet—the colour of Mrs Sinclair's hair, I believe."

He showed her the cloth bearing a smudge of paint. She immediately coloured, stammered her thanks, and then rushed upstairs.

He looked at her longingly and then returned to the dining room to deposit the napkin before searching out his sister to enjoy their walk.

The Darcy siblings ambled along the snow-covered paths for an hour. Georgiana enthusiastically regaled her brother with her pleasure in the gathering. She spoke of the cherished time spent with Elizabeth and Jane and how she had become quite fond of Mrs Sinclair and Lady Holcott. Darcy was gratified by her contentment and was extremely grateful for the attention the ladies had given to his shy sister. He knew such excellent company was a good introduction for Georgiana and hoped it would continue to boost her emerging confidence before her presentation to society.

He had decided to postpone Georgiana's coming out until the next Season. Darcy knew all the young ladies presented this year would be eclipsed by Lady Jane and Lady Elizabeth's introduction, and he had rather not be distracted in his courtship of Elizabeth by having to oversee his sister's presentation. Georgiana was relieved at the delay, quite willing to cede the attention to her friends. After an invigorating walk, the duo returned indoors to relax before the evening's entertainment.

Darcy escorted his sister to the stairs, so she could return to her rooms, and then walked towards the library. He had little hope Elizabeth would still be there, but he determined it was the best place to begin his search for her. All the guests would be departing on the morrow, and he wanted to spend as much time in her company as possible.

As he approached the doors, he heard her soft laughter and quickened his pace, only to be arrested at the sound of a deep masculine chuckle. He hurriedly entered the room and was troubled to find Elizabeth seated near the fire with Dynham in the chair next to her. They both looked up at his entrance, and Dynham rose to greet Darcy with an almost imperceptible smirk on his lips. Darcy bowed to them both before settling in a chair.

"Did you enjoy your walk with Georgiana?" Elizabeth enquired.

"It was a very fine afternoon for a stroll."

"How wonderful to spend some time with your sister," Dynham began, "though I do not envy you in the slightest. Lady Elizabeth and I have been quite cosy here and have enjoyed the last hour together in a discussion of Shakespeare."

Darcy's glance towards the young man was severe, but it did not dissuade Dynham from teasing him.

"We were discussing the merits of the Bard's comedies."

"Yes, Mr Dynham is quite determined that *The Merry Wives of Windsor* is the most entertaining work, owing to the character of Falstaff, but I cannot agree."

"Come now, the bumbling fool is excessively diverting."

"I admit I find amusement in the caricature, but his comedic worth is so obvious that it is not difficult for even the least discerning person to be diverted."

"You prefer more subtle qualities," Darcy stated knowledgeably, "such as those found in Beatrice and Benedict. I remember that you are quite proficient at quoting *Much Ado About Nothing*. I am glad you were able to see it performed this autumn."

Elizabeth flushed slightly at this reminder of that evening. "Yes, it was most memorable."

"As was your introduction to *mille-feuille* if I remember correctly. I see that particular dessert has made an appearance each evening at Grancourt."

"You are as observant as always."

"As I told you yesterday morning, madam, I have a vested interest in being observant in this matter."

Elizabeth's blush increased. "I know that particular dessert is a Darcy favourite, and as a conscientious hostess—"

"Now, now," Darcy interrupted, "it is my understanding that Duchess Agatha failed to inform you that Georgiana and I had been invited."

"True, sir. I confess I was so impressed with the pastry that it has become a favourite of mine. However, I am fortunate that Grancourt's cook is not only willing to prepare it, but can pronounce it as well."

Darcy laughed heartily at this rejoinder. "Touché! I am gratified you have remembered my preference for the orange variety. You are an extremely conscientious hostess."

Dynham saw fit to interrupt their exchange, steering the conversation to books. He appeared annoyed to be reminded of Darcy and Elizabeth's previous acquaintance, which allowed them to converse on subjects to his exclusion. The trio remained in the library until it was time to change for dinner.

When the guests reconvened, Darcy was delighted to finally find himself seated next to Elizabeth. He turned towards Duchess Agatha, who smiled knowingly in response. Dynham was seated at the opposite end of the table near Jane and Georgiana, furthering Darcy's contentment. The meal progressed pleasurably with engaging discourse.

Once the gentlemen re-joined the ladies, a game of

charades ensued. Jane and Elizabeth made quite a winning team, and it was deemed an unfair advantage for them to remain in the same group, necessitating a change. However, once Darcy and Elizabeth were paired with Georgiana and the young Mr Leventhorpe, the resulting success was even more formidable.

Eventually Lady Bradshawe lamented her continuous losses and pleaded for a change in activity. Mr Dynham suggested some dancing and requested the honour of being Elizabeth's partner. She demurely acquiesced, and Duchess Agatha consented to play the pianoforte. Darcy brought Georgiana to the line, and Mr Leventhorpe partnered Jane, while the Holcotts, Sinclairs, and Bradshawes rounded out the set. The party spent the remainder of the evening in this amusement. The duke asked his wife to stand up, pleasantly surprising his lady.

After the group had danced several sets, Duchess Agatha suggested a waltz. Darcy immediately looked for Elizabeth and made his way to her side, and without uttering a word, they took up a position on the floor. He placed his hand on her delicate waist and secured her fingers within his grasp as the soft strains of the music began.

They moved in graceful accord, their eyes locked on one another. Elizabeth's breathing was rapid, and her eyes were bright as Darcy pulled her closer. Neither was aware of the room's other occupants. It felt as though it was just the two of them with the gentle three-count of the music propelling them.

Darcy ducked his head and quickly brushed his lips across Elizabeth's cheek. His first touch was light, but then he placed a kiss near her ear. He felt her sigh softly, and he tightened his grip on her as he felt her almost falter. He became concerned that he had overstepped, but then he beheld her brilliant smile and was comforted that not only had she not been offended, but a passion had been awakened in her. When the music came to an end, the daze caused by their encounter did not dissipate quickly. For several moments, the couple remained in each other's embrace, until Dynham clapped loudly and commented on his enjoyment of the evening. Duchess Agatha briskly rose from the instrument and declared her intention to retire.

Darcy shook his head as though to dispel a fog. "Elizabeth," he whispered.

She raised her face at the sound of his voice, and he was grateful not to see censure, just embarrassment. Then she squared her shoulders, and displaying that indomitable spirit he cherished in her, she curtseyed.

"Thank you for the dance."

He bowed in response. "It was my pleasure, I assure you, madam."

"Duchess Agatha insisted we learn the waltz. Jane and I were initially anxious, but I love the music and movement."

"I have never enjoyed a waltz more, and I hope to repeat it many times."

The duke interrupted their interlude and suggested everyone retire for the night. Darcy escorted Elizabeth to her sister, and the guests departed for their rooms.

THE NEXT MORNING, THE GUESTS GATHERED FOR A FINAL MEAL before returning to their homes. All declared their great enjoyment of the party and many promises of correspondence were exchanged, as well as anticipation of meeting again in London.

The Darcys were the last to leave, due to the clever machinations of Duchess Agatha. She had remembered a keepsake of Lady Anne Darcy's she had discovered only the previous night, one she wished to return. Elizabeth and Jane remained on the steps with the Darcys as Duchess Agatha withdrew indoors to retrieve the item. Jane and Georgiana began a quiet discussion, leaving Darcy and Elizabeth alone to talk.

"It was a most memorable gathering, Lady Elizabeth."

"I am glad you and Georgiana could join us. It was quite a pleasant surprise to see you enter the drawing room."

Darcy drew closer to her and reached for her hand. He turned them so he was shielding Elizabeth from their sisters' view and enveloped both her small hands within his. He brought their joined hands up to his chest and rested them against his heart.

"Elizabeth, I shall count the days until we meet again in London."

"As will I."

"And every supper dance will be reserved for me?"

"Yes, as long as you remember my conditions."

"You are cruel," he replied, adopting a mock haughty tone. "You know how much I detest such functions, and you are forcing me to be present the entire tedious evening."

"It is a perfect way to show your regard. Surely, it is a small sacrifice to make for my company at dinner."

Her playful remark was met by his serious countenance. "I would sacrifice almost anything to have your exclusive company for eternity."

Before she could respond, Duchess Agatha returned. She had a small drawing of Grancourt that Lady Anne had done during a visit to the estate. As she presented it to Georgiana, Darcy surreptitiously bent forward and pressed his lips gently against Elizabeth's before withdrawing quickly. He turned, said a quick goodbye to Jane and Duchess Agatha, and gathered his sister to enter their carriage.

As the coach drove away from the house, Darcy risked a glance backwards and smiled to see Elizabeth frozen on the steps with her fingers pressed to her lips and a dreamy expression fixed on her lovely face.

CHAPTER 30

The remaining weeks before the Season passed in a flurry of preparations for the Everards. Duchess Agatha provided final instructions on what would be expected of the duchess and her daughters. Jane and Elizabeth became quite confident under her excellent tutelage, and soon the trunks were packed, and the loaded carriages were journeying to London.

They arrived only a fortnight before the planned court presentation, allowing enough time for the final fittings of their gowns. Several members of the *ton* left their cards, but all were refused admittance. Only the Gardiners were allowed entrance. The Darcys, being forewarned during their stay at Grancourt of the family's preference, timed their own arrival for two days prior to the momentous occasion and sent a simple note informing their friends of their safe trip.

Six weeks prior, elegant invitations to a ball in honour of Ladies Jane and Elizabeth had been sent to various acquaintances and associates that Duchess Agatha and the duke had deemed suitable. The receipt of these invitations was the most coveted of the Season. Triumphs or tantrums abounded, depending on whether one had been received. Speculation was rampant. What would they wear? With whom would they dance? Who would they favour?

The Gardiners were a font of information about the wagging tongues of the society matrons, and the family derived great amusement from the antics of the *ton*. The ball was scheduled for the evening following the presentation to the Queen and had evolved into the unofficial start to the year's Season.

On the day of the presentation, the three ladies at Everard House donned their heavy, formal gowns and made their way to St. James's Palace. Many eyes were upon them as they entered and followed the footmen to the gallery where they would wait until the Queen summoned them.

Due to their father's title and their precedence over the other ladies present, their wait was short, and they were the first allowed in the drawing room. Her Grace was amazingly poised as she approached the Queen and the other royalty present in the room. After curtseying and receiving the Queen's kiss to her forehead, she gracefully backed out of the room, her train draped over her arm by one of the lords-in-waiting. Jane and Elizabeth also survived their presentations without any mishap, though Her Majesty lifted each girl's chin and surveyed them before bestowing her kiss and acceptance.

Whispers about the young ladies had apparently reached the Queen's ears. When she later told her attendants she thought they were lovely girls, news spread like wildfire throughout the drawing rooms of London that evening. The expectation for the following night's ball became even more pronounced with the Queen's apparent approbation. The Everards enjoyed a family dinner with the Gardiners that evening, and all retired early in anticipation of the busy day on the morrow.

A BEAUTIFUL MORNING GREETED THE INHABITANTS OF LONDON the following day, an auspicious sign for the residents of Everard House. Preparations for the night's festivities were well in hand, the servants of the house being accustomed to lavish events under Duchess Agatha's auspices. The ballroom and dining hall gleamed, and sumptuous floral arrangements and decorations festooned every nook and cranny. The ladies retired to their rooms in the early afternoon where they enjoyed a time of respite and a light repast before beginning their elaborate preparations.

Jane and Elizabeth relished the calm atmosphere. Accustomed to the frantic bustle of Longbourn on the day of a ball —the search for missing gloves and slippers, the screech of their younger sisters, their mother's agitated nerves—the ease with which the servants of Everard House saw to all the arrangements and the services of their own personal maids were a welcome change. Never had they anticipated an event with such pleasure, not even the ball at Netherfield.

Because she was not yet out and unable to attend the ball, Georgiana had been invited to spend the afternoon with Jane and Elizabeth. They enjoyed several hours in pleasant conversation before Georgiana returned to Darcy House, where her brother unsuccessfully interrogated her about Elizabeth before making his way across Grosvenor Square.

Too soon the time of their guests' arrival was upon them, and the ladies exited their rooms and descended the stairs to greet the entrance of London's elite. The Holcotts, Sinclairs, and Bradshawes were some of the first to alight from their carriages, and the friends greeted each other with warmth and reminisced about their winter party. Darcy entered the house and was arrested by the sight of Elizabeth. She was laughing gaily at something Lady Bradshawe had said, and the sound was like music to his ears. She was dressed in a gown of emerald green, and her hair was swept to one side, with most of the tresses allowed to spill over her shoulder and almost halfway down her back. He manfully restrained a vivid image of what she would look like on her wedding night. Her jewellery was relatively simple, only a thin necklace of emeralds and matching jewelled pins adorning her hair, but her skin glowed and the stones shimmered in the candlelight.

He had paused in his progress to drink in the sight of her when she suddenly turned in his direction and smiled. She unconsciously started towards him, and he met her, greeting her by bowing deeply over her hand and placing a kiss on her gloved fingers.

"You are a vision, Lady Elizabeth."

"Thank you, sir," she responded, her famous wit having seemingly abandoned her.

Despite the fact that Georgiana had refused to reveal anything, she had helped her brother choose his evening clothes and had selected a green waistcoat flecked with gold and silver that perfectly complemented Elizabeth's gown. The continuously arriving guests could not help but admire the stunning couple as they softly conversed, oblivious to the others around them.

"Thank you for inviting Georgiana this afternoon. Spending the day with you and your sister allowed her to feel part of the celebration and alleviated her disappointment."

"I should be thanking you for allowing her to come. Jane and I were a little sad our sisters were not present to share this evening with us, and we were glad to have another female in the house. It was entirely too quiet during our preparations!"

Darcy chuckled at this allusion to Longbourn's more hectic reputation. The noise of the guests soon intruded on their conversation, and Darcy knew he must relinquish her to greet them, but at the risk of breeching propriety, he made a request.

"I have arrived in ample time to secure my supper dance with you." She laughed and nodded. "Is it at all possible to secure another before the evening is over?"

Elizabeth thoughtfully chewed her lower lip, no doubt fully aware of the implications of such a request. "There is a waltz planned for later in the evening."

Darcy's dimples made a rare appearance, and he was exceedingly pleased not only with her acceptance, but with her choice of dance.

"Thank you."

Elizabeth made her way back towards her family to welcome the newest arrivals. She looked back to him and smiled, and his heart soared at the affection he saw in her eyes.

Darcy walked around the room, conversing with friends, but always staying within sight of Elizabeth. He watched with a mixture of pride and jealousy as she was introduced to the gentlemen of the *ton*. Their responses to the Everard ladies were predictable. All were thunderstruck by their beauty and manners. Jane's flaxen, angelic beauty, accentuated by her dress of icy blue silk and jewels of sapphire, stood in direct contrast to Elizabeth's raven locks, but side by side, the sisters were breath-taking.

Darcy stiffened when Dynham approached Elizabeth and requested a dance but was secure in the knowledge that she held him in no particular affection. Darcy's friend Newbury arrived at the same time as the Gardiners and also secured a place on the sisters' dance cards before striding towards Darcy. The friends greeted each other jovially.

"Darcy, did you enjoy Christmas?"

"It was very pleasant. And yours? I imagine it was difficult without your parents."

"True, but I spent the time with my favourite cousins in Kent and had a most enjoyable visit. How are you holding up, old man?"

Darcy looked towards Newbury in confusion. "Holding up?"

"The vultures have descended upon your lady. I was barely able to secure a dance with her or her sister! And they both look entirely ravishing tonight."

Darcy frowned at his friend's statement but could not keep it in place for long. "I always knew the Everards would be a sensation, but I am not worried."

Newbury raised a brow at this declaration. "You are certainly more confident than the last time we discussed this."

Darcy's smile grew as he reflected on the progress he had made with Elizabeth over the last six months. "I have much to be confident about."

"Is that so? Would you care to enlighten me? I may need your advice if your methods are as successful as they appear."

"When have you ever needed advice with the ladies?"

Newbury laughed and left Darcy to greet some other acquaintances.

Darcy looked towards Elizabeth to see Bingley speaking to the sisters. Jane was blushing and Bingley was ebullient. Darcy's smile diminished as he observed the entrance of the Hursts, followed by Caroline Bingley. Their reception was decidedly cool from the residents of Everard House, and Darcy assumed they had been invited only because they were Bingley's closest relations. Bingley barely acknowledged his sister before heading towards Darcy. Caroline looked in his direction, but she abruptly turned away, the memory of Darcy's wrath apparently still fresh in her mind.

Darcy and Bingley shook hands and caught up on the months they had been separated over the winter. Bingley was delighted to have secured the supper dance with Jane, and the friends made plans to sit with one another for the meal.

The majority of the guests had arrived, and the musicians performed a final tuning of their instruments. The Duke of Everard led Lady Jane to the dance floor, Mr Gardiner escorted Lady Elizabeth, and the other couples took their places in the set. Darcy silently applauded the clever way the Everards had devised to open the ball. With the sisters dancing the first with their closest male relations, there was no possibility of anyone being either offended or singled out. The ladies switched partners for the second dance, and the ball was officially underway.

During the evening, Darcy partnered Lady Matlock, Lady Holcott, Mrs Sinclair, and other wives of his married friends. He was resolved to make his intentions perfectly clear to the *ton,* and Elizabeth was his sole intention. Darcy manoeuvred to remain close to Elizabeth during the dances, and he was pleased to meet her several times when partners were switched or they passed each other. She always gifted him with a smile. Darcy had never enjoyed himself more at a London ball, and he gave all the credit to Elizabeth and his knowledge of her growing affection for him.

At last it was time for the supper dance, and Darcy, having momentarily lost sight of Elizabeth, began scanning the room for her. He finally caught sight of her conversing with Mrs Gardiner and her mother. Her Grace looked quite handsome, and the company of Duchess Agatha had affected a great improvement in her demeanour, but Darcy was almost immediately entranced again by Elizabeth as she started to make her way towards him. He bowed to her and gathered her arm close to his side to escort her to the floor. The musicians struck the opening chords and their dance began.

ELIZABETH DANCED EVERY SET BUT, ALTHOUGH SHE HAD BEEN introduced to many amiable gentlemen, her thoughts and her eyes never strayed too far from Darcy. She was flattered to notice his continual attention to her, for every time she looked in his direction, his eyes were trained upon her and he smiled. She had been greatly anticipating their dance and some uninterrupted time in his company.

Realising she had not yet spoken to her partner, Elizabeth cleared her head of her ruminations. "Come, Mr Darcy, we must have some conversation."

He laughed softly. "I remember you prefer to talk while dancing, and I assume books are still a banned subject in a ballroom."

"Yes, I can never discuss books while dancing. My mind is

too preoccupied to give the subject its deserved attention. We are supposed to limit ourselves to more conventional subjects. I shall comment that the evening appears to be a great success, as many people have decided to attend."

"You are too modest. I am sure you know perfectly well that no one would have refused an invitation to this particular ball. You and your sister are all the rage of London."

"You give us too much credit."

"Not at all. I have not been to a ball at Everard House in several years, but Duchess Agatha always hosted a splendid evening. Nothing has changed with the addition of your family."

"The servants prepared everything seamlessly. I found I had not much to do other than select my gown."

"Then you performed your task admirably. That shade of emerald suits you beautifully. I have never seen your hair in that fashion."

Elizabeth had been reluctant when Carter suggested the more daring style, but she had eventually yielded after Jane and Georgiana's entreaties.

Darcy surreptitiously smoothed his hand down the length of her unbound hair. He leaned in close and whispered, "You are entrancing, Elizabeth."

His words and actions, spoken and displayed so tenderly, were almost too much for Elizabeth, and the rest of their dance passed in silence, the intensity of their looks saying what no words could.

As the music came to an end, Darcy took Elizabeth's hand, tucked it into the crook of his arm, and led her towards the dining room.

They quickly located Jane and Bingley and sat down to enjoy the supper that Everard House's kitchens had been preparing for nigh on a week. Talk in the room was gay and cheerful. The guests all exclaimed at the beautiful decorations, the superb meal, and the delightful dancing, but the topic most discussed were the undeniably lovely and charming Everard sisters.

CHAPTER 31

Not a single person, no matter how much they wished, could find anything unfavourable to report about the Ladies Jane and Elizabeth. They were beautiful and gracious, kind and artless. They paid sincere attention to the young ladies of the *ton* and their mothers, so they quickly found themselves desirous of forming friendships with the sisters. The gentlemen were enamoured, and although they had only praise for Jane and Elizabeth, the same could not be said for Darcy and Bingley. The fact that the two young men had a previous acquaintance with the sisters, and now had the enviable position as their dinner companions, created a stir of jealousy, but not all the gentlemen were deterred by the obvious intimacy between the friends.

One gentleman in particular acutely observed Darcy and his female companion. Marcus Carlyle, Earl of Dunmore, had arrived from his estate in Scotland to enjoy another Season in

London. He was an exceptionally handsome man, with midnight black, silky hair, a dark olive complexion, and piercing blue eyes. He had an estate, Dunmore Castle, in County Stirling, and derived a handsome income of eight thousand a year from coal and iron mining on his family's vast parcel of land. His mother was a cousin of Duchess Agatha, which accounted for his invitation to the ball. However, had that lady known more about him, she likely would have never supplied it.

Dunmore had attended Cambridge at the same time as Darcy, but they had never befriended one another due to their disparate characters. Darcy's decency was at direct contrast to Dunmore's rowdy and dissolute habits. They had been in fierce competition for many academic awards and achievements, in which Darcy generally triumphed. This fuelled Dunmore's extreme dislike for the young man he considered a prude and bore. In order to spite his rival, he had even sought out Darcy's childhood friend Wickham and had contributed to that man's debauchery.

Dunmore's dislike had only strengthened over the intervening years as Darcy had become one of the most eligible bachelors of the *ton* but continued in his haughty and superior manner, in Dunmore's opinion. There was certainly no love lost between these two men, and Dunmore had been watching Darcy throughout the evening, quickly deducing the man's infatuation with the younger Everard sister.

Dunmore had spent the last several Seasons enjoying the delights of London without any thought of his own matrimonial prospects. However, this year he had decided that he should find a wife and start producing his heirs. Scotland was a long way from what he considered decent society, and he was desirous to have a woman to warm his lonely bed. He was not particularly interested in companionship—that was what mistresses were for—but he knew his duty was to perpetuate his family's name and noble reputation. A woman of Lady Elizabeth's pedigree and wealth—and comely body—was perfect for his wife.

And if it foils Dreary Darcy, all the better.

He began to form a plan and looked forward to the dance he had claimed with the lady directly following supper.

DARCY AND ELIZABETH WERE COMPLETELY UNAWARE OF THE malevolent machinations that were brewing and had immensely enjoyed their meal, though they had begun to garner whispers about their close friendship.

Soon the young ladies in attendance were called upon to perform for the assembled company. Lady Holcott and Mrs Sinclair played an excellent duet, and Elizabeth followed them. She entertained the room with a few short but lively airs, further entrancing the guests with her cheerful manner. A few other young ladies displayed their accomplishments on the pianoforte before the crowd made their way back into the ballroom just as the musicians were again tuning their instruments.

Darcy had not left Elizabeth's side and was attempting to hide his disappointment that she would soon be called away to dance with other gentlemen, but he consoled himself with her promise to waltz with him later. Her next dancing partner arrived to claim her hand, and Darcy's happy demeanour immediately turned suspicious and angry.

Dunmore bowed courteously. "Lady Elizabeth, I believe your next dance is promised to me."

Elizabeth took Lord Dunmore's proffered hand. She turned

to Darcy to excuse herself and appeared taken aback by the expression on his countenance.

"Thank you for your company during dinner, Mr Darcy, and I look forward to our dance later."

The sound of Elizabeth's voice returned him to his senses, and Darcy smiled at her. "The pleasure was mine, I assure you."

He bowed to her and watched with increasing distress as Dunmore led her to the floor. Darcy had not forgotten Lord Dunmore and his degenerate behaviour at university. He was aware of the rumours that circulated about the man, regarding his conquests of the newly married ladies of the *ton*. In fact, Darcy had recently heard a rumour involving Lady Amherst, who everyone knew did not love her husband. Darcy had attempted to caution his cousin Amherst, who waved away the warning but proceeded to drink and gamble throughout the night to avoid returning home to his loveless marriage and cold wife.

Darcy's agony at seeing his Elizabeth in the arms of that rogue was acute, and he was grateful he had not promised a dance to anyone so as to keep a close eye on Lord Dunmore. Elizabeth did not appear anxious, which only somewhat alleviated Darcy's unease.

Darcy was extremely relieved when the music ended, and Lord Newbury approached Elizabeth to claim the next set. Newbury, also privy to Dunmore's unsavoury reputation, caught Darcy's eye, and led Elizabeth to the line. Darcy did not immediately discontinue his vigilance of Lord Dunmore until he watched him take his leave of Duchess Agatha and depart from Everard House.

He was surprised at his sudden retreat and resolved to immediately question Duchess Agatha. He quickly made his way across the room, glancing repeatedly towards Elizabeth as she danced with Newbury, more and more grateful for such a perceptive friend and the providential timing of their set.

"May I have a word?" Darcy enquired once he had finally reached Duchess Agatha's side. She appeared startled by the serious expression on Darcy's face and quickly agreed, stepping towards a small alcove where they could have privacy.

"Are you enjoying yourself? I saw that you and Bingley were the lucky men to sit with the belles of the ball during supper."

"It has been, overall, a splendid evening."

"Overall, but not *everything* is to your satisfaction?"

"I have concerns about some of the guests."

Duchess Agatha smirked. "I am sure I have invited far too many single gentlemen for your taste, but Elizabeth must dance with them. She cannot dance only with you, no matter how much you might wish it."

Darcy quickly understood Duchess Agatha's wrong assumption. He shook his head to stop her teasing. "That is not it at all. I know my dances with Lady Elizabeth will of necessity be restricted, and I want her to enjoy herself, but she was just dancing with Lord Dunmore, and I cannot understand why he was invited."

Duchess Agatha appeared confused. "He is my cousin's son."

"Have you spent much time with him?"

"No, their estate is in Scotland, and I only saw Josephine half a dozen times after her marriage. I had never met her son until this evening, but I could not exclude him from the guest list. He is a relation."

"He is not the proper sort of company for your Everard cousins, and in fact, he could be a danger to them."

"You surprise me, Darcy. What do you know of him?"

Darcy was reluctant to admit such sordid details to a lady but felt a duty to tell Duchess Agatha what she wished to know. "We were at Cambridge together. He associated with an immoral crowd, and I know that his current behaviour is no better. In fact, it is rumoured to be much worse."

Darcy gave as brief a summary as he deemed acceptable. After finishing, he fervently whispered, "I cannot abide Elizabeth being anywhere near him! Dunmore cannot be trusted."

"I know you to be an honest person, and I assume you are not exaggerating or simply jealous of the man's attentions towards Elizabeth. You must be truly worried for her safety. I shall warn the girls."

"And the duke."

She nodded her agreement. "I have the matter well in hand. Now, go and enjoy the rest of the evening."

Darcy swiftly left Duchess Agatha to find his partner.

ELIZABETH WAS BEING LED AWAY FROM THE FLOOR BY Colonel Fitzwilliam and was pleased to see Darcy walking towards them. She had been concerned by his dark humour prior to her dance with Lord Dunmore and had not failed to notice his intense scrutiny while they danced.

She found Lord Dunmore to be an attractive and amusing partner, but he could not compare to Darcy, though she was curious about Darcy's unusual reaction to the man. She was further disconcerted when she could no longer locate him during her set with Lord Newbury, only to discover him in earnest conversation with Duchess Agatha. Her relief was palpable to see his familiar form crossing the room to claim her hand for the waltz. Darcy's former good humour appeared to be restored as he smiled widely at her.

"I hope the good colonel has not injured your feet."

Colonel Fitzwilliam affected an offended mien, and Elizabeth laughed at their silly antics. "Your cousin is a fine dancer, and my feet are quite unharmed, Mr Darcy."

"That is excellent news, for you have promised me the next dance, and I would be heartbroken to have missed it on account of my cousin's clumsiness."

"Now see here," Colonel Fitzwilliam protested, "I have kept Lady Elizabeth in good order and in perfect health. If you are not careful, I shall be forced to relate the incident of your first dancing lesson, and your reputation will not emerge from the telling unscathed."

"Then I shall make a hasty retreat before you can begin."

He whisked a laughing Elizabeth onto the dance floor and into his arms. He pulled her close, and the tension he had been feeling over the last hour immediately dissipated.

"You seem to have recovered your good spirits, sir."

"I must talk with you about Lord Dunmore, but for now I just want to hold you, Elizabeth."

Her breath caught at the tenderness in his look and voice, and she readily acquiesced. She let the three-count melody and the nearness of Darcy envelop her senses and gave in to the moment.

There were fewer couples on the floor, given the somewhat controversial nature of the waltz, and Darcy swirled and twirled Elizabeth around the room, both completely intoxicated with one another and oblivious to the other occupants.

There was little doubt in anyone's mind that an understanding between Darcy and Lady Elizabeth was well underway. There was no mistaking the couple's enchantment with each other. Indiscreet whispers circulated through the assembled guests, and there was more than one matron that declared the couple's actions scandalous.

ALTHOUGH THERE WERE MANY LADIES WITH DISAPPOINTED hopes, Lady Amherst's surpassed them all. As the new daughter of Lady Matlock, she had no choice but to attend the ball. Lady Matlock's close friendship with Duchess Agatha had ensured the entire family of an invitation, and Lady Amherst could not risk her mother-in-law's disapprobation, especially not when she hoped to continue her assignation with a certain Scottish lord.

If Lady Matlock's ire was raised, Lady Amherst's activities would be subject to closer scrutiny and most likely curtailed, and that would make it difficult, if not completely impossible, to meet with Lord Dunmore. He was infinitely more handsome and dashing than her husband, and Frederica had no intention of giving up their affair—not even when she noticed him dancing with that annoying Lady Elizabeth. She had been upset to see him leave immediately following their dance—and without having asked her for a set—but Frederica consoled herself with their plan to meet the following afternoon and settled in to seethe over Darcy's continued attentions to the chit.

He is making a fool of himself over her!

ELIZABETH FELT WONDERFULLY LIGHT-HEADED AS THEY SPUN, and unconsciously clutched Darcy's hand more tightly. He pulled her closer and leaned down to whisper in her ear.

"I must extract another promise from you, Elizabeth."

She was unable to respond, so captivated was she by the soft exhale of his breath against her neck.

He noticed her distraction and whispered again. "You must promise never to waltz with anyone but me."

At that moment, she could not imagine wanting to dance any dance with anyone else ever again and easily surrendered to his demand. "Yes."

"Yes, you promise?"

"I promise."

"Thank you, my love."

She inhaled sharply at the endearment, and Darcy almost missed a step as he realised what he had just said. He looked at her apprehensively but found her smiling at him.

The music ended, and Darcy quickly led Elizabeth through one of the open doors to the softly lit terrace. He guided her towards a corner, and using his body to block her from the view of those in the ballroom, he took both her hands and placed them over his heart.

"Elizabeth, I love you. I have loved you for a very long time. Too long for me even to remember when it began, but my love has only grown and strengthened over time. I know I have hurt you in the past, but I hope and pray that my actions since have proved to you that I have changed, that I am now deserving of you. I shall endeavour throughout my life to make you happy, to please you, to care for you."

She could not let him go on uninterrupted. "You have not changed in essentials, and for that I am grateful. You are the best man of my acquaintance."

"You are too forgiving. I would not be the man I am today without your influence. Elizabeth, I know that it is early in the Season—it is the *beginning*—but I must know if you will be waiting for me at the end of it. As difficult as it will be for me to watch other men vie for your attention and your smiles, I can withstand it as long as I know I have your heart."

"I do not need an entire Season."

"No, you are a woman worthy of being pleased, and I made such a disaster of my first proposal to you, I would never forgive myself if I deprived you of a proper one this time."

Elizabeth knew her heart, and it belonged to Fitzwilliam Darcy, but she would not deny him this demand when he was so earnest.

"Do not keep me waiting too long. I was never good at being patient."

He laughed deeply and gathered her into his arms. "I promise I shall not keep you waiting longer than you will be able to bear. May I call tomorrow?"

"Of course."

"Splendid! Then I suppose we had better return to the ball-room. I am certain some poor gentleman will be distraught to have missed his opportunity to dance with you."

Elizabeth giggled and allowed Darcy to guide her back inside. Fortunately, she had only missed her dance with Mr Bingley, who was more than understanding, even giving his friend a knowing smirk before granting his forgiveness to the errant couple.

Only a few more sets remained before the guests made their sleepy way home. Darcy and Bingley departed with the Gardiners and were the last people to take their leave.

Darcy quickly kissed Elizabeth's gloved hand before he turned into the night and strolled across Grosvenor Square to his townhouse, already anticipating his call on the morrow.

CHAPTER 32

Darcy and Georgiana called the next afternoon at Everard House and were received enthusiastically by the female inhabitants, the duke having left for his club earlier in the day. Georgiana was extremely curious about the ball, and Darcy indulgently listened to the minute dissection of the previous evening's festivities. Jane and Elizabeth were forced to give an exact report of the fashions, the music and performances, and all their dancing partners.

When Elizabeth recounted her dance with Lord Dunmore, Darcy could not repress his frown and Elizabeth quickly assured him that Lady Agatha had warned them of the Scotsman's dissolute reputation. The ladies promised to be on their guard when in Lord Dunmore's presence. When the duke arrived home, he invited Darcy into his study and asked for a more thorough account. He then promised to be particularly vigilant regarding Lord Dunmore. The

Darcys soon departed for their home, happy to know they would meet with their friends often over the upcoming weeks.

THE SEASON WAS IN FULL SWING. PARTIES, BALLS, SOIRÉES, musical evenings, plays, concerts, and dinners occurred most nights of the week. Days were filled with receiving and returning calls, shopping, walks and carriage rides in Hyde Park, visits to museums and gardens, picnics, and other activities. Elizabeth was pleasantly surprised to find herself thoroughly enjoying the merriment, particularly when a certain handsome Derbyshire gentleman was present, as he was at almost every occasion.

The other members of the *ton* could not mistake the romances that were occurring between the Everard sisters and the male residents of Darcy House. Although Lady Jane and Bingley's involvement was more understated, no other gentleman tried to win her heart for longer than a week once he had seen Lady Jane smile at the tradesman's son as they danced together.

The romance between Elizabeth and Darcy was completely incontestable. It was quickly apparent she reserved every supper dance and waltz for him. Once, when Darcy had been unable to attend a ball, Elizabeth sat out the remaining sets, rather than accept an offer to dance the waltz with another man. Darcy had been elated when Colonel Fitzwilliam had related the news.

As he and Elizabeth walked in Hyde Park the following afternoon, the path curved and momentarily shielded them from the view of their group. Darcy delivered a quick kiss to Elizabeth's cheek, and when she questioned him about his impetuous display, he simply began to hum a three-count melody.

Things were progressing quite agreeably for the couples, and Darcy's family in particular was relentless in their hints for him to secure the lady before she was won by another, but he, confident in Elizabeth's feelings, laughed off their jests. Though, six weeks into the Season, Darcy was beginning to become somewhat impatient.

One evening, London's women had been invited to a musical entertainment at a notable widow's house, and the gentlemen were left to shift for themselves. Darcy and Bingley had been invited to spend the evening at Kenton House. After a hearty meal, Lord Matlock, his sons, Darcy, Bingley, and Lord Newbury repaired to the billiards room. The earl retired early, declaring his old age made him unfit to compete with youth, and he left the other men to their brandy. They imbibed frequently in the libation over the next few hours and were all quite in their cups. Bingley was sprawled in a chair, his snoring reminiscent of his brother Hurst. The remaining four gentlemen had settled comfortably in armchairs and were regaling each other with antics from their childhood. Talk soon turned to the current Season.

"So, Darcy," began Colonel Fitzwilliam, "when are you going to propose?"

"Soon."

"Come, man," chimed in Newbury. "Do you not think that you have dawdled long enough?"

"I have resolved to give Lady Elizabeth time to enjoy the Season."

"Perhaps he has finally seen the wisdom in avoiding marriage," Amherst cynically commented. His three companions looked towards him in sympathy.

"Brother," said the colonel, "Darcy is not destined for your unhappiness. You chose poorly, as you well know. You made your bed, and now you must sleep in it."

"Oh, I *do* sleep in it—quite alone."

"I am sorry, Amherst," replied Darcy, truly distressed for his cousin's melancholy.

"I envy you, Darcy. Lady Elizabeth is beautiful and charming, wealthy, connected—and even more important, she appears to hold affection for you."

The liquor having loosened his tongue, Darcy replied more honestly than he otherwise would have. "She loves me," he whispered.

"She has told you so?" enquired Newbury.

Darcy recovered his senses. "No, she has not declared she loves me, but I know it all the same."

"Then you are fortunate indeed," Colonel Fitzwilliam said.

"You have it all, do you, Darcy?" retorted Amherst, his bitterness seeping through every word. He abruptly rose from his chair and stormed from the room.

Colonel Fitzwilliam sighed deeply. "He is absolutely miserable. And how could he not be with such a wife?" The other gentlemen nodded. "I envy you too. You have won the heart of a good and lovely woman. You will be infinitely happier in your marriage than my poor brother. If only you can gather the courage to ask her."

"I hardly lack courage."

"Then what are you waiting for?" Newbury asked.

"A moment alone!" The colonel and Newbury laughed heartily. "She is always surrounded by friends and family. If I could get her away for even a moment, I would drop to my knee and make her an offer!"

Colonel Fitzwilliam's amusement increased with Darcy's display of emotion.

"It is not funny, Richard."

"You are wrong. It is extremely funny. With all your wealth and prestige, you cannot find a way to get your lady alone to propose to her. Newbury and I would have no such difficulties."

"Pray do not bring me into this, Fitzwilliam," Newbury replied.

Darcy frowned at his cousin. "It is not as easy as you think."

"Then let us form a plan. You know her habits better than anyone. When are there fewer people around her?"

Darcy pondered this and reviewed everything he knew about Elizabeth. "She used to walk almost daily in Hyde Park before others had awakened, but the busyness of the Season has precluded that habit. Now she is always in company with someone—her aunt, her sister, Duchess Agatha. It is completely provoking!"

"Could you persuade her to reinstate her former habit, even if just for a morning?"

Darcy thought and began to form a resolution. "Yes, that could certainly be possible. I shall ask her to meet me this Friday morning. Thursday evening's plans are for a family dinner, so they will not keep late hours. That will be perfect. Thank you, Richard."

"Not at all. And if that fails, you can always just ask her father to speak with her."

Darcy frowned. "But that is so unromantic."

Both the colonel and Lord Newbury laughed loudly at this uncharacteristic response. Neither man had ever considered Darcy a romantic.

Their laughter was too loud for the gentlemen to hear the rustle of skirts as Lady Amherst rushed away from the door that had been left ajar by her husband's hasty retreat. She quickly ascended the stairs, penned a note, and sent her trusted maid to Lord Dunmore's home.

THE DINNER SET FOR THURSDAY EVENING WAS IN HONOUR OF the duke's birthday, and as such, only family had been invited. Knowing he would not see Elizabeth that day, Darcy's need to speak to her privately before then and arrange a walk Friday morning became paramount.

A ball on Wednesday presented the perfect opportunity, and Darcy took advantage of her promise of a waltz. As they danced around the room in each other's arms, the envy of most of the guests, Darcy procured Elizabeth's agreement to walk in Hyde Park early Friday morning before the other inhabitants of Everard House awoke.

She reminded him that Thomas would be required to accompany her, to which he immediately concurred. Her safety was of the utmost importance to him. Thomas was discreet and would allow Darcy the necessary privacy to ask Elizabeth to marry him. The wait until Friday would be interminable, but Darcy was confident that their mutual happiness would soon be secured. He pulled Elizabeth close to him as they swirled to the music and silently rehearsed the words he would use to declare his love to the woman who held his heart.

THURSDAY'S GATHERING WOULD BE UNEVENTFUL AS THE DUKE required little fuss to celebrate his birth.

Elizabeth, not being needed for any of the preparations for

her father's birthday dinner, decided to walk in Hyde Park. She needed some time alone to reflect. She entered the park near Grosvenor Square, followed unobtrusively by Thomas, and quickly struck a route west towards the Serpentine.

The afternoon was fair and perfect for contemplation. She cast her mind upon all her previous interactions with Mr Darcy and amused herself with the evolution of their relationship—from their wretched beginning to their subsequent understanding. She was excited and nervous about their talk the next morning. She was certain Mr Darcy intended to propose marriage to her.

Elizabeth thought back to his previous proposal and lightly blushed with mortification to remember her cruel remarks in response to him. She was grateful he had not allowed her rudeness to overcome his good opinion of her. In fact, he had used her angry words to correct and change flaws in his character. Elizabeth was certain she did not know a better man in all of England and was eagerly anticipating their encounter when she could finally declare her love for him.

She rambled along the footpath for over an hour and eventually wandered south along the Serpentine, watching the young children float boats in the water. She had reached the southeast corner of the park when she noticed the sky was rapidly becoming overcast. Catching Thomas's eye, Elizabeth turned to wend her way back home. She decided on a more direct path towards Grosvenor Gate and quickened her pace as a brisk wind began to blow. Large raindrops started to fall, and she and Thomas were practically running, hoping to reach home before the deluge began in earnest.

As she was passing near Stanhope Gate, only slightly south of her destination, Elizabeth heard her name called. She turned and saw Lord Dunmore striding towards her with an umbrella. He stopped when he neared her and angled the umbrella to protect her from the brunt of the rainfall.

"Lady Elizabeth, are you in need of assistance?"

Remembering the warnings regarding the young earl, Elizabeth was anxious to leave his company. "No thank you, sir. I am not far from home."

She turned to leave, but Dunmore halted her progress by grasping her upper arm. "My lady, it is pouring rain, and you cannot possibly reach Everard House without becoming soaked to the skin." His gaze swept up and down her body with this statement.

Elizabeth's alarm increased, and she attempted to free her arm from the earl's grip, but he tightened his hold, almost to the point of causing pain. "Please release me, Lord Dunmore."

"It would be ungentlemanly of me to allow you to continue unaccompanied in such inclement weather."

"I am not unaccompanied, as you see," Elizabeth responded, gesturing to Thomas who by this time had taken a protective stance close behind Elizabeth. "Thomas is more than capable of seeing me safely home."

"Sir, I shall ask you only once to release her ladyship." Thomas interrupted while placing his hand upon the club on his hip.

Dunmore laughed darkly. "But I do not intend to accompany you to your house, Elizabeth. Let us find somewhere less wet to have a little discussion."

"I will not go anywhere with you!"

Dunmore only chuckled in reply and pulled harder on Elizabeth's arm. Thomas started forward, but to Elizabeth's utter astonishment, he toppled to the ground in a heap. She looked up and saw another man wielding a club who had just struck Thomas on the head to prevent his interference.

"Just in time, Archer," called Dunmore. "Pull him off the path and deposit his body where it cannot be seen. I shall take her to the carriage."

Elizabeth panicked. Her protector had been disabled, the extent of his injury unknown, and she was now quite alone with a known rake and completely at his mercy.

"Come, Lady Elizabeth, we shall get you out of this rain."

She could not fight him and could see no immediate escape. She had no choice but to comply. Keeping a tight grip upon her arm, Dunmore directed her out of the park and towards his awaiting carriage.

Elizabeth looked around, hoping to see a familiar face, but the weather had forced everyone indoors and the street was deserted. She reluctantly entered the carriage and sat in the far corner of the seat. Dunmore laughed at her and sat down directly opposite, purposefully brushing his knees against hers as the carriage moved forward. The shades were drawn down tight, affording Elizabeth no glimpse of their route or destination. They drove for half an hour before the conveyance halted.

The door was opened by a footman, and Dunmore exited and offered his hand. Elizabeth ignored it and descended without aid. She found herself at the back of an unfamiliar house, and though she had attempted to keep track of the turns along the way, she surmised they had taken a circuitous route in order to confuse her. They had certainly succeeded, for she had no idea of her current whereabouts.

No one knows where I am! she thought in horror. *What will become of me? How can I escape?* Her mind raced, each thought more terrifying than the one before it.

Lord Dunmore grabbed her arm again and directed her into the kitchen, where he put her in the care of an elderly woman named Mrs Crockett. The woman led Elizabeth up the back stairs, down a long hallway, to a bedroom where she laid out a dress and offered to help Elizabeth change out of her wet clothing. The dress was simple and a little too big, but Elizabeth was grateful to remove her sodden garments. Mrs Crockett then lit a fire and left to prepare some tea, taking Elizabeth's dripping gown downstairs to dry and closing the door behind her.

Elizabeth surveyed her surroundings, her prison. The room was large and well-appointed, the wealth of the owner apparent. She had noted cloths draped over the furniture in the hallway and the hushed atmosphere, implying that the house was currently unoccupied. She assumed Lord Dunmore had not taken her to his own residence—it being the most obvious place to search if poor Thomas recovered and was able to report their encounter in the park.

She was trapped, and as the wretchedness of her situation overcame her, Elizabeth finally succumbed to weeping. A constant refrain resounded in her mind, giving her the only hope she could muster in such miserable circumstances.

Fitzwilliam, you must find me!

CHAPTER 33

Darcy spent Thursday morning occupied with estate and business matters. The busy Season—and Elizabeth— had taken most of his time recently, which he did not in the least repine, but being the diligent and dutiful master of Pemberley, he could not neglect it for long. Signing the final correspondence with an unusual flourish, he stood, stretched his shoulders to relieve the ache, and left his study.

The day grew gloomy as a rainstorm unleashed a torrent upon London, but Darcy was comfortable and completely at ease with a cheery fire, a glass of brandy, an unattended volume of some historic significance, and endless pleasant thoughts of Elizabeth. He was too preoccupied with thoughts of her and his imminent proposal to pay much attention to the highly acclaimed tome abandoned on the arm of his chair.

His mind lit upon and quickly discarded phrases of varying eloquence and expression that he could use, but he eventually decided to open himself to inspiration during the moment. It was an uncharacteristic choice but the most appealing, as it would allow him to respond to Elizabeth's words and actions. He would let her guide the conversation. The only words he absolutely had to say were, "I love you," and "Will you marry me?"

He smiled at the simplicity this thought implied, knowing well how complex its execution would most likely be. *Everything with Elizabeth is more complicated, which is one of the many reasons I love her!*

He chuckled and picked up his book to devote his attention to the description of a war won long ago, but his mind soon wandered. It was brought back to the present with the discernment of some commotion coming from his front hall.

Darcy rose and quickly made his way there to discover the source of the noise. He was astonished to see that Mr Gardiner and Lord Newbury had just arrived, their greatcoats drenched by the downpour.

"Mr Gardiner, I am surprised to see you here. Are you on your way to Everard House for dinner?"

The men exchanged glances and turned their faces towards Darcy, who instantly recognised their seriousness and knew that something was terribly wrong.

"No, Darcy," Newbury replied, "we are just come from there."

"Something is amiss. Is it Lady Elizabeth?"

Mr Gardiner frowned. "Have you seen her today? Did she perhaps come to spend some time with your sister this afternoon?"

"No, Georgiana has been at Kenton House all day and is engaged to stay through the evening." Darcy glanced between the two men and did not fail to notice their looks of disappointment and concern. "Why do you ask? What has happened?"

"May we sit?"

"Of course. I apologise. Follow me." He swiftly led them to his study and had barely allowed them to sit down before resuming his questioning. "What has happened to Elizabeth?"

"She appears to be missing," answered Newbury.

"Appears? She is either missing or she is not. Which is it?"

"She is missing, Darcy," confirmed Mr Gardiner. "She left for a walk in Hyde Park in the early afternoon accompanied by Thomas. Neither has returned home. Duchess Agatha had been looking for her, and when she discovered she had not come back from her walk, especially considering the dreadful weather, she became worried and informed the duke. He summoned me immediately upon realising she had been gone for so long, and we had hoped she had called at a friend's house and had then become trapped by the rain. You and your sister were the first to come to mind, so I am sorry to find she has not been here."

Darcy sat immobile as he contemplated the ramifications of Mr Gardiner's disclosure. "Do you mean to tell me Elizabeth has been gone for several hours, and no one knows where she is?"

"It appears so, yes."

"And what has been done to recover her? What have you attempted?"

"As I said, yours is the first house we have visited, hoping to find her. I learned of this only half an hour ago. Do you know of anyone else she could have called upon that would have been close enough for her to visit?"

Darcy thought of the inhabitants of the streets and squares within Elizabeth's usual walks. "Both the Holcotts and the

Sinclairs live quite close, but I can think of no other particular friends in the vicinity."

"Thank you. We shall try there next."

The gentlemen rose and returned to the front hall. The butler went to retrieve the gentlemen's coats, and Darcy called for his as well. Mr Gardiner gave him a questioning look.

"You cannot believe I will sit idly at home while the woman I love is missing. I could not abide it!"

Darcy instructed his butler to inform Bingley of his departure and implored Haskins to send Bingley to Everard House if he did not arrive home too late from his dinner engagement.

The group then made their way to Newbury's awaiting carriage. He had been spending the afternoon in Gracechurch Street with his godfather and was present when the note from the duke arrived, requesting help in searching for Elizabeth, and he offered his services.

Their calls upon the Holcotts and Sinclairs met with negative results. Elizabeth had not been seen by the inhabitants of either house. The three men returned to the carriage and decided to call upon the Matlocks before returning to Everard House to discuss further plans. Martin, butler of Kenton House, opened the door to three soggy and sombre men.

Darcy asked him not to inform the family of his presence but enquired whether Colonel Fitzwilliam was at home. When informed that the colonel was currently in the music room with the rest of the family, Darcy requested he be summoned as discreetly as possible. Martin left to retrieve the colonel, who appeared only moments later.

Fitzwilliam was surprised to see the trio that awaited him, for Martin had informed him he was required for an army matter. "Darcy, what do you do here?"

"I pretended to an army matter as I did not want to raise any questions from your parents or Georgiana."

"You look quite serious. What is wrong?"

"Is Lady Elizabeth here?"

"No, she is not. Why do you ask?"

The three visitors sighed in disappointment but were not surprised. The visit to Kenton House had been a last resort.

"Elizabeth is missing. She has been missing for several hours." Darcy related the details they knew and what actions they had undertaken. "If she is not here, then we can only assume that something befell her in the park."

"What do you know about this Thomas?"

"He is one of Duchess Agatha's most trusted servants and has been accompanying Elizabeth on all her walks. We have no reason to suspect him of anything."

Fitzwilliam nodded in acknowledgement. "We must quickly start canvassing the park, before we lose any more light."

"Will you help us?"

"Of course, and we can enlist the aid of my fellow officers. They will be discreet. I am certain of it. Let me pen a quick note and send it to the barracks. They can meet us at Hyde Park."

"Tell them to meet at Grosvenor Gate in thirty minutes."

Colonel Fitzwilliam walked away but returned quickly, his coat and hat already in place and followed by a servant who would dispatch the note. The group climbed into Newbury's carriage, and within minutes, they disembarked at Everard House.

They found the family in the striped parlour. Mrs Gardiner had retired with the duchess, who was too inconsolable to meet with any company. Jane sat on a sofa with Duchess

Agatha, unceasing tears streaming down both women's faces. The duke stood rigidly by the window, looking out into the growing darkness. He did not even turn when the other gentlemen entered the room.

"Elizabeth was not at any of her friends' homes." Mr Gardiner addressed his brother-in-law, who still refused to turn away from the window. "Colonel Fitzwilliam has recruited the help of his soldiers to assist us in searching the park. They will be meeting us soon. We will find her."

The duke remained motionless for a moment, then turned from the window. The look of devastation upon his visage was almost unbearable to behold. He began to falter, but Darcy ran to him and caught him just before he dropped to the floor. He brought the duke to a nearby chair and gently sat him upon it. He fell forward, his hands clutching his head, and broke into wracking sobs.

The duke's collapse ignited Darcy. He knelt on the floor near his chair. "Your Grace," Darcy began, but upon receiving no response, changed his address. "Bennet."

The duke slowly raised his head.

"I will find her. I will find Elizabeth. No matter how far I must travel, no matter what I have to do or expend, I will find her." He held the duke's gaze.

"Thank you, son." He gripped Darcy's shoulder in a fierce grasp, and Darcy felt honoured and fortified by the duke's trust.

"We must leave, and you must attend to your family. The ladies are beside themselves with worry and will look to you."

The duke struggled to his feet and sat beside Jane, taking her into his arms. "Do not cry, my dear. Lizzy will be found. She likely tricked poor Thomas into one of her adventures, and they will come through the door laughing and sopping. We shall give her a thorough scolding for worrying us."

Jane attempted to smile at this nonsense but was still too distressed by her beloved sister's disappearance.

"Come, my love, Darcy has promised to find her."

Jane turned towards Darcy. She wiped the tears from her face and rose from the couch with her hands outstretched. Darcy met her halfway, and taking both her hands in his, bowed over them.

"Thank you, Mr Darcy. I know you shall do all in your power to return Lizzy to us."

Darcy released her hands. "We must not delay. The officers will be waiting for us. We shall send you word as soon as we have news."

Darcy left the room and quickly exited the house. He had been holding his emotions in check and knew they were close to overpowering him. The cool air outside was a relief, and he took in several deep breaths, repressing the tears that threatened to fall from his eyes. *I cannot afford to break down now. Elizabeth needs me to be calm and focused.*

He drew upon all his reserves of strength, and when the rest of the men joined him, his usual composure was in place. Newbury had remembered to bring Darcy's coat and hat and gave them to his friend, eyeing Darcy's emotional state. Darcy acknowledged his friend's silent assessment by a quick nod of his head, and Newbury slapped him on the back, directing him into the carriage, which instantly set off for Hyde Park.

The soldiers were already gathered at Grosvenor Gate when Darcy's group arrived. Colonel Fitzwilliam quickly took charge and divided the men into search parties. Armed with lanterns and whistles, the men spread out to hunt for the missing. The storm had abated, but a light and steady drizzle still fell, and the persistent clouds would bring nightfall early.

Darcy knew of Elizabeth's affinity for the path along the Serpentine and had requested to be part of the group looking along the river. They had been searching for over an hour when the shrill blast from a whistle pierced the air. Darcy broke into a run and raced towards the sound. The other men were also converging on Stanhope Gate, where they found Colonel Fitzwilliam and one of his officers pulling a body out of the bushes that lined the pathway.

When a lantern fell upon the man's face, Darcy's breath rushed out of him to see Thomas's familiar features. The footman was clearly unconscious and alone, so the searching parties refocused their attention to exploring the immediate area.

Darcy scrutinised the ground, looking for any clues of Elizabeth's location. His lantern light caught the glint of something metallic almost buried in the muddy soil, and he bent to retrieve it. He instantly recognised the jewelled comb. Elizabeth had worn it to a dinner several weeks earlier. He had noticed it because of the unusual gemstones arranged in a vine pattern. She had informed him that the jewels were peridots, and the Gardiners had given it to her in August for her birthday. At the time, he had been excited to learn the month of her birth and had filed the information away for future use, but today he almost broke into tears to see the comb, knowing that she had been wearing it, and it had most likely come loose during an altercation.

He called to Mr Gardiner, who verified that the jewellery belonged to Elizabeth, and the men determined she was most likely no longer in the park. Darcy's heart sank at this news, but at least they had recovered Thomas, who would hopefully be able to supply some helpful information. Newbury's coach was summoned, and Thomas was carefully lifted and placed inside to be conveyed back to Everard House. The colonel had stayed behind to thank the soldiers and would then call upon Darcy's personal physician, Mr Hughes, and request his presence to see to Thomas's injuries.

The vehicle made its way back to Everard House as quickly as possible without causing excessive jostling to the injured Thomas. Upon arrival, a flurry of activity started with Thomas being carefully carried upstairs to a guest bedroom, and warm water, bandages, medicines, and other possible necessities were gathered in preparation for the imminent arrival of the physician. Duchess Agatha and Mrs Gardiner ordered a sleeping draught for the duchess then returned to help comfort her distraught brother-in-law and niece and directed the servants. All was thus in readiness when Dr Hughes finally appeared.

When the doctor pronounced Thomas in no danger, Darcy asked, "Is it possible for you to rouse him?"

The doctor looked towards the younger man. "I would not recommend it. He needs to sleep for now. He will most likely have a fierce headache when he finally awakens, so we should leave him alone and unconscious of the pain for as long as possible."

"I understand your apprehension, Doctor, but we need to speak with him. It is urgent and concerns the health and safety of a young lady. He was accompanying the duke's daughter at the time of his assault, and she is now missing. We need to ask Thomas if he saw who attacked him so that we may know where to begin searching for her."

"The duke's daughter is missing?"

"Yes, sir, Lady Elizabeth." Darcy's voice broke slightly when saying her name.

"Very well, Mr Darcy." He retrieved a bottle from his bag and opened it, waving it under the unconscious man's nose. Thomas shifted and jerked, and after a few moments, his eyes opened. He looked about, and settling on Darcy's face, he struggled to rise up on his elbows. Darcy gently helped him down and calmed him.

"I tried to stop him, but I do not know what happened. I believe that someone hit me from behind. He took her, sir!"

"Yes, Thomas. Who took her?"

"Lord Dunmore. He came upon us at Stanhope Gate and grabbed Lady Elizabeth's arm and tried to drag her out of the park. I was about to stop him when everything went black. I am so sorry, sir."

"You did what you could, and now we know where to look for her. You took a rather nasty blow to the head, and you need to rest. Mr Hughes will see to you."

Darcy hurried from the room and called for his coat, with Mr Gardiner and Newbury following right behind him. As they exited the house, they encountered Colonel Fitzwilliam waiting in the foyer, and he joined them as they entered Newbury's carriage. Darcy gave the address of Lord Dunmore's London home, and the conveyance made the trip to Belgrave Square.

CHAPTER 34

Dunmore's London house was awash with lights, but when the gentlemen requested to see the master, they were informed he was not at home. Darcy stepped forward to force entry, but was restrained by his cousin's firm grip on his shoulder.

"It is unlikely he would bring her here. He must have known we would find Thomas and learn of his involvement. He most likely would have taken her somewhere else."

Darcy eventually agreed with Fitzwilliam's assessment but was anguished to know their one clue produced no results. The colonel questioned the butler at length, and the poor man, recognising the angry countenances of the gentlemen before him, replied that he had no idea of the current whereabouts of Lord Dunmore. Colonel Fitzwilliam, experienced in interrogation, was satisfied with the man's truthfulness, and dispirited, they left to return to Everard House.

Mr Gardiner disembarked to apprise the family of the current situation, and the remaining three gentlemen rode on to Kenton House. The colonel had made many contacts throughout his military career, and he desired to retrieve some information he hoped would help him in their search. He informed Darcy that his batman would also be useful, as he had served one of Dunmore's friend's prior to his enlistment and assignment to the colonel.

The carriage stopped in front of Kenton House, and the men clambered out, surprised to find one of the Matlock coaches there.

Colonel Fitzwilliam called to the driver. "Mullens! Where have you come from?"

"I have just brought Lady Amherst home, sir."

"From where?"

"Her father's home in Portman Square."

The colonel stiffened and turned straight away towards Darcy, who also understood the implication.

"We need to speak to Lady Amherst immediately!" Darcy said as he ran into the house as soon as the colonel gained admittance. The other gentlemen rushed into the house behind him, startling the butler.

"Martin," Darcy shouted, "where is Lady Amherst? Tell me, man!"

"Darcy, calm down!" exclaimed Fitzwilliam. "Martin, do you know where Lady Amherst is?"

"I believe she has retired."

"Where are her chambers, Richard?" Darcy demanded. His yelling had attracted the attention of the family, who had exited the drawing room and made their way to the front hall.

"What is happening?" asked Lady Matlock.

His aunt's anxious voice finally intruded upon his anger, and Darcy turned slowly towards her.

Georgiana, who was clearly upset by the commotion, was huddled behind her, wrapped in a hug by Lord Matlock. Seeing his sister's distress was the breaking point for him, and Darcy staggered to a nearby chair and collapsed into it.

"Lord Dunmore has taken Elizabeth!" he choked out.

A collective gasp emanated from the Matlocks and Georgiana. "Taken her? What do you mean?" questioned Lord Matlock.

Colonel Fitzwilliam, seeing Darcy's distress, informed his parents, brother, and young cousin about what had transpired.

"And you are certain that Lord Dunmore is responsible?" enquired Amherst.

"Absolutely," Darcy replied, finally regaining his composure. "We found the footman who had accompanied Lady Elizabeth. He had been knocked unconscious, and when we revived him, he told us that Lord Dunmore had taken her. We went to his home, but of course, he was not there." Darcy's fury was rekindled as another thought came to him, and he rose from the chair, a ferocious look darkening his countenance. "But I have good reason to believe I know where he has taken her, and I need to speak with your daughter-in-law."

Lady Matlock was confused by this response. "Frederica? Why would you have need to speak with her?"

"Because," Lord Matlock began, "she has been carrying on an affair with Dunmore for several months."

He looked to his older son, and Amherst sadly acknowledged his father's statement.

Darcy was impatient. "Mullens has just informed us that he has returned her from her father's home in Portman Square.

Is Falmouth not currently in the country due to some emergency that arose on his estate?"

"Yes, Darcy, that is correct," Amherst confirmed.

"It is the perfect place for an illicit tryst. No one would question Lady Amherst visiting her childhood home. They have probably been meeting there, and it is quite possible that Dunmore could be keeping Elizabeth there now. Lady Amherst could be complicit in the entire scheme."

All agreed with Darcy's logic, and Amherst sent the butler to summon his errant wife. The party removed to the drawing room to await her arrival. Darcy sat close to his sister, offering her comfort and explaining the situation to her innocent sensibilities. Amherst began pacing the room in agitation, his parents and brother looking on in sympathy. The atmosphere was decidedly tense, and they waited in silence, knowing a reckoning was forthcoming.

Lady Amherst was extremely irritated to be summoned so ungraciously by her husband. When she entered the drawing room, she was surprised to see the entire family gathered, but she hid her astonishment and gracefully sat upon a chair.

"You wished to speak to me, Amherst?"

Her husband turned towards her with a cold look on his usually amiable face. "Where is Lady Elizabeth?"

She paused only momentarily. "How would I know that?"

"You do know, and you will tell me."

"She does not share her schedule with me. We are not particular friends."

"True, and all of us here know why. Darcy loves her, and you are jealous."

When Lady Amherst refused to respond, Amherst continued harshly. "I was foolish to have married you. I had hoped you had recovered from your infatuation with Darcy and I offered you marriage despite my family's strong opposition. They have been kinder to me than I have been to myself. I know you are having an affair with Dunmore, and it is grounds for divorce."

Frederica finally looked at her husband with this pronouncement. "You would not dare! The scandal would be horrendous to your family."

"I am vastly more concerned with my son's future happiness than with any scandal that would stem from a divorce," Lady Matlock replied. "Besides, apparently all of London knows of your perfidy, so the scandal would be entirely upon your shoulders."

Lady Amherst began to look distinctly uneasy, but her pride outweighed her judgment. "You cannot do this to me. My father will not stand for it."

"Your father gave up all his authority when you married me," Amherst reminded her. "You are my wife, as little as that title has meant to you. But the law is clear in this regard. Now, where is Lady Elizabeth?"

She glared at her husband with contempt and turned away from him.

"If you answer, I promise to remit a portion of your dowry upon our divorce. I do not want to see you destitute, for your humiliation will be enough."

Lady Amherst startled at the mention of her dowry. Her entire fortune of fifty thousand pounds was now controlled by her husband, and although there were conditions in their marriage settlement that ensured her money upon her husband's death, there was no such provision in the case of divorce. She would have no independent fortune were he to divorce her, and her father, though wealthy, would have a difficult time providing such a large sum again. She recognised she was defeated.

"He has her at my father's house."

Darcy sprung from his chair and loomed over Lady Amherst. "If she is hurt, I swear by all that is holy, you will regret it for the rest of your life!"

Lady Amherst cringed back from his rage. "He only asked if he could bring her to the house!"

"What are his plans? What does he intend to do?"

"He hopes to marry her."

"If he has harmed her in any way, I will kill him!"

"Darcy!" Lady Matlock interrupted. "You are frightening Georgiana. Sit down and let us determine what to do."

Darcy reluctantly followed his aunt's directives. The party spent a quarter of an hour more questioning Lady Amherst and making plans before the men left to put them into action.

AFTER A GOOD BOUT OF WEEPING, ELIZABETH'S REASON began to exert itself. She rose unsteadily from her chair and made her way to a basin and ewer. After splashing her face with water, she turned around to survey her surroundings more acutely. She was in a large bedchamber. She tried the door and was unsurprised to find it locked. She then made her way around the perimeter of the room, checking the other doors and windows. The windows opened only to reveal she was trapped on the upper story of the building with no close balconies or possible routes of escape to the outside. One of the inner doors was also locked, and the other one led to a large dressing room with no other outlet. Her frustration mounted as Elizabeth began to realise the hopelessness of her situation. She was suddenly overcome with weariness, and the large bed beckoned to her, but she refused to allow herself to sleep, knowing Dunmore was likely somewhere in the house. She sat by the fire to wait for Mrs Crockett to return with the promised tea.

After another quarter of an hour, a knock sounded on the door and the lock turned. The housekeeper entered, bearing a tray of tea and fresh-baked bread. Elizabeth rose and thanked her for the food.

"You are welcome, my lady. Your dress is still wet, but I shall bring it to you as soon as it is dry."

"Mrs Crockett," Elizabeth hesitantly began, "can you please help me?"

The old lady averted her eyes, clearly uncomfortable with the role she had been asked to perform.

"Please, Mrs Crockett. My family will be worried about me. I do not know what Lord Dunmore has planned, and I am frightened."

"He will not harm you. I have been promised that much. I told Lady Amherst I could not be party to anything that would result in your being harmed. You are to stay here tonight, but they have promised me that you will be safe." The elderly lady patted Elizabeth's hand for comfort.

"Lady Amherst, did you say?"

"Yes, indeed. I have been the housekeeper here at her father's home since she was a little girl. And she has given me her word that you will not be harmed, so there is no need to fret, my dear."

"How can I not worry? I am being kept here as a prisoner. None of my family knows where I am. And how can you be so certain that a man willing to kidnap a young woman will keep his word to you? Lord Dunmore cannot be trusted! You must help me escape."

Mrs Crocket wrung her hands. "My lady has promised me that you will be safe." She would not look Elizabeth in the eye. "I shall be back for the tray later. You should try to get some rest." The old lady bustled out of the room, locking the door again.

Elizabeth stamped her foot in frustration. She now knew where she was being held but did not know the location of Lady Amherst's childhood home.

It is somewhere in Mayfair, at least, so I cannot be far from Everard House. If only I could find a way to escape!

It was disheartening to realise she was so close to her home. Elizabeth had placed some hope on the mercy of Mrs Crockett but understood her loyalty to Lady Amherst, even knowing that lady's actions were wrong.

Elizabeth sighed and returned to the chair near the fire. She partook of the food and drink, knowing she would need to maintain her strength for whatever was to come. She found some books on a nearby table and attempted to distract herself by reading.

Sometime later, she heard a commotion. She could discern raised voices, one male and one female. She assumed they belonged to Lord Dunmore and Lady Amherst, most likely arguing about her.

She reflected on Lady Amherst's actions. Though Duchess Agatha had warned her about Frederica's jealousy, Elizabeth had not truly believed it would affect her. She could bear the woman's scorn quite easily, but she could not begin to fathom why Lady Amherst would help Dunmore in his schemes. She also could not help but wonder why the lady would dishonour her wedding vows to a good man to be involved with the likes of Dunmore.

Elizabeth felt sympathy for Lord Amherst for being

married to such a woman, and she was extremely grateful to have gained the love and respect of an honourable man and could now only hope Darcy would find her before Lord Dunmore could enact any plans he had concocted.

She was startled from her thoughts by the door rattling as the lock was turned, and Elizabeth stood up, expecting it to be Mrs Crockett returning to collect the tea tray. She took a step back and frowned when she realised Lord Dunmore had entered the room.

He smiled and mockingly bowed to her. "Lady Elizabeth, I hope I have not kept you waiting too long. I see Mrs Crockett has provided some dry clothing for you, and I hope you have eaten something. I want you to be comfortable as we need to have a little discussion now."

Elizabeth glared at him. "There is nothing to discuss. I insist you release me and allow me to return to my family."

He shook his head and chuckled. "I am afraid that will not be possible, Elizabeth. You must stay here until morning. Tomorrow there will be plenty of time to visit your family when we announce our engagement to them."

"I will never marry you."

"You will not have a choice. By being alone in this house with me tonight, you will be presumed ruined. We shall need to be married for your sake."

"My father would not require me to marry you based on something as ridiculous as that."

Dunmore moved closer, looming over her. "No? Then perhaps I will have to do more to be sure of his compliance. There are other ways to…force things, my dear."

Elizabeth's breath caught in her throat, and she stepped back to increase the distance between them. This only added to Dunmore's amusement, and he laughed openly at her distress.

"I have given my word not to harm you, and as desirous as I am to see your passionate nature unleashed, I should like to start our marriage off right."

"And how does kidnapping me allow that?"

"It is a bit unorthodox, I admit, but I had to act quickly before your engagement to Darcy became official. You are of age, and I would rather present it all to your father as a *fait accompli*, but I was uncertain how compliant you would be."

"Think of your family and your sisters. How will the scandal affect them? Especially once I inform your father of the activities we engaged in while alone in the house." He leered at her. "Now it is getting rather late, and you should probably get some sleep. I would like you to be well-rested and cheerful when we announce our engagement tomorrow." He advanced towards her, and she immediately stepped back in response. "Elizabeth, there is no need to be so shy. You will be my wife, and I expect you to show me the respect your husband deserves. Let us kiss to seal our future."

He smiled and Elizabeth's gut clenched. "Do not touch me!"

Dunmore's eyes hardened, and before she knew what was happening, he had grabbed her by the arms and kissed her roughly. She stiffened and he soon released her.

"You are in no position to give orders, and I may do whatever I please. Go to bed, and tomorrow I expect a more agreeable companion. You must do as I say. I will not tolerate defiance."

He turned from her and swiftly left the room. Elizabeth sank to the floor, tears streaming down her face. She wept for the lost opportunity of her future with Darcy, for she could no longer hope he would find her before the morning. Her heart was rent, and her future was now bleak.

Elizabeth knew not how long she remained immobile on the floor but was roused by another commotion. She stood and went to the door, hoping to hear better, and was astonished when the doorknob moved in her hand. Dunmore had apparently forgotten to lock it after his departure.

She drew in a deep breath, slowly opened the door, and peeked into the hallway. It appeared deserted, and she cautiously left the bedroom and crept quietly down the corridor in the opposite direction of her arrival, hoping to avoid the main areas of the house and make her way down a servants' stairwell to the ground floor. Elizabeth could hear the raised voices of several angry men coming from the direction of the front hall and the clatter of boots as they made their way above stairs.

Her fear rose, and not wanting to be caught escaping, she slipped into the nearest room to hide. However, as soon as she closed the door, she heard her name being called, and recognising the voice, she threw open the door and ran into the hall.

"Fitzwilliam!" she cried upon seeing Darcy racing down the passageway. He immediately halted upon hearing her shout, turning from the door to the room he was about to enter —ironically the room she had just abandoned.

Darcy swiftly ran to her side and gathered her close to him in a crushing embrace. Her sobs were relentless as she tucked her head into his chest and murmured his name over and over. His tears of relief fell, and he scooped her gently into his arms and cradled her to his chest, whispering assurances into her ear and kissing her hair, her cheeks, her eyes, and finally her soft lips. Elizabeth responded instinctively, opening her mouth and allowing Darcy to deepen the kiss, both receiving comfort from the intimate contact.

Their tears subsided, and Darcy pulled slightly away to gauge her well-being.

"Did he harm you?" She shook her head. "You are safe now, Elizabeth. I will let no harm befall you."

"I love you, Fitzwilliam," she whispered as she buried her face into his neck, her sense of security restored by the strength of his arms. "I was so scared, but I knew you would find me."

"I would have travelled anywhere to find you, darling, and you would never leave my sight again if I had my way, but there are some people who are very anxious to know you are safe, and I promised to let them know as soon as we had recovered you."

Darcy shifted her more closely to his body and began to make his way down the hall towards the foyer. Mr Gardiner, Colonel Fitzwilliam, and Lord Newbury stood guard over an unconscious and securely bound Dunmore, a large bruise already appearing along his jaw where someone—Darcy, she presumed—had punched him.

ELIZABETH WAS EXHAUSTED BY HER ORDEAL AND FELL ASLEEP as Darcy descended the stairs. The other gentlemen, particularly her uncle, expressed their relief at having found her safe and whole, and the party exited the house and made their way to the carriage, leaving behind Colonel Fitzwilliam to keep guard over Dunmore.

Darcy refused to relinquish his precious burden, sitting with the sleeping Elizabeth on his lap for the duration of the short journey, the other gentlemen turning away to allow the couple some privacy.

Darcy's heart constricted as he held Elizabeth, knowing how close he had come to losing her, and he resolved to waste no time before securing her promise to marry him without delay. He surreptitiously placed soft kisses in her hair and stroked the delicate skin of her arms. When she flinched in her sleep, he looked at her more closely and was enraged to see purple marks marring the beautiful skin of her upper arms where Dunmore must have grabbed her. *That brute will pay for what he has done to you, Elizabeth!*

When they reached Everard House, Darcy carried Elizabeth inside, where they were immediately met by her family. All wept to see her safely ensconced in Darcy's embrace. Duchess Agatha and Mrs Gardiner insisted she be put to bed at once, and Mrs Gardiner left to inform the duchess of Elizabeth's return.

A chair was set outside her chamber door, and Darcy settled into it, keeping his vigil throughout the night. A little before dawn, he heard her stirring within and silently pressed open her door. Seeing her under the covers, a maid soundly asleep in the chair beside her, he decided to step inside.

Elizabeth stirred again and opened her eyes. Her gaze met Darcy's intent stare and she smiled sleepily. "Thank you for loving me, Fitzwilliam."

"I could no more stop loving you than I could stop breathing or stop the sun from shining. I love you more than words can ever express, and I want to be able to show you how much I love you for the rest of our lives. Marry me, Elizabeth."

"I love you so dearly, Fitzwilliam. Of course I will marry

you." A tear fell and traced down her cheek, and Darcy leant forward and gently kissed it away.

She pulled on his arm, urging him to come closer. "Please hold me."

Darcy hesitated only briefly, looking towards the maid still asleep in the chair, but eventually he lay down alongside her on top of the counterpane. He gathered her close, fitting her back along his stomach, her head tucked under his chin. He kissed the top of her head and tightened his arms around her.

"Go to sleep, Elizabeth. You are safe now, and I will never leave you."

She sighed and they both settled into a deep sleep, the anxiety of the day eradicated by the promise of their shared future. Neither awoke when the door opened and the maid left the room.

CHAPTER 35

Late that morning, Elizabeth entered the breakfast room where Darcy sat alone sipping a cup of coffee. She could hardly believe it was only a day earlier that she had been forced to face a possible future without him. She shuddered at the thought.

"Good morning, Fitzwilliam."

Darcy's brow creased. "Are you well, my love?"

She shook the negative thoughts from her mind and focused on the man before her. "I am."

He stared at her, evidently trying to gauge her emotions, and apparently satisfied, he nodded.

With a quick glance around to ensure they were alone, Elizabeth went to him, settling herself into his lap. His hands smoothed up and down along her back, tracing her spine and ribs, up along her shoulders and down her arms, again causing her to wince when he touched her bruises.

"What did he do to you?"

"Nothing that will not heal."

"Please, Elizabeth, I must know."

She hesitated, but the distress in his voice broke the dam of her checked emotions, and she recounted her ordeal. He listened without interrupting, tensing at the mention of Dunmore kissing her, of his daring to place his filthy hands upon her. Anger made his body flush hot as she told of Dunmore's plans to force a marriage. As her account came to an end, Darcy held her close, offering words of comfort. She pulled back to look at him, offering a small smile.

"But thankfully, it all came to nothing. You came and you saved me."

"Dunmore could have—"

"Many things *could* have happened," Elizabeth interrupted gently, "but what is important is that they did not. I am well, and you are too. And if my memory serves correctly, we are to marry. Let us rejoice in this, the first day we are engaged."

She watched the rage fade away as other ideas came to his mind, ideas which he almost immediately put into action. He captured her lips in a kiss she hoped would never end, and indeed, did not end until Jane, none too delicately, stomped into the room and coughed loudly.

Darcy wished to return to his townhouse to change clothes and retrieve his sister. He gave Elizabeth a parting kiss, and she clung to him, reluctant to let him leave now that they had come to an understanding, but he reassured her that he would be gone only as long as it took to bathe and gather his sister from Kenton House. Brushing a final kiss across her forehead, he rose and exited the room.

The duke and Duchess Agatha, with knowing smirks on their faces, bid him a good morning as he passed them in the corridor. Hastily donning his coat, he blushed and bowed, told them he would return shortly with Georgiana, and strode down the hall, certain he could hear them chuckling.

But his spirits were too elated to be embarrassed long. Elizabeth was safe, and they were engaged. *And it will be a very short engagement if I have anything to say about it!* he firmly resolved as he made his way across Grosvenor Square to his townhouse.

WHEN DARCY AND GEORGIANA RETURNED TO EVERARD House that afternoon, Darcy lost no time in securing the duke's consent and blessing to the marriage. When Darcy insisted on a short engagement, the duke lifted a sardonic brow before nodding silently.

The two men then immediately repaired to the drawing room where Darcy had left his sister with the ladies of the house. Elizabeth rose from her chair at seeing their entrance, and Darcy's wide smile beckoned her to join him. He wrapped his arm around her waist as her father announced their engagement to the room's occupants. An immediate cry of joy erupted, and congratulations were swiftly given.

"But Mr Darcy!" exclaimed the duchess, "that is only three weeks away! It will be impossible to prepare for such a momentous occasion in such a short time! Your wedding will be a significant event! There is entirely too much to do. We must shop for Elizabeth's trousseau and plan the menu and decorations. I am certain we can accomplish it all in three *months*. Surely you can wait that long!"

"No, Your Grace," he solemnly replied. "I have waited more than a year to marry the woman I love, and after yesterday, I do not want to wait a moment longer. I came too close to losing Elizabeth, and I will not take the chance again merely to plan a wedding breakfast." Darcy turned to Elizabeth and gathered both her hands in his. "Please, Elizabeth, let us not tarry over wedding frivolities. The most important thing is that you marry me."

His earnest plea would have melted a stony heart, and Elizabeth's was far from granite where Darcy was concerned. The love that radiated from him was enough to convince her, and she extracted her hand from his grasp to caress his cheek.

"Nothing is more important to me than becoming your wife."

A brilliant smile graced his face at her heartfelt declaration, and heedless of the others, he gently cupped her face and softly kissed her upturned lips.

Duchess Agatha's discreet cough broke them apart, and they turned to the family with somewhat sheepish expressions.

"Well, my dear," the duke said to his wife, "it appears Elizabeth will wed her young man by the end of the month. I am confident in your abilities to prepare an elegant event, even with so little time. I shall be in my study if you have need of any funds."

The mention of money stirred the duchess into action, and she accosted Elizabeth, demanding she attend the shops with her that very day. Darcy reluctantly released his intended to her mother's care, knowing that over the next three weeks he would see little of Elizabeth, but he was content that his ultimate goal of a short engagement had been successful.

Darcy was correct, and the next three weeks afforded little time alone for the betrothed couple. Elizabeth was consumed with wedding preparations, and Darcy had his own responsibilities to attend to prior to his marriage. A licence was required along with preparing the marriage settlement. Darcy made a brief trip to Pemberley to ready it to receive its new mistress and to retrieve Elizabeth's younger sisters from their northern schools.

They had all been granted a short holiday to attend their sister's wedding. Darcy was pleased with the improvements achieved in the deportment and decorum of his future sisters. Lydia was still more exuberant than Darcy was inclined to accept, but her wild behaviour had been drastically reduced.

Darcy was also kept busy seeing justice done to the perpetrators of the crimes committed against Elizabeth. Lord Amherst wasted no time in petitioning the courts for a divorce from Lady Amherst, and she had returned to her father's home in shame.

It had proved more difficult to seek retribution on Lord Dunmore. Not willing to make Elizabeth's kidnapping public in order to protect her reputation, there was little that could be done to him overtly. Darcy threatened to shoot the villain should he ever approach Elizabeth or any member of the family again, and he ordered Dunmore to remain in Scotland for the foreseeable future, especially during the divorce proceedings of Amherst and Lady Amherst. Darcy was frustrated, but he vowed to keep looking for ways to exact justice against the villain.

THE WEEKS BEFORE THE WEDDING PASSED QUICKLY, AND SOON the day was upon them. Her Grace, with the help of Duchess Agatha, Mrs Gardiner, and even Lady Matlock, had truly outdone herself with the arrangements. The church was beautifully arrayed and filled with family and close friends of the couple.

Darcy waited impatiently at the front of the church,

Colonel Fitzwilliam standing beside him, speaking *sotto voce* to keep his cousin distracted while he waited for his bride. Finally, the doors at the back opened, and Darcy's eyes immediately rested upon Elizabeth's beloved form as her father escorted her down the aisle.

She looked radiantly beautiful and happy as her eyes locked with Darcy's. Their gazes did not waver during the entirety of the ceremony. As Darcy pronounced the familiar words, "With this ring I thee wed, with my body I thee worship, and with all my worldly goods I thee endow. In the Name of the Father, and of the Son, and of the Holy Ghost. Amen," he placed a lovely gold, braided band on Elizabeth's finger. It had belonged to Lady Anne, and Darcy had retrieved it when he travelled to Pemberley prior to the wedding.

Elizabeth smiled up at him as the vicar announced them man and wife. They walked arm in arm down the aisle in jubilation, signed the register with a flourish, and proceeded to Everard House to enjoy their wedding celebration and begin their life together.

EPILOGUE

The Darcys journeyed to the Lakes for their wedding trip. They stopped at Pemberley along the way to allow Elizabeth to see her future home. She was slightly daunted by the grand building and numerous servants, but living at Grancourt with the benefit of Duchess Agatha's guidance helped her quickly overcome her anxiety. She was utterly enchanted by the large park, encouraging her husband to accompany her on long rambles. They remained at Pemberley to direct the changes they wished to be made to the mistress's chambers, then continued their journey north. After several weeks of touring, the Darcys returned to London.

The marriage of Fitzwilliam and Elizabeth Darcy was by no means perfect, and disagreements and vexations happened with regularity—not surprising considering their strong wills and personalities. However, they would remember their turbulent courtship and the times when they had almost been lost to each other, and a quick reconciliation was sought and achieved—generally a rather passionate one! The seven children that resulted from their union came as no surprise to anyone. They divided their time between London and their beloved Pemberley and became a model of a contented couple. Their families prospered alongside them, though there were also times of sorrow.

Jane and Bingley married a few months after the Darcys' wedding, allowing the duchess the necessary time to prepare a truly magnificent event. Jane gave birth to the first grandson who would inherit the Everard dukedom, so the Bingleys made their home at Grancourt to allow their son to be raised there and to learn his duties. That their other four children were girls only somewhat vexed their grandmother, as it was now unlikely she would ever starve in the hedgerows.

Mary was presented at court the following Season, and her debut was a resounding success. She married an earl's son with an affinity for music, but sadly, they remained childless. They devoted their lives to the musical arts and were renowned for their evening musicales and their generous contributions to music schools and charities.

Kitty entered society several years later. She and a particular friend from school married a pair of brothers that same Season and settled in estates not five miles from each other, where they raised their energetic broods almost as one family.

Lydia's entrance into society was much heralded by the *ton*, as she was the last of the wealthy, beautiful, and eligible Everard ladies. Lydia's four years at school had truly improved her. Seeing the happy results of her sisters' refined characters had induced her to emulate them. Lydia would always be lively and vivacious and never one to adhere to serious subjects for a prolonged period of time, but she had learned to comport herself with grace.

To the surprise of her entire family, Lydia completed her first Season and remained single. She married a tradesman at the ripe age of three-and-twenty and sailed with him to India where they spent the first ten years of their marriage amassing a vast fortune and several children.

Georgiana Darcy never completely overcame her natural shyness, but with her brother and Elizabeth's help, her first Season was successful. She was in no hurry to marry, however, and although she accompanied the Darcys to town each year, no gentleman caught her eye.

So, when at the age of five-and-twenty, Randolph Leventhorpe asked for her hand, their entire family was shocked.

It was revealed they had developed a friendship after his visit to Grancourt years before. That friendship, founded on their mutual love of music, had slowly developed into a deep affection and devotion to each other. Darcy granted his blessing, and the couple married in a quiet ceremony at Pemberley. The Leventhorpes, both of reserved dispositions, lived a quiet life at Chetwin Hall. Having Georgiana living so close to Pemberley brought Darcy comfort as he saw his sister often.

They enjoyed connubial felicity until Georgiana died at the age of two-and-thirty while giving birth to her second child, a daughter her husband named after his wife. Leventhorpe never remarried but devoted his life to raising his son and daughter. Darcy was devastated by the loss of his sister, but his loving wife and family helped him slowly overcome the sadness. He developed a special affinity for 'Little Ana,' as his niece was called, who resembled her mother in appearance and character.

The duke and duchess lived at Grancourt for the remainder of their days, helping to raise the Bingley children. Duchess Agatha also remained there, preparing the young duke for his future duties and supporting the duchess and Jane in their responsibilities. No one faulted Duchess Agatha or the duke when either ventured to Pemberley for a prolonged visit.

Lord Newbury and Colonel Fitzwilliam put aside their contempt for wedlock and found happiness in their marriages. Newbury wed a widow with a young daughter, and the colonel married an heiress who appreciated his humour. Their unions resulted from matches made during winter house parties hosted at Pemberley. The Darcys held such a gathering every February, and there was always sleigh riding and waltzing.

Lord Amherst also remarried. Following the successful completion of his divorce and the defeat of Napoleon at Waterloo, Amherst travelled to France. There, he met a charming though somewhat impoverished *comtesse*. She was not a beauty, but she loved her husband. Upon returning to England, Lord and Lady Amherst resided primarily in the country and raised their three sons there.

Lady Catherine never forgave Darcy for marrying Elizabeth, or the family for accepting the marriage. She refused to apologise and isolated herself and her daughter in Kent. She died ten years after the Darcys wed, never having reconciled with her family. Elizabeth entreated her husband to attend the funeral, and he reluctantly agreed to go. While there, his cousin Anne informed everyone she would travel to Italy for her health and was leaving Rosings in the care of Colonel Fitzwilliam and his new wife.

Caroline Bingley never married. She became an embittered woman and her invitations to Grancourt dwindled as the years progressed. Even Lady Jane and Bingley's forgiving natures eventually reached their limits.

And what of the villains in this story? Wickham served long years in prison for his desertion from the militia, and when he was transported to Australia for his unpaid debts, no one in England was sad to see him go.

Though Lady Amherst was forced to return to her childhood home, and Lord Amherst was generous enough to return fifteen thousand pounds of her dowry, there was nothing he or his family could do to repair the reputation she had herself destroyed. Her father was shamed by her dissolute behaviour, and when a widowed and ageing baronet offered for her, he was quick to grant the request and to banish her to the country.

A STORY IN A LONDON NEWSPAPER ABOUT TEN YEARS AFTER his marriage caught Darcy's eye.

> *Marcus Carlyle, Earl of Dunmore, was found dead this morning in a park on the outskirts of London. Lord Dunmore had been shot in the chest. No suspects have been apprehended, and the authorities believe the death was the result of a duel. Dunmore's notorious reputation has led the investigators to believe that a relation of one of his many paramours must have challenged the Scottish lord.*

Though Darcy was a compassionate and generous man, he was not saddened to hear of the reprobate's death.

His small smile elicited a question from his wife, who had been watching his face as it flickered with emotions while he read his paper. The Darcys had made a habit of spending their mornings together in their rooms before they ventured into the world to see to their numerous responsibilities. This precious time alone was one of the ways they maintained the strength of their love and union.

"What makes you smile so, Fitzwilliam?" Elizabeth queried.

Darcy hesitated a moment before handing the page to his wife and pointing his finger towards the proper place for her to read. She quickly perused the notice, handed the paper back to her husband, and took up the letter she had been reading prior to the interruption.

"It is what he deserved. It was so many years ago now, I can hardly recall that wretched day."

Darcy was somewhat astonished by her calm reaction. "I can never forget it, darling. It was the day I almost lost you."

Elizabeth rose from her chair and sat on her husband's lap. He gathered her close to his body and tucked her head beneath his chin, inhaling the scent of gardenias he always associated with his cherished wife. He took a lock of her hair and wrapped it around his finger, an action he always did when feeling troubled. This unconscious habit, so reminiscent of taking the lock she forfeited after the fencing match all those many years ago, always caused Elizabeth to smile.

"It was a frightening day, but I have been too happy these last years with you ever to dwell on it. You may have almost lost me, but I believe that in this case a good memory is unpardonable. You must remember my philosophy."

"Think only of the past as its remembrance gives me pleasure?"

"The very one. No one can ever come between us now."

Darcy gazed into his wife's fine eyes, cupped her face in his hands, and kissed her fervently.

Their family did not see them for the remainder of the day —children, housekeepers, and valets all turned away from the door. An entailment of the amorous kind kept them too occupied for interruptions.

Quills & Quartos Publishing thanks you for reading this book.

To receive special offers, bonus content, and information on sales and new releases, we invite you to sign up for our newsletter at www.QuillsandQuartos.com.

ACKNOWLEDGMENTS

I would like to thank the people at Quills & Quartos Publishing, first for reaching out to me more than a decade after posting this story online and offering to publish it, and then for their hard work and dedication to bring about a completed project. Thank you Jan & Amy & Debbie.

I would like to thank my mother and three sisters for their love, support, and teasing throughout my life that helped shape me into the woman I am today. And to my father, outnumbered though he was with five women in the household, who still managed to encourage us through the years.

Thank you to my Heavenly Father for the strength He gives me each day to accomplish the many tasks and responsibilities given to me and do so with grace and forgiveness when I fall short.

To my children, to whom I devote my heart and efforts.

Thank you to my dear husband, Ben, for stepping up and pitching in more when I had to devote time to editing or other activities. You are my miracle.

And to Jane Austen, whose words and characters have been an inspiration to me through many years.

ABOUT THE AUTHOR

Noell Chesney's childhood love of reading led to an introduction, as a young woman, to the works of Jane Austen. The second of four sisters—though with no fear of starving in the hedgerows—resulted in a special affinity for Elizabeth Bennet. After reading numerous works of fanfiction by other authors, a decision to try her hand at composing her own story was born.

Noell has a Bachelor of Science from the University of Colorado. She enjoys cooking, boating, camping, and of course reading. She and her husband, Benjamin, live in Highlands Ranch, Colorado with their three children and two dogs.

 facebook.com/Noell-Chesney-Author-104933294664461